"ARE ALL SOUTH̶̶̶̶̶̶̶̶̶̶̶̶ YOU? IF SO, I PITY THE WOM̶̶̶ IN THIS BACKWARD PLACE!"

Mark's hand lashed out to lock around Maggie's arm.

"Our women get along just fine," Mark drawled. "Some of them even like it when a man takes charge." Like lightning, he grasped her other arm and pulled her to him.

"Are you so different?" he demanded, lifting her up against his chest.

In complete surprise, Maggie raised startled eyes. He was only inches away, and suddenly the twittering sounds of the grove receded as her other senses flared.

Mark didn't know when he'd been so blasted mad. The feelings he had about this girl were going off in his head like skyrockets—until all he could hear was the crashing of his blood against his temples.

His strong fingers tightened about Maggie's arms, squeezing her against his body. Mark's eyes trained on her mouth. A heavy pounding started in her chest, reverberating in her ears as she watched him bend closer . . .

A SPIRITED YANKEE WOMAN IN A BATTLE OF HEARTS WITH AN UNFORGETTABLE DIXIE MAN. . . .

SOUTHERN NIGHTS

SOUTHERN NIGHTS

MARCIA MARTIN

J
JOVE BOOKS, NEW YORK

SOUTHERN NIGHTS

A Jove Book / published by arrangement with
the author

PRINTING HISTORY
Jove edition / July 1990

ISBN: 0-515-10302-0

Jove Books are published by The Berkley Publishing Group,
200 Madison Avenue, New York, New York 10016.
The name "JOVE" and the "J" logo
are trademarks belonging to Jove Publications, Inc.

PRINTED IN THE UNITED STATES OF AMERICA

10 9 8 7 6 5 4 3 2 1

For my untiring mentor and unfailing friend.
Thanks, Mom.

PART ONE

Oh, what a tangled web we weave,
When first we practice to deceive!
—Sir Walter Scott
Marmion

PART ONE

Chapter One

May 1, 1957
Foxcroft Estate
Charleston, South Carolina

"But, darling, surely you must know how vexed she was. After all, it was he who talked her into letting him live there in the first place! And then, to have a *gardener* telling tales!"

Dolly finished the gossipy story and laughed—the sound lilting across the terrace until it reached William.

He stood discreetly in the shadows where the giant bank of white azaleas cast a pale wave across the lawn. From there he could watch the two boys playing near the gazebo. He could watch, too, the man and woman who stood on the terrace and glanced occasionally toward the children, their gaze returning to each other.

The sound of Dolly's laughter was rare these days. That another man was granted it so carelessly struck William like a blow. His pale eyes sparkled with pain. He shouldn't be surprised. His wife was always lively and vivacious when Art Townsend was about.

A chorus of giggles came from the boys, and William turned his attention to where they played in carefree abandon on the gazebo stairs. Their small forms had barely achieved the stature of boyhood. Mark was nearly seven; that would make Arthur barely five—noticeably smaller than his older playmate but struggling to keep up with Mark's antics as best he could.

William's gaze lingered on Mark. The raven hair was the exact shade of his mother's. Though William was too far away to make out the boy's face, he imagined the rosy cheeks and fine features beneath the shock of dark hair. Mark was going to be a real looker—much like his mother but for the clear green eyes, which were entirely unlike the black eyes of Dolly Fox.

"Boys! Boys!" came Art Townsend's deep southern voice.

"Calm down! Come along now, Arthur. It's time for us to be going."

"Oh, must you go?" Dolly asked in a quick, cajoling manner. "I was hoping you could stay for lunch."

William took in his wife's form. Sunlight danced on the glossy hair, the blue dress swirling attractively as she leaned toward her companion to place a hand on his arm.

Another man might have stormed up onto the terrace, ordered his wife into the house, and punched the usurper squarely in the jaw. But that sort of behavior wasn't in William Fox's nature. He was a southern gentleman for whom an old-fashioned duel, complete with seconds, would have been far more in character than a fistfight.

"I'm afraid we must go," Art Townsend replied, inclining his head intimately toward Dolly. "Isabel is expecting us at lunchtime. And I promised Alicia I'd take her for a carriage ride around the district this afternoon. At three and a half, she's become quite the young lady. And she's grown rather possessive of her daddy."

Dolly stepped provocatively closer to the tall man. "I've grown rather possessive of *that* commodity myself," she purred.

Unseen, unheard, William slipped through a breach in the snowy azaleas and proceeded along the path at a brisk pace. To the left, the towering wall of the house seemed to go on endlessly; ahead, the courtyard gate looked far away. He'd be damned if he'd stand around on his own property and be made to feel like an intruder! He had planned to go into town later; might as well go early and leave Dolly to her designs. She probably wouldn't miss him anyway, since their lives had twisted so drastically apart.

If he had been a different man living in a different place, he would have considered divorce. But in the staid Protestant Southland, divorce was still an avant-garde notion—accepted in New York, perhaps, but whispered about in Charleston.

It wasn't as if Dolly were an adulteress. She merely loved Townsend and no one else. When William had finally grasped that fact, something within him died, and he hadn't touched his wife since. He had lived like a monk the past few years. It was small solace that Dolly had done the same.

He rounded the corner of the house, slammed through the gate, and spotted the massive shape of Harold, who was waxing the black limousine parked in the curving drive while Dolly's cousin John Henry looked on.

The burly chauffeur and the young man seemed to be as thick

as thieves these days, William thought as John Henry looked over with a start. He was well groomed, but looked old, his face pinched and drawn prematurely into disapproving lines.

Stepping away from the car, John Henry nodded respectfully. "Good mornin', William," came the refined southern drawl.

"Mornin'," William answered. "We have an errand," he announced to Harold with uncharacteristic shortness, then reached for the car door and climbed abruptly into the back.

Harold gave John Henry a questioning look, then shrugged into his jacket and settled himself in the driver's seat. "Where to?"

"The harbor," William replied tersely.

It was a brilliant spring day, the sun so bright on the water that it hurt the eyes. A salty wind whipped along the main deck of the *Indies Queen,* bringing with it the tantalizing scent of land and flowers. It tugged at the hats and coats of the small group of passengers lined up along the ship's railing. They craned their necks and squinted for a better view as the vessel steamed into Charleston Harbor. Sea gulls swarmed to welcome the old ship, their cries filling the air, their white wings flashing against the dazzling blue of the sky.

Stella stood apart from the other passengers. She could scarcely believe her eyes. The harbor teemed with boats of all sizes and rang with a cacophony of chugging engines, bellowing horns, and clanging bells. Long dock fingers reached out from a wharf crowded with people hustling to and fro. Beyond the docks, along a boulevard lined with tall houses, men in suits strolled with ladies in frilly dresses.

Even the busiest areas of the port of Kingston had left Stella unprepared for this spectacle. With a sinking feeling, she looked away from the elegant people parading along the docks and stared down at the leather thongs on her feet. Uncoiffed, unpolished, she saw herself in a sudden unflattering light. She failed to notice that the eyes of the ship's male passengers strayed regularly in her direction. Although she lacked the latest couture, she possessed a natural beauty that was only heightened by her homespun attire.

At twenty, she was tall and slim. The product of a dark Spanish mother and a fair Viking-like father, Stella was a colorful blend of the two, with copper hair and startling turquoise eyes. Now, as she stood in the sun, her curling hair glowed like a halo, and her bleached muslin dress shone like an angel's raiment. At home in Kingston she had drawn the eyes of many young bucks. Like moths to a flame they had come, only to have her consume their attentions, cast them away, and burn all the brighter. She knew her destiny lay beyond the boundaries of the island.

She and her mother had planned it for years, this journey to Charleston of South Carolina. It was a place Stella's seafaring father had often mentioned, and although she hadn't seen him in a dozen years, she still remembered his stories of America.

With each year he failed to return to Jamaica, she had pictured him in the fine place he called Charleston. Each year she had listened to her mother invent excuses for John Matthews, her tall American husband who dropped into port occasionally during the first ten years of their marriage and then ceased coming altogether. Although her mother spoke of illness and unknown hardship, Stella knew the truth: He had deserted them. As she grew up in respectable but nearly destitute circumstances, a cold bitterness froze around her heart.

She helped her mother build a modest dressmaking business and save toward the dream of being reunited with her father. She listened with feigned agreement as her mother concocted theory after theory about her husband's disappearance. But each year, as her excuses for her absent husband became more elaborate, Stella's mother became more frail, as if feeding her hopes left her starved and empty. Finally, as she died, "John" was the last word to cross her lips.

Her mother had deserved better, Stella thought once again, her eyes stinging. She had her own reasons for seeking out her father, and first among them was revenge.

Her fingers strayed to the familiar shape of the pendant hanging around her neck. As she stared ahead to the bustling shoreline, the imposing scene was displaced by a fleet of memories. She remembered a rustic frame cottage near a Jamaican beach. The sand glistened milky white where a dark-haired woman waved to the tall man and little girl who frolicked in the azure shallows. Once again Stella felt the rush of exhilaration as her father swept her high above his head to dangle her over the lapping waters.

The image shifted, the dancing sunlight replaced by the flicker of a campfire under the open stars. Nearby, her mother sat quietly embroidering a gentleman's linen handkerchief. Stella lay in the cool sand listening to the call of night birds and the comforting slap of the water against the shore. Her eyes were glued to the hands of the man leaning into the light of the fire as his fingers skillfully polished an ornament.

"There," he said and turned the pendant over in his hand. In a swift, fluid movement, he tipped back his head to take a swig from the ever-present bottle of rum. "It's finished. Come here, my girl."

Her turquoise eyes wide, the eight-year-old scrambled to the knee of her father and watched breathlessly as he threaded a slender gold chain through the top of the carving. Whittled from a flawless piece of red Italian coral, the five-pointed star gleamed richly in the firelight.

"Come, Stella. Turn around so I can fasten it."

The girl quickly obeyed, feeling with a thrill the cool touch of the necklace as it settled about her throat. It was the first present her father had made for her. It would be the last.

"Let's see now," the sailor said with a smile, turning his daughter around by the shoulders so he could gaze at her. His eyes grew misty as he studied the beautiful child—the fiery hair that curled about the heart-shaped face, the twinkling turquoise eyes that had always reminded him of the clear waters of the West Indies.

"Stella . . . my Stella," he murmured, his eyes falling briefly to the red star that glowed against her golden skin. John Matthews's smile turned curiously sad as he reached out to touch her cheek. "Wherever destiny takes you, Stella, you'll always be my star."

"Always . . ." the voice resounded. "Always . . ." it echoed once more, as the dreamy image of the Jamaican beach faded and Stella was again confronted with the fast-approaching docks of Charleston.

Traitorous tears sprang to her eyes. She swiped at them with one hand as the other played nervously about the shape of the pendant. All those years of desertion. All those times when she and her mother had clung to each other fearfully, not knowing where the next meal would come from. Those experiences had honed a spirit harder and sharper than the points of the coral star.

She had thought she was beyond being hurt by melancholy memories of her father. But as Stella looked upon the place he had so often described, she felt the old pain slice into her anew. She yanked the necklace from her throat and sent it sailing over the ship's railing, the golden chain glimmering until it was swallowed by the deep blue water of Charleston Harbor. She stared after it, her thoughts and emotions churning like the white wake trailing the *Indies Queen*.

"Good morning, miss," came the hopeful sound of a young man's voice.

Stella turned with a start. He was an attractive youth with sun-streaked hair and rosy cheeks. But he was no different from the rest of the crew who had stared hungrily at her throughout the voyage, resentfully keeping their distance because she sailed under the protection of their captain. This one seemed to have mustered the courage to speak now that the end of the voyage was at hand.

"Good morning," she replied. He beamed at her, his fair hair and quick smile triggering a fresh image of her father.

"You're Stella Matthews," he said, hesitantly extending his hand. "I've been—uh—hoping for a chance to meet you. My name is Kelly Dawes."

He regarded her in such a shy, hopeful way that after a moment she smiled helplessly and placed her hand in his. "How do you do?" she said, withdrawing her fingers from his grasp almost before he had touched them.

For an instant Kelly Dawes only gazed at her adoringly. Then he cleared his throat and buried his hands in the pockets of his white deck trousers. "I—uh—I was hoping I might escort you ashore. Charleston is a pretty big place. If this is your first visit, you might need a little help finding your way around. I could help you locate a hotel. Maybe take you out to dinner."

Stella looked at him. He seemed to be nice enough, with his well-scrubbed face and easygoing smile. He could probably simplify the process of getting settled by finding her a hotel and buying her dinner, the thought of which made her stomach turn hungrily. But Kelly Dawes was a sailor—he might as well have had two heads.

"Thank you for the invitation," she said. "But I'm looking for someone."

"Oh," Kelly muttered, the disappointment showing clearly on his face.

"Perhaps you know him," Stella offered. "He's a sailor, too. My father, John Matthews."

"Your father?" A glimmer of hope returned to Kelly's eye. Perhaps if he had some link with the father, his chances with the daughter would improve. "John Matthews? Let's see . . . His name doesn't ring a bell. But I'm from these parts. Whereabouts does he live?"

Stella's face took on a distant look. "I don't know." She turned away from Kelly Dawes to grasp the splintery railing and look again to the shore. "That's why I'm here," she added absently.

As she stood on the deck of the *Indies Queen* and gazed on the magnificence of Charleston, the futility of her mission dawned with full force. With only the islands as a frame of reference, she had never envisioned a place as grand as this America, her father's homeland.

Perhaps the old woman of Trelawny had been right. The fortune teller had warned that a journey to Charleston would end in tragedy, and as Stella surveyed the bustling wharf and mentally counted her meager funds, she imagined that tragedy might be about to strike. But if nothing else, her mother had bequeathed her a sense of dignity. She raised her chin, eyed the harbor defiantly, and pulled her shawl close against the sea breeze that had grown suddenly cold.

She was silent for several moments before Kelly Dawes realized she had dismissed him. Finally he sensed that she was no longer with him, her eyes and thoughts on some distance place he couldn't imagine. He had watched her stand like that a hundred times over the course of the voyage—her head held rigidly high, the fiery hair dancing in the wind, the shawl clutched about her like a barrier that would permit no trespassing.

How the beautiful girl did it, Kelly wasn't quite sure, but she managed without saying a word to discourage any approach. She had set herself apart, separated herself from the ordinary scheme of things; she seemed to exist in her own private world. He had watched her for days, even dreamed about her. But now he had to accept what he had suspected all along: Stella Matthews was unattainable, at least for the likes of him.

With a last lingering look, he turned away. Something drew his attention to the quarterdeck, where he found Captain Jack Lewis's eyes leveled on him.

"Taking a bit of a rest, are you, Kelly?" the captain boomed.

"N-no, sir!" Kelly called with a quick salute. He scurried back to his duties, all thoughts of Stella wiped abruptly from his mind.

It seemed to Stella that the ship docked exceptionally quickly. The noise of the engine became a constant roar as a flurry of activity embraced the *Indies Queen*. Lines were thrown, and sailors scrambled across the decks on various assignments as the ship came to a shuddering halt. On the wharf below, she could see a colorful, seething mass of people.

Even before the ship ceased rolling against the pier, the

passengers began to disembark. Stella moved cautiously along the
deck and down the ramp, her eyes bright with apprehension. It
was a moment she and her mother had dreamed of, but now it was
real—frighteningly real.

Keeping her back ramrod straight, Stella trembled as she
stepped alone onto American soil.

William Fox rarely failed to meet the *Indies Queen*. His friend
Jack Lewis, for whom he had financed the ship's acquisition,
always brought him a case of pungent Jamaican rum.

Oblivious to the fine gray cloth of his suit, William lounged
against a wooden crate and enjoyed watching the port activities.
To him the harbor was beautiful; he had captured different views
of it in oils on the canvases that hung in his studio loft above the
library at Foxcroft. Art was one of the few things he took pleasure
in anymore—painting and writing his journals and, of course,
Mark, whom he could watch in the ring for hours, mesmerized by
the young boy's way with horses.

It hadn't always been like that. Seven years before, when he had
married Dolly, he had been the happiest man in the world. How
high his hopes had been! Gone would be the solitude that had
dogged him through life. A wife, a child, a family. How
promising the future had seemed. But that had been seven years
ago. The years in between had taught him the foolishness of hope,
the naïveté of love.

Those years had also taught William about passion. It could lift
a person to a dizzying height or send him plummeting to the earth.
It had taken him a long time to accept the reality of his marriage
to Dolly, to recognize that her passion was as deep and strong as
his own—but it was for someone else.

Gradually a deep silence had stolen over William's soul and
then reached out to embrace the whole of Foxcroft. The great
house was now shrouded with a heavy quiet, broken only
occasionally by the sound of Mark's innocent laughter.

With a self-reproving grimace, William turned his attention
back to the harbor. He watched the *Queen* dock and couldn't help
but notice the unusual woman who was disembarking. Judging
from her suntanned skin and tropical clothing, she was from the
islands. She stood steadfastly on the pier as if waiting for
someone.

He put her out of his thoughts as he boarded the *Queen* and
joined Jack Lewis on the main deck. It had been three years since

the captain repaid William Fox for his new stake in life with the *Indies Queen*. Still, he reported the success of his voyages in full detail. He sensed William's interest in his seagoing life, and he was glad to offer his friend a bit of cheer, for of all the men Captain Lewis had known, William Fox was the finest—and the most unhappy. A man of property, a gentleman, and a scholar, he was rich in many ways. But he was living proof that money couldn't buy everything.

"Who is that unusual woman down there?" William asked.

Jack Lewis shielded his eyes and turned to find William pointing at Stella, who was still standing forlornly on the wharf.

"A sad story, Mr. Fox. She's a brave but foolish girl. Her mother was married to an American sailor some years ago in Jamaica. Seems he hasn't been back to the island in twelve years."

Noting the way William's attention lingered on the bright-haired girl, Captain Lewis went on. "Her mother died a few months back, and Stella came here all alone. I tried to talk her out of making this trip, but she is determined to try to find her father, John Matthews. Seems he used to talk a lot about Charleston, so she came here looking for him. I remember him—Johnny, his friends used to call him. A big, strapping man and a damned good sailor, but he was devilish fond of the rum. That's a demon that's wrecked many a sailor, and some of them seem to just drop out of sight.

"I tried to warn Stella. Tried to tell her that a lot of us had looked for Matthews over the years, that it was no use her coming here. But she just stared me straight in the eye and said she had to come. She spent most of her money on the passage. I suppose she never figured out what she'd do once she got here. I suspect she's got no place to go.

William stared fixedly at the woman on the pier. A moment of silence passed before he took his leave of the captain.

"Well, Jack, I'm happy to hear you had another good voyage. And thank you for the rum. I'll enjoy it often with good thoughts of you." He gave Jack Lewis a firm handshake. "Take care of yourself," he added as he started down the ramp.

"Yes, sir!" Captain Lewis called. "Let me know if there's something I can pick up for you on the next trip!"

William saluted the captain over his shoulder and proceeded along the pier. As he glanced toward his car, his eyes fell once more on the young woman from Jamaica. He approached and tipped his hat.

"Good day," he said politely. She caught him off guard when she bowed her curly-topped head and then looked up at him with the most remarkable eyes he'd ever seen. It crossed his mind that he would be hard-pressed to re-create that vivid color with oils.

Stella realized she was staring at him, but she couldn't help it. He was a true gentleman, the likes of which she had seen only when they brought shirts and trousers to her mother for mending. The rich gold of a pocket watch gleamed beneath his vest, and on his finger was an unusual golden ring crafted into the face of a fox.

Despite his obviously lofty station, the man returned her gaze in a kindly way through pale blue eyes that put Stella's skeptical nature at rest. They were the color of a clear lake, only shadowed somehow. He smiled and removed his hat to reveal thick honey-blond hair. Tall and fair like her father, he was still so different, so clean and polished.

"My name is William Fox," he said. "I understand this is your first trip to America. May I be the first to welcome you to Charleston . . . Miss Matthews?"

Her luminous eyes looked surprised.

"Allow me to explain," William added. "I'm an old friend of Captain Lewis. He has hinted that you haven't had a chance to make contacts here, and I'd like to make you a proposition."

Stella returned the man's gaze levelly. During the past several years, many "propositions" had come her way. The defensive aloofness, which had momentarily slipped, displayed itself again.

"Proposition?" she repeated.

"Yes. I have a rather large home some miles away—Foxcroft. If you have no pressing appointment and aren't afraid of a little work—"

"I'm not afraid of work, Mr. Fox," she broke in. "But I do have a particular purpose in being here."

"Ah, yes. Your father."

Again Stella looked at him with surprise. "It appears you have me at a disadvantage, Mr. Fox, knowing as much as you do of my circumstances. Yes, I'm looking for my father. All I want is a chance to confront him."

"Confront? That seems an odd word. What will you do when you find him?"

"Make him pay."

She said the words softly, but their vengeful ring was unmistakable.

"I see," William murmured, his brows arching. "You want

revenge." As William studied her delicate feminine features, he found her vengeful expression disconcerting, perhaps because it seemed out of place on such a dewy young face.

It occurred to him that he had something in common with this unknown woman: They had both been abandoned. He had withdrawn, given up, and retreated into his paintings and journals, but Stella Matthews had developed a strength of purpose that enabled her to sail to an unknown land on a hopeless mission.

"Valor in adversity"—the Fox family slogan flashed through William's mind as he stared into the turquoise eyes of the young stranger. Suddenly it seemed important that she come with him.

"Didn't you know, Miss Matthews?" he said. "Living well is the best revenge. And live well you certainly will at Foxcroft. At the very least, you can earn an income to support your search. At the most, you can begin a new life. What do you say?"

She continued to look skeptical. William Fox chuckled. "I can assure you I'm quite trustworthy. What's the matter? Haven't you any gambling spirit?"

Stella flared at the challenge. "Oh, yes. I'm a gambler, Mr. Fox. Else I wouldn't be here, would I? What sort of work are you offering at this place . . . Foxcroft?"

William was absorbed in studying her hair and face. Her coloring was dynamic. "What? Oh, let's see. Some light household duties, and I'd like to pay you to be my model."

Stella's eyes narrowed. "What sort of model did you have in mind?"

William threw back his head and laughed wholeheartedly. It was something he hadn't done in a long time.

"A perfectly respectable model, I assure you. I'm an artist. I'd like to paint your portrait—head and shoulders only if you prefer."

Stella's cheeks began to burn. "Why do you want *me* for a model?" she persisted.

William looked at her a little more solemnly. "Surely you know by now that you're quite beautiful. But the reason I'd like to paint you goes beyond that. It's your coloring. I've never seen anything like it." William smiled. "Really. Why, of all the models I've painted, you could be my star."

The young woman's eyes lit up as if he had uttered a magic word.

It took Stella a moment to speak. "*My star* . . ." It must be a sign, she thought, for this stranger to use the same endearment her father had favored.

"Where did you say this home of yours is?" she finally asked.
He led her away from the docks toward a long, shiny black car.

"Harold," he said to a hefty man in chauffeur's livery. "We
have an unexpected passenger."

"Yes, sir, Mr. Fox," the driver replied.

After opening the car door, the chauffeur turned to look at
Stella. His eyes were flat and muddy, disclosing nothing, but
seeming to convey a vague threat. Despite the warm afternoon sun, she shivered as she climbed into the back of the
limousine.

Captain Jack Lewis watched contentedly from the deck of the
Indies Queen. He had anticipated William's actions. The man
simply couldn't pass up someone in need. Look at the way Fox
had helped him by financing the purchase of the *Queen*. Look at
the way he'd hired that churlish bumpkin, Harold, when everybody knew he was as crazy as his drunken fanatic father.

As he stood there, a gust of wind swept across the deck, turning
over a pail. Startled, Captain Lewis looked up at the sky where
dark clouds swiftly gathered.

"Hmph!" he snorted. "You can never predict when a storm will
blow in around here. Look lively, lads!" he called to his crew and
hurried to square away his ship.

It seemed to Stella that she was floating along in the silent
limousine as the imposing city flashed by. She had viewed
Charleston anxiously from the deck of the *Indies Queen*, but it
looked different now. The word that came to mind was one her
mother had always used to describe something lovely and beyond
their modest means: "fine." Everything about Charleston looked
"fine"—the wide, tree-lined streets, the immaculately trimmed
lawns and gardens.

So unlike the wild majesty of Jamaica, Charleston was steeped
in a refined beauty. Its buildings were laced with balconies of
wrought iron, their elegance rivaling that of the people who
strolled along the walks outside the courtyards. Even the palms
stood in stately rows.

The anxiety that had beset her evaporated, and Stella felt a
rising excitement. For the first time since her voyage began, the
thought of her father was not foremost in her mind. Glancing at
William Fox, she felt grateful that, because of him, she was riding
in style instead of walking fearfully away from the docks of
Charleston Harbor. Suddenly she was devoted to the man. She had

never felt that way before, but already she knew that, for her, no one would ever quite measure up to Mr. Fox.

Turning back to the window, Stella watched the beautiful scenes rush past and daydreamed about the new and wondrous things her life would hold. She had no way of knowing that life held the future the old woman of Trelawny had predicted—a future that would find its end at a place called Foxcroft.

Chapter Two

March 25, 1987
Kensing, New York

The rain held off until she was nearly halfway home from the store. Then it began to fall in sheets, an erratic wind whipping it into cold gusts that slapped and stung.

Head down, Maggie huddled within her slicker and hurried along the puddled sidewalk. By the time she reached the familiar gate, the groceries were sopping within their paper sack. She strode irritably through the yard and up the steps. It wasn't until she reached the shelter of the porch that she raised her head and saw him.

"Hi," he offered, lounging against the front door as if he owned the house, flashing straight white teeth that must have cost thousands.

Maggie halted in mid-stride. "What are you doing here, Nathan?"

His smile broadened as he rubbed his palms briskly together. "It's a chilly morning. I was hoping for a hot cup of coffee."

She eyed him suspiciously. "Why here?"

"Come on, Maggie. I haven't seen you in weeks—not since your parents' funeral. I've been concerned about you. After all, you *are* my friend."

"I'm your *wife's* friend," she corrected.

"Any friend of Shelley's is a friend of mine. We all went to high school together. Remember?"

"You were two years ahead of me, Nathan, and I was never part of your country club set. You didn't even know I was alive until your buddy Steve Moore started spreading his little stories."

Nathan chuckled. "Still the same old Maggie. Can't let anything pass, can you? Come on. Are you really going to refuse the husband of your best friend a simple cup of coffee?"

Shifting the cumbersome bag of groceries, Maggie looked him

over. Dressed like a fashion plate in a dark suit and topcoat, he
made a striking impression, especially when he turned on the
winsome smile she recalled from long ago. Nathan Barnes had
always been a charmer, and now he was pouring it on.

"A cup of coffee," she repeated. "And that's all?"

He raised his palms in a gesture of innocence. "What else could
there be?"

What else, indeed? she thought and, acting against her better
judgment, let him in.

As soon as he closed the door behind them and gave her a
heated look, she knew she'd made a mistake. Turning quickly, she
walked through the house to the kitchen, removed her slicker, and
began to prepare the coffee without so much as a glance in his
direction. After a moment she heard him enter the room.

"So how are you?" he asked from somewhere behind her.

"As well as can be expected."

"I've been worried about you, the way you've locked yourself
away in this empty old house."

"I prefer to be alone."

"That's clear. I've come by several times."

"I'm aware of that, Nathan."

"Why didn't you answer the door?"

Maggie drew a deep breath and wordlessly measured dark
coffee into the pot.

"What's the matter, Maggie?"

The voice was closer now, scarcely a foot beyond her shoulder.
Maggie sidestepped to the sink, gracefully eluding him in a
maneuver that had become reflexive.

"Nothing's the matter. I simply had a cold, wet walk from the
store."

Again Nathan stalked her. After a moment she felt the pressure
of his palms on her shoulders.

"I'll bet I could warm you up," he whispered.

Despite his threatening nearness, Maggie spun and confronted
him. "I don't find this amusing, Nathan! I've told you before—
your innuendos are an insult both to me and to Shelley."

"It isn't innuendo, Maggie."

"So much the worse! I must have been crazy to let you in here.
Now please leave!"

Nathan's gaze moved to her fiery hair as he smiled. "I've
always liked your temper, Maggie. It's part of your allure."

She brushed past him and stalked across the room, turning when she reached the counter to give him an angry look. "I can't believe you would do this to Shelley. The smartest thing you ever did was to marry her. You've got the *best*, Nathan, and you don't even know it!"

He moved steadily toward her. "Shelley's great, but she doesn't—"

"If you say she doesn't understand you," Maggie broke in, "I'll puke!"

"It's true!"

She looked at him scathingly. "I'd have expected something more original from the town's most promising young attorney."

"Look. I'm giving Shelley a good home and a good life! I've never run around on her, Maggie. You know that!"

"Then why don't you leave me alone?" she demanded.

"Maybe because I don't believe you really want me to," he said. "You're a woman of the world, Maggie. I'm sure you had no lack of male companionship during all those years in Paris and New York. Okay, then why not me? No one has to be hurt. Shelley will never know."

"How considerate!" Maggie lashed out. "Do you really think her not knowing would make it all right?" She shook her head. "You know, Nathan, for all your money, all your social position, you're not fit for her to wipe her boots on!"

His expression turned grim. Finally, Maggie thought, she had broken through his complacency.

"I'm beginning to think the guys are right," Nathan said. "You *do* have ice water in your veins."

She gave him a hard look. "Hardly an attractive quality, wouldn't you agree?"

"I don't know. Something about you draws me. Maybe it *is* the challenge of breaking through that icy reserve of yours."

Maggie slumped against the kitchen counter. "Just get the hell out of here, Nathan! Now!"

He took a step closer, regarding her in a self-assured, challenging way. "And if I don't?"

She couldn't bear his arrogance, his belief that anything he wanted was his for the taking! With deceptive calm, Maggie reached across the counter for a canister, flipped the top off it, and thrust the can forward. Flour billowed in the air and settled like a white veil over Nathan's dark hair and topcoat.

He backed away, sputtering.

The illustrious Nathan Barnes stared for a moment, then

stomped out of the kitchen, leaving a trail of footprints behind on the flour-dusted floor.

The letter came the following week. It was totally unexpected, and it would change the course of her life. But Maggie had no reason to suspect that. She tore it open carelessly and raced through its contents, a brow lifting as she finished.

For a moment she stared into space. In the blustery New York springtime, she shivered in the old house and wrapped herself in a vision of sunny skies and trailing flowers. Then, with an absent sigh, she replaced the note in its official-looking envelope, stashed it in her pocket, and forgot it altogether.

A smoky twilight haze was draped across the sky, its gray folds shadowing the familiar view as she stood at the living room window later in the day and looked across the patchy lawn that had yet to show a sign of spring. The limbs of the giant elm, where a child's swing still dangled, were black and naked; the hedge lining the picket fence looked brown and straggly. Beyond the fence, an occasional car whizzed by, its headlights shining on the slick street where a freezing drizzle had persisted through the day.

Maggie turned away from the window and went into the den to stoke the fire. She had continued the family tradition of using the fireplace each evening, and she was well into the last cord of wood that had been carefully stacked for winter. Still, try as she might, she couldn't coax any coziness into the house.

After laying aside the poker, she sank down on the braided rug, pulled her knees up under her chin, and huddled in the fire's circle of warmth. Eventually her gaze left the orange flames and moved around the room—to the overstuffed chair where David Hastings once did his reading, the hutch where Myra Hastings had kept photographs, mementos, and some of the sketches Maggie had done as a child.

She opened the hutch and began to study the gallery of snapshots. There she was astride a palomino at the Miles Riding Stables. The love of horses was one of the few constants that had carried her through a difficult adolescence. Now, as Maggie looked at herself in the picture, dressed in her riding habit and smiling as if she hadn't a care in the world, she thought it sad that she hadn't been astride a horse since she was a young girl.

Her gaze moved on to the next snapshot, a picture of herself and Shelley at age fourteen, when Maggie was already a head taller than her diminutive friend. The picture had been taken during the time when she had shot up like a weed and started looking different from the other girls. Her almost painfully narrow waist and hips had contrasted embarrassingly with breasts that had developed early, and although she'd dressed in the same school-girl styles the other girls wore, the clothes had looked different on her—alluring, almost seductive. At fifteen, with the right makeup and outfit, she could easily have passed for twenty.

Fifteen, she thought wryly. *That* was certainly a banner year! That was the summer she found herself fancying Steve Moore. Tall, blond popular Steve, son of one of the wealthiest men in town. Maggie had been flattered when he took an interest in her, a lowly freshman.

But the summer night she "made out" with him in his dad's fancy car, her fate was sealed. Steve swept into his junior year on a liberally embellished story about his conquest of Maggie Hastings. *She* nervously entered a new school full of strangers to discover that she was already known as "that redhead who made it with Steve Moore."

Her denials only made things worse. The girls, except for Shelley, kept a holier-than-thou distance. The boys made sugges-tive remarks. When Maggie consistently refused dates with leering classmates, the rumor spread that she was sleeping around with older men.

It was a painful time of life, and Maggie remembered how she'd felt. She'd had two choices: crumble under the pressure of her peers or rise above them by feigning an attitude that suggested they could all go straight to hell. Pride won out, and in the winter of her fifteenth year, a door slammed shut within Maggie, sealing off a tender innocence and trust that could never be recovered.

She declared a cold war on Steve Moore and his popular crowd, walking the high school corridors with her head high, returning their whispers with a haughty aloofness that became her trade-mark. Steve went on to become student council president; she remained an outcast.

It had happened years ago, but even now Maggie recalled the hurt and lonely feelings she'd hidden away during that turbulent time. She'd turned her back angrily on her schoolmates, throwing herself into her studies and a social life designed to give the high school gossipmongers something to whisper about. Boys from other schools, students from the nearby college—the stream of dates was steady.

It was the beginning of a pattern that seemed to feed on itself, snowballing and sweeping her through four years of college and two years of graduate study in art at the University of Paris. Men came in droves, drawn as much, it seemed, by her aloofness as by her beauty.

Maggie didn't question it, nor did she revel in it. It was simply the way things were. Her female friends were few, her male companions many and fleeting. She spent her days studying the art that she loved, her nights on the arm of one man or another, never veering from the untrusting reserve she'd adopted in high school, never allowing any man to get too close.

The company of men became comfortable, if predictable. The typical pattern, for the men, was an enamored show of attention, hurt surprise at her consistent elusiveness, cold bitterness at her final rejection. Maggie sometimes felt a pang of regret when she moved on, but for the most part their attention was merely something to be expected, something that was often a means to an end.

Her years in Paris, for instance, had been filled with incredible experiences made possible by men. The university was a virtual melting pot of art enthusiasts—intellectual giants, millionaire investors, students of genius, royal benefactors. Maggie hob-nobbed with them all, attending the theater, the ballet, formal balls, and gallery openings, even a candlelit dinner in an ancient castle. She enjoyed herself as long as things remained light-hearted, but when a suitor pressed too arduously, she coolly dismissed him.

As long as one kept one's distance, she believed, the opposite sex was harmless. And for Maggie, keeping a certain distance was automatic. In her tender teenage years a wall had sprung up around her. It had grown more impenetrable with age. Behind the mask of cool charm she approached the male animal with a mixture of caution and disdain. Even in romantic Paris she fended off the many opportunities for *affaires de coeur*.

Until Jean-Paul de Chevalier came into her life, with his open smile, clean good looks, and a love of art nearly as ardent as her own. He showed up one day in her Renaissance Art class, and she was aware from the first that he was watching her. A couple of weeks passed before he approached her after class.

"You're a treat to watch, *mademoiselle*."

"Excuse me?"

"You *play* with men," he remarked. "And I would very much like to join the game."

It was a novel approach, and Maggie looked at him with surprise, her indignation giving way to amusement as she succumbed to the intelligent eyes and smiling face.

"*Bien, monsieur,*" she said. "The ball is in your court."

She spent the last four months of her stay in Paris with Jean-Paul, and though she was not certain she was in love with him, she enjoyed him as she had no other man.

She had known from the beginning that he was a count or marquis or some such thing, but he'd never made anything of it. Not until the end, when she gained her master's degree and he announced that he was about to marry a countess.

"It's expected, *chérie*," he said simply, then implored her to stay on in Paris as his mistress.

She had run from Paris . . . just as she had run from New York a few months ago when her boss's unwelcome attentions forced her to resign from her position as an assistant curator at a museum in the city.

A log fell in the fireplace grate and sent a crackling shower of sparks flying up the chimney. Maggie opened her eyes, unaware that a bitter look had crept into them. She had learned well her lesson about men. She would never fall prey to one of them again.

A gusty night wind pummeled the walls, drawing creaks and groans from the old house, but failing to penetrate the warm, firelit den. Maggie's gaze returned to the hutch, and she scanned the shelves until she found the familiar photo portrait. Unlike their adopted daughter, David and Myra Hastings were blond, short, and plump. Unlike their hot-tempered daughter, they were invariably serene. Their cherubic faces beamed at her from within the wormwood frame, and she stared back until a lump rose in her throat.

They had always been her safe harbor. Always she had been able to run home to the couple in the house on the shady lane. And for a time her restless spirit had found the comfort of being loved—if not of belonging.

But no more. They were gone.

Maggie had refused to believe they were dead until she saw unarguable proof. After the devastating snowstorm subsided, a search party had found the small party of college scientists, bringing to a tragic end the week-long search of the mountains of upstate New York.

She recalled that day a month ago, the casual wave she tossed them as they embarked on another expedition. Once again she cringed, realizing their last thoughts of her had been tangled between the hope that she would finally settle down and the certainty that she was about to set off on another escapade.

"It's not that I want to leave you two," she'd said as she helped them pack the station wagon. "It's just that I need to find myself a niche, now that things haven't worked out in the city."

She didn't tell them about Nathan and his sly propositions.

"Besides," she added with a shrug, "you know how hard it is for me to stay put."

That much, at least, was true. The older Maggie grew, the more pronounced became her restlessness. At first she'd thought it was just Kensing. She was different. She didn't belong there. Later she'd discovered it was something she carried with her wherever she went. At times she thought the feeling coursed in her blood, so deeply was it embedded. Some allegiance or direction cried out to her, and had for as long as she could remember, driving her from place to place, taunting her with the notion that she was connected to *something*, if only she could find it.

David Hastings had heaved a suitcase into the back of the wagon and turned to Maggie. "Can't stay put," he repeated with a somber look.

Placing a warm hand on her shoulder, he looked into the vivid eyes of the daughter who stood head-to-head with his five-foot-eight frame.

"Long ago we made a decision concerning you," he resumed. "During all the years you were growing up, we believed we'd been wise. But now, since you've come back from the city, we've been wondering . . . Maybe some things run deeper than conscious thought. Maybe memories go back farther than we know. At any rate, when we return, we want to discuss something with you, Maggie. Something we've put off for a long time."

Now Maggie would never know what that mysterious "something" was. They were never coming back.

Never. The word seemed to echo through the room, so dreadfully silent but for the whispering of the dying fire.

Maggie crossed her arms, absently hugging herself as she continued to study their picture. Deep in reverie, she jumped when a loud ring split the quiet. Not the phone; the doorbell.

"Damn!" she muttered. Again the jangling of the bell reverberated down the hall.

"All right, all right. Coming!"

Closing the hutch, she moved into the hall, and stopped

to assess her appearance in the mirror. She wiped a smudge of soot from her chin as the bell sounded once more. "Coming!" she called again, and was all the way to the front door before a warning thought leapt to her mind: Maybe it was Nathan. He had called a couple of days earlier, and she'd promptly hung up on him.

She peeped through the diamond-shaped pane, her eyes widening as they beheld Shelley. Maggie had avoided her friend the past few months, and now as she looked at the familiar face, a hot rush swept over her. With considerable irritation, she recognized the feeling as guilt.

Quickly she threw open the door, and a blast of evening air shot past her, lifting the curls from her forehead. "Shelley! What are you doing here?"

The dark-haired woman stepped inside and gazed up at Maggie with devoted gray eyes. "I hope you don't mind my barging in like this, but you don't seem to answer the phone anymore."

"You know you could never barge in on me, Shelley. But what brings you all the way over here on such a cold night?" A half-formed worry stabbed at her chest. Surely Nathan hadn't said anything. "Is everything all right?"

"Everything's fine," Shelley replied, removing her muffler and coat. "And we only live on the other side of town, you know." She smiled reassuringly. "I came to find out if you're okay. Since the funeral I haven't heard a word. I've been calling and calling, but you never answer."

The mention of the funeral brought a familiar ache to Maggie's throat. "Sure, I'm okay," she said flatly. When she noticed her friend's concerned expression, she managed a lighter tone. "Can't you tell just by looking?" She assumed a fashion model's pose that mocked her sloppy appearance.

"You look pale," Shelley replied as she handed over her heavy coat. "And a little thin. But the fact is, you grow more beautiful with time, Maggie. You could still have any man you wanted."

Coming from Shelley, it was an unusual remark, and Maggie again regarded her friend uncertainly. "Pity I haven't found one I want, huh?"

She hung Shelley's coat in the closet, and together they walked into the cozy den that had harbored their get-togethers for twenty years. It wasn't until later, when Maggie poured them a sherry and began to rebuild the fire, that Shelley broached the subject that had brought her across town.

"Maggie, come here. I want to talk to you." She said the words tenderly, her gray eyes locked on Maggie's face. Obediently Maggie approached the sofa and sank to a cross-legged position, her heart beginning to thud disquietingly.

"Maggie, what are your plans?"

"My plans?"

"Yes. Nathan made a puzzling remark yesterday—"

"Oh! My plans!" Maggie interrupted with a rush, her brain racing to make up a plausible reply that would turn Shelley's thoughts away from Nathan and his treachery.

Suddenly the answer burst upon her. "My plans! I can't believe we've been chatting for an hour and I haven't mentioned the letter."

"Letter?"

"Yes, it arrived today," Maggie said quickly. "From our lawyer." Retrieving it from her pocket, she thrust it at her friend. "Here . . . read this."

"Miss Margaret Elizabeth Hastings," Shelley began to read. " 'Dear Miss Hastings, I have been unable to reach you by phone. I must make you aware of a document, an addendum to your parents' will. We discovered it among the papers in their safe deposit box.

" 'As you are aware, I drew up your parents' will. Perhaps you already know that they owned property in South Carolina. I, however, was unaware they had any such holding, nor did I know that it was being held in trust for you. If you are unfamiliar with this property, I suggest you consider visiting it. A firsthand view would help you decide if you wish to maintain the property or sell it.

" 'These are matters we should discuss. Please call me at your earliest convenience. Very truly yours, Albert Morely.' . . . How intriguing!" Shelley exclaimed, looking up from the letter with wide eyes. "Did you know about this property?"

"No. I've never heard anything about land in South Carolina. All I know is that Mom and Dad went to the university there, in Columbia."

"But they've held this property in trust for you all these years. Fascinating!"

"Yes. Isn't it?" Maggie returned, and rushed headlong into a decision she'd barely considered. "That's why I'm going away . . . to South Carolina."

"Really?" Shelley breathed.

It broke Maggie's heart to see the unmistakable relief that leapt to her friend's gray eyes.

The next morning a telephone call to Albert Morely produced a clipped tenor voice and the mental image of a sharp-featured face with beady eyes. The attorney extended eloquent expressions of sympathy, but he was not a man to waste words. As soon as he had paid his respects, he turned to business.

"Suffice it to say, I shall greatly miss David and Myra. They were valued friends as well as clients. Now then, as for your inheritance: Their will, as I recorded it, leaves you in a comfortable situation, Miss Hastings. But I'm at a loss about this South Carolina property. I must confess I find it odd that such a document should be found in their safe deposit box. This was completely unknown to me; your parents never alluded to it in any of their records or conversations."

Morely seemed a bit put out by the discovery, as if his trustworthiness had fallen under question.

"Exactly what sort of document is it?" Maggie asked.

"It's a simple, handwritten—hand-*scribbled*, actually—and duly witnessed document. It describes a plot of land stretching from, and I quote: 'the markers to the marsh and including the house that stands thereon.' At the moment that's all I know about the property . . . that and the fact that it was granted to your parents in trust until you reached adulthood. At that time, the gentleman stipulates, the property became legally yours."

"What gentleman?"

"The man who transferred the land to your parents." Albert Morely paused for a moment. "Does the name William Fox mean anything to you?"

Never before had Maggie heard the name. Yet at the sound of it a chill raced up her spine.

The inherited property was located in a rural area outside Charleston, South Carolina. In one of his many calls, Morely had reported that the name of Mark Fox had cropped up. Apparently the man and his mother were residents on or near the inherited property, and making the connection with the name of William Fox, Maggie imagined them to be distant relatives of her mysterious benefactor—perhaps caretakers of some sort.

She had not corresponded with them. Morely had handled everything, beginning with contacting Mark Fox who, according to Morely, had seemed quite surprised—demanding that a copy of

the document be sent for his review. Finally Morely had tele-
graphed the man and announced that Maggie was flying down to
survey the property. The next day Mark Fox had sent a reply wire
saying Maggie would be met at the airport.

When the plane landed, Maggie followed the flow of passengers to the baggage area. It took a full half-hour to collect her
luggage and move to the waiting room. She watched the majority
of her fellow passengers depart, and checked her watch for the
third time. It was 5:10 P.M. Someone should be here by now.

Eventually a bulky, middle-aged man in chauffeur's livery
ambled toward her. Glancing about, she saw that no one was
standing nearby. He must be coming for her. A chauffeur?

Five or six paces from her, the man came to a halt as a look of
bewilderment crossed his blunt features. He was a most
unpleasant-looking person, Maggie decided. Ragged salt-and-
pepper hair escaped his cap to fringe about a heavily lined face
with bushy eyebrows. There was a coarseness about him that
contrasted with the dark formality of his uniform.

"Miss . . . Miss Hastings?" he stammered in a hoarse voice.

"Yes, I'm Maggie Hastings."

"I'm here to drive you." He mumbled the words, then gathered
her luggage and began to move toward the exit.

Her eyes fixed on the man's broad back, Maggie followed him
to the door. But when she stepped into the warm afternoon
sunshine and looked around, her thoughts left him. It was
beautiful! Palms and bright splashes of hot pink azaleas graced the
green lawns surrounding the airport, and although quite a few cars
wheeled along the driveway, there was not the frenzied atmosphere she had become used to in New York. Even the air was
different. Heavy with the salty aroma of the sea, it held the
promise of summer.

Maggie took a deep breath and, as she followed her escort,
shrugged out of her jacket and slung it casually over her shoulder.
She looked ahead to the long black car where the man had
stopped. Slowing her pace, she watched as he loaded her bags into
the trunk of the sleek limousine. He slammed the trunk lid shut
and stepped around her to swing the passenger door open in a
grudging manner.

As she climbed into the back of the car, her eyes flickered up at
the driver from beneath lowered lids. Unaccountably, he called to
mind a presence she hadn't thought of in years—a face she had
seen in a childhood nightmare, a threatening man who had peered

at her from behind the screen of bushes that scratched against her bedroom windowpane.

"Who are you?" she demanded when he took his place in the driver's seat.

He muttered a slow, raspy reply. "I'm Harold. I've worked for the Fox family for thirty years."

"Where are you taking me?"

"You'll see," he answered.

Indignantly Maggie leaned forward and injected a tone of authority into her voice. "I demand to know where you're taking me."

His response was to push the button that closed the glass panel between driver and passenger. "Foxcroft," came his one-word reply. The privacy panel snapped shut, and Maggie was effectively plunged into solitude.

Her first impulse was to bang resoundingly on the window. On second thought, she snapped her mouth shut and fell back against the plush seat. There was something intimidating about the man, something that went beyond his size and appearance. Within his eyes was an absence of feeling and understanding, a kind of ignorant meanness. The less she had to do with him, the better.

From the airport they drove south onto the peninsula and into the city. As they entered the Historic District of Charleston, Maggie was struck by the aura of antiquity pervading the place. Boulevards were lined with tall royal palms and pastel town houses trimmed elegantly with wrought iron. Ancient churches were surrounded by lush gardens protected by tall iron fences. A cobblestone street drew her eye to a horse-drawn carriage that rattled along toward the harbor.

The place was breathtaking, and she wished the insolent driver would slow down. But she held her tongue and did her best to take in the scenery as they raced through the city. It seemed only minutes before they crossed the Cooper River by means of an enormous bridge and continued north, leaving the city behind.

The highway dwindled to a two-way thoroughfare, and the roadside buildings thinned to an occasional convenience store. Still gazing through the limousine window, Maggie noted road signs to Georgetown, Myrtle Beach, and an estate called Boone Hall. Every few hundred yards, blacks dressed in colorful clothes and bandannas looked up at the limousine from roadside stands brimming with handwoven baskets of all shapes and sizes.

Eventually the chauffeur slowed the great car and turned onto a narrow shady road flanked by jungles of plant life—palmettos, pines, and the dark ghostly shapes of cypress. Kudzu and honeysuckle twined through the trees and formed a tangle of greenery that seemed to hover over the road, admitting only an occasional shaft of golden sunlight. In a flight of imagination, Maggie half expected to hear the call of a tropical bird. But there was no sound save the smooth purr of the limousine's engine.

She felt suddenly like an intruder in a strange land. Along with the feeling came a sense of danger that stirred the hair on the back of her neck. With each mile that rolled under the luxurious car, Maggie's apprehension mounted.

Chapter Three

The wild trees and brush came to a halt as a white fence appeared on the left side of the road. Beyond it was rolling meadowland and, in the distance, a pine forest. About a mile farther on, Harold turned between two tall brick gateposts bearing plaques inscribed with the name Foxcroft. They cruised down a wide avenue shaded by twin rows of giant live oaks, vivid with the green of spring. Their black limbs twisted across the road to form an arch draped with silvery trails of Spanish moss.

Maggie caught her breath at the grandness of the place. On both sides of the road, beyond the white fence, lay manicured lawns dotted with beds of camellias, jonquils, and white azaleas. A lacy white veil of dogwood blossoms hung over the dark magnolia trees and evergreens that grew alongside the lengthy drive. Straight ahead, just visible among the trees, stood a massive white house.

She turned questioning eyes to the driver's capped head, but he maintained his brooding silence behind the glass, and Maggie was left to watch mutely as they approached the mansion—although to call it such seemed an understatement. The drive carried them into a courtyard enclosed by a brick wall with a white wrought-iron gate. A side drive branched off to a garage. In the center of a circular courtyard, a two-tiered fountain propelled sparkling water into the air.

Harold stopped the car in front of the mansion, but Maggie paid no heed. She was staring through the window at the most magnificent house she'd ever seen. Bathed in the golden light of late afternoon, the white structure glowed, its wrought-iron-trimmed windows and towering walls creating the impression of a majestic castle. It was the kind of place pictured in history books, a place so grand and imposing one would never expect to stumble across it in present-day America. A light-headed sense of unreality swept over her as she pressed close to the glass and craned her neck to follow the shape of the house as it rose monumentally toward the sky.

It was three full stories, its sloping roof crowned with a dozen chimneys. Dazedly Maggie brought her gaze back to ground level. To the left stood a separate wing connected to the main house by a rose-covered ambulatory. Tiled steps led up to a semicircular veranda, capped with a crescent-shaped roof supported by white columns. On one side of the porch she saw a swing and a love seat, on the other a white tea table and chairs. A jardiniere of red geraniums stood on either side of the double doors which, she noticed, were slowly opening.

A distinguished-looking man in a conservative suit emerged from the house. He stood between the jardinieres and stared in the direction of the limousine. He was followed by a round black woman with silver hair, dressed in a gray maid's uniform and apron. She hobbled—more side to side than forward—to the front steps and peered down at the car through wire-rimmed glasses. Eventually the man moved to join her.

"Speak up, Harold," the woman called. "Did ya fetch her?"

Maggie suddenly realized she was sitting motionless in the back of the car, although the driver had already opened the passenger door. A look of wonder on her face, she climbed out of the limousine and started up the steps, her fingers gripping her jacket nervously, her eyes on the silver-haired woman who squinted against the low afternoon sun.

"Why, you're jest a young thing," the woman rumbled and broke into a chuckle.

Encouraged by her friendliness, Maggie relaxed somewhat and moved to stand before her and the man, who had yet to speak. A look of horror swept over his pinched face before he quickly averted his eyes, ostensibly to study the broken red tiles that covered the porch floor. He was perhaps fifty years of age, though the carefully darkened hair was designed to belie those years.

"Mr. Fox?" Maggie ventured hesitantly.

At that, the man's brown eyes snapped in her direction. "Hardly!" he gasped. His sharp look impaled her for an instant; then he attempted a smile that was more forbidding than his sharpness.

"Forgive me, my dear," he drawled. "I'm afraid I'm not at my best today. I am John Henry Alexander—administrator of Foxcroft, you might say. When Mark Fox is away, I am in charge here."

Tentatively Maggie extended her hand to the man, but he only glanced at it disdainfully and backed away a step.

"I'll let Rachel take charge of you now," he said with a nod to the black woman. "I'm afraid I've grown quite unused to guests. It's been years since we've *invited* anyone to the house. I fail to grasp the modern code of etiquette that would allow a young woman simply to show up on our doorstep. But nonetheless we've prepared a room for you and hope your *brief* stay will be pleasant. . . . Rachel?" he concluded, arching a brow at the old woman.

The man spoke in such a refined, polished way that it took Maggie a moment to realize she'd been thoroughly insulted. By that time John Henry Alexander had walked away. A hot blush dappled her cheeks as she turned to the woman called Rachel.

"Pooh!" the old woman huffed with a frown in the direction of the man's fast-disappearing back. "That's Mrs. Fox's cousin. He fancies himself the boss here, but he's the only one who does, if you know what I mean. My, my," she added with a smile, cocking her head and assessing Maggie through thick bifocals. "A pretty young thing come to visit us all the way out here!"

Her voice had a pleasant, guttural timbre, and she chuckled again as she shooed Maggie into the house. "You come on inside now, honey. . . . Harold!" she called over her shoulder. "You jest bring Miss Hastings's things up to the green room!" Turning back to Maggie, she said, "It's been too long since we had a guest out here. Why, it used to be we'd have parties and guests, but now . . ."

As they entered the house, Maggie caught her breath. The place was immense—grander than she had imagined during the quick assessment she had made when she first saw the mansion. A thick red carpet muffled her steps, stretching across a parquet floor and continuing up a wide freestanding staircase with glossy mahogany banisters. Halfway up, the staircase split to left and right, then curved up to the second floor. A tremendous crystal chandelier hung in the center of the entrance hall, which was decorated with mirrors, paintings, and small tables bearing porcelain figurines, silver pieces, and vases of jonquils.

The wainscoted hallway was broken up by elaborately embellished double doors, some of which stood open. To the left, Maggie glanced quickly into a rose-colored parlor with a love seat and a piano, then into a large dining room with a massive table and china-filled breakfront. Here a slight blond woman, who was dressed in the same starched gray garb as Rachel, looked up briefly from polishing the table, then returned to her chore. Maggie walked along silently, following Rachel toward the staircase.

Lengthening shadows crawled over the rich brocades and velvets, over the polished glow of the antique furniture. Perhaps it was just the hour of the day, but there was an odd darkness about the house, and despite Rachel's friendly chatter, a solemn hush— an almost morbid quiet—hung in the air. Once again the hair on the back of Maggie's neck stood straight up.

"What *is* this place?" she finally murmured.

"Home," Rachel chuckled. "This is home, honey. That's all it is," she added with a little puff as they reached the staircase and she began to pull herself up, leaning on the banister. "You got plenty o' time to see everything and everybody. You jest get yourself settled and take you a little rest before supper."

As they reached the landing where the stairs split, Maggie exclaimed over an ancient grandfather clock that towered two feet above her head. The old woman merely smiled, apparently so conditioned to the splendor of the house that it no longer had any impact on her. When they had climbed to the second story, she opened the first door along the hall and hustled Maggie into a spacious bedroom. Harold appeared behind them, deposited her luggage, and disappeared without a word.

"There, now. You jest make yourself right at home, Miss Hastings. You want some iced tea or lemonade to sip on?"

Maggie shook her head.

"Well, then, let me just say welcome to Foxcroft. Mr. Fox told me your folks were real good friends of Mr. William, and I do believe I met 'em years ago one time. Anyhow, I was real sorry to hear they passed on. But I'm happy you decided to come visit us. I got to go now and get supper ready."

She was almost out the door when Maggie snapped to attention and called out, "Excuse me . . ."

"Yes, honey?" The old woman turned to face her.

"I believe I'm supposed to meet Mr. Fox."

"Why, you will, honey. You'll meet Mr. Fox tonight at supper—him and his mama, too. You jest rest for a little while and be downstairs at seven-thirty sharp. Mr. Fox likes for supper to be on time, now, you hear?" She closed the bedroom door.

Maggie turned in a slow circle in the center of the bedroom. Obviously designed for a woman, it was furnished with a gilded

French provincial dressing table, divan, chest of drawers, and canopy bed. The ivory of the walls and the moss-green of the carpet were repeated in the brocade drapes and bedspread. Doors in the east wall opened into a roomy closet and a bath. French doors curtained in sheer lace led to a wrought-iron balcony. Excitedly, Maggie drew open the doors, and a breeze gusted in, caressing her face with the scent of flowers.

She stepped out onto the balcony, her hands finding the cool metal of the railing, her eyes growing wide at the beauty before her. The grounds unfolded gracefully around the house—just what one would expect to find on a bona fide southern plantation. Jonquils hugged the foundation of a weathered gazebo. Gardens of brightly blooming azaleas and greening rosebushes, sculptured hedges and rolling lawns stretched to the dark blue-green of a pine forest. Beyond the pines ran a silver ribbon of water. And beyond that, for as far as Maggie could see, lay a marshy wilderness.

Slowly her gaze traveled to the green lawns dappled with the hot pink of azaleas, then to the stone terrace below, where a fringe of pear trees boasted snowy blossoms. In New York, winter still hung on with a vengeance, but here spring had danced across the land, leaving in its wake bright flowers and lush green color.

When she was able to tear her thoughts from her surroundings, Maggie turned to questions that ran around and around in her mind. Why had her parents never mentioned this place? What was their connection with the obviously wealthy Fox family? Did her newly acquired property adjoin this fabulous estate?

Time drifted by unnoticed as she stood on the balcony. When she looked again at the ribbon of water, it was red with the reflection of sunset. A misty haze rested on the treetops, and she was suddenly aware of a chill in the air. Looking quickly at her watch, she discovered it was almost time for supper.

Ten minutes later she stood before the dressing table mirror and smoothed the skirt of her suit, blessing it for not having wrinkled. The turquoise silk blouse mirrored her shining eyes. Her cheeks were flushed. The shining mass of fiery hair was pulled back neatly with combs, then tumbled gracefully about her shoulders.

Many men had been lured by her exotic beauty—the vivid dark-lashed eyes, the high cheekbones with their natural blush. Slender to the point of being wraithlike, Maggie moved with a fluidity that some mistook for invitation.

But she had long ago come to terms with the mixed blessing of her looks. The most thought she ever gave the matter was to recognize that when she looked her best, she turned heads. Tonight she looked her best. With a wry memory of her ill-conceived notion that the Fox family would be down-home country folks, she donned her jacket and left the room.

As she descended the stairs, she overheard Rachel's voice coming from the dining room she had glimpsed earlier. "Poor thing," Rachel was saying. "She probably fell asleep up there after that long trip she had today. I'll jest go up and fetch her."

Maggie smiled at the woman's thoughtful defense of her and, picking up speed, was at the bottom of the stairs when a sneering male voice stopped her cold.

"She's a quarter of an hour late. The soup is getting cold. I would think she could improve her Yankee manners enough to be on time for *supper*!"

The voice was deep and rumbling, seeming to echo out of the dining room and reverberate through the huge entrance hall. Maggie's already pinkened cheeks flamed red. Mark Fox. That must be *his* voice deriding her to everyone within earshot!

She strode briskly across the foyer and into the brightly lit dining room. Head high, blind with indignation, she stalked to the table. At the head sat a dark-haired man she presumed to be Mark Fox. As he and the others looked up, startled, she swept them with a haughty glance.

"I apologize for my tardiness, Mr. Fox," she said coolly. "I hope the soup isn't as cold as your welcome!"

Mark Fox scraped his chair back from the table and leapt to his feet, his gaze settling on the woman who stood at the far end of the table. His eyes raced over her, then suddenly slowed their pace to absorb a tall, slender vision topped with a curling mass of coppery hair. As she turned her head to survey the group at the dinner table, light from the chandelier glanced off the curls, setting them afire. . . . What was it she had just said?

Several things seemed to occur at once, and still dizzy with anger, Maggie saw them unfold as if in slow motion. At the far end of the table, the dark-haired man sprang to his feet. Rachel, who stood on Maggie's right, covered her mouth to suppress the laughter that shook her round shoulders. On the left, the self-important John Henry Alexander clutched at his chest as if he'd been stabbed. And beside him a woman with dark graying hair and a sculptured face stared.

Maggie stared back defiantly, uncaring that the woman was

probably Mrs. Fox, the mother of the man she'd just confronted.

Mrs. Fox's hollow dark eyes grew wider. She put a slender hand to the throat of her high-necked black dress, then suddenly closed her eyes and slumped in her chair. Her chin plopped limply against her breast. She had passed out.

Maggie was riveted where she stood. Had her abruptness actually caused the poor woman to faint? A wave of regret washed through her as she watched John Henry lean over the woman in alarm while Mark Fox rushed around the table. Kneeling, the younger man grasped the woman's wrist as if to take her pulse. After a moment, his eyes left the woman in black and he looked at Maggie. The silence was tense, but he seemed oblivious of that as his look traveled over her.

Close up, the girl was even prettier. Pretty? Hell! She was devastating! As she stared at him with a tremulous expression, Mark's gaze roved from the startling turquoise eyes to the smooth, blushing cheeks. When it lit on the moist pink lips that had fallen slightly open, his heart slammed up to his throat.

Maggie couldn't move or speak. Under his penetrating stare, a shiver tingled along her limbs. As if hypnotized, she stared back. One by one, his features registered on her mind. Green eyes. Straight, narrow nose. Ruddy lips. Full dark hair, brows, and lashes, and a suntan that made the whites of his eyes fairly jump from his face—a face, she fancied, that was shadowed with the same brooding air of darkness that filled the rooms of the mansion.

Although the confrontation seemed to float in time, it must have been only seconds before Rachel waddled to Mrs. Fox and commanded, "Carry her up to bed, Mr. Fox. She'll be all right. Jest the excitement is all. Don't you worry." She patted one of Mrs. Fox's lifeless hands, adding, "I'll get John Henry to take her some of her favorite soup. Now, you go on and get her to her room. She'll come around all right."

At Rachel's instructions, Mark snapped back to reality and tore his eyes from Maggie, who continued to stand dumbfounded at the end of the long table. Feeling somewhat foolish—after all, hadn't he been staring at her as if spellbound?—he hid his irritation behind a scowl and turned back to his mother. John Henry stood up and went into the kitchen.

Scooping up the dark-haired woman as easily as if she were a doll, Mark Fox straightened his over-six-foot frame and strode away. Only when he reached the doorway did he hesitate and turn to address Maggie. The lines of his face were contorted with hate-filled arrogance, the shape of his mother's black-clad form etched severely against the white of his shirt.

"Wait here," his deep voice boomed, and then he was gone.

As if in a daze, Maggie turned to Rachel—confusion, amazement, and distress fighting their way across her features.

"Don't you worry about him," the old woman consoled with a quick nod toward the doorway. "Mr. Fox's bark is worse than his bite! And his mama? Why, I wish I had a nickel for every time she's fainted. It's her way, that's all. Now, why don't you jest have a seat and I'll bring you some soup."

Maggie refused the offer of supper, but allowed the old woman to pour her a cup of coffee from an exquisite silver service. Rachel disappeared into the kitchen, and moments later John Henry emerged carrying a covered tray. As he passed, the carefully groomed man clucked his tongue scoldingly in Maggie's direction.

She lowered her eyes, but when John Henry stopped by Mrs. Fox's place, she looked up long enough to see him retrieve a walking cane before quietly making his exit. Then she felt even worse.

Dolly Fox began to stir as Mark carried her into her room and gingerly placed her on the bed, but it wasn't until her cousin bustled in that her dark lashes flew open. Setting aside the silver tray, John Henry sank down on the side of the bed and leaned over her, his face a mask of concern. Dolly's black eyes searched his wildly, then turned to the towering form of her son.

"Did you see her? Did you see her face?" she demanded, her voice rising.

Mark's scowl deepened. "Calm down, Mother. You're going to upset yourself again."

"But you *did* see her, didn't you?" Dolly insisted. When she received no reply from her son, she jerked around to face her cousin.

"John Henry?" she questioned in a pleading tone, raising herself from the bed, clutching at his arm. "Surely I'm not imagining things! Surely you saw the same person I did!"

The man covered her thin fingers with his own. "Yes, Dolly," he muttered through tight lips. "I saw."

"You *saw*!" Mark repeated sarcastically. "How can you be sure *what* you saw—or *whom*—after all these years?"

John Henry turned to look indignantly in Mark's direction. "I'm sure, and I'm not the only one. Harold knew who she was the moment he set eyes on her."

"And what of Rachel?" Mark pressed. "If anyone would remember, *she* would! And she hasn't said a word!"

"Rachel is old and nearly blind!" John Henry returned impatiently. "Listen to me. Harold and I told you what to expect! We told you who this woman is!"

"Yes, you did!" Mark thundered, taking a step toward the bed. "And it was probably no more than your power of suggestion that planted this notion in Mother's head!"

Dolly Fox shook her head sadly. "No, Mark," she murmured. "You were only six or seven at the time, too young to remember. The resemblance is uncanny! I admit that my own memory has been blurred for many years, but one look at her brought it all back. That hair, that face, those eyes! Why, they're identical," she breathed with an expression of horrified awe.

"That's quite correct, Mark," John Henry chimed in. "They *are* identical. And if she's *not* who we say, how do you explain her being here? How do you explain the will?"

Mark searched for an answer, but could find none. A heavy sigh of defeat escaped him. "I don't know," he rumbled and ran his long fingers distractedly through his hair. He was nonplussed now, as he had been since this whole mess had dropped out of the sky to explode into his world.

Dolly fell back onto the pillows, her ebony-draped body seeming to sink deeper and deeper into the bed as she stared blankly at the ceiling. "All these years," she whispered. "Weren't all these years of imprisonment enough? Did she have to come back and haunt me?"

"Don't be ridiculous, Mother," Mark snapped.

"What are we going to do?" John Henry asked.

When Mark shifted his gaze to the man, he found a turmoil of emotions—fear, anger, horror—writhing across the sallow face.

"We'll do exactly as we planned," Mark said. "We'll buy her out, no matter who she is."

"But what if she has some silly idea of attachment to the place?" John Henry persisted. "Buying her off may not be easy."

"Selling out is the only sensible course of action for her," Mark returned. "I ran a check on her. She's from an average middle-class background. The sum I'll offer will bowl her over."

"But what if she fancies the idea of finding her roots?" John Henry pressed. "What if—"

"Look!" Mark interrupted. "We don't know *what* she may be thinking! I'm not certain she fully understands the circumstances of this inheritance—or that she knows her true identity, for that matter. Her attorney, Morely, never mentioned a word about it. In fact, he seemed unfamiliar with the name Fox."

John Henry's brown eyes were bulging. "Are you saying this girl may not know who she is?"

"Oh, God," Dolly whimpered. "Please let her know nothing. Please let her take the money and leave us alone!"

"She's not a demon, for God's sake!" Mark grumbled. "She's just a woman. And even if you're right about who she is, maybe luck is on our side. Maybe she doesn't know, and we can simply pay a long-overdue debt and send her on her way. Let's just play our hand close to the vest. Okay?"

John Henry raised a manicured hand to stroke his chin. "Now that I think about it, I wonder how much she *does* know."

Mark gave him a grim look. "That's what I intend to find out."

John Henry studied the younger man's threatening expression and relaxed. At any time, Mark Fox was someone to be reckoned with. And when his back was up, no one was his match!

Maggie took a sip of coffee and felt the soothing warmth course down her throat. Ten minutes passed, then fifteen. She poured a fresh cup and found herself wishing she were anywhere but the elegant dining room at Foxcroft, squirming in the antique Chippendale chair, awaiting the return of the formidable Mark Fox.

She should have told Albert Morely to order an appraisal and sell the mysterious property. What did she think she was doing traipsing around the South Carolina countryside, imposing on strangers who obviously resented her intrusion into their home?

Once again the dinner table scene played itself out in her head: Mrs. Fox's white-rimmed black eyes, her body slumping in the chair. Maggie chewed at her lip in embarrassment. What a bizarre turn of events! But then, everything today had been bizarre—the limousine, the grand southern plantation, the people. Such an odd, hostile group they were—Harold, John Henry, Mark Fox. As if summoned by her thoughts, the latter appeared in the doorway, and Maggie nearly spilled her coffee as she shakily replaced the cup in its saucer.

Tall and lithe, Mark Fox moved into the room with smooth

grace. She took note of a crisp oxford cloth shirt with sleeves rolled casually to the elbow, close-fitting jeans, and cowboy boots. As he drew near, her gaze lifted to his face—the high planes of the cheeks, the firm lines of nose and brow. Once again her eyes locked with the green ones that reminded her suddenly of a wintry ocean.

With the warnings of his mother and John Henry ringing in his ears, Mark looked at Maggie Hastings with new eyes. Earlier he had been caught off guard and had seen only a beautiful woman; now he saw a threat.

He rounded the table and stopped directly across from her to rest his hands on the back of his mother's chair. Silently, warily, he watched her like some great cat ready to pounce. Maggie cleared her throat and broke the silence.

"Your mother—"

"Is resting now," he cut in and briskly changed the subject. "I'm glad you came to Foxcroft, Miss Hastings. Obviously there are several matters to be worked out. According to the codicil . . ."

His words rolled out in the lazy southern manner, but there was a commanding edge to the voice. For a moment Maggie sat quietly, her mind less on what he was saying than on the arrogant way in which he'd taken charge of the conversation.

"Mr. Fox!" she broke in finally. "Before we talk about anything else, I must insist on a report about your mother. I feel responsible for her . . . condition."

He seemed surprised at having been interrupted. He hesitated, then replied somewhat graciously, "My mother hasn't been well for years. The slightest thing can set her off. As it happens, you look remarkably like someone she once knew."

He let the statement hang in the air, waiting curiously to see what she would do with it. But she refused to rise to the bait.

He stalked to the head of the table and sat in the chair he had occupied earlier. "Tell me, Miss Hastings. Why are you here?"

Maggie returned his intimidating stare. "After my parents died, I needed a change of scene. I wasn't aware they had property here until I got a letter from my lawyer, Albert Morely. He suggested I come to South Carolina. I'm between jobs right now. So here I am."

"You say you didn't know about the property? Or the will? You mean your parents never mentioned Foxcroft? I find that difficult to believe!"

A single brow shot up. "Your beliefs, Mr. Fox, have nothing to do with the facts."

His eyes snapped to hers, and she watched them narrow. He was dashingly handsome. The dark hair curling over the collar of his shirt was a bit too long to be regarded as conservative, but he had the symmetrical features Maggie's art instructors had sought in models. Still, there was a grim hardness about his face.

"How old are you?" he demanded.

Maggie raised her chin. "Twenty-seven."

Damn! he thought. She was exactly the right age.

"And how old are *you*?" she countered.

Mark looked at her as one would look at a bothersome insect. "Thirty-six. What does that have to do with anything?"

"What does *my* age have to do with anything?" she challenged.

Mark glared at her. "Let's get this little confrontation over with, shall we?" He glanced away, continuing in a flat, impersonal tone. "David and Myra Hastings were close friends of William Fox, my father. He was extremely fond of them. They went to the university together in Columbia.

"My father died more than twenty-five years ago. After his death I took control of Foxcroft. But now Morely has found that odd document in your parents' safe deposit box. It was written several years after the original will, and there's no question of the authenticity of William Fox's signature. You say you knew nothing of this?"

"Nothing but what Albert Morely told me," Maggie replied simply.

His expression was skeptical, but Maggie only gazed at him in silence. The coffee cup before her remained full, its contents neglected and cold.

"The document puts Foxcroft House and the surrounding grounds in your hands. I must point out, however, that Foxcroft operates several successful businesses and owns a number of holdings on which you have no claim whatever. The newfound document grants you only this house and a strip of land."

It took a moment for what he had said to sink in. Then Maggie blinked in disbelief. "This house? You mean . . . *this* house?" In the quiet room, her voice was a loud croak.

"Of course *this* house! What other house would it be?" He spat the words and glared as if her stupidity were beyond belief. Didn't she know *anything*?

Maggie quickly recovered her wits. When her voice came, it

dripped with ice. "Mr. Fox, you know I'm a stranger here. You could reply civilly to a perfectly understandable question."

Mark's face turned as dark as a thundercloud. "I fail to find it understandable that you're pleading ignorance of all this."

"Are you insinuating that I'm lying? Why would I?"

"You could have your reasons," he remarked. "Look, Miss Hastings. Whether you know more than you're telling or not, this whole matter is inconvenient. A group of investors will meet here a few days from now. I don't have time to devote to this business of my father's will. I intend to make you a generous offer—an amount of money that will buy you any kind of life you want. The papers will be ready to sign tomorrow, and I hope this matter can be settled immediately. We can meet with my attorney for lunch, and there's a flight to New York at four."

Maggie's head was spinning. Men usually tried to charm her. She wasn't accustomed to being treated in such an offhand way. "Tomorrow," she repeated dazedly. "Let me get this straight. You're telling me that I own this house and that you want me to sell it to you and leave . . . tomorrow?"

"Yes."

"But surely you must realize how strange this is."

"How so?"

"You've just told me I've inherited this house. I haven't even had a chance to think. I'd at least like to look around!"

Mark Fox studied her for a moment. "All right, I suppose we can put off your departure for a day. We'll meet first thing day after tomorrow, and you can make the eleven o'clock flight."

The conversation was turning into a fencing match. Settling back in her chair, Maggie tilted her head to one side and regarded the man assessingly. "Why the big rush?" she said softly. "Why are you in such a hurry to get me to sign your papers? Is there something you're not telling me?"

The challenging questions were out of her mouth before she knew they were coming. But they gave her a brief advantage. Apparently Mark Fox was unaccustomed to being put on the defensive. He stared at her, speechless.

"A sweet young thing with nothing to do," he finally muttered, his eyes boring into hers. "I suppose I can see how an art student might have time to waste on all of this."

"I am *not* a sweet young thing," Maggie returned hotly. She rose to her feet so she could look down on him. "Nor am I a student. I hold a Master of Fine Arts degree, and I was an assistant curator at one of the finest museums in New York. So please don't talk down to me as if I were a schoolgirl!"

"I simply meant that we're in different positions." Mark gritted the words from between his teeth. Rising from his chair, he planted his fists on the tabletop and leaned toward her. "I'm a businessman! This situation is a costly interruption. But I'm sure you must be just as anxious to put this matter behind you as I am. After all, the South Carolina countryside can't offer you the glamorous New York life-style you must want!"

"You can't possibly know what kind of life I want!" Maggie returned, her eyes flashing. "I'm sorry I'm a 'costly interruption,' as you put it. You've made it quite clear you wish I'd never come here. But I *am* here! You can't just snap your fingers and make me disappear."

In a slow, fluid movement, Mark straightened from the table and folded his arms across his broad chest. "I don't intend to snap my fingers," he replied coldly. "I intend to make you rich. The rest will take care of itself."

Everything about him brought out the tiger in her. All the careening emotions Maggie had stored up, all the grief, shock, and confusion, suddenly culminated in rage toward this arrogant man.

"Not everyone is bought so easily!" she blazed. "I'm no simpleton you can bully, Mr. Fox. Don't expect me to make a rash decision just because it's convenient for *you*!"

"Just how long *do* you intend to stay here?" he barked.

"It's *my* house. I'll stay as long as I like!"

Her voice rang through the quiet room, and Mark Fox glared at her murderously. A flush rose under his suntan as his fists clenched spasmodically.

Maggie stared up the tall length of him, took in the seething anger that had the man fairly trembling, clearly fighting for self-control. A pang of fright shot through her. He was so big; his handsome face was distorted with a rage so black it seemed positively demonic! For an instant she froze, her heart seeming to stop within her breast. But then her pride kicked in, and she lifted her chin, meeting his glare with a bravado that dared him to challenge her claim.

Mark gradually willed himself under control. "Looks like you're holding all the cards, lady," he said evenly. "Just don't expect me to be happy with the deal."

For a few seconds they stared at each other in mutual defiance. Then Mark spun on his heel and stomped away.

"Where are you going?" Maggie demanded.

"Out!" He threw the word over his shoulder, then on second thought halted at the doorway and turned to give her a short bow. "With your permission, ma'am," he added mockingly and was gone.

Maggie hurried away from the table, reaching the dining room doorway in time to watch the tall man stride out the front door. For a few moments she remained in the foyer and stared angrily at the closed door. The great house was silent at his departure; the oppressive quiet cooled her temper.

She turned wearily toward the staircase. Now that the tense scene with Mark Fox was over, she felt a rush of weakness. It was still early evening, but the day had delivered a series of shocks that had her head reeling. She sought the green bedroom as a haven and forgot even the strange, imposing grandeur of the house as she retreated up the stairs toward solitude.

Mark's thoughts raced ever faster as he strode through the night and into the dark stables. It wasn't until he neared Gray Lady's stall at the far end of the barn that he stopped to flip on a light. The mare whinnied a greeting, having recognized his footstep long before the overhead lamp illuminated his shape.

"Evenin', girl," he murmured and reached over the rail to caress her velvety muzzle. "How are you feeling tonight?"

His gaze traveled down to her bulging belly. The dappled Arabian would foal in about a month. Gray Lady nuzzled his fingers, then raised her trusting doelike eyes to his.

"You're doing fine," Mark encouraged and dipped his hand into a nearby feed bin. Extending the grain on his open palm, he watched the mare bend her sleek head and crunch happily away.

"Yes, ma'am," he added. "You're the best-looking lady it's ever been my pleasure to come across."

His words triggered an unwelcome memory of a woman who challenged the compliment. The mare continued to munch the oats as Mark's gaze strayed between the pointed ears to a spot on the shadowed, rough-hewn wall of the stall. A vision formed of flaming hair curling about a heart-shaped face, of clear turquoise eyes that looked straight through him.

Maggie Hastings. The sight of a beautiful woman had heretofore elicited only pleasurable thrills in his masculine libido. The sight of this one struck fear into his heart—a fear he would conceal at all costs from his mother, his cousin, and everyone else.

Without the will to stop himself, Mark surrendered to the same self-pity he had heard so often from his mother. Haven't I endured enough? he thought. Why this? Why now?

Gray Lady finished the oats, and Mark folded his arms casually on the top rail of the stall. From outside, cooling shafts of air wafted through the stables. The mare snorted at the invigorating scents of night, but Mark's face grew hot, his eyes remaining glued to the dark wall where the image of a female face lingered teasingly.

He had said he would find out what she knew, and he felt certain he had: nothing. She knew nothing of the peculiar circumstances of her inheritance. For some unfathomable reason, she had been kept completely ignorant.

Ignorant of this one situation, yes, but she wasn't dumb. He sensed an incisive intelligence in her well-spoken manner. And she had spirit. Hadn't she defied him in his very own dining room? Mark admired spirit. He liked it in a horse, and he liked it in a woman. But not this woman!

"Damn!" he sputtered and tore his gaze from the vision on the wall. Yet Maggie Hastings's fair features continued to swim before his eyes, refusing to disappear even when he buried his face in his crossed arms.

Maggie took a long, hot, luxurious bath, then slipped between silky mint-green sheets. As she turned off the light on the bedside table, moonlight filtered into the room, creating a faint glow and soft shadows. Through an open window near the French doors, a cool breeze brought the night sounds of crickets and an occasional frog.

"Foxcroft." She whispered the name, relishing the feel of it on her tongue. Foxcroft—which Mark Fox expected her to sell. She thought for a moment of how furious he must be at having to buy back something he thought he already owned. And what if she didn't want to sell? After all, she could live comfortably, albeit not grandly, on the estate her parents had left her.

The thought of them triggered the questions all over again. Why had they never told her about this part of their lives? Why had they kept Foxcroft a secret? And why did a stranger named William Fox leave his home to her rather than to his family? Mysteries.

Maggie had no solution to any of them. She would figure things out, but not now. She was too tired.

As she drifted closer to sleep, her thoughts turned again to Mark Fox. He was devilishly good-looking, but his looks weren't the only thing that put her in mind of the devil. There was an aura of darkness about him, a bleak fury that was both cold and blazing. She recalled the moment in the dining room when she'd been intimidated by his anger. Yet as his lanky image lingered in her mind's eye, Maggie experienced a sensual stirring.

Stop it! she scolded herself. Stop thinking about him! Shifting her position, she settled more comfortably between the silky sheets.

But when sleep overtook her, Mark Fox came to her dreams. She cringed at his booted feet as he stood like a giant above her. Wind whipped his hair into a writhing black halo, and his eyes burned like red coals as he pointed to the road leading away from Foxcroft.

Chapter Four

Morning sunlight poured in through the window, collecting in a warm, shimmering pool across the foot of the bed. A clean breeze from the same open window wafted through the room and brought the scent of newly mown grass. Coming slowly awake, Maggie wriggled her toes beneath the covers and watched dreamily as the sunlight danced along the golden threads of the brocade.

From the bedside table came the faint ticking of an antique clock. Under its crystal dome, gilded components whirred with steady precision, and slender hands responded with minute movements across a porcelain face. It was a beautiful piece, and she wondered how she could have failed to notice such a lovely thing the day before.

She recalled the tide of events that had stunned her. No wonder she hadn't noticed the clock or the oil hanging over the mantel or the fireplace of carnelian-flecked marble. As Maggie scanned the room, it came alive with interest and beauty. So, she imagined, it would be with the whole of the estate.

It was nearly nine o'clock, well past her usual hour of rising. Yet she stretched languidly, reluctant to give up the luxury of the silky sheets, reveling in the memory of her surprising inheritance. She felt a sense of well-being, even a glorious impression of belonging. How odd that only yesterday she had been a nervous intruder. Today she felt totally at home in this bed, this room, this house. It was as if Foxcroft, during the night, had embraced her.

It wasn't so, Maggie knew, with the inhabitants of the house. Somewhere in the lofty rooms languished the ailing Mrs. Fox. Somewhere, like a captain at the helm of his ship, Mark Fox dictated daily routine, just as he sought to dictate to her.

But even the thought of the intimidating Fox family couldn't dampen Maggie's spirits. Now, in the light of day, her anxiety of the night before seemed baseless and exaggerated. She was exhilarated as she hadn't been in months. A smile curved her lips as she sprang from the four-poster bed.

She began by looking through her suitcase for something to wear, but found herself putting things away—hanging most of her clothes in the roomy closet, folding away lingerie in the chest of drawers. It felt good. It felt as if she'd settled in. Besides, Maggie thought with a grin, small as the rebellious gesture might be, if Mark Fox suspected what she was about, he'd be furious!

She dressed casually in slacks and shirt, crossed to the vanity, and took a long look at herself. Was it only yesterday that she'd woken up in Kensing feeling groggy and hung over after another fretful night? Today the bright yellow of her ensemble enhanced the fiery highlights in her hair, and a glow of vitality lit her face. Other than that, she looked the same and thought it odd; she felt like a different person.

Her spirits lifted even higher as she descended the stairs and took in the magnificence of the house with a fresh eye. Maggie could barely wait to explore it, to learn everything about Foxcroft and the mysterious way it had fallen into her hands. She had no idea what the day held in store. She knew only that she was filled with excitement and that—oddly enough, considering her strange surroundings—the dismal feeling of displacement that had plagued her for a lifetime was gone.

She wandered into the dining room and investigated the swinging door at the far corner. Beyond it was the kitchen, where an aging woman dressed all in white was stirring a big pot on the stove. Near the butcher block in the center of the room, the slight blond woman Maggie had glimpsed the day before looked up curiously from her sweeping. A short distance away, Rachel stood with John Henry.

"Why, Miss Hastings," Rachel said, beaming as Maggie entered. "Aren't you looking bright this morning? You must have slept well."

"Very well, thank you, Rachel," she answered, turning her eyes reluctantly to John Henry. "Good morning," she added.

The dark eyes flickered to Maggie's face. "Miss Hastings," he acknowledged with a short, formal bow.

He could have been an attractive man in his youth, but his impeccable apparel and tinted hair couldn't hide the toll that time had taken. The years had etched lines of arrogance across his face so that his expression seemed a permanent sneer of superiority. His complexion had yellowed, as if a sourness from within had risen to the surface.

"Is this ready for Mrs. Fox or not?" he demanded of Rachel.

"It's ready," the woman replied with a disapproving frown. John Henry took the silver tray Rachel offered and strode from the room, leaving the door to swing behind him.

"Isn't Mrs. Fox feeling well enough to come down to breakfast?" Maggie ventured.

"No. I'll tell you the truth, honey," Rachel answered. "We don't have a formal breakfast around here. Mr. Fox is usually out before seven and just has coffee. And Mrs. Fox, she hardly ever comes down these days. John Henry takes most of her meals up to her, takes care of her like she was a little baby. Now, I don't want you to go getting worried about that spell she had. She's doing just fine."

"Okay, I'll take your word for it." Maggie smiled and added hopefully, "I'd sell my soul for a cup of coffee."

She followed Rachel around the kitchen and met the cook—a stolid woman named Mrs. Phipps—and the maid, Annie MacGregor, who smiled shyly and spoke with a pleasant Scottish burr. Annie and Rachel, Maggie suddenly realized, were the only pleasant people she'd encountered since her arrival at Foxcroft. Why, then, when hostility was the overwhelming atmosphere of the house, was she so drawn to it?

The airy, sprawling kitchen was a remarkable facility. Polished hardwood floors. Giant pantries. Along the far wall was a breakfast nook with a bay window overlooking the terrace and a door to the outside. A stove, sink, refrigerator, dishwasher, and microwave oven stood near the west wall. In the center was a large butcher-block table, and on the east side of the room copper pots and utensils hung on a wall broken by a large brick fireplace. Maggie wandered to the hearth and, in examining it, discovered a stone bearing the date 1730.

"Rachel!" she exclaimed. "Was this house built that long ago?"

"Yes'm, that's what they say," the old woman replied. " 'Course it's been added on to in lots of ways over the years, but it was built way back then by the first Mr. Fox who came over from England. The king himself gave Mr. Fox the land, and it's been the family home ever since."

"Amazing," Maggie breathed, as a fleeting vision of generations of Foxes flashed before her.

Although Rachel protested, Maggie insisted that she sit with her at the breakfast table while she had coffee and delicious homemade muffins with butter and strawberry preserves. Maggie wanted information, and it took very little prodding to start Rachel talking about the family she had served for a lifetime.

"Yes, ma'am. The household is a lot smaller now than when I first came. Now there's just Mr. Fox and his mama. 'Course, I live here, and John Henry and Harold—he does the driving and looks after the grounds. Mrs. Phipps and Annie drive out together from Charleston every day except Saturday and Sunday. And then there's Mr. Thompson who lives down the road a piece. He comes over every week and does the gardening. And his boy, Jeremy, tends the stables. We take care of everything, but in the old days, we had us a houseful."

"What was it like then?" Maggie prompted. "When you first came to Foxcroft?"

A distant look swept across Rachel's round face. "Lord, honey, when I came out here from the poor side of Charleston, I was barely fourteen years old. Mr. William was a baby, and his mama just been put in the grave. It was a sad thing to see. His daddy never did forgive poor Mr. William for being born. It didn't matter that Mr. William was his only child, with no brothers or cousins, nobody else to carry on the Fox name. All he could see was his wife being dead, and he avoided the boy like the plague. That was a shame 'cause there was never a more loving soul born than Mr. William.

"William grew up with his daddy always being in town or in the stables. Then he started painting, and he would go off by himself for hours. He was a real artist, he was, and good with his hands. He built himself a painting place up at the library."

"You mean a studio?" Maggie asked quickly. William Fox—an artist?

"Yes, that's it! He made himself a studio out of that old attic, and that's where he stayed most of the time, even after he came back from college and married Mrs. Fox. But then Mr. William died and Mrs. Fox got sick. And now nobody comes out here to the house, and even if they wanted to, Mrs. Fox wouldn't let 'em. She jest wants to stay to herself now. Mr. Mark, he's real good to her. When he has to go into town for business, he goes, but then he comes right back."

At the mention of Mark Fox, Maggie felt a tug of interest. "I guess Mr. Fox has been running Foxcroft for a long time. I'm surprised he doesn't have a family of his own. Has he ever been married?"

"No, he never has. But the Lord knows there's been enough

ladies chasing after him all these years. There was one who really went after him, but—"

Rachel stopped suddenly, tipped her head, and looked knowingly over her bifocals. "You ain't had a chance to see it, but that boy can turn on the charm when he wants to. Reckon Mr. Fox might never get married now, but I sure wish he would. He's awful good at providing, and keeps the place mighty nice. But it jest don't seem to make him happy. No, ma'am. He's a young man, but seems like he's turned all old inside."

Over the rim of her coffee cup, Maggie regarded the old woman thoughtfully. "Why do you say that, Rachel?"

"Well, honey, people can be real unkind, and I reckon the people in town ain't no different from most. You know, everybody's got some stories that's best left untold. I reckon Mr. Mark has been told things he never should've known. And now it's like he's getting back at 'em all, showing 'em he's better than all of 'em put together, what with all the money he makes and how they write about him in the papers and call him a genius and all.

"But that hasn't put the light back in his eyes, not like when he was a boy. Even when he rides that big old black horse of his, it's like he's riding fast and furious to get away. Like the devil himself was on his trail!"

At that point Mrs. Phipps called Rachel over to sample the aromatic dish she was creating, and realizing that the old woman needed to get back to her chores, Maggie excused herself. She was pensive as she strolled through the dining room, her thoughts lingering on Rachel's comments about Mark Fox.

The man was rude, arrogant, and infuriating, but there was no denying his fierce masculine appeal. Even Maggie, who considered herself immune to men's charms, had experienced a surprising response when she looked into those emerald eyes. Like it or not, she was intrigued by Mark Fox, and she found herself wondering what events of the past had caused the bleakness he wore like a cloak.

Mark thrust the shovel into the ground, but it sank only a couple of inches. The earth around the dead tree was stubborn. It hadn't been disturbed in a hundred years and was giving up its hold grudgingly.

He glanced around the trunk, where Harold was digging with equally questionable success. They'd been battling together for over an hour—the only result, a large circle of upturned topsoil.

The stump of the live oak, which had perished during the winter, was planted as firmly in the Foxcroft back lawn as ever.

Mark stripped off his shirt, passed a gloved hand across his sweating brow, and resumed his work. The morning sun was hot, but the spring breeze was reviving. He threw his strength behind the shovel, thinking that it felt good to do some physical labor for a change. Far too often these days, his only exercise was a fast horseback ride. He had the opportunity for little else, considering the amount of time he spent at the office.

He thought briefly of Foxcroft, Inc., and imagined what everyone would be doing at this time of the morning. He knew they were wondering where the boss was. Mark hadn't missed a day at the office in over a year and was often there on weekends. But today? Today he'd felt the need to stay home.

His flushed face turned grim as his muscular body kept up a thrusting rhythm with the shovel. He had wakened with Maggie Hastings on his mind and promptly decided to take the day off. Something told him not to leave the estate—that possession was nine-tenths of the law. Intellectually Mark accepted the fact that the woman had legal claim, but his feelings said that Foxcroft was *his* and that no piece of paper was going to change that.

Ever since he'd heard the shocking news, he'd told everyone—including himself—that things would work out, that it was only a matter of time before a contract was signed. But that was before he'd met Maggie Hastings. She was no pushover. Now he didn't know what the hell might happen.

Mark turned to gaze across the lawns at the towering white walls of Foxcroft. Until this thing was settled, he intended to stake out his territory like a lion.

Harold moved around the massive tree trunk and noticed Mark standing there, his task forgotten. The master of Foxcroft was usually a good worker; it wasn't like him to daydream and dally the way he'd been doing. Today Mark Fox was different, and as Harold followed his line of vision up to the house, he realized what had Mr. Fox worried.

That redhead! That jezebel! She could mess up everything!

"Hmph!" he snorted in loud disapproval.

The sound brought Mark out of his reverie. He turned to his companion with an absent look. "What's the matter?"

Harold looked toward the house, his bushy brows drawing together in a frown. "Nothin', Mr. Fox."

"Well, I guess we'd better get on with it, then," Mark muttered, returning his attention to the old oak.

Harold threw a last threatening look across the lawns. When he went back to work, he passed the time by imagining the redhead's face beneath each bite of the blade.

Maggie spent the whole of the day exploring the great house. The Georgian details were graceful and airy; the furnishings, exquisite. The upholstery fabrics were satins and velvets; the furniture, predominantly mahogany and cherry; the interior was studded with antiques and works of art so that each look revealed a treasure. Even so, a dark air of times long dead hung over the dignified rooms and hallways.

Downstairs she found a receiving parlor, a music room monopolized by a concert grand piano, the enormous dining room and kitchen, the servants' quarters, a formal living room with a marble fireplace, and—to Maggie's surprise—a mirrored ballroom with a glossy hardwood floor.

Here the brooding atmosphere of the house seemed oppressively thick. It was obvious the room had been closed off for years. The mirrors were layered with dust, and the giant chandelier was shrouded in a protective cover. At the far end of the ballroom, between two sets of French doors, dozens of chairs were lined up against the wall, as if they had long ago performed their duty and would never again be required. After a last look around the mausoleumlike room, Maggie made her way back to the foyer.

Upstairs she toured six bedrooms, each with its own bath and fireplace, each in a different color scheme—blue, peach, her own green room, and so on. Across the landing from her bedroom at the rear of the house were two sets of double doors beyond which, she deduced, was Mrs. Fox's domain.

Exploring the great house was like having a museum all to herself. Time flew, and through all of her wanderings, Maggie met no one, except when she dropped into the kitchen to have lunch.

Rachel and Mrs. Phipps were busy, and Annie moved so quietly about her chores that you scarcely knew she'd been there until she passed. Except for the four of them, the house seemed deserted, although Maggie supposed that John Henry was keeping Mrs. Fox company in her suite. Mark Fox was decidedly absent. No one had mentioned where he might be, and Maggie hadn't asked.

It was late in the afternoon when she decided to call Albert

Morely. The Carolina legacy had turned out to be something quite different from what they'd expected; and the memory of Mark Fox's pressure for a quick sale had nagged her all day.

When she got the attorney on the phone, she spilled the story in an excited rush. She was unprepared for his gloomy response.

"If it's as grand as you say, Miss Hastings, you could be in trouble."

Maggie's face fell. "Why?"

"Because the taxes and upkeep on a place like that would be staggering. David and Myra left you in a position of comfort, but certainly not wealth. I don't mean to frighten you, Miss Hastings, but if I were you, I'd start looking for a buyer right away."

She chewed her lip. "A buyer?"

"Yes. If you can unload that place, you'll be sitting pretty. Of course, I don't know enough details about the property to estimate its value, but from your description, it could be worth a fortune. The problem is, it might prove difficult to find an investor willing to spend such a sum for a house in the middle of nowhere."

"Maybe not," Maggie said quietly.

"What do you mean? Do you know someone who's interested?"

"Mark Fox. He's having the papers drawn up."

"Wonderful!" Albert Morely nearly sang the word. "Then your problems are over. Just send me a copy of his offer and leave everything to me! Congratulations, Miss Hastings. It looks as though you're about to become a rich young woman."

Thoughtfully Maggie replaced the receiver, her fingers trailing off the phone to caress the antique mahogany sideboard on which it sat. She would be rich. Why did the idea fail to excite her? She glanced about the sweeping foyer and knew the answer. It was this house, this place. Twenty-four hours ago, she hadn't even known Foxcroft existed. Now it was under her skin.

The sun hung low in the sky as Mark made his way across the rolling back lawns toward the house. His sweat pants were rolled up, his shirt tied around his waist. He and Harold had managed to sever a few of the major roots of the old oak, but it had taken a good deal of hot, sweaty work. Harold would have to blast the stump out with dynamite.

Mark was tired. His shoulders were sunburned, his arms and legs ached. But it was worth it. The physical labor had been cathartic, and he'd managed to keep his mind off his troubles most of the day.

Now, however, as he approached the house and recalled that Maggie Hastings was somewhere within, his feet dragged and his mood turned black as night. She couldn't know how her presence affected him.

There was more to it than just her claim. There was his own betrayal. If what everyone suspected about Maggie was true, he could understand the provision William Fox had made. But understanding did nothing to relieve the secret hurt that twisted in Mark's gut like a knife. The only cure was to get Foxcroft back.

As he walked along, he pictured her, face flushed and eyes flashing as she announced she'd stay in *her house* as long as she liked! But by the time he reached the terrace steps, he'd slipped into memories of the way her fiery hair shone under the light of the chandelier. She was a beauty, all right.

Mark brought himself up short. To think of Maggie Hastings as a desirable woman was blasphemy! He slammed the door behind him as he stomped into the kitchen.

Maggie completed her tour of the house by climbing the stairs to the third floor. There she found the only rooms that departed from the opulent style of the rooms below. From the moment she looked into the spacious chambers, she recognized Mark Fox's stamp; it was so strong that it repelled trespassers. She halted just inside the doorway.

It was a sprawling suite, apparently comprising study and bedroom. The walls of knotty pine were nearly covered with hunting and horseman prints. There were bookshelves, a desk on which several hefty books lay open and face-down, a television and stereo—the first Maggie had seen in the house. Modern rustic furniture blended with the knotty pine for a totally masculine effect. On the far side of the room, beside the open door to the bathroom, was a king-sized bed, a far cry from the diminutive four-posters on the second floor.

She was sorely tempted to browse through the man's quarters, but she had no idea where he was, or if he might come strolling in at any moment. Backing away from the doorway, she turned and all but collided with someone who had come up behind her without a sound. Even as she recognized John Henry's face, she gasped, her hand flying to her throat.

"A *lady* doesn't invite herself into a gentleman's rooms," he scolded with a flourish of his hand toward Mark Fox's open door.

A blush raced to Maggie's cheeks, but a spark of anger sprang to her eye. "And a *gentleman* doesn't sneak up on people."

John Henry tossed his head and chuckled. It was a hollow sound, devoid of mirth or goodwill.

"My dear Miss Hastings, I doubt very much if what *you* know of gentlefolk would fill a thimble. Women of your sort are typically lacking in—how shall I put it?—a grasp of etiquette."

Maggie glared at the man. "Women of *my* sort?"

He spread his hands impatiently, as if any fool could take his meaning. "It's obvious you have no breeding at all—gallivanting around the country, barging into men's rooms—"

"Excuse me!" Maggie broke in and started to step around him. "I don't have to listen to this—"

"But perhaps you *should* listen," John Henry insisted while moving adroitly to block her way. "You're not in New York City now. You're in *our* world. There are social rules to be obeyed, customs of courtesy to be observed. You can't just wander through Foxcroft House as if . . . as if—"

"As if I *owned* it?" Maggie supplied and watched with satisfaction as the haughty man cringed. "That's what really bothers you, isn't it? Through a strange turn of events, I *own* Foxcroft. You have no right to question what I do or where I go!"

John Henry's face turned scarlet. "I have every right!" he cried. "Do you think you can just waltz in here and take over when I've lived here—taken care of this house—for more than thirty years?"

Without seeming to realize it, he curled his hand into a fist and brandished it in Maggie's face. "I am as much a Fox as anyone in this house! When Mark is away, I and I alone am in charge here!"

Mark heard the ringing voice from the second-floor landing. What the hell had his cousin in such a stew? Curious, he vaulted up the last flight of stairs to his rooms, arriving in time to see John Henry threatening Maggie Hastings with a clenched fist.

"What's going on here?" Mark boomed, his long legs taking him quickly to the two people who stood outside his suite.

"She was trespassing!" John Henry accused.

"I was *not* trespassing!" Maggie flashed.

Mark stepped abruptly between the two, who were faced off like a couple of bulldogs. Maggie was so angry she barely noticed the rippling muscles in the bare chest and arms that were right in front of her. Instead, she leaned around Mark to carry on her row with John Henry.

"And furthermore—" she began.

"And *furthermore*," John Henry jumped in. "You haven't the manners of a billy goat! Otherwise you'd never have come in the first place. Everyone knows you don't belong here!"

Mark pivoted so he could look down at John Henry. "Now, hold on, cousin. Why don't you just calm down?"

"I can handle this, Mr. Fox!" Maggie cut in.

Turning in surprise, Mark noted her flushed cheeks and sparkling eyes.

"That's obvious," he remarked sarcastically and, in spite of himself, found his attention turning to the fine smooth texture of her skin.

"I don't need anyone to fight my battles for me!" Maggie flared.

Mark's softening regard went suddenly hard. "I can see that, Miss Hastings. But it just so happens the two of you are parked outside my door! May I request that if you want to continue your brawl, you do it somewhere else?"

John Henry stepped from behind the taller man and gave Maggie a scathing look. "I have no intention of continuing *anything* with this woman!" he announced, and retreated down the hall.

Maggie was left standing there with Mark Fox. She was furious, but fast beginning to feel silly. John Henry was, after all, a harmless aging man. And yet his slurs were maddening! She stared up at the remarkably handsome face of Mark Fox and released her frustration on him.

"I'll thank you to let me handle my own arguments after this," she snapped.

Below a shock of dark hair, the man's chiseled brows drew low over his green eyes.

"Count on it!" he thundered.

Maggie turned and walked away.

She changed into an elegant black dress for supper, but as it happened, she needn't have bothered. The dining room table was set for only one. Rachel bustled in bearing a decanter of wine, a fruit salad, and the information that Mrs. Fox was having a tray sent to her room and Mr. Fox had some business to attend to. John Henry was also absent.

Maggie supposed their absence was an insult. But she wasn't insulted; she was relieved. Mrs. Fox would have cast a pall over the dinner table. John Henry would have continued his bellicose remarks.

As for Mark Fox, Maggie's thoughts were mixed. It hadn't been quite fair, the way she snapped at him earlier. But she resented the man beyond endurance—his snide remarks, his arrogance, and most of all the fact that she was losing her newfound inheritance to him.

According to Morely, she had no choice. Mark Fox was her answer—the savior who could deliver her from financial disaster. But the idea that she'd be forced to submit to the domineering man was almost more than Maggie could swallow.

Pushing away the thought, she welcomed the fact that she was alone and enjoyed her meal in silence. As she sipped an after-dinner demitasse, her gaze wandered over the room. Elaborately carved moldings outlined the ceiling; wainscoting and brocade-patterned paper graced the walls against which stood graceful antique chairs and tables, the luster of their polished wood glowing warmly in the soft light. Never, not even in Paris, had she dined in more elegant surroundings.

Gazing into the small flames that danced atop the silver candelabra, she decided to call Shelley. What fantastic news she had! But the flare of excitement faded as she thought of all the things she *couldn't* tell Shelley, things that she herself didn't understand. Why had her parents never told her about Foxcroft? Why had she, Maggie Hastings, inherited the mansion? A wisp of a thought kept tugging at the back of her mind, but it had yet to come forward.

Maggie gathered her plates and went into the kitchen. Rachel was standing by the bay window, peering out into the night.

"Lord have mercy!" the old woman exclaimed at the sight of Maggie carrying her own supper dishes. "Give me those things, honey. You're not supposed to be cleaning up after yourself!"

Maggie smiled and proceeded to the dishwasher. "It's the least I can do after such a delicious meal."

Rachel smiled broadly at that, and Maggie went to join her at the window. The old woman pulled aside the curtain and once again looked out across the terrace.

"What are you doing?" Maggie asked curiously.

"Just watchin', honey. Just watchin' that man over yonder eat his heart out."

"Who?"

"Mr. Fox. He's in a state, that one. Has been ever since you got here." Rachel looked over her shoulder. "Don't get me wrong, Miss Hastings. You got every right in the world to be here. It's what Mr. William wanted, and it's what you deserve."

"Why did he do it, Rachel?" Maggie asked softly. "Why did Mr. William leave the house to my parents and me?"

For a moment Rachel's ancient eyes searched the pretty young face. "I'm sure he had his reasons," she said and turned back to the window. "But that don't mean it's easy for Mr. Fox. It's hittin' him pretty hard, honey. Pretty hard."

The statement surprised Maggie. She couldn't imagine Mark Fox being "hit hard" by *anything*. She leaned over and looked curiously beyond Rachel's silvery head. It was just as the old woman had said: Mark Fox was sitting alone in the shadows of the terrace, head bowed and shoulders slumped as if he'd lost his only friend.

Albert Morely's unwelcome suggestion came to mind. Distasteful as the idea of selling was, she couldn't ignore reality; sooner or later she was going to have to negotiate with Mark Fox.

"Maybe I should go speak with him," she suggested finally.

"Mebbe so," Rachel affirmed so quickly that Maggie wondered if the old woman had had that in mind all along.

Mark looked up when Maggie opened the terrace door, then straightened in the chair as he recognized her. Light spilled in patches across the terrace from within the house. It wasn't until she came to a stop beside his chair that he could see her clearly. His look traveled up the slim figure in the black dress and touched her face. His jaw set a little harder as he dropped his gaze.

Maggie looked down on the dark head of hair, noting the rigid way he stared ahead. "You weren't at supper," she said.

"Does that surprise you?"

"Because of me?"

He glanced up, his stern expression discernible even in the shadows. "Good guess."

Maggie folded her arms across her breast and regarded him critically. "Funny. You didn't strike me as the type to run from a problem."

Mark gave a short, harsh laugh. Shaking his head, he got to his feet and looked down on her with scorn. "Believe me, lady. It has nothing to do with running."

"What, then?"

"I don't see why you have to ask. It seems obvious to me that we find each other's company offensive."

His insult stung. "You're so right!" she flared. "But in spite of that, we're going to have to deal with each other."

"Is that what your attorney said?"

Maggie blinked. "How did you know I talked to Morely?"

"Come on," Mark admonished. "Don't you think I know everything that goes on in this house?"

She stared up the vast height of him, took in his self-satisfied expression.

"I see I can add eavesdropping to your list of sterling qualities," she flashed.

He stared at her with what looked to Maggie like utter loathing.

"We can stand here and trade insults all night," she went on, "or we can talk. Which will it be?"

Mark shifted his weight onto one leg with infuriating calm. "The only thing I have to say to you, Miss Hastings, is that I'm picking up the papers from my attorney tomorrow."

"Fine!" she snapped. "I came out here with the idea that we could call a truce. But I can see you're not up to that!"

She whirled away, but he was hot on her trail.

"Wait just a minute!" he yelled.

Maggie halted, turning slowly to confront him.

"Just what the hell do you expect from me?" he said angrily. "You come here, claiming you own *my house,* announcing you'll stay as long as you like! What do you want me to do? Pretend I don't mind?"

"No!" she returned just as angrily. "Be civil, that's all! You call yourself a businessman! Any businessman knows that the best way to expedite a deal is by opening lines of communication. You want me out of here, Mr. Fox? All right! Then stop behaving like an angry bull! Try being a little cooperative and informative for a change. Because I assure you I'm not leaving here until I've seen everything I inherited—the house, the land, *everything.*"

Mark glared down at the woman, who met his ferocious look with one of her own. Spitfire, he thought derisively. Hellcat! But then one of Rachel's sayings flashed through his mind: "You catch more flies with honey than with vinegar." He forced a long, steadying breath.

"All right," he said finally, his deep voice rumbling. "I'll be civil. I'll be informative. And if it will help expedite the deal, I'll show you around."

"Don't do me any favors," Maggie said caustically.

"Dammit, woman!" Mark exploded. "If I'm going to make an

effort to get along with you on this deal, then you're going to make an effort too! We're *both* going to be civil and get through this thing as painlessly and quickly as possible! All right?"

"All right!" she said.

"Well, then, when do you want a tour?"

"As soon as possible."

"Do you ride?"

"Do I ride what?"

He rolled his eyes in frustration. "Horses."

"I've ridden."

"Then we'll go on horseback. Tomorrow. At two."

"Fine," she replied succinctly.

"Fine!" he boomed.

They glared at each other for another strained moment, then retreated in opposite directions—she to the shelter of the house and he to the darkness of the Foxcroft grounds.

The next morning Maggie scanned her wardrobe in search of a sporty ensemble appropriate for a horseback ride later in the day. The best she could do was a pair of snug-fitting jeans and a short-sleeved white sweater that hugged her waist.

By pulling her hair sleekly back into a French braid, she created an effect that made the startling color of her eyes leap from her face. A reckless excitement raced through her. Perhaps Albert Morely was right. Perhaps she *would* be forced to part with Foxcroft. But she didn't have to think about that now! For the time being, this place was hers.

She leaned across the vanity and picked up a small glass vial. It was a unique fragrance, a special perfume blend that she continued to order from Paris. Unscrewing the cap, she closed her eyes and held the open bottle beneath her nose. It was a rich scent, an enticing brew that hinted of warm spices and gardenias. Liberally she dabbed the potion at her wrist, throat, and earlobes.

She had no boots, and so completed her ensemble by donning knee socks and tennis shoes. They would offer some protection against the rub of stirrups. She thought briefly of the last time she had ridden. She hadn't been on a horse since before she went away to college! As she bounded down the staircase, she nursed a silent hope that her equestrian skills would come back to her once she straddled a mount.

She drank a quick cup of coffee in the kitchen with Rachel and the ever-silent Mrs. Phipps, then wandered to the front of the house where she gazed out through beveled glass windowpanes. The bright flowers were so cheerful, the sunshine so inviting, they seemed to beckon. The freshness of the spring morning burst upon her as she stepped outside.

Maggie ambled across the veranda and took a sweeping look beyond the fountain to the azalea gardens, the stately lawns, the giant live oaks twisting gracefully across the drive. Surely no place on earth was more beautiful. She skipped down the steps and into the courtyard, where she strolled aimlessly around the corner of the house and was confronted with the flower-draped ambulatory. White trelliswork was nearly hidden by a trailing mat of talisman roses, forming a floral bridge to the detached east wing. Wisely the gardener had restrained himself from overpruning. The crimson flowers tumbled over one another in magnificent disarray. As Maggie approached the blossom-thatched corridor, their scent filled her nostrils.

Stepping inside the walkway, she marveled at the rose-covered roof that blocked the warm sunlight. The ambulatory was cool, and patches of moss padded the brick walkway, which was laid in a herringbone pattern broken every so often by a round millstone.

Ahead, through dappled sunlight, was the door of a freestanding two-story structure. Maggie walked toward it, but at the threshold she hesitated. The door seemed to mark the entryway to something more than just a separate wing of the old mansion. With an unconscious shiver, she shook off the feeling that she was about to open Pandora's box and reminded herself that she had the right to go wherever she pleased. Half expecting the oak door to resist, she was surprised when it easily swung open.

The deserted room she entered comprised the entire ground level and had the sedate look and feel of a museum. A large mahogany desk and some filing cabinets filled the foyer area; beyond it, the room opened into a large library with banks of towering bookshelves extending from the far wall.

The shelves that lined the walls were intermittently broken by elaborately framed portraits and scarlet-draped windows. Maggie walked farther into the room and began to look at the portraits. On examination she found small plaques bearing names and dates on the bases of the frames. The portraits were of the Foxcroft heirs.

Major George Thornton Fox, 1740. Jane Harrod Fox, 1740. James Leighton Fox, 1798, and his twin, John Thornton, painted during the same year, both of them dressed in the velvet and lace garb of the eighteenth century.

Maggie made a leisurely tour of the cavernous room and studied each oil. George Harrod Fox, 1860. Depicted against a landscape of acres of rice, he epitomized the gentleman planter. Next to his portrait hung that of a fair-haired woman wearing an off-the-shoulder emerald gown that pinched her waist, then flared out over a large hoop. Maggie looked down at the plaque. Nicole Justine Fox, 1860. All the Fox males were appropriately noble; their ladies, appropriately ladylike.

Her tennis shoes treading softly on the old hardwood floors, Maggie moved from portrait to portrait. William Justin Fox, 1875. Anna Leigh Fox, 1880. William Tate Fox, 1925, and beside him, a pretty blue-eyed woman—Margaret Elizabeth Fox, 1925. With a slight start at the coincidence, Maggie looked long into the serene face of the woman whose name was the same as her own. Her gaze slid to a neighboring framed work, an embroidery of the Fox family crest. The design was executed in bold red and black, the head of a fox surrounded by three crowns and resting on a shield bearing crossed lances. At the top was stitched a slogan: "Valor in Adversity." And at the bottom the proud words: "The Mark of a Fox."

Maggie felt as if history were coming to life. She perused the crest of the family whose roots lay buried in the annals of English nobility, and she wondered dreamily how many family members had marched gallantly behind a banner bearing the head of a fox and the stirring motto, "Valor in Adversity."

There was something sad about the state to which the clan had dwindled. From what Rachel said, Maggie surmised that Mark Fox was the sole survivor of his forefathers. And Maggie herself? An unlikely heiress to the manor that had long been the family seat.

Thoughtfully she turned and walked back toward the front of the room. She thought she'd seen all the portraits when she spotted three more on the front wall. The first arrested her attention by the warm smile on the face of the subject, a contrast to the stark, stalwart air exuded by the other Fox males. She read the name—William Marcus Fox, 1948. Slowly, it came to her that she was looking at the man who had bequeathed Foxcroft to her parents and ultimately to her.

With growing interest, Maggie backed away a few paces and gazed at the painting. Now she could understand Rachel's words about the man. What was it the old woman had said? "Never a more loving soul born?" It was all in the painting—the openness of the smile, the kindness in the clear eyes. She must have remained absorbed in the painting for a full ten minutes before realizing that the next portrait over was of Mrs. Fox.

Dolly Alexander Fox, the plaque read, and Maggie was stunned by the dark-haired beauty who had been the young Mrs. Fox. Wearing a smart navy suit, her dark hair clipped flatteringly in the style of the fifties, Dolly Fox lounged on a velvet settee in the Foxcroft parlor. Her enigmatic smile rivaled that of the Mona Lisa.

Quickly Maggie compared the vision in the painting with the frail woman she had seen two nights before. The woman in the flesh was only a shell of the woman in the portrait, as if all the color and life had been drained away. The solemn black eyes had once sparkled and teased; the painting testified to that. Dolly Fox had been a striking woman. It was easy to see where her son got his good looks.

With a last glance, Maggie moved on to the final painting. As she approached, she discerned a young boy astride a large dappled gray. It took only a moment to recognize Mark Fox. The crop of dark hair and the green eyes were unmistakable. Sitting erect in his riding habit, the boy grinned mischievously. The artist had recorded a mixture of discipline and devilishness so that Maggie got the impression that the boy had restrained himself only momentarily and was about to dig his heels into the horse's sides and go tearing across the manicured lawns of Foxcroft.

She found herself absently returning the boy's devilish grin. There was no plaque on the frame, but her eye was drawn to the lower right corner of the painting where the artist's signature was diminutively but clearly inscribed. W. M. Fox, 1957—William Marcus Fox. Her benefactor!

With great surprise she found herself impressed by his skill. When Rachel had said he liked to paint, Maggie had imagined, with academic snobbery, an amateurish hobbyist. But William Fox could legitimately be called a painter—at the very least, an excellent portrait artist. Not only were his technique and use of color professional but he had managed to capture the ebullient spirit of his subject.

It was then that she remembered Rachel had mentioned a studio above the library. Glancing around the enormous room, Maggie spotted a black cast-iron spiral staircase in the east corner. Her eyes followed its graceful curve upward until it disappeared through the ceiling. As she crossed the room, the top disclosed itself. There was a small landing, and in the poor light she could just make out the shape of a door.

Grasping the hand railing, she put her weight gingerly on the first grated step. The iron hinges cringed in protest, but the staircase seemed strong enough. With her eyes on the landing above, she licked her lips decisively and began to climb. When she reached the top and hurried to the old, massive door, she was disappointed. The locked barrier sternly refused her entrance.

She took a last impatient look at the forbidding door and climbed back onto the staircase. She was halfway down when she heard the murmur of voices and had time only to turn in surprise before the library door swung open and Mark Fox strode into the room. John Henry followed. Behind him lumbered the massive Harold.

"You're overreacting," Mark Fox said as he walked to the desk and picked up a sheaf of papers. His back was to her, and from where Maggie stood on the shadowy side of the staircase, she was certain she wasn't visible to him or the other men. She was just about to move out of the shadows and announce her presence when John Henry's voice stopped her.

"No good'll come of *her* being here!" he said loudly, his dark head bobbing.

"No good," Harold echoed hoarsely.

"The two of you sound like a couple of doomsayers," Mark accused as he rummaged through a filing cabinet. "What are you so afraid of? Miss Hastings will be gone soon. I promise you that. Now let me be. I've got to get to Charleston and back in time to take the lady on a tour." He selected a file and turned to go.

"If she stays around here, it'll kill your mother," John Henry challenged.

Mark Fox glanced at his cousin. There must have been a threatening look in his eye, for both his companions shrank away.

"Your devotion to my mother is touching," he said. "But your concern is misplaced."

Still, John Henry refused to be placated. "What if she refuses to go?" His shrill voice rang out in the quiet room. "What if she won't sell?"

"Yeah," rumbled Harold.

Mark's tone was menacing when he answered the question. "She'll sell. But if by some chance she doesn't, you two won't have to worry your old heads about it. *I* can take care of her."

With that they were gone, the door slamming harshly behind them.

For a few seconds Maggie stood like a statue. Then she flew the rest of the way down the creaking stairwell, bolted to the door, and put her ear against its solid wood to listen. Hearing nothing, she cautiously pulled open the door, peeped through the small crack, and confirmed that the flowered walkway was deserted.

Stepping outside, she closed the door quietly behind her and hesitated. She heard only the friendly chirping of birds and the industrious buzzing of bees among the roses. With a burst of speed, she ran down the floral pathway, exiting at the far end and following a worn path between the house and the library. Finally she reached the azalea-banked boundary of the back lawn, glistening rich green in the morning light. Without hesitation she turned to one side, slipped through the waist-high snowy azaleas, and hurried into the sunshine.

The narrow path became a hard-packed dirt walkway bordered on either side by half-buried bricks. As she darted along, a fresh breeze coursed across her hot face. Eventually it cooled her feverish cheeks. Only then did she slow her pace, allowing herself simply to follow the meandering walk—past a well-tended garden of newly budding roses, around a giant dark green magnolia, past an old granite statue of a woman carrying an urn, and back up the lawn to the weathered white gazebo.

At this point the path swelled into a circle and split—one branch of it encircling the upper lawns, the other curving away from the house and disappearing in the direction of the distant pines. The gazebo, mildly shaded by a nearby oak, offered repose in the form of a swing. Maggie scaled the three steps, took a seat on the old swing, and pulled her knees up under her chin.

Statement by statement, she reviewed the conversation she'd overheard in the library. It had frightened her. There was more behind the men's words than just resentment. There was also a threat—as if the three cutthroats would stop at nothing!

The longer Maggie thought, the more her emotions tumbled—from intimidation, to curiosity, and ultimately to a cold-blooded decisiveness. She intended to find out exactly what was going on. She raised a brow as she remembered her date at two o'clock. What better place to start than with the master of Foxcroft himself? She was experienced with men. Men could be charmed, and Mark Fox, after all, was only a man.

So he thought he could "take care of her," did he?

"We'll see," Maggie murmured. "We'll just see."

She stood up and walked to the top of the gazebo steps, letting her gaze travel up the rear wall of the house. It was then that she spotted a dark shape at one of the balconied French doors. But as soon as her gaze lit on the figure, it darted out of view.

Chapter Five

Mark pulled his Porsche neatly into the reserved space in front of the offices on Meeting Street. The building sparkled in the sun, a fresh coat of white paint defining the proud lines of the three-story antebellum structure. Like most of its neighbors, it was fronted by a flowering courtyard and a sweeping veranda supported by tall Doric columns. From the outside the building presented the undeniable impression of southern history carefully tended and preserved. The image left one unprepared for the stark contemporary look of the interior.

It was unlike other offices in the Charleston area, most of which were furnished with dark, polished antiques. Mark preferred the clean, sleek lines of modern furniture for a business environment, an atmosphere that bespoke an awareness of the present and suggested a corporation that was not dwelling in the past but marching boldly into the future.

With a sense of pride, he stepped into the receiving area where a black carpet and a white wall made a striking backdrop for the company's chrome logo: Foxcroft, Inc. The chiseled capital letters gleamed with dull richness.

The spacious room had the feel of a gallery rather than an office, with paintings and modern sculptures placed on and near the walls, a curved flying staircase in the far corner, and lamps and glass tables scattered about. Yet it was comfortable, the low-standing gray sofas and chairs splashed with pillows of magenta, white, and turquoise. A chrome receptionist's desk was positioned directly beneath the logo.

Mark's gaze fell from the chrome letters to where Sally Ann lounged behind the desk. As he began to walk toward her, she smiled invitingly, her blue eyes traveling slowly down his body before again rising to his face.

She was a pretty woman, her round, dimpled face framed by cascading blond hair that danced enticingly above the ample curves of her bosom. Her fair looks and southern charm dazzled many a male client who stepped into the front offices, often opening a door of goodwill that made business dealings far easier. As he stopped before her desk, she stretched out a rounded arm to offer him his mail.

"Hello, Sally Ann," he rumbled.

"Mornin', boss," she returned lazily.

He dropped his gaze to the full bosom that strained against the pink sweater and enjoyed the spectacle—until an unexpected image sprang into his mind. A slender form in a tailored black dress that only hinted at slim curves beneath. Fiery hair curling about a fine-boned face; wide turquoise eyes the likes of which he'd never seen.

Mark's grin faded as the tight sweater and provocative smile before him seemed suddenly tasteless. In baffled irritation with himself, he commanded Sally Ann in a harsher tone than he intended. "Buzz Todd Williams and tell him I'm on my way up. I want to have a look at the renderings before I go." He bounded up the flying staircase, his long legs taking the steps two at a time. He proceeded to the architects' and draftmen's offices on the third floor where, without knocking, he strode into Todd Williams's sunny room. A mammoth drawing board was positioned to catch the north light.

The older man looked up from his work with a typically serene expression. "Mornin', Mark . . . or is it still mornin'?" he added, grinning around the stem of the ever-present pipe.

"Just barely," Mark admitted. "I can't stay long today. I've got to get back to Foxcroft, but I wanted to check with you about the renderings. How are they coming along?"

"Just putting the finishing touches on the last one. They'll be ready in plenty of time for the meeting. Here, why don't you take a look?"

Todd Williams spread a collection of drawings across the top of a nearby table and regarded them confidently. He took pride in the work he did for Foxcroft, Inc., having been with the company for nearly twenty years, even before Mark took over at the ripe age of twenty-two. At first Todd had been leery of what such a young man could accomplish, but he had revised his opinions in short order. Over the years, he had come to respect Mark Fox enormously, not just for his financial acumen and progressive, environmentally oriented views on development, but also because of his drive for success. Mark was like a bulldog when it came to finishing what he started, and Todd took special pleasure in the way his young boss admired his work.

Mark studied the nine colorful renderings. As always, Todd Williams's skill had brought to life the sterile blueprints the architects had devised, surpassing even Mark's own dreams for the development of Canadys Isle. The overall view of the island showed that the undulating hills and streams would remain undisturbed. Clusters of condominiums and homes and recreational facilities had been tucked into the natural hollows of the land. Even much of the tropical forest and many of the crushed-oyster-shell roads would remain untouched, while the buildings themselves would be constructed of natural wood that would blend into the landscape.

The close-ups of residences and shops, clubhouse, pools, and tennis courts were no less impressive than those of the marina and golf course. With the help of a brilliant interior designer, Todd had even provided a drawing of the club's spacious dining hall—a combination of rusticity and elegance, with linen-covered tables set against a backdrop of screened terraces that seemed to bring the palms and bright flowers of the outdoors right into the dining area.

Mark's heart swelled. As he dreamed it, Canadys Isle would be the most beautiful, the most ecologically sound, development along Charleston's island-studded coast. After seeing Todd's renderings, the investors would be crazy to do anything other than adopt Mark's plans wholeheartedly. His shining eyes rose to meet those of the gray-haired artist.

"Outstanding!" he said enthusiastically. "If this thing goes through, and I don't see any reason it shouldn't, I owe you a bonus."

A strange look came over Todd Williams's face as he removed his pipe from his mouth and thoughtfully tapped its spent contents into an ashtray. "It *should* go through. It's one of the best plans I've ever seen, maybe the best. But you *do* know Townsend and Company is going after the project too?"

"What?" Mark blurted the word out as his bright mood burst like an overfilled balloon.

Todd repacked the bowl of his pipe and looked sympathetically at his companion.

"Townsend?" Mark exploded. Granted the bidding for such a project as Canadys Isle was open, but Townsend had never gone in for anything resort-oriented. His cup of tea had always been institutional properties. Mark's expression turned menacing as the thought surfaced: Townsend's attraction to the development had nothing to do with Canadys Isle—it was the builder he'd be going up against to get that contract.

Todd Williams shrugged. He understood that threatening look was meant not for him but for the man whose development offices were but a few blocks away. "Last night I ran into a friend I haven't seen in quite a while—a free-lancer. He said Townsend came bursting into his place a few days ago asking for a quick set of renderings. The deadline was so short that my friend refused until Townsend offered him an exorbitant sum. I wouldn't worry about it, Mark. If Townsend is throwing together a proposal as hastily as it sounds, there's no way it will be of a caliber to compete with ours."

On the way back to Foxcroft, Mark's expression grew darker by the mile. Townsend! Throughout Mark's life, he had hovered like some nagging fly, returning to buzz all the louder after every swipe. And now he was after Canadys Isle! Mark's fingers flexed tightly around the steering wheel.

Jumping from one threatening subject to another, he glanced to the passenger seat and saw the file he'd picked up from Jim Wilkes.

"She seems a bit stubborn," Mark had told the attorney. "I'm not sure if I can get her to come in."

"It isn't necessary for us to meet," Wilkes replied. "Everything is in order. All you have to do is get her to sign before a witness. It's a strong offer, Mark. Maybe even too strong for a first round. Why don't you start low and negotiate if the lady proves greedy?"

"No," Mark returned quickly. "I don't want her to find *anything* objectionable. I want her to see that it's completely fair."

"Oh, it's more than fair," Wilkes had assured him.

But as Mark considered that word—"fair"—his conscience stirred. As far as Maggie Hastings was concerned, he was dealing from an unfair advantage. She didn't know how things really stood. If she did, would she cling to Foxcroft, as John Henry suggested?

The mere thought obliterated any sense of guilt. There was no room for charity in the world of business. Maggie Hastings's weak position only strengthened his own. Now he had no time or energy to spare on a fight for Foxcroft. He needed every bit of concentration he could muster to cement the deal for Canadys Isle.

Maggie Hastings. She was a dangerous interloper to be eliminated at any cost. A cold feeling of purpose settled in Mark's chest as he sped along the sunny highway.

At one end of the terrace at Foxcroft was a grouping of patio furniture—a table with a dark green umbrella, two chairs, and a long rocking couch with plump dark green cushions. Maggie decided to wait there for Mark Fox. She brushed a few twigs off the couch and lay down, lacing her hands behind her head. Above her the white blossoms of a pear tree danced in the breeze, creating shifting patterns against the brilliant blue of the sky.

But for the sounds of the birds and the wind, everything was quiet. The warmth of the sun, where it peeked from behind the towering roof, was soothing. Minutes later she was dozing in a twilight of semiconsciousness.

Gradually she became aware that a shadow had fallen across her face. She opened one eye. Mark Fox. He was standing silently over her, and she quickly scrambled to her feet.

"Good afternoon, Maggie," he said briskly. "I hope it's all right for me to use your first name?"

"Fine . . . Mark," she answered nonchalantly.

So totally in control he was—his manner courteous but distant, his expression pleasant, but cool. Comfortably dressed in jeans, he appeared to have taken no trouble with his appearance, yet his white shirt was crisp. A suede vest matched the rich tooled leather of his boots, and a worn cowboy hat sat comfortably on his head, its tan brim dipping low over the bridge of his nose. He seemed taller than ever, so that Maggie had to lean backward to look him in the face.

"I've been looking for you," he said sharply. "You might have told someone where you were."

Her first impulse was to lash back at his scolding, but then she remembered her strategy—to be courteous, to win him over and get him talking.

"I didn't think of it," she said.

He glanced irritably at the gold timepiece on his wrist. "It's twenty-three minutes past two. You've been running late ever since you got here. Don't you own a watch?"

Maggie bit her tongue. "Yes," she replied sweetly. "I have a watch."

Mark knew he was being a jackass, but couldn't seem to stop. "Maybe you should try looking at it now and then!"

The gleam in her eyes belied the smile Maggie forced to her

lips. "But why should I bother wearing a little old watch?" She mocked in a heavy southern drawl. "When you, kind sir, seem *so* to enjoy keeping me abreast of the time?"

She ended with a coquettish flutter of her lashes and watched a chain of expressions flicker across Mark's face. His brows arched in a look of surprise that turned into amusement. A spark kindled in his eyes, and suddenly he smiled, a bright warm smile shining white against his suntan.

"Touché," he rumbled, absently placing a large comradely hand on Maggie's shoulder.

The touch generated unexpected warmth through her sweater. She looked at his hand, then slowly up to his face. The touch on her shoulder tightened, the smile faded, and almost imperceptibly Mark Fox leaned toward her. As before, when he had stared at her so fixedly, Maggie found herself immobilized. Her heart beat wildly with anticipation.

Mark stared down at the beautiful woman. The shining hair was pulled back from the exquisite face; the eyes were a shifting blue-green like a tropical sea. He caught wind of a sweet fragrance, something like gardenia, and beneath his tightening fingers, he could feel the inviting curve of her shoulder. Then he realized what he was doing.

A curtain fell across his features, and the appearance of warmth receded before the look of cold indifference with which Maggie was more familiar.

Mark retrieved his hand and stuck it in the pocket of his jeans. "If you'd like to go now?" he said quietly, his eyes distantly questioning.

"Sure," Maggie replied, lowering her gaze to stare intently at the toes of her tennis shoes.

She stuffed her hands into her pants pockets and followed him down the terrace steps. She was too preoccupied to notice the person who witnessed their scene from the balcony above.

The sun was hot on her back, and the heat of the horse crept through the saddle. Although a breeze whistled by as they cantered, small beads of perspiration broke out on Maggie's upper lip.

Her mount, Lorelei, was a trim mare, well schooled in five gaits. But though she moved smoothly, Maggie could already feel the rub of the saddle on her unaccustomed flesh. She wouldn't dream, however, of complaining to Mark Fox, who maintained his detached, arrogant manner. He was obviously a master horseman, and she wouldn't consider showing him anything less than composure and competence.

The stables of Foxcroft had proved to be large and thriving. The young stable boy, Jeremy, had offered to hold her horse, but Maggie had declined and made quite a show of mounting the chestnut mare and swiftly wheeling her in a circle to display her skill.

Her actions had elicited an amused look from Mark Fox. He rode a black stallion at least seventeen hands tall, and astride the mammoth destrier, the man looked even more forbidding than usual. Almost warlike.

"Whoa, Sonny. Whoa, boy," he had muttered as he swiftly mounted the prancing animal.

"Sonny?" Maggie questioned. "That seems an odd name for such a huge horse."

Mark glanced at her disdainfully. "His registered name is True Son. His lines go back to the sire of Secretariat." With that, he loosened the rein, and Sonny immediately broke for the path out of the stable yard.

As she released Lorelei and began to follow, Maggie studied the tall man astride the towering horse and was struck by the incongruity of Mark Fox's western boots and hat coupled with the diminutive saddle and rigid posture of the English tradition. His riding style was a study in contradiction, and she absently imagined it might be an apt symbol for the man himself.

With all the formality of a tour director, he guided her around the grounds, elaborating on particular points of interest. The stables and foaling barn, one of the first topiaries in America, and at the base of the rolling lawn, virtually hidden behind a stand of pines, a row of a dozen brick huts with tile roofs—grim, weathered reminders of the slaves who had lived there more than one hundred years before.

"These houses were built by the slaves back in the middle of the eighteenth century," Mark pointed out. "They're constructed of brick and tile made right here on the plantation, which probably accounts for the fact that they're still standing. The house servants lived here. Contrary to the custom of the time, Major Fox had these quarters built in the back of the house instead of along the front avenue, where they were often placed as a status symbol. It seems the major didn't care much about appearances."

He grinned at the thought as if in admiration, then caught

himself and looked sharply at Maggie. "Stop me if I ramble. I don't know if you're interested in history."

"Oh, yes. Very."

"Then come this way."

He took the lead to the east, and eventually, as they trotted along the back edge of the lawns, they approached a graveyard surrounded by an elaborate cast-iron fence and a screen of oaks dripping Spanish moss above the markers.

"This is the family cemetery," he said, bringing Sonny to a halt. "Beginning with the major, seven generations of Foxes lie here. Back in the 1700s, the major received a land grant from the king of England—fifteen thousand acres to one of the first British settlers in the Carolinas. According to the history books, the land was virgin forest in those days. It was cleared in the eighteenth century by slaves, who later became the caretakers of the plantation. They produced cotton, indigo, rice, pecans . . ."

For more than a hundred years, he told her, the plantation traded its crops for goods from Europe and the northern states. Then came the Civil War. Sherman's march reached a crescendo with the burning of Atlanta, then turned north and wreaked destruction through the Carolinas. Fortunately, Foxcroft sustained relatively little damage—the partial burning of one wing, the library, which originally was part of the main house and now was connected only by the rose-covered walkway.

After the war Foxcroft ceased to function as a plantation, and the Fox family incorporated and began to invest in real estate. Over the course of a century the family corporation had grown into one of the state's foremost land developers.

Maggie had no need to ask questions. In an impersonal, knowledgeable way, Mark Fox thoroughly covered every issue. Only at the end of his monologue did he make even a vague allusion to her own connection with Foxcroft.

"Things haven't changed much in the past fifty years. I'm proud to say the company is thriving. But Foxcroft House . . . it's not just a pretty place to live; it's a piece of history that I intend to see preserved." With a brief challenging look, he spurred his horse and moved ahead, squelching any opportunity for Maggie to comment.

They rode south on a wide dirt road bordered by open fields stretching as far as the eye could see. Ahead was a solid stand of pines and, Maggie recalled, a river. Slowing to a trot, Mark led her into the quiet forest. His stallion slowed to a walk, and Maggie reined in behind him as he wound silently through the pines. The air was thick with the clean scent of the trees, and a carpet of brown pine needles muffled the sounds of their progress.

The path curved languidly and eventually took them out of the forest to the edge of the river. Along the bank stood a cluster of gnarled trees, their twisted branches reaching grotesquely sideways to dangle Spanish moss above the water. Beyond them was a stand of dark cypresses. Up the way an old wooden bridge stretched across a narrow curve in the water's path.

Mark abruptly stopped, and Maggie reined in beside him. On close inspection she found the river to be narrower than she had imagined, but remarkably clean. No litter, no stagnation, only the salt-laden wind, the sun sparkling on the water, and the calls of seabirds. The far bank appeared to be wilderness, completely untamed and overgrown, splendid in its wildness.

The mare shook her head, snorting loudly, and Maggie became suddenly aware of the silence and the man beside her. Evidently he was deep in his own thoughts as they stared at the river.

"It's beautiful," she said, hoping to break the silence. But he only nodded without looking at her. "The river is narrower than I thought."

"It's big enough, for a tributary," he answered shortly. "It empties into the Cooper farther south."

"Is it the boundary of Foxcroft?"

"Might as well be." He turned his head, finally seeming to focus his attention on her. "The rest, all the way to the Cooper, is a bird sanctuary. Has been for years." As an afterthought he muttered, more to himself than to her, "Of course, some people would like to change that."

"Really? Why?"

Mark looked at her quickly, then nudged his horse around to face her. "It's not important. Anyway, I should point out that this wilderness acreage completes the strip of land that belongs to you."

She looked at him in surprise, then turned back to the beautiful marshlands.

"Are you ready to go?" he demanded.

"No, not yet. Can't we cross the river and take a look?"

Mark's back straightened as he came suddenly alert. "No, you're not to go there!" he commanded rudely. "It isn't safe. That bridge is old and rickety, hasn't been used in years. And there's nothing to see. That land out there is only good for the birds. It has no other value, except, of course, to you, since I'll be paying you a handsome price for it."

He whirled his prancing horse around and began to move away from the river.

"Mark!" she called irritably, nudging the mare forward. "You seem to think everything hinges on money. There are some things in this world, you know, that don't have a price."

Their horses plodded side by side at a slow pace, and Mark looked at her intently. "So far, that hasn't been my experience," he said evenly. "Particularly when the sum is as attractive as the one I'm offering you. Now that you've had a chance to look around, I hope you're ready to get on with the negotiations."

Maggie bristled at the man's attempt to push her. "And what if I don't want to sell?"

His head snapped around as if he'd been slapped. "Then you're a fool, Maggie."

"Why do you say that?"

He turned and stared ahead through the pines. "Don't be absurd. For one thing, you don't know the first thing about how to run this place, or how much it costs! For another thing, you're a woman."

"And what's that supposed to mean?" she countered indignantly. "That women are only good for cooking and having babies?"

Mark looked over at her swiftly, his eyes glinting beneath the brim of his hat. "Among other things," he drawled.

With that he clucked to his horse and moved in front of Maggie, dismissing her. He stayed a good six feet ahead as they passed through the pine forest, and as soon as they were out of the trees, he cast a casual look back and spurred his horse to a canter.

He's anxious to be done with me, Maggie thought. Apparently Lorelei was anxious, too, for she broke into a canter of her own volition.

About a quarter-mile from the stables, with an unspoken command for her to do the same, Mark slowed his horse and dismounted. Carelessly draping the reins over his shoulder, he stuffed his hands in his pockets and ambled along the dirt road. The late afternoon sun glistened on the dark back of the giant horse that followed tamely, cooling down from the run.

The warm sunshine was mellowed by a refreshing breeze, and the green fields surrounding them made a beautiful picture, but Maggie was miserable. To an observer's eye, she appeared to be strolling along normally. In truth, she had to concentrate to prevent her legs from wobbling, and her jeans seemed to constrict every movement. The white sweater was damp and drooping. Mark looked as fresh as a spring morning.

He was a strange, complicated man. Most of the time he was brooding and distant; other times, sarcastic. Now he conversed in the manner of a polite host. Not knowing what to expect from him, Maggie was constantly at a loss. Earlier this afternoon she'd seen his first genuine smile, and the effect had been startling. But since then he'd been abrupt and short—except when he was talking about the estate. Of that, she'd learned plenty. But of the man? Nothing. Her plan to win him over seemed hopeless.

"Where did you learn to ride?" he asked.

"At home. In Kensing."

"You're not too bad."

"Thanks. You're not so bad yourself."

"I was unaware the Hastingses had children," he said matter-of-factly.

Maggie glanced up, but he was looking ahead. "They couldn't have children of their own. I was adopted as a baby."

Her thoughts darted back to that winter day when she was twelve. They had waited until she was old enough to understand, they said. They loved her as if she were their own blood, they added tearfully. Maggie had embraced them and believed them, but as of that moment she had stopped taking anything—or anyone—at face value.

"You were adopted," Mark repeated absently. "How much do you know about your natural parents?"

The question took Maggie by surprise—that a virtual stranger should voice what she had whispered to herself most of her life, never daring to speculate for long, as if the question were some sort of betrayal of the Hastingses. Her face was tilted up, her eyes fastened on Mark's stern visage—the strong line of his jaw, the chiseled features set in the habitually grim expression, the eyes looking down at her curiously from beneath the brim of his hat. Suddenly she realized he was pumping her for information just as she had designed to do with him.

"All I know is that they died long ago," she returned with crafty nonchalance. "But enough about me. Tell me about you, Mark. Have you lived here all your life?"

"Naturally," he answered.

"Did you go away to college?" she pursued.

"I didn't need to go away," he drawled without looking at her. "I learned everything I needed to know to run this place right here. I took a few business and math courses in town. That was it."

With a careless shrug she plunged headlong onto personal ground. "Didn't you ever fall in love and get married?"

He swiveled toward her, obviously startled by her personal question. Maggie gazed innocently up at him as they walked along, only three feet between them, yet worlds apart. After a moment he averted his eyes and stared at the dirt. She didn't expect him to answer.

"No, I've never married. Never had the inclination or the time. . . . And as for *love*," he added with a gruff laugh, "do you really think there *is* such a thing? I've seen people who thought they had it. All it ever did was tease them into destroying each other."

He continued walking at a calm, steady pace, but Maggie could sense the inner turmoil she had triggered. He was like a proud wild animal brought to bay, and her taste of victory turned unexpectedly sour.

"I'm sorry," she said finally. "I didn't mean to remind you of anything painful."

He whirled to face her. "What do you mean?"

"Oh, nothing," she replied softly, shifting her eyes to the dirt.

"Nothing, huh?" Mark demanded, his harsh tone commanding that she look at him.

A golden spark of ferocity glinted in the green eyes, and Maggie suddenly gathered that he couldn't bear the thought of revealing any vulnerability in himself.

"You didn't mean anything at all by what you just said?" he thundered.

"That's right!" she finally exploded. Losing patience with his pride, she also quite suddenly remembered his threatening remarks from earlier in the day. "You know, it's a real challenge to talk to you about *anything*, Mark! I never know what's going to set you off. You're like some big ferocious cat, ready to pounce at the slightest thing!"

He turned a glittering gaze on her and flashed a crooked smile. "Relax, lady. You don't have to worry about me pouncing. Although that is what you expect, no doubt!" he added with a raking look at her figure.

"Of all the nerve!" she gasped. "I expect nothing of the kind. Nor do I invite it!"

He infuriated her by tugging the brim of his hat low over his eyes and laughing heartily. With an exasperated huff, Maggie shot him a glare of indignation and sped ahead, leading the mare behind her.

Mark caught up to her at the white-fenced ring that bordered the stable yard, but if he'd been planning to speak to her, he didn't get the chance. Harold was lumbering hurriedly around the ring to meet them.

Except for the stolen glimpse of him in the library, Maggie hadn't seen the hulking man since he delivered her to Foxcroft. Now he impressed her even less favorably. Now that the chauffeur's livery had been replaced by coarse work clothes and a floppy straw hat, Harold had lost his only semblance of refinement. A faded flannel shirt was open at his thick neck, and as he came close, her eye was drawn to the scowl contorting the blocky face. Snatching the reins of both horses, he looked urgently to Mark.

"Arthur Townsend is here. Showed up about fifteen minutes ago."

Having uttered the words as if they were a pronouncement of doom, Harold clucked to the horses and tramped swiftly away toward the red-roofed barn.

A tall dark-haired man in a gray suit rounded the corner of the barn and strode toward them. It took only instants for him to bridge the distance, and as he drew near, Maggie noticed the sanctimonious smile he gave Mark.

"Well, well," he drawled. He extended a hand, and slowly Mark joined him in a handshake. "It's been a long time, Mark. You never come into town these days, so you force me to make house calls."

Without giving Mark a chance to respond, he looked to Maggie. "And this must be Miss Hastings."

The assessing hazel eyes were sharp as they studied her, but then his smile warmed as he grasped her hand and, in a courtly fashion, planted a kiss upon its back.

"I heard of your arrival, Miss Hastings," he resumed, straightening his tall, slender frame. "But I wasn't told how lovely you are."

His rich southern voice flowed like wine, and Maggie found herself smiling into the angular close-shaven face. He was about the same age as Mark, and attractive, though in a somewhat dandified way.

"Maggie, allow me to introduce this . . . gentleman," Mark broke in. "This is Arthur Townsend. He, too, is in the real estate business. Apparently someone in my company has something to learn about professional confidentiality." His eyes leveled on Townsend. "Who told you about Miss Hastings's arrival?"

"Oh, come now, Mark. Be a sport! You know how active our industry grapevine is. You didn't think you could keep this beautiful visitor a secret, did you?"

It was easy to recognize the rivalry between the two men. Arthur was glorying in his competitor's discomfort, as Mark attempted to restrain his anger.

"In fact," Arthur continued, turning back to Maggie, "now that we've been introduced, I have a wonderful idea! Please come to the party I'm giving Saturday night."

He nodded in Mark's direction. "You too, Mark, of course. It's a celebration of my sister's upcoming marriage, and it's going to be a grand affair—good food, music, interesting people. A lot of the people who are sponsoring the Spoleto Arts Festival next month will be there. You'll meet Charleston's finest and have a wonderful time. What do you say?"

"I'm afraid I must decline for both of us," Mark rumbled. "Miss Hastings will have departed for New York by then—"

"Perhaps not," she interjected, her eyes darting sharply to Mark. Her indignation was flying like a flag, easily blotting out any earlier notion of charming the man. She was fed up with Mark Fox's take-charge attitude.

"I'd hate to cut my visit short," she went on, "particularly if I have the chance to attend a party. It sounds like such an enjoyable affair. And I'm very much interested in Spoleto. The festival has a grand reputation."

"Wonderful!" Arthur beamed. "I'm sure you'll have a good time. And I can't wait to show you my home. If you're at all interested in historical restoration, I think you'll enjoy seeing it. It was built back in 1752, and it's located in one of the most fascinating parts of Historic Charleston."

"It sounds lovely," Maggie said smoothly, noting from the corner of her eye that Mark seemed about to explode. "I've had only a glimpse of the historic area of your city. But judging from what I've seen, it's a beautiful place."

"I'm pleased to hear you say that. It's nice to talk with someone who appreciates our beautiful restorations." Arthur cast a scornful look in Mark's direction. "It's all settled, then. I'll pick you up at eight."

"That won't be necessary!" Mark's deep voice thundered. The cowboy hat sat low across his forehead, yet it was easy to see the glare he fired at Maggie from under its brim. "If Miss Hastings wants to attend the party, *I'll* escort her."

He turned back to Arthur, the angle of his jaw tense and sharp. "We'll see you Saturday night, Townsend. I'm sure you can find your way to the drive. Good-bye."

Iron fingers closed about Maggie's elbow, pulling her deftly away from Arthur Townsend and steering her efficiently toward the grove of oaks sheltering the path to the house.

"And I'm sure you can find your way to *my* house, Mark!" Arthur called with a sarcasm that puzzled Maggie.

She had the opportunity only to toss a good-bye over her shoulder as Mark dragged her out of the stable yard. She had to choose between causing a scene or going along, so she did her best to keep up with his long strides and to ignore the strong fingers clamped about her arm. She refrained from snapping at him when they fled, but as Mark propelled her along the path through the oaks in silent fury, Maggie's mounting temper promptly erupted.

"What do you think you're doing?" she shouted at his profile and, with an angry burst of strength, wrenched her arm from his grasp. She came to an abrupt standstill, and Mark whirled to face her.

"You have no idea of what you've done, Maggie! You've just played right into Townsend's hands!"

"I don't know what you're talking about, and I don't care!" she retorted. "What makes you think you have the right to order me around? To, to *drag* me away like an ill-behaved child?"

"Well, that's about how much sense you've shown! You don't know what's going on here, and yet you rebel against everything I say! Maybe if you were less concerned with trying to take charge of things like a *man*, you'd be a more sensible *woman*!"

Maggie opened her mouth to shout back at him, but then tossed her head disdainfully and managed to voice her words in a cool, level way. "Are all southern men as chauvinistic as you? If so, I pity the women in this backward, outdated place!"

She tried to step around him, but his hand lashed out to lock again about her arm.

"Our women get along just fine," he drawled, his anger adding a hard edge to the accent. "Some of them even like it when a man takes charge."

Like lightning, he grasped her other arm and pulled her to him. "Are you so different?" he demanded, lifting her up against his chest, securing her so that only her toes touched the ground.

In complete surprise, Maggie grabbed at his waist and raised startled eyes. His green ones sparkled back through dark lashes only inches away, and suddenly the sounds of the grove receded as her other senses flared. Her fingers clasped his shirt and through it felt the warmth of his skin where it was stretched taut over a hard, muscular midriff. The scent of leather and a clean-smelling after-shave filled her nostrils. A warm wave rocked her stomach and spread through her body, finally reaching her face where it flamed in her cheeks. She hung limp in Mark's grip, gazing trancelike at the strong lines of his face as he regarded her from under the brim of his hat.

Mark didn't know when he'd been so blasted mad. The conflicting feelings he had about the woman were going off in his head like skyrockets, blinding him, deafening him, until all he could hear was the crashing of his blood against his temples.

His strong fingers tightened about Maggie's arms, squeezing her against the support of his body. Above her upturned face, Mark's brows knitted in a dark line, his eyes training on her mouth. A heavy pounding started in her chest, reverberating in her ears as she watched him bend closer. His breath was warm on her face, and then his lips were forcefully on hers, his tongue prodding open her unresisting mouth.

Maggie's eyes closed of their own accord as an electric charge ran through her. It was something so new, so unexpected. But she could barely acknowledge that thought as it flitted through her mind to disintegrate in the face of Mark's onslaught. The hot, moist taste of him was devastatingly male; the lips, firm and demanding as he allowed her to slide down the front of him. Placing a hand on the back of her head, he eased her mouth farther open.

There was no room for surprise, or for any feeling other than that of the man who held her. Maggie's arms reached up around his neck and clasped him to her so that her body was molded pliantly to the full length of him. They spun around and around in a silent, dark void. Vaguely she realized his hand had slipped under her sweater and his warm fingers caressed her back until her bones went fluid. His other hand moved from the back of her head to cup her face. Finally his lips slid to her cheek, then her ear.

"My God, Maggie."

The male voice came from somewhere far away and then with barreling speed smashed into her consciousness. His words broke the spell. Maggie's eyes flew open, and she awoke to the situation—herself in the woods, responding wildly to a man she barely knew and didn't trust. Instantly, she began to push him away.

As if his limbs had gone leaden, Mark slowly adjusted his grasp until his hands gripped her shoulders. Still holding her, he backed an arm's length away and turned glazed eyes on hers. The look of surprise on his face mirrored hers. They stood like that for a few seconds, looking at each other in stunned silence. He withdrew his hands, as if the touch of her burned his fingers.

"I need to go back to the stables for a minute," Mark said in a thick, deep tone. "You go on to the house."

He threw the last at her as he turned to stalk through the oaks. Maggie began walking blindly away, but then he called her name. She stopped, looked dazedly over her shoulder and saw him standing thirty paces away where the path curved toward the stables. Afternoon sun lit on the brim of his hat, a shadow obscuring his face so she couldn't read his expression.

"Let's just forget this happened, shall we?" he called. And then he was gone.

Mark strode furiously through the stable yard and into the shadowy barn. Once under its cool, private eaves, he came to a halt. Whipping off the hat, he slouched irritably against the wall and ran his fingers through his hair.

"Have you lost your mind?" he muttered before slamming the hat back onto his head.

Yet even as he spoke the words, his thoughts hovered on the memory. The desire to overpower Maggie Hastings, to subdue the proud rebellion that had flashed from her eyes, had prompted him to take her angrily into his arms. But his intent had been twisted, leaving *him* to feel like the conquered one!

Her slim body had seemed to melt against him, washing over his length until it settled like fire in his loins. Her lips had parted tremblingly, her mouth opening, welcoming, offering a sweet taste that hinted of even sweeter bounties. And her scent! Even now the heady gardenia fragrance entwined about him like a lover's arms.

Mark began to stalk along the corridor between the horses' stalls. His eye fell on an empty metal pail, and then his booted foot connected with the thing, sending it airborne until it clattered to the floor some three stalls away. At the raucous sound, Gray Lady protested, sending forth a whinny from the far end of the barn.

Chapter Six

"Let's just forget that happened," he had said. Maggie could as soon have forgotten being struck by a lightning bolt.

By the time she was ready to go downstairs for supper, she had relived the episode in the oak grove a hundred times. And each time she had shaken her head more emphatically, refusing to admit her reckless abandon, horrified that one minute she'd been so angry she could have strangled the man, and the next, she'd been wrapping herself around him so tightly she would have climbed inside his skin if she'd been able.

The woman out there had not been Maggie Hastings! That was not the woman who had waltzed through one casual relationship after another, never really caring, never really feeling. That woman was someone new, someone who had been carried away by a kiss from a stranger.

Even Jean-Paul had never had such an effect on her. Never had he sent her to that dreamy, heretofore unknown place where wrenching sensations exploded like colorful stars behind eyelids so heavily closed that they sealed out the world but for one man.

As Maggie stood before the vanity and fastened a gold chain about her throat, his image materialized—the strong outline of his face, the white teeth between parted, ruddy lips. Her fingers trembled on the filigree clasp.

"There," she whispered as it finally caught.

She leaned forward to inspect her face, but when she looked at her lips, her breathing went once again all racy and shallow.

Come on now, Maggie, she told herself. Don't make something out of nothing. It was only a kiss, for heaven's sake! Thousands of people are kissed every day, and it doesn't mean a thing.

By invalidating the disturbing memory, she was able to calm her breathing, and she felt more like her cool, collected self.

Stepping back, she surveyed herself in the gilt-framed mirror. She wore a matching sweater and skirt of a peach color that brought out the sunny color she'd gotten that day, and her curling hair was pulled back to reveal gleaming gold earrings. It was not yet in her makeup to realize that she wanted to impress the man who had kissed her so suddenly in the secluded grove; yet he was the reason behind the few extra pains she took with her appearance.

After slipping on her pumps, she swept out of the bedroom. But as she started down the stairs, she slowed her pace. The muscles all the way down her legs had begun to stiffen from the ride, and they ached complainingly with every step.

As it turned out, her careful preparations were for naught. She entered the dining room and saw that, once again, the huge candlelit table was set for only one. She did her best to bury her disappointment as Rachel served a delicious but silent meal.

Although grateful she'd been spared the company of Mrs. Fox and John Henry, Maggie couldn't help but be offended by Mark's absence. She thought that, considering this afternoon, he'd have deigned to eat supper with her.

By the time she finished the meal and started on an after-dinner demitasse, she had transformed her quivering feelings into ambivalent ones. Who could tell *what* to expect from the man? One minute he was insulting; the next, cold and silent; the next, shockingly passionate. Like a chameleon, he could change before her very eyes, the only constant being the bleak aura of anger that had shadowed even his kiss.

Maggie replaced the cup firmly in its saucer, rose swiftly to her feet, and then caught herself. She had forgotten her strained muscles. During the supper hour they had stiffened appreciably, and as she stepped away from the table, she felt a wave of pain from her backside down to her calves, a sensation that persisted as she made her way to the kitchen to ask Rachel if there were any Epsom salts in the house.

A few moments later, the old woman was handing over a box of salts when the kitchen's back door swung open and Mark walked in.

Maggie's heart lurched, and she noted that he hesitated in mid-stride when he saw her. He had not changed clothes since their outing, and he looked uncharacteristically unkempt—his white shirt soiled, his beard a strong shadow over the lower portion of his face. His eyes flickered furtively in Maggie's direction as he swept the cowboy hat off his dark head and ambled across the room toward her and Rachel.

"What are you up to?" he rumbled.

"Lord have mercy, Mr. Fox," Rachel exclaimed, her silver head bobbing from side to side. "You done left this child on the back of a horse too long today. She's gonna be plumb black-and-blue tomorrow!"

"Oh, it's not that bad, Rachel," Maggie said quickly.

Glancing up at Mark, she found his gaze fastened morosely on her, and as she looked into the eyes that had blazed so passionately only hours before, an unfamiliar pang of shyness began to twitch within her. Her words came out in an untypical nervous rush.

"I guess I was a bit overconfident today. I forgot how long it's been since I've ridden, and my muscles are a little sore. But these salts will be just the ticket. Oh, and Rachel, I just remembered. Is there a radio I could use?"

"I can help you with that," Mark offered.

Immediately he began to move away, and Maggie got the impression that he, too, felt uncomfortable in this encounter and was anxious for an excuse to take his leave.

"I've got a small radio I hardly ever use. I'll bring it to your room." With long strides, he exited the kitchen, leaving the door to the dining room swinging behind him.

With a quick look at Rachel, Maggie discovered the old woman was staring at her, wide-eyed. "And what does that look mean?" Maggie asked.

"That look means it ain't like Mr. Fox to go falling all over himself like that. I got a feeling," Rachel said, a smile spreading across her round face. "And it's a feeling I'm mighty glad to have, yes, ma'am. I got a feeling that it's gonna take a pretty little thing from up north to catch a sly old fox in his den." She broke into a cackle.

As Maggie grasped her meaning, she shook her head scoldingly.

"I can see it now," the old woman went on. "Eveything's gonna work out just fine. Yes, ma'am! It sure is funny the way things turn out. The Lord works in mysterious ways. Mighty mysterious!"

"Rachel, you're a hopeless romantic!" Maggie accused and left the kitchen with the old woman's gleeful laughter ringing in her ears.

She had just limped her way up the stairs when Mark came bounding down from his rooms, bearing a small but sophisticated radio.

"You really are in bad shape, aren't you?" he commented with a sidelong look. Leaning ahead, he pushed open her bedroom door.

"I'll survive," she quipped.

Striding confidently through the green bedroom to the chest of drawers, he began to rearrange the knickknacks to make room for the stereo. As usual he took command of the situation, and Maggie sat down on the vanity stool, crossed her legs, and watched.

He had discarded the suede vest, and as he crouched to plug in the unit, she caught herself admiring the way the white shirt stretched across his broad shoulders, and the way they tapered down to slim hips. She knew now how hard and muscular was the waist above those hips. A blush made its way up her face.

He straightened, adjusted a knob on the radio, and classical music flooded the room.

"Is that all right?" he asked, turning and nearly catching her in the midst of her heated perusal. "Sometimes I listen to this when I'm reading."

The full sound of a concert orchestra wafted through the air. "Yes, that's nice. Thank you."

He walked away from the dresser and came to tower directly above her. "I've been in the stables since this afternoon. There's a mare, Gray Lady, who's having a rough time. She'll be foaling in about a month."

"I see."

Without actually saying so, he seemed to be explaining his absence from supper. But he made no allusion to their interlude— preferring, Maggie gathered, to behave as if it had never occurred. Still, he looked at her in that strange way of his, a sort of head-to-toe examination, and she could feel her body responding with a tingle of anticipation, though she willed it to be still.

"Here . . . what's this?" he said abruptly and knelt at her feet.

"What?"

She followed his gaze to a tennis-ball-sized spot on the calf of her crossed leg, where a colorful bruise had unfolded into a blossom with chartreuse petals and a purple center. With all the detachment of a veterinarian, Mark began to examine it—the touch of his fingers electrifying through the smooth veil of her stocking.

"Stirrups," he muttered. "Let's see the other one."

She complied, and he repeated his examination, little realizing that at his touch, she was once again beginning to slip, once again succumbing to that strange charisma that was at once exhilarating and drugging.

"Well," he finally said and stood. "It's not as bad as the other one. But both of those bruises will be there for a couple of weeks. Damn, Maggie!" he blurted suddenly. "You know enough about riding to prevent something like this. Those buckles must have been damned uncomfortable to cause those bruises. Why didn't you tell me? I could have adjusted your stirrups!"

Her mellow mood disintegrated like mist before the sun. "I'm perfectly capable of adjusting my own stirrups."

"Yes, I can see that!" Mark glared at the ugly bruise on the otherwise perfect leg. An idea hit him. "Take off your shoes," he ordered.

"My shoes?"

"Yes. Take them off, and give them to me. Hurry it up!"

"What do you want with my shoes?"

"Never you mind," he replied sharply as he snatched them from her and strode to the doorway, already berating himself for what he was doing. He grasped the doorknob and hesitated. When he turned, his face was stern.

"I spoke with my attorney today," he announced. "Just wanted you to know. You don't have to meet with him if you don't want to."

"Why not?" Maggie asked. Perhaps Mark had reconsidered. Perhaps he would not push her so hard to part with the beautiful estate that had so quickly, so completely, infatuated her. But his explanation dashed her newborn hopes.

"It isn't necessary for any attorney to oversee the transaction. I think you'll find the documents thorough in every way. I *have* handled a few real estate matters in my time, and to be frank the deal I'm offering is damned sweet. If you feel the same, all you have to do is sign."

"That's *all*, huh?"

Her eyes searched his face for some feeling, some understanding of her reluctance to sell Foxcroft. But she found nothing, only a cold curiosity that seemed to misread the emotions playing across her face.

"About this afternoon," he said abruptly. "I don't want you getting the wrong idea."

"What do you mean?"

He took a step toward her, looking her over languidly. "You're young. It's been my experience that young women tend to jump to conclusions about such things."

As she caught his meaning, Maggie's cheeks began to burn. "I certainly am jumping to no conclusions, and I fervently hope that *you* aren't. If you'll recall, Mark, it was *you* who initiated that little scene!"

He rubbed his chin as a corner of his mouth dipped into a crooked grin. "Perhaps, but I seem to remember your hearty participation."

She opened her mouth to retort, but he cut her off.

"Look, it doesn't matter, as long as we understand each other. Just take your salts and get into a hot tub."

He slammed the door behind him and left her sputtering. If anything breakable had been handy, she would have thrown it at the closed door marking his departure.

Outside the green bedroom, Mark slumped against the door, one hand resting on the knob behind him, the other dangling a pair of ladies' heels. He glanced at the shoes, remembering with disbelief the sudden idea that had prompted him to ask her for them. Boots. He was intending to take her shoes into town and have her fitted for boots!

It was the sight of those bruises, Mark thought defensively—that, and the knowledge that she would be staying longer than he'd first thought. There would be opportunities for other horseback rides, and he wasn't about to let the woman—and a damn good rider at that—go without. . . .

Suddenly he stopped himself in the midst of the rationalization. If Maggie Hastings weren't so attractive, he'd never have had the impulse in a million years. The truth was that part of him was glad Townsend had shown up and invited them to that blasted party. It was an excuse for her to stay the weekend.

Mark shook his head in frustration. When he was away from the woman, his purpose was clear. But when she was around . . . He thought back to the way he had felt as he knelt before her there in that bower of femininity where her fragrance had assaulted him with every breath. She had looked all fresh and peachy and golden, and when his fingers touched her calf, all he could think of was running his hand up her leg and under her clinging skirt.

His eyes opened wide as a look of irritation swept over his face. What the hell! You're acting like a schoolboy! You've got a group of investors flying in from New York tomorrow morning. You should be thinking about Canadys Isle, not Maggie Hastings!

You'd do well to take your own advice, old boy; forget that little kiss in the oak grove. In a few days, after she signs the agreement, she'll be gone and you'll be damned glad. Pushing away from the door, he stomped along the hall.

Soon after Mark left, Maggie drew a hot bath, poured in a healthy portion of salts, and settled into the steaming water with a sigh. The bath and the classical music soothed her aching muscles and ragged mood. But even as she luxuriated in the water, her mind raced: Foxcroft, the inheritance, William Fox . . . Mark!

The thought of him was lodged in her head like a splinter. When Maggie crawled into bed and turned out the light, his changeable face flashed before her—first with the haughty expression she recalled from when they had met; then with the cool look of appreciation he had turned on her as they went horseback riding. An unbidden image flared across her memory like a comet, and only inches away, his half-closed eyes burned through dark lashes.

She abruptly sat up in bed and flipped on the light. What is the *matter* with you? she asked herself, and yet she wouldn't risk entertaining an answer.

Restlessly she climbed out of bed and crossed the room, where she pulled open the French doors and stepped onto the balcony. The night was cool and clear, delivering a loud chorus of cricket song and the rich scent of fresh earth and flowers. Breathing deeply of the crisp air, she grasped the rail and turned her eyes to the gibbous moon that shone brightly, high in the indigo sky.

"Nice!"

The hiss of the word cut through the night and fell sharply on Maggie's ear. Her head swiveled as she realized the sound was coming from a nearby open window.

"Nice?" the female voice repeated. "How can you say that? You're blind. You're just as blind as your father was. Poison, that's what she is! Poison!"

"I hate to say it, Mother," came Mark's resonant voice, "but the only poison in this house is in your mind!"

The quick, loud slam of a door followed, and Maggie stood motionless. The night was now quiet, but the words still echoed in her ears. She knew with intuitive certainty that *she* had been the subject of the mother-son argument. A sudden chill swept over her, and she stepped quickly inside, drawing the French doors closed.

* * *

The next morning brought a sunny sky and a cloudy mood. Perhaps it had something to do with her still-aching muscles, but Maggie found herself looking at the world from a somber point of view. In retrospect, her time at Foxcroft seemed to have passed in a blur, and now she felt as if she'd just wakened from a Cinderella dream.

The excitement of discovery that had buoyed her through the past two days had receded, leaving her to face the possibility that she would soon be leaving, that Foxcroft would become nothing more than a memory. It was only a matter of time before Mark presented his offer. She'd managed to put him off on the premise of learning about her inheritance. But now that she'd explored the house and toured the land, how much longer could she postpone the deal that both Mark Fox and Albert Morely considered inevitable?

And why should she even try? Mark was promising a great deal of money, enough to give her any kind of life she wanted. It was the chance of a lifetime.

She thought of the beautiful house and grounds of Foxcroft, the captivating feeling of having stepped back into southern history. She imagined having morning coffee in the enormous kitchen and chatting with Rachel, whom she now regarded as a friend; she imagined riding through the open fields with Mark who, despite his infuriating qualities, was the most compelling man she'd ever met. Ever since she arrived at Foxcroft, Maggie had felt so alive, as if not just her senses but her spirit was swelling to take it all in.

Oh, but she was tempted to forget all the reasons it was ludicrous for her even to *think* of keeping the estate—her life was in New York; after the sale, she'd be rich; she didn't know the first thing about managing such a place; and besides, she didn't belong at Foxcroft. *Did* she?

That was the one objection she couldn't quite get around. It was the Fox family who belonged here, not her. Some strange set of circumstances must have prompted William Fox to give that document to David and Myra Hastings so long ago. And now, years later, it had come to light after her parents were gone, unable to explain. Perhaps William Fox had meant it to be a safeguard, to be used only if some extraordinary event occurred.

The startling mystery of the document made Maggie feel unworthy. Much as she would have liked to enjoy the feeling that

Foxcroft was hers, deep in her heart, she felt she had no right to it.

She dressed in a cool top and jeans and was downstairs by nine o'clock. She picked up a cup of coffee in the kitchen, where Rachel announced with elaborate winks for Annie and Mrs. Phipps that "in case Miss Hastings might be interested, Mr. Fox left early for Charleston and will return in the afternoon."

Maggie rolled her eyes and left the kitchen, leaving the old woman to her matchmaker's fantasies.

The downcast mood lingered. Maggie walked to the front of the house and cast loving looks into the rooms she passed. But today each look was bittersweet, shadowed by the feeling that she was just passing through.

She looked out through the beveled-glass windows. The sunny outdoors lured her onto the veranda, and she took a fresh look at the bricked-in circular courtyard. The water in the fountain danced and glimmered in the sunlight; the red geraniums nodded brightly against the backdrop of emerald lawn. Feeling her love for the place swell anew, Maggie clasped her hands behind her back and strolled onto the grounds.

A rhythmic hacking noise rang from the back lawns. She wandered in its direction and after meandering around a stand of pines, discovered Harold at the edge of the formal lawns viciously attacking a fallen oak with a long machete.

For a moment, from only a few yards away, Maggie studied the overall-clad man from the side. His bulk bulged from beneath the suspenders, and around his girth was a wide belt from which the empty machete sleeve hung. Again and again, his arm rose and fell, the long blade flashing in the sun between merciless slashes against the oak limbs. As she watched him at work, Maggie shivered. He was like an old battered prizefighter; there was something not quite right about him.

Suddenly he turned, his eyes widening at the sight of her. Then they narrowed, the bushy brows drawing together across his forehead.

"Hello, Harold," she said bravely.

He made no reply, but only grunted as he slipped the machete smoothly into its sheath. Effortlessly he hoisted a heavy limb and dragged it to a pile that was apparently being saved for firewood. Maggie found herself unable to move. It was like being mesmerized by something awful that stopped her dead in her tracks even as her feet sought to drag her away. Only when Harold came close and spoke did she again become mobile.

"Looks like you got here just in time for the fireworks," he muttered.

"What fireworks?" she asked as she began to back away.

Reaching into the pocket of his overalls, Harold produced a pack of matches and proceeded to strike one. "I'd back off a little bit if I was you," he said, an uncharacteristic chuckle trailing behind him as he bent swiftly to touch the flame to a white cord that stretched along the ground.

The cord began to sizzle, and a golden spark raced away toward the massive stump of the fallen tree. Harold lumbered to an oak some distance away and darted behind it for shelter.

Suddenly Maggie understood there was about to be an explosion. She turned and took several wild steps before the dynamite exploded. She clapped her hands over her ears and bolted, slowing her pace only when she reached the oak grove.

Slumping against one of the large shady trees, she caught her breath and stared accusingly toward the back lawn. Harold had taken a perverse pleasure in frightening her, and now that she had put distance between herself and the incident, she wished she had acted more courageously. Feeling foolish and angry, she glanced ahead toward the stables and started impulsively in their direction.

As she approached the fenced pasture surrounding the stable yard, she saw that the horses had been let out to graze. Crossing to the fence, she propped her elbows on the top rail and watched the beautiful animals. There were seven or eight of them—roans, chestnuts, bays. Their coats shone in the sun as they bent their sleek heads to the grass, and even her uneducated eye could see that they came from champion lines. Mark's stable was inhabited only by the best, and she grudgingly admired his high standards.

"Hey, how ya doing?" a friendly voice called, and she turned to see Jeremy walking toward her. He was wearing faded jeans, a plaid shirt, and an open smile.

"Hey!" Maggie responded in kind. Yesterday she'd been too preoccupied with Mark to pay much attention to Jeremy. Now, as she moved to meet the boy, she guessed him to be twelve or thirteen years old.

"We're on spring break from school this week," he said in a friendly way. "I'm not usually around on weekday mornings. If you want to go for a ride, I'll saddle up Lorelei for you."

"No, thanks, Jeremy. Not today," she answered firmly, her thoughts straying to her aching backside.

"I just finished out in the pasture and thought I'd visit Gray Lady. Want to come along?"

Gray Lady. That was the mare Mark had mentioned, the one that would soon be foaling.

Following the boy into the cool shade of the barn, Maggie was assaulted by smells of hay and leather that triggered a fresh thought of Mark. Jeremy led her to a large stall at the end of the barn. He perched on the gate, produced a carrot from his pocket, and held it out to a dappled gray mare. She was a beautiful Arabian, her lineage announced unquestionably by the small, sculptured head and flaring nostrils. She whinnied softly and moseyed over to the gate where she munched on the carrot.

"She seems to like you very much," Maggie offered.

"Sure, she likes me all right," Jeremy said. "But the one she really depends on is Mr. Fox. He brought her into the world. She was born right here, and Mr. Fox delivered her. He knows everything about horses." The boy turned briefly from the mare to glance at Maggie, and it was easy to see the admiration in his eyes.

"You think a lot of Mr. Fox, don't you?" she asked.

"Sure I do," Jeremy answered loyally. "He's the best horseman around these parts, and he taught me everything I know."

To hear Mark spoken of so highly brought a surprising tug at her heartstrings, but Maggie had little time to think about the odd sensation. At that moment Annie MacGregor scurried into the barn.

"Miss!" she called. "I'm sorry to disturb you, but Rachel told me to find you and tell you that some flowers came for you."

"Flowers? For me?"

"Yes'm. Two dozen long-stemmed roses just arrived," came Annie's purring, accented voice. "And the card has your name on it!"

"Who in the world . . ." Maggie murmured as she went to join Annie.

"I've never seen so many roses all in one place," the Scottish woman exclaimed as they walked along the oak-lined path to the house. "Do you think they're from your boyfriend?"

"I hardly think so," Maggie returned. "I don't have a boyfriend."

"Now, that's hard to believe! You're so pretty, I'd give

anything to look like you," she stated simply, brushing her limp blond hair from her eyes. "Maybe then Mr. Fox would look at me the way he looks at you." Annie quickly covered her mouth with stubby fingers and added, "You won't repeat that, will you? If Mrs. Fox ever heard me say such a thing, she'd fire me on the spot!"

Maggie grinned at the impish expression on the pale face. "Don't worry, Annie. I won't say anything, but Mr. Fox doesn't look at me in any special way."

"Rachel says he does. She thinks he's smitten with you!" the Scotswoman said, her blue eyes wide.

Maggie chuckled. "I'll tell you what I told Rachel. She's a romantic. She loves romance, and she sees it in the people she cares about, even when it's not there. How long have you worked here, Annie?"

"Well, let me see. I started working out here right after Mr. MacGregor died, God rest his soul. That's been almost ten years."

"So you've known Rachel for a long time. Don't you think she's a bit of a matchmaker?"

"Maybe," Annie said, squinting as she considered the idea. "But what if Rachel is right? Wouldn't that be something! I mean, Mr. Fox is the handsomest man. Doesn't he just send you?"

Maggie smiled at the old-fashioned expression. "I guess so, Annie. I mean, he's a nice-looking man."

"'Most every lady around here has given him her invitation. Why, if Mr. Fox started courting you, you'd be the envy of every woman in these parts!"

"I don't think I'm going to have to worry about that."

"I wouldn't worry either, I'd be tickled pink. Wouldn't it be just grand if you and Mr. Fox got married?"

At that, Maggie burst into laughter. "Annie, I'm beginning to see that you and Rachel are like two peas in a pod."

The slight older woman smiled warmly. "Well, I for one would be happy for the both of you. What a lovely couple you would make. And I sure like you a lot better than that hoity-toity Miss Townsend."

They had reached the terrace and were approaching the house. "Who is Miss Townsend?" Maggie asked casually, her memory seizing on the name that was the same as Arthur's.

"She's the one who chased Mr. Fox so hard, trying to get him to marry her. But Mr. Fox, he dropped her on the spot."

Rachel burst out through the French doors ebulliently, and Annie hurried into the house and out of sight.

"Lord, Miss Hastings, it sure is nice to have a young lady in the house! Just wait till you see these roses!"

Rachel had placed a huge vase of American Beauties on the dining table. "Would you look at that!" She beamed as Maggie approached the flowers with bewilderment. "The florist brought 'em all the way out from Charleston."

"Really?"

Maggie reached for the small white card that was nearly lost in the profusion of greenery. Sure enough, the name on the envelope was her own, and with an irritating wisp of hope the roses might be from Mark, she pulled the card from its envelope and read the words with disappointment: "How about dinner tonight? I'll call you. Arthur."

Of course, they wouldn't be from Mark, she thought irritably. She glanced at Rachel, who was regarding her with such strong curiosity that it was visible through her thick glasses.

"Isn't that nice?" Maggie murmured and stuffed the card in the pocket of her jeans. "They're from Arthur Townsend."

"Townsend!" Rachel exclaimed. "When did you meet Mr. Townsend?"

"Yesterday, after Mark and I came back from our ride. Why?"

"Mr. Fox ain't gonna like this," the old woman pronounced, shaking her head. "No, ma'am!"

"Why should he care?"

"Oh, he'll care, believe you me. For lots o' reasons. Those two have been at each other, trying to outdo each other, since they were children. And now," she said with a laugh, "now it looks like those two overgrown boys are gonna be fighting over a new lollipop."

"Rachel!" Maggie said in as reproachful a tone as she could manage. "I want you to listen to me. Mark is not going to care if Arthur Townsend sends me flowers. I'm afraid you've got a wrong notion about Mark and me, and I don't want it to go any further."

Rachel paid no attention to Maggie's scolding and continued to enjoy the image she had conjured up of Mark Fox and Arthur Townsend dueling over a fair damsel.

"You say what you will, Miss Hastings," she huffed. "But I know Mr. Fox, known him since he was a baby. And I know what he's like when he wants something. He doesn't show he wants it, but he doesn't give up till he's got it, either. No, ma'am!" With one more shake of her head, the old woman waddled away to the kitchen.

Left alone in the dining room, Maggie eyed the beautiful roses and considered Arthur Townsend's invitation. She wasn't attracted to him, but he seemed nice enough, and certainly any man who extended a dinner invitation by means of roses had to be respectable. It would be a pleasant change to go out to dinner. She was tired of dining alone.

Leaning over the scarlet buds, she took a long sniff of their rich scent and decided to accept the invitation.

Sunlight streamed through the north windows of Todd Williams's office, spotlighting the renderings spread across the tabletop, silhouetting the shapes of the three men who clustered about the table, leaning over the work and exchanging comments. Mark and Todd stood a short distance away, holding their tongues and allowing the drawings to speak for them. Occasionally they shared a questioning glance before turning to focus again on the three businessmen.

To Mark they resembled so many vultures as they clutched and clawed at the precious renderings, turning beady-eyed looks on each other and communicating in low voices. He lounged against the wall and watched them from beneath hooded lids, finding it difficult to read the thoughts of the three investors.

He couldn't fault the shrewd air of business know-how that pervaded the group. It was a worthy testament to the legendary commercial sense of the Yankee trader. Odd that a property like Canadys Isle should fall into their hands.

Several centuries before, the Canady family had been among the first elite settlers of the Charleston area, their holdings far outstripping those of Major Fox and most of the other landowners. But during the Civil War the Canady plantation had been demolished and the family had fled north. Over the course of a hundred years, their descendants had gradually sold off the family's Carolina lands until all that remained was Canadys Isle. Now it, too, had been snapped up by a New York conglomerate with an eye toward its money-making potential as an elegant resort. The process left Mark with a sour taste in his mouth, but at least he could try to develop the island in a way that would preserve its historic and geographic integrity.

"It's a good-looking development," one of the visitors finally pronounced.

"Good-looking, yes," another admitted. "But is it practical? There seems to be a great deal of wasted space."

"Not wasted, I think," the third man put in. "Invested, perhaps. Let's not forget what we're after. We don't want row upon row of high-rise condos. Hell, if we want that, we might as well build in New York. What we want is a sense of tropical grandness—spacious, elegant estates where people can enjoy the fine life and natural splendor at the same time. It seems to me that Fox here has designed just such a place, and I for one am looking forward to seeing this paradise island with my own eyes."

"And see it you shall, gentlemen," Mark rumbled as he moved away from the wall. "I've arranged a trip to Canadys for tomorrow afternoon. The ferry leaves at two o'clock. Until the four-lane bridge is built, that's the only way over."

When the meeting was concluded, Mark turned to another errand. He stepped into the saddlery shop, his eyes scanning the carefully crafted livery hanging on the walls, his nostrils soaking up the scent of leather that hung in the air like a cloud.

"What can I do for you?" the shopkeeper asked.

"Hello, Tom," Mark returned and thrust a paper sack across the counter.

Grasping the small package, Tom withdrew a dainty pair of ladies' pumps and looked up at his customer with questioning surprise.

"Boots," Mark uttered tersely, an irritable edge coming into his voice.

That afternoon Maggie returned to the library. The sedately quiet place, so like the museums where she'd spent much of her life, was a fit environment for her thoughtful mood.

She took a long while studying the painting of her enigmatic benefactor, William Marcus Fox. Somehow the portrait managed to draw her, to call out with suggestions of what he'd been like—this man from the past whose actions were reshaping her present and future.

He had been a gentleman—that much was easy to see—from the top of his well-groomed head to the tips of his long fingers. For the first time she noticed his ring, a heavy gold band molded into the head of a fox with rubies for eyes. It looked like a symbol of nobility, but somehow as Maggie studied the likeness of

William Fox, she suspected that authority had not been of the utmost importance to him. He exuded an inner serenity that transcended the richness of his garments and jewelry, even the ruby-studded ring.

Her gaze lingered on the kindly, intelligent face, where smile lines crinkled at the corners of clear blue eyes. She found herself wishing she had seen that face in the flesh, wishing that she had been the cause of that smile and those twinkling eyes.

Thinking of William Fox reminded her of his attic studio, directly overhead. She moved to the stairwell in the corner and, upon reaching the top, tried the door. Again it refused to give. But then she had an inspiration that drove her down the stairs and back to the main house. Rachel had keys to every room at Foxcroft.

She made directly for the kitchen, but finding only Mrs. Phipps, she searched the ground floor, calling Rachel's name all the while. She had circled back to the foyer when she heard a door open upstairs.

"Are you calling me, honey?"

Rachel's voice drifted down the stairs, and Maggie began the climb to the second floor. Dressed in her usual gray, the old woman stood just outside Mrs. Fox's rooms. As Maggie drew near, she noticed one of the doors was open just a crack.

"I hope you can help me, Rachel." She was excited by the prospect of seeing William Fox's studio, and her words tumbled out enthusiastically.

"I've been in the library. It's really a fascinating place. Many of the books are old and rare, and there's a wonderful collection of art books. I studied art in college, you know. I saw the portrait of Mark that Mr. Fox painted, and I'd love to see his studio. But the door is locked, and I was hoping you had the key."

As she finished, Rachel pulled a large brass ring from her apron pocket and selected a hefty antiquated key.

"Great!" Maggie exclaimed. But before Rachel had time to remove the old key from the ring, a frail but commanding voice called out from the hidden bedroom.

"No one goes in the studio. No one!"

Maggie's excited expression turned to one of puzzlement, and Rachel rolled her eyes behind her thick bifocals.

"Nobody's been in there since Mr. William died," Rachel whispered. "And that's a fact."

"Why?" Maggie whispered back, but Rachel only shrugged.

"I'll tell you why," Mrs. Fox's voice came again, now from just behind the door. "Because I say so. That's why. And no one—no one who wants to keep her job—is going to let you in there, not as long as *I'm* mistress of Foxcroft!"

The door slammed shut, and Maggie heard the distinct click of the lock.

Rachel put the ring of keys back in her apron pocket and glanced at Maggie sympathetically. The thought immediately sprang to Maggie's mind that *she* was legally the mistress of Foxcroft. But no one on the estate viewed her as such, and she found she couldn't voice the idea. She stepped to the door and knocked firmly.

"Mrs. Fox? I'd like to discuss this with you. I'm a student of art, and I won't disturb anything. Please, may I come in for a moment?"

"No!" The answer came sharply from the other side of the door. "I don't want you in here. Do you understand? I never want to see your face again!"

"Come on, honey," Rachel said softly and guided Maggie to the head of the stairs. "Sometimes she gets her mind set on something, and she's stubborn as a mule!"

"Does she dislike everyone?" Maggie asked. "Or is it just me?"

"Oh, child, it's everybody! She's been hiding from the world for so long I reckon she's not about to change now. Don't you fret over it."

For the moment Maggie dropped the subject of Mrs. Fox and the studio. But she didn't dismiss it from her mind. With some thought, she was sure she could figure out a way to enter the studio without getting Rachel into trouble.

Chapter Seven

She lay on the terrace couch. The first edition of *Gone with the Wind* was propped open beside her, the warm afternoon sun shone overhead. Thinking she'd never felt so at peace, Maggie marveled at the way Foxcroft had stolen her heart. In all the places she'd wandered, even in Kensing, she'd never felt at home. Now she did. The irony was that she couldn't stay.

Her conviction that Foxcroft belonged to the Foxes was inescapable. Its history was their history, its life was their life. Maggie Hastings had no part in it. The best she could do was stretch the time she'd been allotted here and treasure it always.

Rachel's voice startled her out of her daydreams. "There's a telephone call for you, Miss Hastings!" the old woman called. "You can take it in the foyer."

"I'll be right there," Maggie answered, thinking that it must be Arthur Townsend. Once in the foyer, she noticed that Rachel was attempting to mask her eavesdropping by concentrating on dusting a table a short way down the hall. Maggie rolled her eyes in amusement and picked up the receiver.

"Hello . . . Oh, hello, Arthur. Thank you for the roses. They're lovely."

"I'm glad you like them," he returned warmly. "I was hoping they would run some interference for me. It's not often I meet a woman I'd really like to get to know. Tomorrow night at the party we won't have much of a chance to talk, so I hope you'll agree to have dinner with me tonight."

"I appreciate the invitation, Arthur. Yes, I'd love to."

"Good! I'll treat you to the best seafood dinner you ever put in your mouth!"

He concluded the arrangements by saying he would pick her up at seven.

"Who was that?" Rachel asked as Maggie hung up the phone.

"You know very well that it was Arthur Townsend," Maggie

replied good-naturedly. "I'm going to have dinner with him tonight."

"O-o-oh, Lord have mercy," Rachel exclaimed. "Things are gonna get hot around here."

"Rachel!" Maggie muttered in exasperation and climbed the stairs to her room, shaking her head at the old woman's prediction.

She washed and dried her hair. As usual when it was freshly shampooed, its volume and curl seemed to double and it glistened with golden highlights from the sun. Even after she pulled it back from her face with combs the fiery hair was flamboyant and eye-catching.

As Maggie looked through her wardrobe, she realized it had been selected to play down her flamboyance. Everything she'd brought was conservative. She chose a navy pinstripe pants suit that would hide the bruises on her calves. An ivory silk blouse and a string of pearls helped dress up the suit for evening and added a feminine touch to the severely tailored ensemble.

There was no need to apply blusher. The sun had provided all the color she needed on her cheeks. But she spent extra time on her eyes, using shadow, heavy mascara, and eyeliner. When she finished, the vivid blue-green of her irises fairly glowed in her rosy face.

She was ready early, and it was only a little past six when she left her bedroom. But when she opened the door, she stopped cold. On the floor just outside were the shoes Mark had so crudely relieved her of the night before. Next to them stood a pair of black riding boots.

Boots? He had bought her a pair of boots? They were of superior quality, obviously expensive. The leather was beautiful—soft and pliable, yet thick enough to provide protection against saddle and bramble.

Boots, Maggie thought again in wonder. With a last caress of the smooth leather, she stood them inside her door and, wearing a pleased smile that sprang from somewhere deep inside, began to trip down the stairs, slowing her pace only when her sore muscles cried out in protest.

She was surprised when she entered the dining room and found Mark already there. He sat on the settee in the corner, sipping a cocktail and reading the *Wall Street Journal*. As she entered, he rose to his feet, laying the newspaper aside.

"Good evening, Maggie," he said formally.

In stark contrast to his rumpled appearance the night before, he was dressed in gray slacks—obviously European—with a white shirt and silk tie.

"Mark," she said simply. Her first odd impulse was to rush to him, but his cool, aristocratic manner nipped the notion. She walked casually across the room, but she couldn't suppress the smile that played about her lips. "The boots are beautiful. Thank you."

"It was nothing," he returned nonchalantly. "If you're going to ride again while you're here, you ought to have a decent pair of boots."

His reply sounded indifferent, but as Mark studied her glowing face, he felt anything but casual. He'd convinced himself the boots were a peace offering, a door opener to business dealings, nothing more. Now, as he looked at her, he knew he'd been kidding himself. Damn! She was more enticing each time he saw her!

Mark didn't like playing games. When it came to women, he was used to reaching out and taking what he wanted. And right now, with Maggie standing before him in a masculine suit that somehow made her look utterly feminine, he wanted nothing more than to take her in his arms, feel her body against his once more.

Maggie noted how impressive he looked in his tailored clothes. She had never seen him in formal attire, and she wondered if his polished appearance was for her benefit. With any other man, she would not even have questioned it. But Mark Fox was not any other man.

For a moment he held her gaze in a way that conjured up the memory of the oak grove, his eyes communicating a sense of intimacy. A heated feeling began to spread within Maggie.

"Would you like a drink?" he asked.

"Some white wine would be nice."

He stepped over to the liquor cabinet and proceeded to serve her, his eyes flickering to hers and lingering. How long had she been here? Three days? It was hard to predict just what might happen if Maggie hung around much longer—Foxcroft or no Foxcroft.

"Thanks," she murmured when he handed her the crystal goblet. Maggie took a long swallow, hoping the wine would calm her nerves, which always seemed to tingle when Mark was near.

"Would you like to sit down?" he asked, gesturing to the settee. He waited for her to lower herself onto the small sofa, then resumed his seat less than a foot away. "What did you do today?"

"Oh, not much. I took a walk around the grounds this morning. Then I got a book from the library and read for a while."

"I knew you must have spent some time outdoors. You're beginning to get a tan."

"Yes, I know. I wasn't out very long, but I guess your South Carolina sun is pretty strong."

"After a while, you build up a certain immunity."

"I don't suppose I'll have time for that," Maggie said, and was surprised the sobering comment had popped out.

Mark glanced at her sharply. "Just how much time do you suppose you'll have?"

Perhaps it was best to get it out in the open. She'd been depressed all day, dreading the time when Mark would approach her with a document in his hand. She met the emerald eyes. They were hard and unyielding.

"I have no idea," she answered. "You're more experienced than I. How long do these business matters take?"

Ever since she'd arrived, Mark had been trying to get rid of her. But at this moment, his feelings were damnably complicated!

"No time at all," he said irritably.

Maggie's spirits sank. "I see."

He took in her look of dejection and was about to utter a comforting comment before he realized it. "There's no need to think about it now. You've decided to stay through the weekend. After all, you made a commitment to attend Townsend's party tomorrow night."

Maggie refused to be consoled. "Maybe we shouldn't go."

"What?" Mark blurted, his brows flying up. "Yesterday you nearly jumped down my throat when I tried to refuse the invitation!"

"I know," she said with downcast eyes. "But maybe it's not such a good idea. I don't have anything to wear."

In spite of himself, Mark was amused by the age-old feminine complaint. "Go out and buy something, then," he suggested. "Harold will drive you."

She made a wry face, and Mark surrendered a grin. "Yeah, you're right. Harold has been here since I was a kid, and I'm used to him. But I guess he *would* seem odd to a newcomer. He was raised in the upcountry hills by his father, a strict old circuit preacher turned drunk. Harold's a little strange, but he knows the land."

"I don't really mind Harold," Maggie lied. Something made her hold her tongue about her experience that day on the back lawn.

Mark looked at her questioningly. Her subdued mood made her seem softer, more approachable than he'd ever seen her. He found himself wanting to put the liveliness back in that beautiful face. He reached into his pocket, produced his keys, and separated one from the rest.

"Here," he said brusquely. "This goes to the Mercedes in the garage. Why don't you get out tomorrow and see a little of Charleston? It would probably do you good."

Maggie looked up at him with shock. "Won't you need the car?"

"I drive a Porsche," he replied shortly and dangled the key in front of her nose.

Eyes wide, she reached out to take it. "Thank you, Mark," she said when she could find her voice.

"My pleasure," he returned smoothly and stretched an arm across the back of the settee.

He began to look at her in that fixed way of his so that Maggie took another long drink of wine. He certainly was behaving oddly—boots, polite conversation, the offer of a car. The deference she'd have expected from another man was startling from Mark Fox.

When she glanced back at him she saw that his gaze hadn't wavered, but she still couldn't read it. For all she knew, the formidable man could as easily consider killing her as kissing her, and she'd have no idea what was coming until it was upon her.

Staring into the clear depths of her wine, she asked, "Did you have a good day at work?"

It was a simple question, but it opened the door to another side of Mark Fox. He took the lead in the conversation, and Maggie was astonished at how charming he could be when he set aside the aloofness that so often surrounded him. He told her about his offices in Charleston and described the town house on Wentworth Street, which he maintained to entertain real estate clients. He talked about the upcoming polo match to be held at nearby Boone Hall—an activity he took part in every spring and fall.

He was interesting, articulate. Occasionally, as when she asked a question about polo, he flashed a smile. The dark aura lifted, leaving behind a drawling, rakish air that was devastatingly sexy. Maggie supposed she was seeing at first hand why every woman in the area had "given him her invitation," as Annie had put it.

Mark told himself he was simply being a good businessman, that being on speaking terms with Maggie Hastings was a necessity. But it was more than that. She was damned bright. He enjoyed talking to her, *and* looking at her.

Eventually he brought up the subject of art. "I understand you're an art scholar. Do you paint?"

"I used to, but I was never very good," Maggie replied modestly as Rachel walked in from the kitchen. "I don't consider myself an artist, more an admirer of art."

"I admire realism," he said, surprising her with the comment. "Still lifes especially. I think it takes talent to capture something real, like those roses."

He gestured to the American Beauties on the dining table and added, "By the way, Rachel, it just occurred to me that the gardens aren't in bloom yet. Where did those roses come from?"

"They came from the florist in Charleston, that's where they came from. Mr. Townsend sent 'em out to Miss Hastings."

"Townsend!" Mark exploded.

As his voice thundered in her ears, Maggie felt the blood drain from her face.

"Yes, sir," Rachel continued, ignoring the pleading look Maggie turned on her. "He must be mighty taken with Miss Hastings, and I can't say I blame him. He's taking her to supper tonight, too."

"What?" Mark sprang to his feet. He looked at the roses and then back at Maggie with blazing eyes that seemed to accuse her of the ultimate betrayal.

How swiftly he had turned on her! The charming man of the past half-hour was gone. Now he was again the dark, angry lord of the manor, looking just as he had that first night. The transformation happened so quickly that Maggie wondered if the charm had been only an act, a veneer beneath which the dark and hostile Mark Fox had lurked all along. Looking up at him from the settee, she said nothing, only shrugged her shoulders.

"Well, well," he began coldly. "Riding boots, roses. You've had yourself quite a day, haven't you? And now you're looking forward to a night on the town! Rachel, I'll have a tray in the study later. At the moment I've lost my appetite!"

With long strides he stalked out of the room.

Rachel chuckled quietly. "Don't you worry about a thing, Miss Hastings," she said. "I know that boy, and I know what I'm doing."

But Maggie *was* worried and confused. As she watched Mark Fox storm away, she had the unfamiliar urge to call out to him, to go out of her way just to be once more in the light of his smile.

The maverick urge passed. She managed to smile at Rachel, but inside she felt completely off-balance. She thought of Arthur Townsend and dreaded his impending arrival. No longer did the idea of going out to dinner seem appealing. She longed for some quiet time to think, to sort out and resolve her conflicting feelings. Yet she knew she couldn't resolve all of them. There was no doubt Mark had a powerful effect on her, just as Foxcroft did.

Rachel departed for the kitchen, and Maggie wandered into the front parlor. She gazed moodily out the window. Night was falling, and she was reminded of a twilight only a week and a half before when she'd stood in the familiar house in Kensing, looking across the street she'd known all her life. Now she gazed upon the dusky lawns of a magnificent Carolina estate. So much could change in a week.

With every hour New York seemed farther away as Foxcroft reached deeper into her soul. In some cosmic way Maggie sensed its ancient brick walls harbored the destiny that had called to her for a lifetime. Foxcroft—mysterious, beautiful, eternal. She could hardly bear the thought of leaving it.

She shook her head as she mused. Mark Fox and Foxcroft— they were as one. Both had bewitched her.

It seemed only minutes before a black Jaguar sedan rolled into the courtyard. Arthur was early. Since Rachel was conspicuously absent when the bell rang, Maggie met him at the door.

He looked urbane in a dark three-piece suit, and his eyes shone as he took her hand in greeting. Arthur's narrow face was changeable. When it was alight with pleasure, as now, he was quite handsome.

"You look breathtaking!" he said in a low, intimate voice.

"Thank you," she replied, smoothly retrieving her hand. "Come in, won't you? I just need to get my purse."

He followed her into the dining room where she had left her bag on the settee.

"I must thank you again for the flowers," she said, gesturing to the long-stemmed roses, which were clearly the focal point of the room.

"I'm glad you like them. I patronize a small shop in the District. The owner is, to my way of thinking, the *only* florist in

Charleston. At any rate, the roses seem to have performed their appointed task."

When she only looked at him questioningly, he added, "You're having dinner with me tonight, aren't you?"

A few minutes later they were cruising along the highway in the silent splendor of the sleek, vintage-model Jaguar. It seemed that Arthur's taste ran to classics. Maggie sensed that he expected her to admire the automobile, and she did so. As she suspected he would, Arthur beamed.

"I really enjoy this beauty," he commented, then turned to her and added meaningfully, "but then, I've always had a fondness for beautiful things."

They drove into Historic Charleston, and this time Maggie had the opportunity to be completely charmed. Twilight accented its antebellum character, and as they rolled along the palm-studded streets, she watched the lights come on in picturesque town houses and noticed for the first time quaint shops and galleries and restaurants, their fronts lit by old-fashioned street lamps.

Maggie began to relax. The change of scene was just what she needed to improve her tumultuous mood, and Arthur was a pleasant companion. He drove slowly through the streets of Charleston, pointing out interesting landmarks and seeming to enjoy the role of guide.

A few moments later they arrived at the Colony House, an elegantly renovated restaurant which, Arthur informed her, was originally a waterfront warehouse.

"I think you'll find the food excellent," he said as they were seated at a table set with white linen and sterling silver.

The restaurant was lovely, and Arthur was a gourmet. Gradually Maggie surrendered herself to the posh atmosphere, the superb meal, and her escort's flattering manner. This was her realm, her element. Dining in elegance, engaging in repartee with a man whose single aim seemed to be to please her, she felt more at home with herself than she had in months.

Most of the diners had departed by the time their waiter arrived with coffee. The restaurant had grown quiet with the late hour, and from some distant anteroom drifted the soothing notes of violins. It was then that Arthur leaned back in his chair and regarded her thoughtfully.

"So, the New York art scholar has come to South Carolina. I must admit, Maggie, I was surprised to hear of your arrival. To be more specific, I am curious about the reason for your visit. Do you mind if I ask how you became tied up with Foxcroft?"

He had wined and dined her into laziness, but his new line of conversation cut through the mood.

"Not at all. Part of the Foxcroft estate, only part of it, was left to my parents by William Fox. As I told you earlier, they died recently, and a document was discovered in their safe deposit box."

"But the part of the estate you inherited . . . it includes the house, doesn't it?"

"Yes, it does. Why are you so interested in all of this?"

"I'll be frank with you, Maggie." Arthur's gaze fell to his coffee cup, the gesture seeming to bely his claim of frankness. "The primary reason I want to get to know you is because you're a beautiful, intelligent woman. A second reason is that I'd like to do business with you."

"Business?"

"Yes. My sources tell me that Mark is going to buy back Foxcroft and the acreage you inherited. Is that right?"

Maggie looked sharply across the table. "He's going to make me an offer," she corrected.

Arthur leaned forward, fixing his eyes on hers. "Maggie, I'm going to tell you something I'm sure Mark would never make known. In fact, he's undoubtedly been keeping you squirreled away in the country to make sure you don't hear about this. I'm very much interested in Foxcroft. I have been for years, and Mark knows it. I'll top whatever offer he makes by a very attractive margin. That estate," he continued heatedly, "is a historic landmark. And Mark Fox just sits out there like some . . . squatter."

Curiously enough, Maggie reacted defensively. "Squatter? That's a harsh word for someone whose family has lived there for generations."

"You're using the word 'family' loosely," Arthur replied. "Most of the people in our circle don't recognize the current Fox 'family.' They certainly don't have enough claim on the estate to forbid the opening of Foxcroft to the public."

As she listened to Arthur's biting remarks, Maggie began to gather something about the southern elite of which he was a member. The leisurely pace of their lives, their hospitable and gracious manner, might fool an unsuspecting outsider. But Mag-

gie sensed that underneath the superficial civility was a ruthless-
ness which would rival that of any "crass Yankee."

"Mark has a perfectly respectable town house here in the
Historic District," Arthur went on. "But he insists on wasting the
entire Foxcroft estate housing two people."

"I see," she said quietly. "And how would you change all
that?"

The man's hazel eyes seemed to catch fire. "I would make
Foxcroft one of the great showplaces of Charleston. I would turn
the house into an inn, enlarge the stables. By the marsh I'd build
a landing and operate paddle-wheel steamboat service up the river.
With my connections, Foxcroft would fast become the playground
of the crème de la crème."

Arthur's dream left Maggie cold, and she amused herself briefly
by imagining Mark's reaction to such a scheme.

"Very . . . imaginative," she began casually. "Why haven't
you approached Mark with your idea?"

"I have! A dozen times!"

"And he doesn't agree?"

"No," Arthur said. "He refuses to consider it. The only
explanation I can think of is that he's reluctant to bring that mother
of his back into the city. She's as mad as a hatter, you know."

"Mrs. Fox?"

"Good God, yes! Mark wouldn't tell you this, of course, but if
it weren't for the Fox name and money, Dolly Fox would be in
prison right now."

"Prison!" The word burst from Maggie's mouth and she quickly
glanced around to see if anyone had heard.

"Yes! And everyone in Charleston knows it!"

Arthur clearly relished releasing a skeleton from the Fox closet.
"Years ago—I was just a child at the time—she burned down one
of the outbuildings late one night. The fire killed a couple of
people, and one of them was her husband, William Fox."

Maggie's head began to spin with the disclosure, and she barely
heard Arthur's continuing remarks.

"Of course she said she didn't do it, that she couldn't remember
anything about it. The doctors called it circumstantial amnesia,
and the family attorneys got her off because of the lack of
indisputable evidence. But she was found near the burned building
in her nightdress, having been thrown from a horse. Even today,
I'm told, she has to walk with a cane."

A cane! Yes! On Maggie's first night at Foxcroft, after Mrs.

Fox's bizarre fainting spell, John Henry had returned to the dining room and retrieved a cane!

"But as I said, that was decades ago," Arthur continued. "It seems a shame to let a gold mine like Foxcroft remain unexploited just to shelter a madwoman who would be just as comfortable in the family town house. All these years, Mark has refused to listen to me. But now *you've* arrived, and I hope I can persuade you to see, as I do, a magnificent future for Foxcroft."

Slowly Maggie was able to switch her thoughts from the incredible story about Mrs. Fox to Arthur's dream of making Foxcroft a glorified resort for the rich. She eyed her escort steadily, a look of distaste forming on her face.

"I'm sorry to disappoint you, Arthur, but the idea of turning Foxcroft into an inn doesn't appeal to me. For one thing, I don't think William Fox would have approved."

A flush rose to Arthur's face, and his voice took on an edge. "William Fox is the past, Maggie, long dead and buried. This is the New South. All of the major plantations—Magnolia Gardens, Middleton Place, Boone Hall—*all* have opened to the public!"

The man was pushing her, not realizing the effect such pressure would have on Maggie's rebellious nature.

"All the more reason to make sure that Foxcroft is preserved with its original identity, as a private residence. I've been here only a few days, Arthur, but already I've developed a special kind of respect for the place. The land was granted to Major Fox for settlement. The house was built in the 1700s as a home. It has survived time and war, even Sherman's march. Far be it from me to end all that."

Annoyance showed in Arthur's expression, and it was a tense standoff the waiter interrupted when he delivered the check. Arthur deposited a credit card on the silver tray, and by the time the card was whisked away, he seemed to have recovered his poise.

"Apparently I haven't made you see things my way, Maggie. But perhaps you'll change your mind."

When she started to object, he raised a hand to stop her.

"There are several options open to you. Many people would be interested in your property if they knew it was available. The main thing I advise against is putting too much confidence in Mark Fox. Don't be taken in by his charm, as so many other women have."

A single brow shot up. "What do you mean by that?"

Arthur settled back in his chair and stated the facts bluntly. "I've known Mark for most of his life. He has a way with ladies. Many times during his rise to power he's been helped along by one woman or another. Whenever one of them had something he wanted, he managed to romance her out of it. Those women included my sister, I'm sorry to say."

"Your sister? The one who's getting married?"

"Yes. Several years ago he and Alicia were quite an item. But oddly enough, about a month after Mark talked her into selling him some of her riverbank land, he stopped calling. It took Alicia a long time to get over him. I wouldn't bring up the subject except that I want you to know what Mark Fox is like so you'll realize what you're up against."

Hot spots of color stained Maggie's cheeks. "I appreciate your advice, but maybe I'm not so easily manipulated as the other women Mark has known."

Apparently sensing her irritation, Arthur closed the subject. "I'm sure you're right. Sorry to be presumptuous. Shall we go?"

He escorted her out of the restaurant and smiled as he held the door, but Maggie had the feeling her tilting match with Arthur Townsend was far from over.

On the way back to the plantation, Arthur chatted about the next evening's party. Occasionally Maggie tossed him a smile or a question, but her thoughts were centered on the disturbing things he had told her earlier. The macabre story about Mrs. Fox chilled her to the bone. Was the fragile woman she had seen capable of such a violent act? It had happened years ago, but time could change people. It had changed the vibrant young woman of the library portrait into an embittered recluse.

The other nagging image Arthur had planted in her mind was that of Mark. Lately the magnetic man had managed to make her forget his unattractive qualities—the cold arrogance, the bleak air of darkness that made one wonder just what he was capable of. Arthur's words served to remind her of those qualities and to acquaint her with an additional one—deceit. Being a playboy was one thing, but the man Arthur described was cold-blooded and cruel.

Why are you so surprised? she asked herself. You're no babe in the woods. You know the ropes. It's just his looks, or that sensual air, or *something* that's been throwing you off lately. Apparently the man is good with women, just as Arthur says, just as everyone says. Good at using them, manipulating them. Isn't that exactly what he's doing with you?

She thought of the expensive leather boots sitting just inside her bedroom door and saw them in the sudden new light of a bribe. A hard look came to her face. When Arthur glanced her way—grinning at some silly joke she hadn't even heard—he must have found her expression disconcerting. The smile faded, and he was far more quiet for the remainder of the ride.

As for Maggie, by the time they reached the estate, she was newly armed against Mark Fox.

The Jaguar pulled into the circular courtyard and came to a slow halt beside the porch. Arthur engaged the brake, flipped off the ignition, and pivoted in the driver's seat to face her. It had arrived—that awkward moment—and as Arthur gazed at her, Maggie reached for the door handle.

"I've had a lovely evening," she lied politely. "I know you've got a long drive home, so—" As she started to let herself out of the car, he reached over and touched her arm.

"Wait a minute, Maggie. I'll walk you to the door."

He came around the car, took her hand, and helped her out of the sedan. He continued holding her hand as they ascended the steps and crossed the dark veranda where no one had thought to leave a light burning.

The crickets sounded like a huge invisible orchestra, backing up the chortling chorus of katydids. Maggie glanced over her shoulder at the courtyard, where the gurgling splash of the fountain added a final, lovely touch to the sounds of the spring night. A cool breeze rustled by, lifting the curls from her face and carrying the scent of flowers. The serene moonlit grounds of Foxcroft were incredibly romantic, and she couldn't help thinking the night would be perfect if only the man beside her were someone else.

They came to the double doors, and Arthur took her other hand so that she had to face him. In a swift, unexpected move, he pulled her to him so she had no chance to object as he kissed her. His lips were soft and smothering, eliciting no passion, only a wish for the moment to end. She pulled away as diplomatically as possible, and Arthur spoke in a breathy voice, "I want to see you again, Maggie. Next week, perhaps?"

"We'll see," she said noncommittally. "There's the party tomorrow night. I'm looking forward to that."

"Me, too. I realize that Mark will be your escort tomorrow

night, but I want you to save at least one dance for me. Maggie,"
he added, giving her hands a squeeze, "I definitely want you to be
there. Sometimes Mark can be a little—how should I put
it?—unreliable. If by any chance he should renege on bringing
you to the party, call me. My number is in the book."

"Don't count on it, Townsend," Mark's voice suddenly thundered so that Arthur dropped Maggie's hands, and both of them
spun around to peer toward the far end of the veranda. The
invisible porch swing groaned as if a weight had been lifted from
it, and melting out of the inky blackness, Mark emerged.

Dressed in black jeans and shirt, he blended eerily into the
darkness. In the deep shadows of the doorway, where only the
faint glow of a single hallway lamp spilled through the side panes,
the whites of his eyes and teeth seemed to float disembodied in the
air.

He folded his arms across his broad chest and eyed Arthur
steadily. "After you've gone to so much trouble to welcome Miss
Hastings into Charleston society, I wouldn't dream of disappoint-
ing her about the party. And I wouldn't give you the satisfaction
of proving me—as you put it—'unreliable.' "

Arthur acted as if Mark Fox had never appeared.

"Maggie," he said urgently, drawing her gaze back to his
narrow face. "I had a wonderful time, and I look forward to
tomorrow night. Don't forget what I said," he concluded with a
meaningful look, and bounded down the steps.

"It's been great seeing you, Townsend!" Mark called sarcastically.

Arthur glanced swiftly up to the porch where Maggie stood in
surprised silence, then climbed into the Jaguar and roared away
from the house. She looked blankly up the drive until the car lights
disappeared, then, directing a brief glare in Mark's direction,
stalked into the house.

She was halfway down the dimly lit hall before he caught up to
her, grabbed her arm, and whirled her around. Holding her by the
shoulders, he forced her to look at him.

"What are you in such a huff about?" he demanded.

"You amaze me, Mark!" she blazed, pushing his hands away.
She was frustrated and angry—angry that he could be the villain
Arthur described, frustrated that her own emotions seemed determined to ignore the fact. "Is this the way you treat everyone? How
dare you spy on me and embarrass me in front of Arthur?"

The familiar grim look settled on his features, creating lines about his mouth and eyes. "Sorry, lady. I didn't know you cared that much about what Arthur Townsend thinks."

"Well, now you know!" she spat and turned on her heel.

He followed her to the stairs. "Since you're in the mood to set me straight, I'd like to know one more thing. Did Townsend talk to you about Foxcroft?"

The question was abruptly revealing. Mark's interest lay only in Foxcroft, and his blatant reminder of the fact cut into Maggie's ego like a blade. She whirled on the bottom step, raking him with an angry look.

"I should have known," she answered in a harsh tone. "All you care about is your precious Foxcroft. Okay, the answer to your question is yes! Arthur *did* talk to me about Foxcroft, about some ideas that he's had for years. And to tell you the truth, they don't sound half bad!"

She didn't mean it, but she was surprisingly hurt and angry, striking out at Mark in the most damaging way she could devise. As she watched the lines of his face deepen, she knew her words had hit their mark.

"Miss Hastings," he began in a calm, deadly voice. "If turning Foxcroft into a tourist attraction sounds like a good idea to you, I need to revise my opinion of your taste. But I imagine the bottom line in this situation, as always, is money. And since I'll top any offer Townsend makes, the matter is academic. It's time you learned that what's mine stays mine!"

With that, he bounded around her and took the steps two at a time. She was moved to fury.

"Don't be so sure your crass assessment is correct!" she hurled at his back and began to stomp up the stairs.

"You just hold on a minute!" he called back angrily. "I've got something for you!"

She had not waited a full minute outside her bedroom door, tapping her foot impatiently, before he returned.

"Here," he said abruptly and thrust a sheaf of papers into her hands. "I must have been crazy to put this off. I've had these papers for two days. There you are, madam, your ticket to riches. I'm sure you'll be very happy!"

She looked from the file in her hands to Mark's stormy eyes. When her voice came, it rang with an uncharacteristically high pitch. "I intend to have these checked out thoroughly by my lawyer."

"Do whatever you want," Mark responded coldly. "Just put your name on the dotted line so I can have my house back!"

"I'll sign when I'm good and ready!" she fired. "You're not the only one interested in Foxcroft, you know! Arthur tells me quite a few people like this property!"

Mark's face turned hard as stone. "Like who? Him? The man is a conniving snake! Years ago I made a vow I'd never again set foot in the Townsend house. If you had any brains, you'd see what he's up to and steer clear of him, instead of planning to waltz into his lair tomorrow night!"

Maggie's eyes narrowed. "I'm *going* to that party, Mark, with or without you! If you want to back out, why don't you just say so here and now!"

He threw her a sneer. "You won't get rid of me so easily! If you're going, I'm taking you, and that's that! Might as well get used to the idea, Miss Hastings. Until your backside is on its way out of here, I intend to be your damned shadow!"

Spinning on his heel, he made for the stairs.

For a long time after she retired, Mark's angry face and the papers lying on the dresser were all Maggie could see. Even after she climbed into bed, her thoughts tumbled as she relentlessly replayed the evening's events.

Once again Arthur's voice resounded in her ears: "She's as mad as a hatter . . . burned down one of the out buildings . . . killed her husband." At the recollection, a feeling of horror prickled up Maggie's spine, and for the first time since coming to Foxcroft, she experienced an eerie fear at the thought that Mrs. Fox resided in seclusion just down the hall.

Maggie's mind raced back in time and forced an image from the shadows that shrouded her only meeting with Mrs. Fox. Gradually the picture of the woman's face materialized—so pale, slender, and gaunt that it seemed barely able to support the large dark eyes that were its unquestioned focal point. That first night, when Maggie had walked angrily into the dining room, Mrs. Fox had said nothing, only stared with those eyes that seemed to grow larger and blacker as Maggie watched. Then the lids had dropped, like shades over two dark windows.

Arthur's voice once again played in her head: "Don't be taken in by his charm." The vision of Mrs. Fox was transformed into an image of Mark.

Maggie shifted her position again, fluffed her pillow, and tried to settle into sleep. But her efforts were in vain. Finally she got out of bed, slipped on a filmy shell pink peignoir, and began pacing the room. A quarter of an hour later, she decided to slip down to the kitchen and fix herself some warm milk.

After stealing out of her bedroom, she trod softly to the staircase where she stopped and, looking down the hall, noticed the narrow strip of light shining from beneath Mrs. Fox's door. Unconsciously, she picked up speed as she started down the stairs.

A single lamp burned far below in the foyer. It provided just enough dusky light for her to see her way, but cast looming shadows through the vast empty rooms. Her bare feet skimming across the carpet, Maggie moved like one of those silent shadows and found herself walking ever more briskly across the foyer and dining room and through the swinging door into the kitchen.

As the tall door closed behind her, she was immersed in silky darkness. Feeling her way along the wall toward the light switch, she brushed something that jangled and caught her breath. Then her fingers touched the switch she sought. She quickly flipped it, and the large room was flooded with light.

Relaxing at the sight of the familiar furnishings, she stopped in her tracks when she saw the object that hung on the wall near the light switch. Rachel's keys! They had jangled as she fumbled in the darkness!

She heated the milk, and after she poured the warm liquid, leaned back against the counter and plotted. Slowly she drained the glass, her gaze lingering all the while on the key ring across the room.

It was too good an opportunity to pass up. She had the use of the Mercedes and would be driving into Charleston. Although she didn't know her way around the city, she was sure she could find a locksmith. She would have a copy made and then return the original key. Rachel couldn't be held responsible if anyone discovered Maggie had ventured into William Fox's studio.

She deposited the glass in the sink and walked slowly to the kitchen entrance. The ring dangled teasingly at about shoulder height, from a wooden peg. Casting a cautious glance about her, she reached for it. The metallic keys clinked together before her grasp muffled the sound. The metal was cold in her hand, and she marveled at the weight of the collection.

The clasp was spring loaded. She managed to release it without any trouble and quickly sorted through the array of keys until she found the oddly shaped one she sought. She had just replaced the ring on its hook and breathed a sigh of relief when she heard something and looked over in time to see the kitchen door swing forcefully open.

Mark, clad only in faded blue pajama bottoms, stepped in and looked quickly around, his eyes widening when he saw her.

"What are you doing here?" he demanded.

Splendid in his half-nakedness, he stood like a lord defending his castle. The pajamas hung low on his hips, calling attention to the flat belly and muscular chest that was sprinkled with dark curling hair. But Maggie was still smarting from their argument. Ignoring the masculine spectacle he made, she raised her chin and gave him a look of defiance.

"I've been having trouble getting to sleep," she said, her tone implying that it was all his fault. "I came down for some warm milk."

Mark regarded her silently, his eyes traveling slowly up and down her body. She remembered the translucent peignoir she was wearing.

"Well," he said impatiently. "Go ahead and get some milk."

"I've already had it," she answered shortly. "I was just leaving."

And with all the dignity she could muster, she swept by, leaving him to douse the light. Her fingers strayed guardedly into her pocket and closed on the stolen key as she heard him coming up behind her when she reached the foyer.

"Good night," she muttered and, looking saucily over her shoulder, placed a bare foot on the step. "Sorry I woke you."

"I wasn't asleep," he grumbled.

Her eyes met his, and though the devil's green ones frowned at her, there was within them a seductive look—a searching, exciting intensity that made her feel suddenly as if she had no clothes on. Unconsciously she put a hand to the neck of her robe. He had no doubt used that look with utter success on a hundred other women. At the thought, she tossed her head and turned away.

Raising the hem of her gown to ease her progress, she reached the landing and turned to continue to the second floor. Only then did she permit herself a glance toward the bottom of the stairs. Mark was still there.

From the base of the staircase, he watched her ascend and pass quietly out of sight. He knew the way he'd been looking at her, and so did she. Yet she turned up her nose and huffed away as if he'd insulted her. What did she expect? Gallivanting around his house dressed in nothing more than a veil!

In the kitchen, with the overhead lights glaring, her body had been silhouetted quite clearly through that pink thing, her nipples showing like two rosebuds behind a piece of gauze, until it was all he could do to keep from staring. Later on, in the shadows of the hallway, the nightgown—if you could call it that!—turned opaque. But it was too late; for as he watched her move up the stairs, it was too easy to imagine the curves he'd already seen swaying beneath that shifting pink film.

His eyes still glued on the spot where she'd disappeared, Mark felt his loins throb. Whirling, he stomped to the table and killed the lamplight that glinted off his glistening brow.

Damned redhead! She couldn't be out from underfoot soon enough!

Chapter Eight

Maggie slept away half the morning and woke to a gray, drizzly Saturday. After showering and dressing in a comfortable seersucker dress, she pulled her hair into a ponytail and stepped to the balcony.

The beautiful panoramic view had become so familiar that it was hard to believe she'd been at Foxcroft only a few days. The rain came down in a comforting pitter-patter, and the lawns seemed to grow greener even as it fell. Her gaze drifted back inside, to the file of papers that Mark had so crudely thrust at her the night before. With renewed anger, she grabbed them from the dresser, picked up her umbrella and bag, and went downstairs.

"Why, good mornin', Miss Hastings," Rachel said cheerfully as Maggie walked into the kitchen.

"Good morning," Maggie returned. Her eyes darted to the key ring peg and saw that it was empty. Presumably the keys now resided in Rachel's apron pocket. "Where is everybody?" she asked.

"Well, now, Annie and Mrs. Phipps don't come out on Saturday and Sunday, you know. And Mr. Fox, he's gone into town to meet some business folks. And you look like you're on your way somewhere, too," she added, nodding toward Maggie's umbrella and handbag.

"Yes, I'm going into Charleston today. I think I'll just make myself a sandwich."

"You sit right down, honey. I'll fix it. That's what I'm here for. Let's see now, we got some chicken, and we got egg salad . . ."

As Rachel bustled about the huge kitchen, Maggie settled in the breakfast nook, opened the manila folder, and began to study the documents Mark had given her. Part of their hefty weight was explained by the fact that all eight or ten pages were in triplicate. Brimming with small type and complicated legal language, the proposal was in three parts: land survey, property list, and financial settlement.

From what Maggie could gather, her land was a comparatively narrow strip that extended from the two-lane access road through the Foxcroft estate and on to the Cooper River—"from the markers to the marsh," as William Fox had stipulated. The property's crowning glory was the house, including all outbuildings and furnishings that had been there at the time of her benefactor's death. The financial settlement was arranged in the form of a fund that would pay Maggie an exorbitant yearly stipend for ten years.

When her layman's brain had absorbed all that it could, Maggie sat back and gazed out the window and across the terrace where the white pear tree blossoms were dancing in the rain. The papers in her hands made everything suddenly real. The dreamlike aura that had surrounded her time at Foxcroft vanished.

As she sipped the last of her coffee, she decisively began to strip the top perforated sheet from each of the pages. These she would mail to Morely. There was no way she could judge the fairness or legality of Mark's offer, and she could delay the sale by getting Morely's opinion before taking action. After procuring an envelope and stamp from Rachel, Maggie placed the letter in her handbag. She would mail it in Charleston.

As she walked through the deserted house toward the front doors, her eyes fell on the telephone in the rose-colored parlor. Impulsively, she detoured into the room.

"Maggie? Where are you?"

The sound of Shelley's voice was the comforting boon she had hoped for, a familiar port in an uncharted sea.

"I'm in South Carolina. You won't believe what's happened."

As if she'd had an unknown need to purge herself, the words welled up and rushed out in a torrent. Beginning with her arrival at the airport and Harold's rude behavior, she related the events that had befallen her, describing the house and grounds, the stables, the wild acreage that comprised the bird sanctuary, the people she had met. She spoke eloquently about Rachel and Arthur and John Henry, even Mrs. Fox. But when it came to Mark, she was tongue-tied.

"Tell me more about this Mark," Shelley prodded.

"There's nothing to tell."

"Tell me what he looks like."

"Oh, Shelley! Come on!"

"No, really, Maggie. Just tell me what he looks like."

"Well . . . he's tall, about six-two or three. Good build, dark hair. The suntanned outdoorsy type. I'll admit he's a good-looking man."

"Aha! I thought so. You're interested in him, aren't you?"

"Shelley!"

"I'm serious! There was something about the way you avoided talking about him. I had a feeling he was something special."

"Oh, he's something special, all right." Maggie's voice took on a sharp edge. "He could charm the birds right out of the trees, but he's also arrogant, chauvinistic, has to have everything his own way. And there's this dark quality about him, as if something dreadful has been done to him and he's cut himself off from any feeling . . . as if he could do something terrible and then turn and walk away without a thought."

"He sounds frightening," Shelley breathed.

"He is," Maggie replied, and decided not to go into the frightening aspects of Mark that had her on the defensive.

There was a moment of silence before Shelley asked, "When are you coming home?"

The thought of Nathan and his threatening attentions dashed to Maggie's mind. "I'm not sure. I may need to stay here awhile, at least until I hear from my attorney. You know, it's strange, but somehow I feel tied to this place. Shelley, why would William Fox leave the estate to my parents?"

"I don't know. There must be a reason. Maybe he was closer to Myra and David than anyone realized."

"And why didn't they tell me about Foxcroft? Why did they keep it a secret?"

"Maybe they intended to tell you someday. Uh-oh, Maggie, Nathan just arrived for lunch. I'd better go. When you decide to come home, call me. I'll pick you up at the airport."

The brief contact with Shelley left Maggie with mixed feelings. As always, it did her volatile spirit good to meet with Shelley's serene one. But the idea of Nathan spoiled any thought of returning to New York.

The rain was falling quietly, washing the outdoors, giving the world a clean, fresh smell. Raising her umbrella, Maggie crossed the veranda and carefully stepped around occasional puddles on her way to the garage.

It was a large structure, and she imagined it must have been built originally as a carriage house and later transformed into a garage. Like huge dark eyes, the doors on all four bays were up. The one on the left was monopolized by the black Lincoln limousine. The second featured an antiquated truck that looked forty years old if a day. In the third bay was the Mercedes. The fourth was empty.

Mark's Porsche, she thought sourly as she climbed into the silver Mercedes sedan. It had leather upholstery, polished wooden accents, and although it was several years old, it was in excellent condition. The engine purred contentedly, and Maggie wondered who, if anyone, ever drove it and why it had been kept so impeccable. Perhaps such tasks were Harold's realm, but she guessed that Mark—with all of his perfectionistic tendencies— was the force behind such high standards.

She was just about to shift the transmission into drive when a loud knock came on the window by her head. She jumped in her seat, swiveled her head, and saw—just on the other side of the glass—a bleary-eyed, threatening face. She recognized Harold, but before she could stop herself, she screamed.

He yanked open the door of the Mercedes and leaned toward her, balancing himself by grasping the roof of the car. His clothes were disheveled, and his unshaven face was pallid behind a grizzly beard. The flat, vacant eyes were streaked with red. When he spoke, his breath reeked of alcohol.

"And just where do you think you're going, missy?" He smirked as he wobbled closer.

"I'm going into Charleston," Maggie replied firmly, her manner masking the fear that had her blood racing. "I'm in a hurry, so—"

"So what?" he interrupted coarsely. "You gonna catch a plane when you get there?"

"No."

"Well, then, I don't care if you're in a damned hurry or not!" he slurred. "The only place I care about you getting to on time is on a plane back to New York. Now, what do you think of that, miss high-and-mighty?"

She surprised herself by becoming suddenly calm. "I don't think anything of it, Harold. Now, why don't you close the door so I can be on my way?"

He laughed, the sound echoing shrilly above the purr of the Mercedes engine. "You don't think. That's right . . . You don't think!" he accused, then looked away toward the steadily falling rain.

"What are you talking about, Harold?" she snapped.

His head spun back in her direction, and he fixed her with

bloodshot eyes. "Don't think I don't know you!" he said, his voice falling to a whisper. "Don't think I don't know you for what you are . . . you she-devil!"

With a frightened gasp, Maggie pressed the gas pedal to the floor. The Mercedes shot out of the garage, the door was snatched out of Harold's hand and slammed shut as the car bounced over a gulley and careened into the circular courtyard.

Only then did she glance into the rearview mirror to discover that Harold had stumbled out of the garage and into the rain. His drunken body slouched, but his arm was raised firmly as he shook a fist at her departure.

She was shaking as she turned off the avenue of oaks and onto the road where the rain pelted the car roof with light, steady precision. The image of Harold's craggy face refused to disappear. There was a hatred in him—not just a general unpleasantness, as she had first presumed, but a fuming hatred targeted toward her personally. As had no one in her lifetime, he terrified her.

She would tell Mark, she thought frenziedly. But as her nerves settled, she shook her head.

Why tell him? *He's* not your ally! Just because, through some base chemical reaction, he makes your pulse race, there's no reason to think you can trust him. In fact, quite the opposite!

She recalled Mark's comments about Harold—how he might seem a little strange, but he had been at Foxcroft since Mark was just a boy. Here was a man who had served the Fox family for thirty years. What could Maggie hope to accomplish if she, an unwelcome stranger, voiced a wild-sounding complaint?

Much as she wanted to, she couldn't depend on the unpredictable Mark Fox, only on herself.

Although the landscape was shrouded in gray mist, the drive to Charleston was beautiful. She passed green rolling fields trimmed with a darker green border of timberland and dotted with bright yellow and blue wildflowers. Eventually the outskirts of the city appeared in occasional buildings and neighborhoods. And just after passing a city limits sign, Maggie turned into a shopping center and parked the car, thinking that a complex of that type usually had a locksmith.

She immediately spotted a bright storefront with a sign that stated simply: Keys. An oily man slouched behind the circular counter, but as she approached, he came to his feet.

"Can I help you?" he said around the cigarette that hung from his lips. Then he gave her a once-over from head to toe.

"I hope so," Maggie answered in a businesslike manner that interrupted his vulgar examination. "I have an old key that's beginning to wear down. I'd like to have a new one made."

He took a magnifying glass and studied the key. "I'll say it's old. What does it go to?"

"A door."

"Well, it's a door that's got a mighty hefty lock on it." He stubbed out his cigarette and rubbed his chin thoughtfully. "You know, this here key looks like it goes to one of those old brass locks folks used during the Civil War, with a compartment where the ladies hid their jewelry when the Yankees came through. Where did you say you were from?"

"I didn't say," Maggie answered brusquely. "Can you duplicate the key?"

"I can give it a try, but it's gonna take awhile. And it's gonna cost you."

Maggie left the key in the man's possession and wandered through the mall, window-shopping. She passed a mailbox where she posted the letter to Albert Morely, and it wasn't long before she came across an attractive boutique with a window display that lured her inside.

It was after three o'clock when she returned to the locksmith. The new steel key gleamed brightly in contrast to the old one, but other than that they looked identical.

When she left the shop, she saw that the spring shower had turned into a downpour. She raced across the parking lot, but by the time she climbed into the shelter of the car, she was soaked, despite her umbrella.

The return drive took twice as long as the trip out, and when she finally turned into the estate and moved under the shelter of the arch of oaks, she breathed a sigh of relief. Not wanting to run into Harold again, she looked carefully around the empty garage before climbing out of the car. She held her purse and shopping bag close to her breast, raised her umbrella, and raced through the driving rain to the house.

She burst through the doors and nearly collided with Rachel. The old woman was dressed in a summery floral-print dress and sported a straw hat.

"Lord have mercy, Miss Hastings! I was beginning to get worried 'bout you."

"Don't you look pretty, Rachel!" Maggie smiled as she halted, dripping, in the foyer. "Where are you off to?"

"Why, my nephew, Jonas, is coming over to take me to the church social," Rachel replied, her eyes beaming behind her thick bifocals. "Lord, honey, you're soaked to the skin. You better go get right into a hot bath. Mr. Fox got back about an hour ago and went on out to the stables to tend to that mare. He said to tell you he'd take you out to supper."

"Supper?" Maggie questioned. What was the man up to? Probably trying to get a quick signature on his offer, she thought sourly.

Rachel bustled off in the direction of her quarters, and Maggie watched quietly until the old woman disappeared. Then she bolted to the kitchen, her fingers busily searching out the studio key within her purse. The key ring hung innocently on the peg, and with practiced sureness, Maggie swiftly replaced the old key. Pausing only for a quick smile to herself at the success of her mission, she hurried up to her room.

Mark had brushed Gray Lady until her coat shone. As he let himself out of the stall, she strutted proudly within its boundaries, despite the bulge of her belly. Pausing at the slatted gate to look the marc over one last time, Mark allowed his thoughts to stray elsewhere.

His plan for showing off Canadys Isle to the investors had gone completely awry. The island didn't show well in the rain—the natural paths losing their charm to become muddy rivulets, the usually turquoise waters reflecting the gray of the sky until they became a dark mirror of the clouds. Reluctantly, Mark had canceled the ferry and scrambled together arrangements for a trip the next morning. All he could do now was hope that the rain would pass and the sky clear, so that Canadys Isle would sparkle the next day with the tropical, flower-bedecked beauty he knew it possessed.

The original plans postponed, he'd been forced to entertain the three men from New York and had taken them to that age-old sanctuary of southern gentlemen, the City Club. Later he had questioned his judgment. The three drank too much and spoke too loud, their occasional bursts of laughter drawing scornful looks from Charleston patriarchs at the vintage bar.

And then, quite matter-of-factly, they had told Mark that a messenger from Townsend & Company had come to the town house that day, bearing an invitation to review a counterproposal to the development of Canadys Isle.

"Rest assured that we'll take no time during this trip to look at anything Townsend has to offer," one investor had stated. "Not while you're kind enough to act as our host. But I must be frank. On a project of this magnitude, we can't afford to bypass *any* proposal without at least a look."

Mark had steered the three men out of the City Club and dropped them off at the town house. Had it not been for his date with Maggie Hastings, he would have felt obliged to entertain the men that night as well. As it was, he prevailed on Sally Ann and Todd Williams. Between her charm and Todd's easygoing know-how, Mark knew he couldn't put the investors in any better hands.

His thoughts turned to his own plans for the evening. Maggie Hastings. Now, there was a can of worms. Somehow she always managed to stir him into rash, impulsive behavior he later regretted.

Ever since he had picked up the papers from Jim Wilkes, he'd been mulling over the right time and place to present them to Maggie. Last night, as they'd sat together in the dining room, talking and enjoying each other as never before, he'd decided to tender his offer in the relaxed atmosphere of the Atlantic House restaurant. Mark knew women. He'd felt certain that in such surroundings he could bring Maggie around—woo her to his point of view and maybe even open the door to a personal relationship, the thought of which titillated his imagination more than he cared to admit.

Then came the revelation that she was going out with Townsend! And later when Mark saw her kiss the man, something inside him had snapped. Instead of making his offer in a tender way, he'd pushed the papers on Maggie like an angry schoolboy, succeeding only in fortifying the barrier between them, making it necessary for him to swallow his pride and start anew in trying to get into her good graces.

Now more than ever, such self-effacing efforts were necessary; Townsend was on her trail like a bloodhound!

Outrage spiraled within him, giving his face the look of a warrior's. Want to fight? Mark thought fiercely as he imagined Townsend's smug face. Then come on out in the open instead of slinking around behind the skirts of a woman!

The mental image changed abruptly to one of Maggie, and Mark's feeling of self-righteousness was promptly deflated.

You're no better, he told himself with a slump of his shoulders. You're not being honest with her at all!

Maggie was innocent of the reason behind her inheritance, of her past—hell, of her true identity! Who could tell what she might decide to do with Foxcroft if she knew the truth? The question spurred a spasm of fear, but even that didn't erase Mark's sense of guilt.

Perhaps she was not the woman they believed her to be. If so, he could proceed in the Foxcroft negotiations with the clear conscience and cool logic that always marked his business dealings. Maybe they were wrong—John Henry, Harold, and his mother. They were old, bitter, scarred by a long-ago tragedy. Maybe their crazy idea had simply sprung from tortured night-mares. If only he knew.

Like a bright light, an idea came into Mark's mind. He hadn't been there in years, but when he was a boy he had hung around the library studio frequently. Hadn't he noticed . . . ? Yes! He could envision it there on the studio wall as clearly as if it were yesterday! It *had* been there, and chances were that it still was!

With burning conviction, he bolted out of the barn and into the pouring rain. In minutes he was on the millstoned floor of the vine-covered walkway.

Maggie stripped off her soggy clothes, unfolded a fluffy towel, and began to rub the rainy dampness from her body. Her eyes fell on the shopping bag. Tenderly she extracted the shimmering turquoise cocktail dress and laid it across the bed. It was one of the prettiest things she'd ever owned, and she couldn't prevent a thrill of exhilaration when she remembered that she'd be wearing it for Mark Fox. But as soon as the thought came, she reproved herself and strode irritably into the bathroom.

She turned on the hot water and watched the tub begin to fill. But as she gazed into the steaming depths, her thoughts strayed to the library wing and the locked door to William Fox's studio. The bathtub was nearly full when she succumbed to her curiosity and turned off the faucets. Swiftly she shrugged into jeans, pulled a T-shirt over her wet hair, and with a cautious glance in the direction of Mrs. Fox's closed door flew down the stairs, along the deserted hall, and onto the veranda.

The rain was still falling in steady sheets, and raising her umbrella, Maggie bounded down the steps and into the midst of it. Promising herself she wouldn't linger, only test the key to be sure it worked, she turned toward the library. Her tennis shoes squished rhythmically on the sodden lawn as she trotted around the corner of the house and into the ambulatory, where water trickled in sporadic streams through the thatch of roses.

She had time only to turn in the direction of the door when she realized that it was opening. Someone was exiting the library. Instinctively, she leapt outside into the rain and retreated along the outside wall of the walkway. The downpour masked the sound of her movements; the thick bank of roses concealed her presence. She was standing only a dozen feet away when Mark emerged from the passageway and hurried toward the house without so much as a glance in her direction.

Without benefit of raincoat or umbrella, he ran, carrying with him a rectangular package wrapped in a sheet. The fabric covered the object, but Maggie's trained eye immediately recognized it as a framed picture. She waited until he disappeared on the veranda. Then she stole back to the passageway and on into the library.

Once inside, she propped her streaming umbrella against the wall and looked quickly about the cavernous room. It was deserted, the air heavy with a silence broken only by the pounding cadence of the rain. With the swiftness of a thief, she scaled the spiral staircase and approached the forbidding door. As if in protest, the cantankerous old lock refused to respond to the shiny new key. Then, with a metallic groan, the lock gave and the key turned smoothly clockwise.

"Eureka," she muttered under her breath, hastily grasping the knob and pushing firmly against the giant door. It swung open with a loud creak, and for a moment Maggie stood rigidly still. She felt an odd sense of secrecy, mystery, even danger. But curiosity won out. Hesitantly, she leaned across the threshold and was assaulted by a dank, musty smell. Although the long deserted room was cool, it seemed to be sound. No windows were broken. No rain or wind whistled through.

Gray light streamed in from a long row of north-facing windows that would afford an artist the light desirable for painting. Cautiously Maggie ventured inside. The north side of the room was dominated by easels, a multitude of canvases, and a long table covered with brushes and palettes and jars of paints. On the south side was a makeshift living area, complete with a bed, a wing chair, an old potbellied stove, and a large oak desk covered with books.

But for the obvious age of the furnishings, the studio presented

the impression that the artist was due back at any moment. It was
as if William Fox had walked out one day, bent on a small errand,
and never returned.

Everything was covered with a fine coating of dust so that her
wet tennis shoes left tracks on the hardwood floor. As she looked
down at her feet, she noticed another set of wet tracks. An alarm
sounded in her head, and she followed the tracks across the room.
They led to the far wall where a clean rectangular space glared like
an empty socket. A painting had recently been removed from the
wall—a painting the size and shape of the package Mark had been
carrying.

With a sense of foreboding, Maggie withdrew from the silent
room, locked the massive door, hurried back to the house, and
deposited the umbrella on the veranda. She was deep in thought as
she stepped inside. Why would Mark remove a picture from a
studio that no one had entered in more than twenty-five years?

"Maggie!"

The name cracked like a whip down the foyer. Like a child
who'd been caught at the cookie jar, she jumped and turned.

Wearing only jeans, with a white towel draped around his neck,
Mark descended the steps and sauntered toward her, his suntanned, muscular chest gleaming dully against the white of the
towel. He said nothing else until he came to stand before her,
stroking the wet dark hair from his forehead and locking her gaze
with his.

"You're not going out, are you?"

"No, no . . . I left my umbrella outside," she said quickly.
As he watched, she stepped onto the porch, fetched the umbrella,
and came back inside. Slowly she began to walk to the stairs, and
Mark strolled with her.

"Did you take a look at the papers?" he asked.

"I looked at them."

"Well, what do you think?"

Maggie turned to face him. "I don't know *what* to think, Mark.
Not yet."

"Why don't we discuss it over dinner? I've got reservations at
a favorite spot of mine."

She gazed up at him guardedly, wondering if she was the
newest target of his celebrated manipulations. "And then we can
go to the party?" she pressed.

"If we must."

With a lingering, assessing look into his eyes, Maggie acquiesced. So what if he tried to persuade her to sign his papers? To romance her into doing his bidding, as Arthur had warned? She was ready for him.

"Okay, but I'll need to hurry," she said with a grimace at her jeans and T-shirt.

"Don't worry about it," Mark said abruptly. The solemn expression dissolved into a devilish grin as he added, "Even at your worst, you look damned good."

He began to scale the stairs two at a time, leaving Maggie to wonder once again at the changeable moods and gestures that were Mark Fox.

She stood before the mirror and scrutinized herself a final time. The turquoise dinner dress was made for her. Cut in simple lines from a mesh fabric interwoven with silver threads, the garment seemed to hover lightly over her body, calling attention to her slender legs, gleaming with the vivid color of her eyes. The mass of fiery hair was pulled back on one side with a comb, leaving her sun-kissed shoulders and throat bare but for narrow straps and a string of pearls.

She had never seen herself look quite this way. Normally she played down her dramatic coloring and seductive allure. But tonight she reveled in it, vaguely realizing her appearance was designed to taunt the man who awaited her, to show Mark that she, too, could emit the kind of sexual energy he flaunted.

"*Magnifica!*" David Hastings would have pronounced. A vision of her parents flashed across the surface of the mirror. They smiled lovingly, and then they were gone.

With a heavy sigh, Maggie turned her thoughts from the past, picked up her black bag and cloak, and left the room.

Her mood brightened as she reached the head of the staircase and paused. Looking below, she felt as if she'd stepped into an old romantic movie. The foyer of the antebellum mansion was the perfect setting; the tall, dark man at the foot of the stairs, the perfect hero dressed in a white dinner jacket. Mark glanced up as he heard her, then did a double take, his glance turning into a long look.

Damn! He had known she was beautiful, but he hadn't expected anything like *this*! She had always dressed so conservatively, as if to play down her startling attractiveness. But now she appeared in a completely different light, that of a woman confident, even arrogant, in her sensuality. He took a step toward the staircase.

As Maggie descended, the lights of the chandelier shimmered

on her dress, streaking across the curves of breast and hip as the fabric shifted. Mark seemed frozen at the foot of the stairs. Rachel joined him, followed by a tall young man Maggie presumed to be her nephew.

"Why, Miss Hastings, you look just lovely!" Rachel beamed, then nodded to her nephew so the straw hat danced on her head.

"Yes, she does," Mark agreed, his deep voice drawing Maggie's eye.

The dinner jacket was perfectly fitted to his lanky form, accentuating his aristocratic bearing. His casual slouch only added to his air of confidence. Here was a man who was just as comfortable in evening clothes as on the back of a horse, a man who seemed unaware of his devastating appearance even as he wielded it to his advantage.

Maggie was able to repress her response to him with the simple memory of the documents resting on her bedside table. She reminded herself that Mark Fox wanted only one thing from her—Foxcroft. She was determined not to forget that, and a cool smile came to her lips as she moved slowly, provocatively, down the stairs.

She met his eyes boldly in an age-old feminine come-on. Even when he raised a dark brow in surprised recognition of her unspoken message, Maggie refused to look away. Confident of her own appeal, secure in her strength of will, she would meet this man on terms she had heretofore avoided.

Even the appearance of John Henry, bearing the silver service, didn't dampen her spirits. She kept her eyes on Mark. When she reached the foot of the stairs, he offered her his arm.

"Are you ready to go?" he asked in the husky voice she remembered from the oak grove. She nodded silently and glanced at Rachel, who was grinning from ear to ear.

"You two have a good time, now," the old woman said, placing a plump arm around her nephew's waist.

With a quick wink for Rachel, and a determined lack of recognition for John Henry, Maggie returned her attention to Mark. A dreamy, unreal quality hung over the foyer. Everything but the action of her pulse seemed to slow as Mark looked down at her, matching his long gait to her own, seeming to devour her with his eyes. She failed to notice the brief conversation that flashed through the group as they left.

"The sooner that vixen gets out of here, the easier I'll rest," John Henry muttered.

"You hush your mouth!" Rachel snapped.

"Really!" the distinguished man objected.

"Go on, now," Rachel added and shooed him toward the stairs. "Take that tray up to Mrs. Fox."

As John Henry huffed away, the old woman turned her failing eyes toward the front door as Maggie and Mark walked outside arm in arm.

"I hope to the Lord she stays," Rachel said quietly to her nephew. "That young lady can put life back in this house just as sure as she's put the light back in Mr. Fox's eyes. She's just like her mama, God rest her soul."

They drove along the coast. The rain had stopped, but the clouds lingered, lighting up the sky with a peculiar glow that threatened a storm.

Mark glanced in Maggie's direction and found her gazing out the window at the distant breakers. His gaze swept from the shining hair to the curves shown off by the clinging dress to the long, demurely crossed legs.

God, she looked good! His purpose in this outing was pure and simple: Reestablish communication with Maggie and get her signature as quickly as possible. But there was no law that said he couldn't enjoy himself while he was at it.

She turned and caught him looking at her. Mark casually turned his eyes back to the road, a grin tugging at his mouth.

Eventually they approached a large building that reached out into the sea like a pier. "The Atlantic House," Mark said as he turned off the highway.

Perched on stilts amid the breaking waves, the building seemed appropriately named. Unlike the formal restaurant where Arthur had taken Maggie the night before, it offered a rustic elegance that was captivating. They entered the candlelit dining room, and as Mark seated her at a table by a window overlooking the sea, his hand briefly caressed her back.

Maggie glanced up in surprise and met a steady look that spoke more clearly than words. It was the intent regard of a red-blooded male on the prowl, a look made threatening by the dark aura that was an inescapable part of Mark Fox. An uncomfortable, prickling sensation raced over her, and she turned quickly away, but not before she caught Mark's irritating look of amusement.

The waiter called him by name, presented a wine list, and then congratulated Mark on his choice. Maggie suspected they were receiving preferential treatment when the maître d' himself delivered the bottle and poured a taste of the vintage wine for Mark's approval. Peevishly, she found herself wondering how many other women her escort had entertained at the Atlantic House. With revived feelings of distrust and wariness, she watched as Mark sniffed the wine's bouquet, took a sip, and gave the nod to fill the glasses.

The maître d' faded unobtrusively away, and Maggie's fingers had barely closed on the crystal stem when Mark spoke.

"May I offer a toast?" he drawled, his gaze burning a path from her breasts up to her face.

Maggie returned his look confidently. "All right," she agreed, raising her glass. "A toast."

He extended his hand until the rim of his glass met hers. "To dreams soon to come true," he began with a rare twinkle in his eye, "and to unions soon to be made."

He looked at her teasingly. Maggie didn't flinch.

"To unions soon to be made," she answered firmly.

In silent challenge, the two touched glasses and drank, their eyes on each other's all the while.

Mark placed his goblet on the table and perused her shimmering dress. It was the same vivid color as her eyes. "I thought you didn't have anything to wear tonight."

She shrugged with feigned nonchalance. "What? This old thing?" When he gave her a faint smile, she added, "I took your advice. I drove into Charleston today and bought it."

"It's very pretty." Pausing for a moment, he added, *"You're* very pretty."

Maggie cocked her head to one side. "I'll bet you say that to all the girls."

"A few," he admitted slowly, his green eyes leveling on her. "This time I mean it."

"Thanks. I'm flattered."

"And will flattery get me everywhere, as the saying goes?"

Maggie regarded him steadily. "That depends."

"On what?"

"On where it is you want to go."

Slouching in his chair, he grinned. "How about as far as I can?"

This was a new, bold, sexy side of Mark. Maggie steeled herself against a traitorous thrill.

"How far is that?" he added with a cocked brow.

He was daring her, fully expecting her to back off from his

suggestive banter. She leaned toward him and smiled seductively.

"Perhaps the night will tell," she said and watched with satisfaction as a look of surprise crossed his face.

Their waiter approached and interrupted the exchange. The topic of conversation shifted to the meal, but a charged air of awareness lingered at the table.

The wine was plentiful, the soft music and candlelight enchanting, the man who sat across the table, intoxicating. For a while Maggie was able to maintain a cool detachment. But as Mark's usual solemnity vanished, he began to break through the barrier she had so carefully constructed.

Arthur Townsend's warnings ran through her mind, and Maggie straightened in her chair. At the moment Mark Fox was the epitome of charm, but she knew how quickly he could turn angry and fearsome.

As the meal progressed, she told herself that she had to remain on guard, that she must not take Mark seriously. She reminded herself that real estate negotiation was supposed to be the purpose of this dinner. Yet he didn't mention the plantation or their odd, antagonistic situation. Instead, he treated her purely and simply like a woman, and despite her resolve, Maggie began to mellow.

Sometime during the main course, she shrugged off her tiresome armor and succumbed to the lure of a lovely evening with a devilishly attractive man. She began to blossom as Mark talked entertainingly about real estate and horses, and even teased her lightheartedly about having been saddle sore after their ride.

"You ride well," he said. "It never occurred to me that you might be a tender greenhorn."

"Greenhorn!" she admonished with a light smile, "I'll have you know I spent *years* on the back of a horse. The only problem is, those years were a long time ago. Until the other day, I hadn't been in a saddle for . . . well, longer than I care to remember. I was afraid I'd forgotten how to ride."

"You certainly have not. You hold your own mighty well." Mark paused. The thought of the ride brought another memory—of this beautiful woman in his arms, melting against him, filling his head with her fragrance, stirring a passion that left him reeling. His gaze dropped to her mouth.

"You hold your own, all right," he added. "Both in and out of the saddle."

"Out of the saddle? What are you talking about?"

His eyes returned to hers. "I'm talking about that little kiss in the oak grove."

Maggie's heart lurched. She hid the sensation behind a winsome look. "I thought you wanted to forget that *little* kiss."

"I find I'm not quite able to," he returned.

The brilliant eyes were fixed on her, drawing her the way they had that day under the oaks.

"Neither am I," she murmured without thinking.

A look of amazement covered Mark's face, breaking his intense, hypnotic gaze. Hurriedly, Maggie dropped back into a teasing mode.

"My first kiss in an oak grove," she quipped. "How could I possibly forget it?"

He nodded slowly, a skeptical grin curving his lips. "Are you certain it was the trees that made it so memorable?"

"Oh, yes. It was definitely the trees," Maggie replied, and gave him a suggestive look that implied just the opposite.

Mark's grin broadened. Damn, but he enjoyed this woman! Propping his elbows on the table, he leaned toward her. "Can I ask you something?"

"Sure."

"What the hell is that perfume you wear?"

Caught off guard, Maggie blinked. "Why? Don't you like it?"

"*Like* isn't the right word! That stuff is downright dangerous! What's it called?"

Other men had complimented her on her fragrance, and she had brushed them off uncaringly. This time she was inordinately pleased. "It doesn't have a name. A friend of mine in Paris is a perfume maker. It's his own special blend. I liked it so much that he agreed to send it to me here in the States."

Mark glanced at a gardenia blossom floating in a crystal bowl on their table.

"It reminds me of this," he said and reached out to remove the flower.

After drying the stem with his napkin, he leaned over and gently positioned it behind her ear, then smiled as he obviously approved the effect of the white blossom against her fiery hair. Feeling helplessly warm and tingling, Maggie smiled back.

As Mark withdrew his hand, he allowed a single finger to trail along her jawline. He sought her eyes and found a knowing look as she leaned subtly into his touch. She'd been different all night, a Maggie he had not anticipated, a siren whose tempting manner was filled with unspoken promises. Mark's pulse quickened at the thought of what the night would bring.

Time flowed by in a languid stream. As the hour grew late, many of the diners left, and the candlelit Atlantic House became quietly romantic, the only sounds the distant murmuring of a few other couples and, from far below, the muted crash of ocean waves. By the time Mark ordered a flaming dessert, the restaurant was nearly empty. Only then did the memory of Arthur Townsend's party cross Maggie's mind, and she realized they were exceedingly late. But she said nothing, dismissing the thought almost as soon as it appeared.

As they awaited dessert, Mark told her about the investors who were staying in his town house. Maggie listened attentively, but as Mark continued to speak in that deep, unique voice of his, the words rolling out lazily, intimately, she looked at him with new eyes. She studied the strong lines of his face, the shapely brows arching beneath the dark hair, the clear green eyes, the brief smile that flashed white against suntanned skin. Capped by the suave charm he'd been exuding all night, he was having an overpowering impact on her.

Mark Fox affected her more deeply than anyone she'd ever known. Like a Picasso, she responded to him with bold strokes, with colors that were vivid to the point of bedazzlement. It occurred to her that despite the warnings her mind continued to cry out, her heart was falling . . . Could she even think the word?

"Maggie?"

She heard her name as if from far away.

"Maggie, are you listening?"

"Oh . . . sorry," she said quickly.

Mark regarded her quizzically. "You're different tonight."

"So are you."

He leaned back in his chair and studied her. "Formidable," he muttered. "You refuse to be overlooked. No matter how a man might try."

"And are you trying?"

His brows rose. "Not at the moment," he admitted with a smile.

As they sipped after-dinner liqueurs, Mark's words became few and long, raking looks became frequent. Behind the polite facade lurked a sexual energy, restrained for now, but showing clearly in his face, his manner, in everything about him. Maggie responded, looking silently into his eyes over the rim of her glass, allowing the liqueur and his presence to warm her blood.

Mark took a slow sip of the liqueur as his gaze roamed over

Maggie's face. He hadn't forgotten who she was, what she represented, but right now he pushed all that away. What had started as a business dinner had turned into a seduction, and in the back of his mind, he knew that was what he'd wanted all along. Before she disappeared from his life forever, he intended to *know* Maggie Hastings in every sense of the word.

How much of his thoughts she could read, Mark had no idea. But if body language was any indication, she was issuing an invitation. Gracefully, she leaned across the table, imitating his posture with a faint smile, meeting his eyes in the glow of the candlelight. Rolling the tiny crystal glass sensually between her palms, she returned his quiet scrutiny with her own.

"Do you realize," he said finally, "that this is the first time we've spent more than fifteen minutes together without getting into a fight?"

Maggie laughed softly, but the sound died when he reached across the table, took her hand, and looked at her piercingly. "You've turned out to be quite different from what I expected, Maggie. Quite different."

Turning her hand over in his long, warm fingers, he stared down at her palm. "But everything is much more complicated than you know. I didn't plan on this happening."

"Plan on what?" she asked.

Mark's eyes rose to her face. "This," he rumbled quietly. "Us. Tonight you can have whatever you want—Townsend's party or me."

They had teased each other all night behind a veil of innuendo, but his sudden bluntness took Maggie by surprise. His meaning was clear. All she had to do was nod and the two of them would leave the restaurant, go to some out-of-the-way place, and get on with the business of enjoying the electricity that had been building between them all night. A lump of uncertainty sprang to her throat, and she pulled her hand out of his grasp.

Mark glanced at his empty palm, then slumped back in his chair. "Don't tell me you're surprised, Maggie. Wine, candlelight—what do you think we've been doing all night?"

The romantic notions that had been dancing in Maggie's head suddenly stumbled and fell flat.

"I assumed we were having dinner," she said, raising a brow.

A familiar look came over Mark's face—that taunting expression he had turned on her so often. "Come on, Maggie. You know what's going on here. This is the major leagues. If you're not gonna play fair, don't go up to bat. Don't behave like a knowing, desirable woman all night and then become a schoolgirl at her first prom. There's a word for women like that, you know."

Maggie's cheeks turned crimson. It was not the first time she'd been labeled with the term.

"I'm not a tease, Mark," she snapped. "Neither am I a witless woman to be pressured into an assignation by you or by any man! I can't stand it when a man takes a perfectly innocent evening and turns it into a seduction!"

"Perfectly innocent!" Mark's brows flew up. "You might be able to fool yourself, lady, but you're not fooling me. The way you look tonight, the way you've been acting . . . you've made me want you. But I'd better warn you—what I want, I get!"

Maybe she *had* flirted with him, Maggie admitted, but she hadn't expected him to call her bluff so directly!

"The way I've been 'acting'? I haven't been 'acting' any differently with you than I have with lots of men I've been out with," Maggie lied heatedly. "And *they* certainly didn't pretend that I'd invited them to the bedroom!"

To her increasing fury, Mark only grinned. "If they chose to let you get away with it, that was their problem," he stated. "It certainly isn't mine."

"No, your problem is that you've always had everything—and everyone—you've ever wanted! Maybe if a woman or two had turned you down along the way, you'd realize there are some things you can't just grab!"

His gaze dropped to her neckline, where the smooth swell of high breasts rose above the turquoise fabric. "With all due respect," he said lazily, "I don't think I've come across them yet."

His eyes twinkled merrily at her as he drained the liqueur from his glass.

Searing heat flashed to Maggie's face, but she couldn't come up with a riposte. It seemed the man could see right through her to a truth she couldn't even admit to herself. Like a slumbering giant suddenly awakened, her long-established disdain for the male sex leapt to her defense. Huffily, she plucked the gardenia blossom from her hair and pushed away from the table.

"Hadn't we better go?" she asked with scornful courtesy. "We're late for the party."

As she stood, Mark's gaze traveled lingeringly up her body until it found her eyes. The look of amused challenge left his face.

"By all means," he said.

He had bungled it again, Mark thought as he followed Maggie's swaying back out of the restaurant. Fleetingly he imagined her as a fine piece of porcelain and himself as the proverbial bull in the china shop. The tantalizing prizes that were wrapped up in her—the recovery of Foxcroft, the electrifying feel of a slim body against his own—both had seemed within his grasp only moments ago when Maggie had smiled at him with such inviting warmth. But then the blue-green eyes had turned as cold as a frozen lake, and she had snatched the prize from his grasping fingertips.

He sure as hell hadn't expected *that*! Most women responded enthusiastically to his bold overtures. But then, he reminded himself, Maggie wasn't like most women. In fact, she was unlike any woman he had known.

Her elusiveness was intriguing, but Mark Fox was unaccustomed to being rejected. A defiant gleam lit his eyes as he snatched open the door and silently ushered her into the car.

Chapter Nine

It was eleven o'clock when they drove down a palm-lined street to the Battery and turned onto the coastal drive. The pretty town houses gave way to mansions secluded among walled gardens and graced with balconies facing the sea. The street was crowded with expensive cars, their owners in attendance at the party in the huge brick house where lights blazed on all three floors. As she and Mark cruised slowly past, the sound of music and laughter floated on the night air through the open windows of the Porsche.

They had barely spoken since leaving the Atlantic House. Mark was in one of his moody silences. Whether it was due to her rejection of his proposition or his reluctance to attend Arthur Townsend's party, Maggie wasn't sure. For her own part, she, too, had sunk into a black mood.

The nerve of the man! To imply that she'd led him on! She'd never led a man on in her life!

Liar, her conscience whispered. Tonight, in a dozen subtle ways you invited him to make love to you as clearly as if you'd spoken the words.

Maggie squirmed in her seat and snapped her head around to peer out the window. Suddenly Mark wheeled into an invisible driveway, and after pulling into a courtyard hidden by a profusion of trees and Spanish moss, they were swallowed in shadow.

"That's the Van Averys' house," he muttered, pointing to a distant iron gate, beyond which loomed a dark, massive house. "They only winter in Charleston."

He switched off the headlights and ignition, and Maggie adjusted her black cloak about her shoulders. For a moment Mark stared straight ahead into the darkness. Then he turned and stretched an arm across the back of her seat. Her heart began to thud as she faced him.

"I'm used to speaking my mind," he said. "More than some people."

"More than *most* people."

"Look! This is the closest thing to an apology you're going to get from me, so you'd better listen."

Mark's rumbling voice filled the car, but the hint of a grin took the bite out of his words. Maggie lowered her eyes as a smile came unbidden to her lips.

"Maybe I came on too strong," he added.

"Maybe?"

"Okay, so I came on too strong! Let's just forget it!"

With a rush he climbed out of the car and circled around to her door.

The Townsend mansion was a fair distance away due to the size of the estates on this, the most coveted drive of the Battery. To the right, a garden wall stretched high above their heads, crowned by a mass of royal palm fronds that reached over the wall from within. To the left, across the wide street, was a sea wall that the ocean winds hurdled as they raced across the pavement to rustle the palms.

As if it were the most natural thing in the world, as if he had every right to invade the privacy of her person, Mark planted a warm arm about her shoulders, securing her cloak as they strolled along the windy lamplit street. An unwelcome shiver crawled over Maggie as Mark pressed her against him, but she stared wordlessly ahead, pretending his touch made no impression whatever.

The sky hung low with threatening clouds. As they approached the massive iron gate in front of the Townsend home, a peal of thunder rumbled up the street.

Mark pointed to the intricately wrought gate, and as Maggie's eye followed his direction, she realized that the ironwork was crafted into the design of a peacock.

"This type of gate is a tradition here in the Battery," he explained. "You may have heard of the Swordgate Inn, which is named for the swords on its gate. By and large, I think the tradition is an exercise in snobbery. But in this case," he added, gesturing to the peacock, "I have to admit that the symbol is appropriate."

Maggie immediately understood his reference to Arthur Townsend's vanity. She laughed brightly, and Mark smiled down at her in a way that made her forget his earlier effrontery. Reaching toward her, he made a barrier of his hand where the wind was relentlessly tossing locks of hair into her eyes. After only a moment his smile faded into the morose expression that so often sat upon his features.

"Come on," he said. "Let's get you inside."

Within the circle of his arm, she fairly floated through the courtyard and up the steps to the brightly lit veranda. As they reached the landing, Mark rapped sharply on the door. It was opened by a wizened black butler. A crescendo of lights and music and laughter spilled out from inside.

"Why, Mr. Fox," the old man said, a broad smile breaking across his face. "Come in! Come in!"

"Good evening, Isaac," Mark said, gripping the elder man's hand. "I'd like you to meet Miss Hastings. Maggie, this is Isaac Wilson, an old friend of mine."

"Good evening, Miss Hastings. I'm proud to meet you. Here now, let me take your wrap."

Isaac closed the door behind them, and when Maggie turned to discard her cloak, she found herself confronted with the over-whelming grandeur of the Townsend mansion. The entry hall stretched to a wide, ornate staircase. From the foyer, she could see the open doorways to a half-dozen rooms filled with people.

The entire house seemed to be decorated in the Louis XVI style. Paintings and mirrors were everywhere. All the furnishings were gilded. Everywhere were crystal chandeliers so that light danced through all the rooms, accompanied by a melee of conversation and music.

Mark looked around, apparently charting their course. Ab-sently, his hand reached for hers, and a resented warmth washed over Maggie. His long fingers had only just closed when they squeezed hers warningly. Leaning down, he rumbled, "Get ready."

Maggie looked at him questioningly, but he was already turning to a dumpy older woman in a blue chiffon gown. Her salt-and-pepper hair was piled high, and she dripped diamonds from her tiara to the tips of her fingers. Her dark eyes smiled at a distinguished silver-haired gentleman, but when they lit on Mark, the smile disappeared.

"Mark Fox," she declared in an imperious southern drawl. "When Arthur said you were coming tonight, I didn't believe him. I didn't believe you'd break your word about never again entering this house."

"Good evening, Isabel," Mark returned smoothly. "I'd like you to meet Maggie Hastings. Maggie, Isabel Townsend."

Maggie nodded to the older woman, who only glared at her contemptuously.

Mark broke in with a reassuring look. "It's Mrs. Townsend's party we're about to enjoy, and I guess we ought to get on with it. Thanks for having us, Isabel."

With smooth efficiency, he swept away with Maggie in tow. She had no time to question him about Mrs. Townsend's insulting behavior before the noisy crowd began to close around them.

The party was in full swing, and Mark led her into the fray. Stepping ahead and pulling her along in his wake, he carved a path through the crowd that spilled into the foyer from adjoining rooms.

"Mark . . . hi!" came a female voice. Maggie heard him respond to one of the elaborately dressed women they passed, but he didn't slow his pace.

"Hey, Fox! I want to talk to you about that bottomland."

"Sure, Dave, sure. Let me get a drink first."

Several others called out as Mark steadily moved through the crush. By the time he and Maggie made it through the foyer, it seemed all heads had turned to them. The eyes first lit on her tall escort, then moved to rest curiously on Maggie.

"Who is she?" "Arthur told me . . ." "Foxcroft, you know," came the whispered fragments. Eventually it became so embarrassing that Maggie ceased trying to acknowledge the questioning faces and focused on Mark's white-jacketed back. She was grateful when they arrived at a bar between the dining and living rooms.

From the large, crowded living room where a dance floor had been cleared came the brassy sounds of a nine-piece band. Mark stepped away to fetch drinks, and Maggie watched from the doorway as formally dressed people moved awkwardly to the romantic strains of a tango. As she watched, she revised her opinion. The dancers *were* awkward but for one couple—a man who called to mind Fred Astaire, and a curvaceous dark-haired woman in a low-cut black gown.

The couple moved in ever more intricate steps until the dance floor eventually cleared, the guests forming a circle about them. From the bandstand draped with gold and white bunting the music grew louder as the band played to the single couple who swept across the floor.

Mark arrived in time to watch the finale. As the music reached a crescendo, the man twirled his partner out to arm's length, and she began to circle him, her hips swaying provocatively with the Latin beat. Suddenly, as if on cue, the man drew the black-haired woman to him. As the musicians blared a final flourish, he dipped with her to leave her hanging dramatically over his arm, one leg extended so that the slit in her skirt opened halfway up her thigh. The music stopped, and the dancers held their pose.

An instant of silence was followed by a crash of applause. Only then did the man pull his partner to her feet, and together they bowed to the approving calls of the guests. The woman curtsied and turned a blazing smile on the crowd. Maggie watched as her gaze swept the room and froze upon Mark.

The musicians began to play. Conversation resumed. The crowd milled. Still, the woman stood like a statue, her stare like a knife cutting through the noise and commotion. Maggie glanced up and saw Mark returning the gaze. With a sinking feeling, she watched as the woman in black excused herself from her partner and moved to join them.

"Mark . . . darling," she cooed as she arrived. Her red lips parted in a dazzling smile, her black lashes fluttering coquettishly.

"Hello, Alicia," Mark said. "It's been a long time."

Alicia Townsend. She was a beautiful woman—her almond-shaped eyes, large and slanted, her shining black hair in a sleek pageboy, her ample figure that of a young woman perhaps thirty years of age. Her low-cut gown cried out that it was a one-of-a-kind French design, and the pearls at her ears and throat suggested the same high quality. Darker than her brother, she bore a strong resemblance to her mother, particularly in the air of disdain that played across her features.

Dark and voluptuous, she was the opposite of Maggie in every way. Like night and day, they were converse reflections of womanhood, their only bond the man who stood between them.

"Yes, it's been a long time, Mark. Too long. And here I am about to be married. Ironic, isn't it?" Alicia tossed her head, sending the glossy tresses flying as her dark gaze slid to Maggie.

"And who, may I ask, is this? Oh, yes," she added in a rush, her eyes glinting. "This must be the little girl Arthur told me about. Well, we're certainly happy you could squeeze our little old party into your visit." Arching a dark brow, Alicia shot Maggie a condescending look. "Annie, isn't it?"

Coming from the sophisticated woman, the mistaken name was an insult. It implied that the effort to remember correctly was far beneath Alicia Townsend.

"That's close enough," Maggie returned, her eyes glittering.

"Alicia," Mark interrupted. "Allow me to present Maggie Hastings."

"Charmed, I'm sure," the woman murmured as she turned back to Mark. "Come along, darling. They're playing our song." She grasped Mark's arm, jostling him so that his drink spilled. Maggie felt the blood rush to her face.

"No, Alicia," Mark said, trying diplomatically to disengage her grip. "We just got here. Maybe later."

"Come on, Mark. Just one dance for old times' sake?"

Her words were slurred, and Maggie suddenly realized the woman was a bit drunk.

"No, Alicia," Mark repeated firmly.

"Well, at least get me a drink, then," she prodded.

"Here. Have mine," he returned smoothly and pressed his glass into her hand.

Alicia gave him a smoldering look and was about to reply when she was interrupted.

"Alicia! Alicia dear, I've been looking everywhere for you," came a refined masculine voice. Maggie glanced around to behold a slender man with graying blond hair. In a black tuxedo that matched Alicia's ebony gown, he looked exceedingly elegant.

"The senator and his wife are leaving, my dear," the man continued. "It simply won't do for you not to bid them farewell." As he finished, he flashed a wide smile at Mark and Maggie, a white, even smile that somehow in its perfection seemed to be absolutely empty.

"All right, Grover," Alicia muttered. As she turned to take his arm, she looked at Mark. "I'll see *you* later!" she promised and, with a final challenging glance at Maggie, stepped away.

"That was Alicia's fiancé, Grover Harward," Mark said as the couple moved out of sight. "Very big in politics."

"I see."

Maggie looked up at him with questions dancing in her eyes. He read them, and a supplicating expression came over his face.

"Not now, okay?"

With that, he stalked off to the bar to get himself another drink. When he returned, they moved closer to the band and mingled with the crowd.

Mark put on a new face for her to consider—no longer the arrogant land baron or the bold male who challenged her with passion. Ignoring their ambivalent relationship, which teetered between cold anger and hot awareness, he now played the adoring escort—guiding her from group to group with an attentive hand at her elbow, introducing her as if with pride to the guests, managing to impress her with his debonair manner as he conversed with bank presidents, real estate developers, civic leaders.

"What about that new highway plan, Mark?" a commissioner asked.

"The residents will never go for it," he replied casually.

"Fox, what's this I hear about you expanding your offices?" a builder queried.

"You'll be the first to know, Bob."

"Mark dear, I know I can depend on you to make a contribution to Spoleto," a silver-haired woman said.

"Why, Mrs. Tate, I would never let you down." Gallantly, Mark bent to kiss the matronly woman's hand so that she giggled like a debutante.

Maggie found herself following comfortably in his wake, chatting only occasionally, the conversation usually terminating in a flurry of compliments to her escort. He seemed to occupy a unique place among these people. He was not quite one of them; yet she had the impression that his aloofness was purely his own choice. People treated him with an almost palpable deference, and the image of a rogue stallion sprang to mind—one that ran ahead of the herd most of the time, dallying only when something captured his fancy. Maggie caught herself staring thoughtfully at his profile, but when he turned her way, she quickly looked aside, pretending she had been casually glancing through the crowd.

She had yet to see Arthur. The mere thought of him was unpleasant, for with it came the nagging memory of his warnings about Mark, warnings that were becoming ever more difficult to heed.

They were standing with a half-dozen guests when the band began the old nostalgic tune, "April in Paris." Maggie stood chatting with Mrs. Tate while Mark talked with an elderly gentleman whom he addressed as "councilman."

"Excuse me, Mrs. Tate," Mark interrupted. "May I borrow my date for a moment?"

He looked at Maggie. "Dance with me," he commanded, taking her hand and giving her no chance to reply.

Aware of the nods and knowing glances that circulated behind them, Maggie followed him onto the floor. A dozen couples were on the dance floor, and when he found a spot to his liking, Mark turned and drew her toward him.

With complete confidence, Maggie had danced with million-aires, maestros, even noblemen. Yet a wave of nerves swept through her as she moved against Mark Fox and raised a hand to rest on his shoulder. Gradually, she settled her cheek against his.

"April in Paris," he murmured close to her ear. "I know you lived there for a couple of years. Is it as beautiful as they say?"

"Yes. Paris is beautiful year-round."

He raised his head and gazed down at her. "Perhaps you could show it to me sometime," he suggested. He placed her hand around his neck so he could enfold her with both arms. She was crushed against him, her turquoise dress a blue splash against the white of his dinner jacket. She squirmed momentarily in protest until Mark stopped her with a challenging question.

"Is the schoolgirl back?" he whispered tauntingly.

Maggie stiffened in his arms, then reached determinedly around him, clasping him to her intimately.

"I guess not," Mark answered himself, a note of surprise in his voice.

They danced without conversation, just the communication of their bodies swaying together. After a while Maggie didn't care that the crowd whispered or that she was betraying herself by enjoying the heady feeling of holding him close. All she could hear was the music. All she could feel was Mark. Perhaps that was why she didn't notice the irritated clearing of a throat nearby. When a feminine voice spoke, it had to repeat itself before Maggie paid any heed.

"I said this is ladies' choice!" came Alicia's rich southern drawl. "Or don't they have such a custom up north?"

Maggie whirled around with a start, but Mark's arm stayed about her.

"Or perhaps they don't have any *ladies* up north," Alicia added venomously.

"Alicia . . ." Mark began in his deep voice. But the dark-haired woman kept her attention on Maggie, her eyes glinting ferociously.

"I'll handle this, Mark," Maggie broke in, sweeping Alicia Townsend with a haughty look. "You're perfectly welcome to finish this dance, Miss Townsend. There's no need to be insulting. Or is that part of being a *lady* here in the South? Excuse me," she added with a cool nod to Mark, failing to notice his look of amused appreciation as she walked away.

Maggie's cheeks were on fire as she broke through the fringe of people surrounding the dance floor and threaded her way through the crowd. She reached the back of the room and began to move along the edge of the throng. Near the double doors to the foyer she found a good vantage point from which she could view the dancers without being easily seen. She leaned against the wall and watched Mark and Alicia. He wasn't holding her particularly close; yet the sight of them together caused a twitch in the pit of Maggie's stomach.

"Never thought I'd see Mark and Alicia together again," came a high-pitched voice.

Maggie's gaze flew to the source. A couple of spindly-looking women in pastel dresses stood only a few feet in front of her. They resembled each other so much she thought they must be sisters.

"Doesn't surprise me," said the other. "Alicia Townsend has never gotten over him and doesn't make any secret of it."

"Scandalous! I don't care how rich the Townsends are. I don't care if her mother's family *did* help found the city. Alicia should show a little dignity. It's unnatural, that's what it is. And at her own engagement party, for heaven's sake!"

"Poor Grover Harward! Well, you know what they say— politics makes strange bedfellows. I wouldn't be surprised if politicians' brides do the same!"

The two ladies began to titter, and Maggie took the opportunity to move into the foyer and lose herself in a fresh group of guests. Passing a friendly, matronly face, she asked directions to the powder room, and with a driving urge for escape, entered the nearly deserted sanctuary.

Several women sat on plush sofas in a small sitting room. Maggie smiled briefly and proceeded into the washroom, where she ran cool water over her hands and stared into the mirror. Her eyes stared back at her brightly, then fell to her crimson cheeks. It was happening again. She had begun the evening so confidently, so sure of herself. And once again Mark Fox was reducing her to a mass of nerves.

She dampened a towel and pressed its coolness against her forehead. Why had she insisted on attending this wretched party? Somewhere during the course of the night she had lost her power of reason.

She left the washroom and selected a slender chair at the vanity in the sitting room. Two ladies remained on one of the sofas. They were in the midst of a heated exchange about something, and their muted chatter was comforting.

Maggie began to brush her curly hair. Moments later the door swung open, and Alicia Townsend descended on her like a dark crow. She stared fixedly at Maggie's reflection in the mirror until the two gossiping ladies took the hint and left. Maggie wasn't surprised to see the raven-haired woman. Her feminine intuition had told her to expect a confrontation with Arthur's sister. The door had barely closed behind the exiting ladies when Alicia began.

"You are *such* a fool that I can't bear to let you go on in your ignorance," she said in a lethal tone.

Maggie laid the brush on the counter and turned to face her. "Please," she said levelly. "Do go on."

"I've been watching you out there mooning over Mark. It's enough to turn my stomach."

"Oh?" Maggie replied, turning back to the mirror. She began to check her makeup. "I'm surprised at your interest, Alicia. After all, this is your engagement party. You *are* planning to marry Mr. Harward, aren't you?"

The dark woman strolled a few paces closer, her eyes burning into the looking glass. "He's rich and he's powerful. That's what Grover Harward is, money and power. He'll make a good husband. But when it comes to love, *that* is reserved for Mark!"

Maggie finished applying blusher. "I see," she said, replacing the compact in her purse. She stood and turned to confront the angry woman, who was shorter yet far heftier than she. "And is Mark aware of this . . . arrangement? Or did you cook it up all by yourself?"

"You Yankee fool! There's no way *you* could understand the way things are here in the South. Families are close. Ties go back generations. You couldn't possibly grasp the special bond that exists between me and Mark!"

The woman's words were slurred, and she swayed slightly. It was obvious she was drunk, and her anger increased as she raved on.

"No other woman can *ever* be what I am to him. No woman in the world! Oh, there have been lots of them, I admit. Since we broke up, Mark has gained a reputation as a veritable stud! But none of them lasted. None of them meant anything. Just like *you*," she finished with a sneer. "*You* don't mean anything to him either!"

"I don't claim to," Maggie returned briskly.

"You don't have to *claim* to!" Alicia accused. "It's plain for anyone to see. Why don't you wise up? *I'm* the one Mark loves! I'm the only one he'll *ever* love!"

"If that's true," Maggie countered, "I wonder why you're marrying Mr. Harward instead of Mark."

"Because . . . because . . ." Alicia's face was bright with rage. "Because his bitch of a mother couldn't stay away from my father! Because when Dolly married William Fox she was already pregnant with Mark! Because my father is his father, and Dolly felt compelled to reveal it when Mark and I were about to become engaged!"

A look of amazement registered on Maggie's face.

"Aha!" Alicia exclaimed. "I see I've finally made you understand. For the sake of convention, Mark keeps his distance. But don't make the mistake of thinking he'll ever care for anyone but me! If you've set your cap for Mark Fox, Little Miss Yankee, you're in for a big disappointment!"

Maggie blinked in speechless surprise. All she could see was the pathetic picture of Alicia Townsend—proud southern belle, prominent socialite, drunk and pretending indifference to a fact that obviously tormented her. Without realizing it, Maggie allowed a sympathetic expression to cross her features.

Alicia's head snapped up, and she blinked back the tears that glistened in her dark eyes. "Don't you *dare* look at me with pity," she growled. "Mark loves me. Save your pity for yourself!" With a swish of her black gown, she was out the door.

Maggie felt as if she'd just been through a whirlwind. For a moment she stared at the closed door; then she turned and looked in the mirror. The reflection that returned her gaze appeared flushed but calm.

Mark was not the son of William Fox! Slowly her brain began to assemble the implications. This could explain the rivalry between Mark and Arthur, who were actually resentful half brothers. It could explain why William Fox had left part of his estate to someone other than Mark. It might even be the reason behind the threatening darkness that surrounded Mark like a thundercloud. Suddenly Maggie recalled a conversation with Rachel. "He's been told things he never shoulda known," the old woman had said. "And now he's out to show he's better than the lot of 'em."

Alicia Townsend was his half sister! *That* was why Mark had dropped Alicia—not because he had managed to romance her out of some land, as Arthur had told her.

Alicia had shed light on some of the mysteries that plagued Maggie. She took a last reassuring look in the mirror and walked purposefully from the deserted room and into the sweeping entry hall. The door had just closed behind her when she heard Arthur's voice.

"Maggie! My God, am I glad to see you! I had begun to think you weren't coming!" Arthur's face was beaming above his stiff black tie. "Let me look at you. You're beautiful!"

"Thank you, Arthur," she replied and began to scan the foyer for Mark. It was after midnight, and the crowd was beginning to thin. She spotted him across the hall in the next room, speaking with a man who had voiced interest in bottomland.

"Maggie," Arthur pressed, "here's someone who's been waiting to meet you. This is George Haley, one of Charleston's foremost newspaper columnists. And this is Mr. Leonard, a photographer."

"Hello," Maggie said, extending her hand to Mr. Haley, a plump man in an outdated brown suit, who regarded her with sharp blue eyes. The photographer was young and gangly and had a camera hanging about his neck.

"Miss Hastings," Haley said, "I'm happy to make your acquaintance. From what Mr. Townsend tells me, there's an interesting story behind your visit to Charleston. I wonder if I might ask you a few questions."

"Well, I—suppose so," she stammered as the man whipped out a pad and pen.

"Where in New York are you from?"

"Kensing. It's near Rochester."

"You grew up and went to school there?"

"Yes."

"You later studied art in college?"

"That's right. I attended college in New York City and then spent two years at the University of Paris."

"Your parents . . . I understand they died recently?"

"Yes, in a snowstorm."

"And the document in which William Fox bequeathed part of Foxcroft to you was found among their papers?"

"Yes."

"Mr. Townsend says the inheritance was a surprise to you. Right?"

"Yes."

"Will you consider other offers on the property, or does Mark Fox have an exclusive?"

At that remark, Maggie's eyes flashed to Haley and she found her tongue. "Perhaps I'll keep Foxcroft for myself. As you know, it's a very special place."

A stricken look crossed Arthur's face. "But—" he began.

"Keep it for yourself?" Haley interrupted. "You mean you'd *live* there?"

"Why not?" Maggie returned lightly. Her temper had flared, and she enjoyed shocking Arthur. After all, he had set her up with this barracuda.

"And what would become of Dolly and Mark Fox?" Haley pressed.

"Why, I'd throw them out into the street, of course," she responded outrageously and watched a slow grin spread across Haley's face.

She laughed, but before she could go on, Mr. Leonard snapped a picture and the flash of the camera momentarily blinded her. Before she could recover, he snapped another so that she raised a hand to shield her eyes.

"So you plan to stay on in Charleston?" Haley continued. The flash of the camera had drawn attention. A small crowd was gathering around them, and at the back of the group Maggie caught a glimpse of Alicia, glaring with satisfaction before tossing down the contents of a cocktail glass.

"What's going on here?" Mark's voice suddenly boomed so that Maggie spun around.

"Just getting the news, Mr. Fox," George Haley replied smoothly. "Would you like to make a comment on the arrival of the surprise Foxcroft heiress?"

"No comment!" Mark said stonily and turned to Arthur. "What's the meaning of this, Townsend?"

"The meaning?" Arthur repeated, his angular face alight with a wide smile. Obviously he was thrilled at Mark's rage. "Why, surely you can grasp the meaning! I'm rectifying the wrong you sought to commit by secluding Miss Hastings in the country. I'm perfectly aware that you planned to whisk her away from here before anyone knew what was going on. The public has a right to know!

"In short," Arthur added, lowering his voice and staring Mark down from three feet away. "The more people who know Foxcroft is up for grabs, the less chance *you* have of getting it back!"

Mark's eyes narrowed to slits. Maggie, Foxcroft, Canadys Isle, the harassment of a lifetime. Suddenly Mark exploded. With lightning swiftness, he dropped his drink, drew back his right fist, and punched Arthur square in the jaw. A flashbulb went off, and Arthur fell back into the crowd and down to the floor, taking a half-dozen ladies and gentlemen with him.

Maggie stared at the spectacle. Elegant men and women in all their fine plumage scrambled and squawked like colorful birds beneath the twinkling lights of the chandelier. If it hadn't been so mortifying, it would have been hilarious. Suddenly Mark took her arm and hurried her through the crowd so rapidly that she stumbled and nearly lost a shoe.

"Mark!" she protested. "Mark, slow down!" But he only tightened his grip and threw her a venomous look.

"Isaac," he said tersely when they arrived at the door, leaving a trail of jostled people behind them. "Miss Hastings's wrap, please."

"Yes, sir, Mr. Fox," the old man replied, his big eyes shining. "I got it right here. It's storming out there now. Y'all better be careful on the road."

"We will," Mark replied.

He pulled open the door, letting in a rainy gust of wind that drew a new round of startled gasps from the guests. After placing the cloak over Maggie's head and draping a strong arm around her shoulders, he plunged into the raging storm with her at his side.

They vaulted down the stairs, through the courtyard, and out the gate. When they reached the street, the storm greeted them with full force, the rain driving relentlessly from the sea as if it would hurl them against the garden wall.

A jagged streak of lightning lit the street, followed by a deafening crack of thunder. Maggie's cloak flew behind them like a flag, and the rain pelted them furiously. Finally Mark ducked off the street and into the shelter of the Van Averys' drive. He helped her into the car, then skirted around, climbed in, and started the Porsche.

"Mark!" she exploded.

He looked at her briefly, the water streaming down his face. "I hope you're satisfied!" he blurted as he backed the car out from under the trees and into the street.

"You hope *I'm* satisfied!" she exclaimed incredulously, swinging her dripping hair over her shoulder so that it sprayed him.

"You're the one who insisted on going to that blasted party!" he snarled.

"Well, I didn't know you were planning to use it as a boxing debut!"

"Oh, good!" he chuckled harshly. "Just what I need, a little dry humor on a wet night. Do me a favor, will you, Maggie? Save it! And what was that rubbish about throwing me out into the street?"

"I was just giving George Haley a bit of what he was dishing out!"

"Are you kidding?" Mark exclaimed in disbelief. "You were giving him a headline!"

"So? Maybe I *will* decide to keep Foxcroft. You've never once *asked* me if I want to sell it to you! You just make insulting remarks and act as if I couldn't possibly handle the responsibility of running Foxcroft myself. You're wrong, you know. I *could* manage the estate."

"Alone? Don't make me laugh, Maggie. You wouldn't stand a chance alone. The heating system in the library needs replacing. How would you handle that? I was planning to have the house painted this fall. How would you foot that bill? On an income like yours, you couldn't *begin* to run Foxcroft. The taxes alone would break you!"

Her eyes snapped angrily to his profile. "How do you know that?"

"I know. *Believe* me, I know."

With an expression of mixed astonishment and belligerence, Maggie started to challenge his right to snoop into her financial records. But before she could get the words out of her mouth, the speeding shape of an approaching car intruded. Headlights glared across the drenched windshield, momentarily blinding them.

"Fasten your seat belt!" Mark bellowed. He turned his attention to the road and retreated into the stony silence she had come to hate.

Chapter Ten

The savage spring storm raged through Charleston, frightening travelers off the road and clearing a path for the solitary sports car that wound through the deserted streets. It seemed as though the heart of the storm pulsed angrily above the towering Cooper River Bridge as they sped across it.

Maggie gripped the door handle, her eyes frozen on the window. Clouds of fog rushed past, lightning flashed, and thunder cracked deafeningly just outside the insignificant little car as it left the lights of the city behind and raced into the inky darkness of the countryside.

She had barely moved a muscle. Her dress was like wet film clinging to her legs, and every so often a drop of water slid off her hair and down her back. The drenched cloak lay on the backseat. By the time the highway narrowed into the familiar two-lane road, her jaws were aching, so tensely had she clamped them together to keep her teeth from chattering.

The storm seemed to worsen as they drove deeper into the country, but perhaps it was the dense blackness surrounding them that made the lightning seem so bright, so fearfully spectacular, as if it were showing off its power to its audience of two. Rain assaulted the car in ragged sheets, and the meager beam of the headlights dissolved only a few feet ahead. Still, Mark pushed the car at breathtaking speed, as if he were in some sort of blasphemous race with nature itself.

Maggie glanced in his direction. He sat rigidly hunched over the wheel, his eyes straining to cut through the stormy night. The angry distance between them was so great that they might as well have been at opposite ends of the earth. Her eyes flashed back to the passenger window until she could no longer keep silent.

"Mark, please slow down."

Her voice sounded shrill against the roar of the storm. His eyes remained glued ahead, but he slowed the automobile somewhat.

"I'm in complete control, Maggie. I know this road like the back of my hand."

"I'm not worried about the road. Or you. I'm worried about the other guy—"

Her voice broke on the last word, then rose to a shriek as two lights raced toward them from around a curve. Maggie's mouth remained open, but the scream died as Mark yanked at the steering wheel and they veered off the road. A tree flashed by, only inches away. They hit a sloping embankment, the front of the Porsche lurched up and over, and they barreled down the grassy hill like a roller-coaster car. Out of the darkness, the ground rose to meet them, jolting them with the impact as the car bucked from slanted bank to flat plain.

The rear end fishtailed on the wet grass. The car spun around and stopped. As if nothing had happened, the windshield wipers clicked back and forth with calm regularity.

After a few seconds of shocking stillness, broken only by the pounding of the rain like some fearful drumroll, Mark's voice came from far away. "Maggie! Are you all right?"

He gently turned her around to face him. "Maggie!"

Slowly the image of fast-approaching headlights dissipated and Mark's face came into focus. Damp hair clung to his forehead, and across his face danced the unfamiliar ghost of fear.

"Maggie!"

"I . . . I . . . I'm all right," she stammered, watching the fear leave his face.

He pushed his door open, and as he climbed out of the car, the rain and wind gushed in.

The car was sitting on a plateau. To the right was a barbed wire fence. To the left, a twelve-foot embankment. Ahead, Maggie could see a steep, grassy hill. She watched dazedly as Mark passed in and out of the glow of the headlights. He circled the car, apparently checking for damage, and then scaled the bank toward the road, his white dinner jacket like a disembodied shape floating through the rainy darkness. When he returned, he was again soaked to the skin.

"Whoever it was, they're long gone now."

He stripped off his dripping jacket and tossed it into the backseat.

"They didn't stop?" she asked hollowly.

"That's right. You can always count on that good old southern code of honor." He turned to look at her sharply. "Are you sure you're all right?"

She could only nod.

"Okay. Here's what I think we ought to do."

Leaning forward, he scrubbed a clear circle in the clouded windshield and looked long and hard at the raging storm. When he turned back to her, his voice was low against the relentless pounding of rain on the roof.

"I can't get the car out of here. It's going to have to be towed. The property we're on belongs to the Flauberts. They only drop in every few months. Their house is a few miles away, but there's an unused gamekeeper's cottage in the forest not far from here. When we were kids, Marie Flaubert and the rest of us used it as a meeting place. It was always stocked with firewood, and it probably still is. What do you say? Shall we make a run for it?"

Maggie blinked in disbelief. "Out there?"

He looked at her irritably, but then a softer expression came to his face, as if he understood the terror that had her in its clutches. In an uncharacteristically tender gesture, he took her freezing hands in his own. "Maggie, we've got to do something. We can't stay here, soaking wet, all night."

It was amazing how persuasive he could be. She consented.

She started to step cautiously out of the car, but for a moment she froze, her arms rising to shield her face as she cringed away from the onslaught of the storm. Mark gave her no time to think, no time to let shock take hold. After taking her arm and helping her to her feet, he fought his way to the barbed wire and pried the rows apart so she could climb through. He followed swiftly and then led her across the grassy meadowland and into the forest. The tall pines sheltered them somewhat from the rain, but added a new dimension of fear as their spindly limbs thrashed about in the fierce winds.

Mark forged ahead, Maggie holding on to his arm for dear life. Thunder crashed and time crawled as they fought their way through the black forest. The wind snatched at her hair. Pine branches clawed at her arms and legs. A quarter-mile? A half-mile? Maggie no longer knew how to judge. They finally reached a clearing, and she could make out the shape of a small structure.

When Mark and Maggie emerged from the forest, the rain assaulted them with fresh fury. They dashed across the clearing to the door of the cottage, where he darted to a shuttered window and returned with a key. Swiftly he threw open the door and followed her inside.

Blackness enveloped them like a warm, dark cloak. Maggie had no idea what kind of shelter he had led her to. But whatever it was, she was grateful. The sound of the storm was muffled, overridden by the clatter Mark stirred up as he fumbled nearby in the darkness.

There was a loud bang as something fell to the floor, and then "Dammit! There's a lantern over here somewhere. Ah, here we go."

She heard the sound of a striking match, and a small flame flickered where Mark stood across the room. Motionless, Maggie watched as he lit an oil lamp and moved toward her, bringing a trail of light with him.

Mark held the lamp high and studied her, but she only stared at him, unable to voice a word. Her wild red hair was dripping steady streams down her breasts, where taut nipples thrust impudently through the wet dress. With a reluctant grin, he reached out and wiped a long streak of mascara from her cheek.

"You're all right now," he said. "Trust me."

There was nothing glamorous about the cottage, but Mark turned it into a cozy place Maggie would later remember with painstaking clarity. After settling her in a wooden chair by the cold hearth, he began to rummage around the small hut, which was but one rough-hewn room with a bed, a pantry, an old stove, and a woodpile that reached nearly to the ceiling.

It was to the woodpile that Mark directed his attention. With a few deft moves, he stacked a monument of kindling and logs in the fireplace and put a match to it. The wood was so old and dry that it caught immediately. He moved to the kitchen area and searched through the pantry. Maggie watched as if from a great distance. The warmth of the fire had yet to penetrate the chill that held her frozen. Bearing a large bottle of amber liquid, Mark walked over to where she sat.

"Drink a little of this," he said, handing her the bottle. "It's brandy."

The first swallow burned like liquid fire down her throat. She offered the bottle back to him, but he motioned for her to take another swig. Obediently, she tipped the bottle. This time the fiery drink had warm fingers that glided down her throat and into her stomach. Several gulps later, the strong brandy had performed its task—heating her blood so the chill unclenched its icy grip on her bones. She handed the bottle to Mark and looked at him with new life in her eyes.

"Welcome back," he muttered and raised the brandy to his lips. Crouching before her, he drank. Firelight played across his handsome face and glistened on the wet dark hair. Maggie's gaze lingered there, then traveled down his throat to where the rain-soaked shirt was but a veil on his suntanned shoulders. Mark's eyes found hers, and the sound of the storm receded, consumed in the crackling of the fire.

"You'd better take that wet thing off."

The rude command shattered Maggie's dreamy state. "What?"

"Your dress," he rumbled. "Take it off."

"Take off my dress?" Rising quickly to her feet, she added, "And replace it with what?"

His gaze traveled up her body, reaching her face as one corner of his mouth dipped mirthlessly. "I'll see," he muttered and got up from his crouched position. He crossed the room to a curtained corner and returned with a couple of old blankets smelling strongly of cedar.

"Here," he said, pushing one of the blankets into her arms. "Wrap up in this." When she only stared, he took her by the shoulders, turned her around, and gently pushed her toward the hearth. "Go on."

She stood indecisively for a moment, clutching the soft old blanket and watching Mark warily. He ambled away from the fire, sank onto the bed, and seemed to forget her presence as he turned his attention to his left arm. He sat a distance away in the flickering shadows, and it was difficult to tell what he was doing. He seemed to be examining his shirtsleeve, and then came the sound of a sharp intake of breath.

Despite the cold wetness of his shirt, Mark's arm felt as if it were on fire. Gingerly he brought it to rest against his side, leaned back on the bed into the shadows, and rolled his eyes to the ceiling. The old cabin. Thank God it still stood.

The moment of thankfulness passed as he began to deride himself. He should have driven more cautiously. He should have held his temper at the party. But damn! Townsend's behavior was the last straw!

With a snort, Mark hoisted himself from the bed and began to remove his trousers. Across the room, Maggie quickly pivoted to turn her back on him. Only then did his thoughts turn to her.

Maggie Hastings—the only innocent in all of this. After going to the library studio that afternoon, he'd had no further doubt about who she was, nor did he question her complete ignorance of the circumstances of her inheritance. What was he doing but perpetuating that ignorance? Perhaps he deserved the misfortunes that had been dealt him today.

Guilt didn't sit well with Mark, and it wasn't long before the emotion gave way to irritation. His eyes traveled down Maggie's body—across the proud, rigid back, beyond the hem of the short dress, along the lines of her slender legs. The urge to touch her swelled within him as it had done more frequently with each passing day.

He allowed his trousers to drop to the floor and stripped off his underwear before wrapping the blanket about his waist, but his eyes remained on Maggie where she stood so woodenly by the fire. With firm determination he suppressed his attraction to the woman as he approached her.

"I thought you were going to change," he said.

Maggie regarded him steadily. "Where?"

He looked amused that she imagined herself to be of interest to him.

"I'll stay here by the fire, and you can go over by the bed. You're perfectly safe, I assure you."

He approached the fireplace, retrieved the brandy, and took a long swallow.

Maggie left the hearth and moved away from the fire and into the cold darkness. She stripped away the ruined garments—the soiled pumps, torn stockings, and the rain-soaked dress, which seemed to shrink even as she pulled it over her head. Without realizing it, she had been emotionally numbed by the accident and was only now recovering. Her mind only now began to recall and assess what had happened to her. Holding the dress out before her, she saw it was ruined.

What a pity, she thought. How thrilled she had been at its beauty; how confident she had felt as the evening began. The dreamy dinner at the Atlantic House, the grandeur of the Townsend mansion. Now she was in a hut in a forest discarding her beautiful dress, having been in an accident that could have killed her.

Yet Mark seemed to take it all in stride, as if plummeting down an embankment in his Porsche were an everyday occurrence. From the concealing shadows, she watched as he squatted by the dancing flames, raised the bottle to his lips, and took a long draft.

He settled himself more comfortably on his haunches and stared moodily into the fire.

Leaving on her damp undergarments, Maggie took awhile arranging the blanket in the most concealing fashion she could devise. By the time she finished tucking it under her arms like a sarong, her teeth had begun to chatter. Quietly, she moved toward the warmth of the fire and Mark's forbidding back. He glanced up as she drew the chair chose to the hearth and sat beside him so that she, too, could look broodingly into the flames.

They had faced disaster, had looked into the jaws of death, and had emerged to share the victory of life. The experience didn't erase the guarded way in which Maggie viewed Mark, but there was a new, unique bond between them. These, at least, were her thoughts. She had no idea what Mark's were as she became aware he was studying her.

"I'm sorry about all this," he said finally. "But at least we're dry."

Her eyes fixed on the fire, Maggie nodded silently. Time passed, the wind whistling about the cottage, the flames leaping in response to every gust.

"It could have been worse, you know," Mark added.

"I know," she admitted.

She didn't look at him. Something was happening to the atmosphere in the little cottage. Before, she had felt as if they were refugees, a pair of lucky fugitives who had found sanctuary. Now the man beside her was changing from her anonymous partner in flight to the inimitable Mark Fox—virile, powerful, threatening. "What I want, I get," he'd boasted in the restaurant. Suddenly she remembered Arthur's dire warnings, Alicia's haughty face, and she felt totally alone and defenseless.

Where was the self-confident aloofness that had always been her Rock of Gibraltar? Lately, as never before, it seemed prone to desert her.

Abruptly Mark rose and moved away from the fire. Maggie kept her back to him, yet she could feel his eyes boring into her. Her hand rose to clasp the blanket to her breast.

A half-hour had passed, and now there was but one all-consuming thought in Mark's mind—that of the flame-haired woman who sat before him. The firelight touched the smooth skin of her bare shoulders, dappling it in shifting patterns of rose and gold. He could almost smell her rich, unique scent. No other woman had affected him in such a way, calling him to reach out even as his brain told him such a move would be unwise.

Yet here they were, alone in their private world. The urge to touch her was overpowering.

Behind her, Maggie heard the shuffle of his feet.

"Here," he said and dangled the brandy bottle over her shoulder.

Silently, one hand still on the blanket, she took the bottle and sipped from it. There was a faint rustling noise as Mark crouched behind the chair. When, without turning, she held up the bottle and offered it to him, his voice came from just behind her.

"You keep it," he said gruffly.

And then it came—the touch she'd been dreading and longing for. On her shoulder his mouth was like a warm, moist shock. She felt it move along her back and open to suck the side of her neck.

"No! Stop it!" With a rush, Maggie stood and moved to the far end of the hearth. She nervously shifted the bottle in her hands as the pounding in her temples reminded her of the brandy's presence in her blood.

"I don't want to be—I *won't* be another of your conquests!" she announced.

"What are you talking about?"

From the corner of her eye, Maggie saw him rise and step toward her. Her back went straight as a rod as she stared at the rough stones of the hearth.

"I asked you what you're talking about." Mark gripped her shoulder and would have turned her around to face him, but she jerked away and stepped closer to the fire.

"Exactly what I said," she replied firmly. "Is this what you meant when you were talking to Harold and John Henry a few days ago?"

"When I was—"

"Is this how you planned to take care of me, as you so quaintly put it?" Over her shoulder Maggie looked at him coldly, the imperiousness of her stance in sharp contrast to the old blanket in which she was clad.

"I'm well aware that I have something you want, Mark. But I must warn you that no romantic tryst in the woods is going to influence my decision about Foxcroft."

In seeming surprise, he hesitated a moment.

"If you could be honest with yourself," he said, "if you could bring yourself to listen to reason, you'd see that I'm right.

Foxcroft is a special place, with special needs. Taking care of it is a full-time job. It's very demanding and very expensive."

Mark's voice dropped intimately. "I'm not your enemy, Maggie. In this instance I know what's best for you. Can't you trust me?"

Her resolve against him was strong. Even so, she could feel it weaken and wouldn't risk further damage by offering a reply. A minute passed, and she could feel Mark studying her even before she heard him move closer.

"Forget Foxcroft," he said in that deep, authoritative voice. "We can settle that tomorrow. Right now, tonight, there's nothing here but you and me."

The last words came from just above her ear, softly stirring her hair. Maggie sidestepped away.

"Forget Foxcroft? And then what? Let you sweep me off my feet? Sorry, Mark. Your reputation precedes you."

"Who's been filling your head with nonsense?" he demanded. "Who?" he repeated, so loud that she jumped and finally turned to face him.

"Everyone!" she retorted. Her doubts rallied, once again overpowering the unnerving attraction she felt for the man. She gave him an accusing look that turned into a smirk. "You don't seem to realize, Mark, that your masculine prowess has become legend! Rachel, Alicia, *everyone* mentions the long line of women who have filed through your life!"

Mark gazed at her in stunned surprise. He'd had his fair share of ladies, all right, but he usually selected them from outside Charleston. That way the gossips had nothing to talk about, and when the time came, it was easier to make a clean break. He thought he'd been discreet, but Maggie was painting him as the biggest Casanova in the Carolinas.

"And on top of that," she went on, "Arthur says you *use* women. You string them along until you get what you want, and then you drop them without a thought! Well, I certainly don't intend to become another notch on your pistol!"

"I don't *use* women, Maggie."

"That's not what Arthur Townsend says!"

"Townsend! Good God! Don't you know by now that he'd say or do anything to undermine me? I've been out with plenty of women, sure—"

"Sure," she cut in cattily.

Mark stared at her for a moment, then ran his hand distractedly through his hair. "I knew my instinct was right from the beginning. You're better off leaving and not getting involved in all this . . . scandal."

The fact that he was again pushing her to leave Foxcroft struck her like a slap in the face.

"You came down here like a wide-eyed kid," he continued. "And you didn't know what you were walking into. Things are very complicated, Maggie. There's a lot you don't know."

"Perhaps I know more than you think," she snapped, brushing past him and putting an end to the conversation.

Her dismissal was so clear that she might as well have slammed a door in his face. Mark's mouth settled in a grim line as he watched her turn the wooden chair away from him. She sat down with all the primness of a schoolmarm and in a swift, incongruous gesture, hoisted the bottle to her lips like a sailor.

He studied the squared shoulders, the proud, disdainful mien that would brook no approach, then shook his head in irritation. Maggie had been teasing him all night, but every time he made a move, she put him off. At the restaurant, and now—with some cock-and-bull story about him being a playboy! Well, he was damned tired of it! With a snort Mark knelt on the hearth and threw his angry energy into rebuilding the fire.

Maggie kept her eyes carefully trained away from him, nursing her mistrust of the man, contenting herself with hasty gulps of the disappearing brandy. Eventually he settled again before the hearth, and in morose silence they passed the bottle back and forth.

Another half-hour passed, the storm continuing to howl about the cottage, its windy breath rattling the old door, its rainy fists beating at the roof. Inside, however, it was safe and warm. And the brandy was nearly gone.

A feeling of mellowness invaded Maggie's bones. Now, as she glanced away from the fire, the lines of the rustic cabin—and even of Mark's face—were soft and hazy. She was getting drunk. She hadn't been drunk in years, but she didn't care. If ever there had been an occasion that justified it, this was it. Her thoughts turned again to the strange events of the evening, and images flew across her mind—the faint outline of a car behind blazing headlights, Arthur falling into the crowd of horrified guests, Alicia's almond-shaped eyes.

The hand with the bottle extended itself in Mark's direction, the rosy light playing along the bare skin of her arm.

"Tell me about Alicia," she said.

He was reaching for the brandy. At the sound of the name, he froze, then snatched the bottle from Maggie's hand.

"What about her?" he uttered through tense lips.

Perhaps it was the brandy that made Maggie bold. "She enlightened me about a few things at the party. Is it true that you're in love with her?"

Mark sputtered in the midst of his drinking. He wiped his mouth with the back of his hand and looked at her piercingly.

"So that's it," he said. "You know, don't you? She told you. I'm not the son of William Fox, just Art Townsend's bastard."

Maggie returned his look with blurred surprise. It was not the answer she had expected.

"I didn't say that," she began. "I simply asked—"

"About Alicia," he broke in. "Do I love her? You tell me. What does a brother feel for a sister? Protectiveness? Guardianship? That's what I feel for my half sister—nothing less, nothing more. It's a fact Alicia seems to have difficulty accepting."

He looked away. The line of his profile was etched in the firelight, and his voice took on a solemn tone.

"I dated her for a while years ago. Nothing ever happened between us. When I found out about my father, I stopped seeing Alicia immediately. I stopped doing a lot of things."

"But do you love her?" Maggie pressed, remembering too well the long, unreadable look he'd given the raven-haired woman at the party.

"No!" Mark exploded, his eyes snapping back to her face. "Try to imagine . . ." He lowered his voice, but stared at her heatedly. "Try to imagine finding out that you're not the person you always thought you were, that you're someone else entirely!"

"It would be a blow," she allowed, her words slow and clumsy. "But it's still better to know the truth."

"No matter the consequences?"

"No matter." Her eyes glowed at the handsome face. "No matter what the truth is, it's better to know. If people have no honesty between them, they have nothing."

He regarded her steadily, a strange, questioning look crossing his face. "Are you accusing me of something specific?"

Maggie blinked at him. "I don't have the right to accuse you of anything."

An expression of irritation raced over his features. "You are the most infuriating woman," he muttered under his breath.

Grabbing the poker, he began to stoke the fire. As he did so, he leaned into the light. It was only then that Maggie noticed the long lines of blood that stained the left sleeve of the shirt he still wore.

"What have you done to yourself?" she demanded, her words rolling out in a slurred stream as her eyes widened in alarm.

Mark turned his head to follow her gaze, his eyes coming to rest on the blood-soaked sleeve.

"It happened when we came through the forest," he mumbled. "A broken limb slashed my arm."

"My God," Maggie whispered. Her eyes rounded in horror as the stain seemed to gape larger and darker. How could she have failed to notice it? "We've got to do something!"

"It's okay," Mark replied irritably. "Don't worry about it."

"Are you crazy?" she cried, searching his face. Pausing for a moment, she ordered, "Take it off."

When he only stared, she repeated, "Take off your shirt."

In reluctant obedience, he unbuttoned the formal shirt, wincing only as he shrugged it over his shoulders. Maggie knelt by his side and retrieved the discarded garment. She ripped off the damaged sleeve and tore several clean strips, one of which she saturated with brandy from the nearly empty bottle. When she looked again at Mark, she found his eyes resting on her bare shoulders.

"Let me see it," she commanded, her hands poised, ready with the alcohol-saturated fabric. Slowly, he raised the wounded arm.

There it was, a gash about four inches long in the smooth skin of his upper arm, as if a swordsman had slashed at him with a blade. Maggie drew a sharp breath as she watched a small pool of blood spill out and run in a slow stream along the muscular arm. Carefully she began to clean the long red streaks from around the wound.

"Say something," she ordered.

"What?"

"Talk to me. About anything. About when you were a child growing up at Foxcroft."

He hesitated. "Well," he began and then grimaced as the brandy-soaked rag brushed the torn flesh. Maggie glanced at him briefly, apologetically, and went back to her task.

"Everything was different then," he finally said.

The words came slowly, as if he was unaccustomed to talking about his past.

"I spent most of my free time riding. Even back then Townsend was at me like a bulldog. One thing after another—football, polo, everything. He seemed to be trying to prove something. Later, when I found out the truth, I wondered if he had always known."

Mark winced as Maggie began to wind a strip of cloth about his arm. She paused, her eyes rising from his arm to his face. That small show of pain was all he would allow, and his green eyes looked into hers steadily. She turned back to her bandaging.

"Go on," she commanded.

"I remember when Art Townsend Senior died. Young Arthur and Alicia stayed out of school. Mother got sick. Dad just got quiet. He'd seemed happy for a couple of years—talking more, laughing more. Now, as I look back, I think I understand what happened to him."

Mark lifted his gaze from her hands, settling it on the bright head bent over him. "You see, a woman came to Foxcroft."

Maggie glanced up. "A woman?"

He felt suddenly as if he could fall into the turquoise depths of her eyes and drown. "Yeah," he mumbled thickly. "I guess Dad fell in love with her."

Maggie looked back to complete the bandaging, and with a quick, deep breath, Mark repressed the curious feeling that surged through him—something beyond physical desire, something he didn't want to think about at all! He focused his thoughts on the tale of his past, the poignant story of having lost not only two fathers but his own sense of identity as well.

"Whatever the reason," he muttered harshly, "my *supposed* father, William Fox, had become happier, more active, and more interested in everything, including me. He took me to all the competitions, every race, every show. Of course, that was before I knew he wasn't my father at all."

Maggie finished tying the bandage and met his eyes. They were filled with pain and with a fierce denial of that pain.

"Maybe now you can understand something you must have wondered about all along," he went on. "Why didn't William Fox leave his estate to his only son? Easy. He had no son. Maybe you can even understand why I must keep Foxcroft: Without it, I'm no one . . . nothing."

His voice died away, his eyes giving her the impression of a confused plea for—for what? Understanding? Acceptance? Forgiveness? The look lasted only seconds. With a swift movement, he jerked his head to one side, flinching as the forgotten, wounded arm twisted out of her grasp.

Maggie studied his profile, outlined clearly in the firelight. His jaw tightened threateningly, but she saw beyond that, to a depth of feeling she had not imagined in Mark Fox.

"You want to know something?" she ventured. He turned to her, his features solemn and tense. "I understand how you feel. I really do. It's strange, I know, but ever since I came to Foxcroft, I've had the odd feeling I belong here."

Mark's throat went dry.

"For years I've wandered around," she went on. "New York, Paris, back to New York again. Something kept me moving on. I never felt settled anywhere, and it all seemed so pointless. Then out of the blue, I come across an old plantation in the middle of nowhere. All of a sudden, I feel as though I've come home. It's ridiculous!"

"Maybe not so ridiculous," Mark mumbled. "Foxcroft has that effect on some people."

"What's going on, Mark?" she asked.

He looked at her abruptly.

"I mean, why did William Fox want me to have part of the estate?"

This was it. She was asking him point-blank. His answer would be the truth or a lie. God, she was irresistible, and Mark leaned toward telling her the truth. It might not be so bad, her staying around awhile.

Straighten up! his logic suddenly warned. You've known this woman for only a few days, and Foxcroft has been your home for life. Don't even *think* of jeopardizing it!

"I told you," he said grimly. "William Fox wasn't my father."

Maggie gazed at him intently. "If there was anything more to it, would you tell me?"

Mark's eyes snapped to hers. "Anything more? Like what?"

She shrugged. "I don't know. *Would* you tell me?"

"Yes, dammit!" Mark lied. A wave of self-loathing swept through him.

Maggie searched his face. "I just get this feeling—"

"Look!" he interrupted, his stomach sinking. "I'm another man's bastard! I'm not William Fox's son! I can understand why he didn't leave everything to me!"

"I can't! I've seen his picture, Mark. There's something wonderful about his face. I can't imagine him doing such a thing without a good reason."

"Well, he did it!" Mark barked. "Whatever the reason, he

yanked my home right out from under me and gave it to you!" He clamped his mouth shut.

Maggie looked into his glittering eyes, and something within her wrenched. She took a long, heavy breath. "Don't worry, Mark," she said finally. "If I thought I had any right to Foxcroft, I'd give you one hell of a fight for it. But it seems to me you're more William Fox's son than you believe. You're all that's left of the Fox family. I wish things were different. But you're the one who belongs there, not me."

Mark stared in disbelief. Her face was alight with sincerity, and for the first time he sensed the integrity behind her beauty. Oh, God, woman! he thought. Guilt welled up inside him, collecting in his eyes, which were like warm, tortured pools.

Maggie mistook the shimmering look for pain. He had always seemed so strong and invulnerable. Now, even in her inebriated state, she could see that Mark was tormented. Suddenly he struck a chord in her that had never been touched before, and she had a strange urge to comfort him.

As if outside herself, Maggie watched her hand reach out to him. He flinched as her fingers touched his cheek, but then submitted as she gently stroked the hair from his brow. It was a simple gesture, but as Mark stared at her, she found more in his eyes than simple warmth. There was a hot look, the look she remembered from the Atlantic House. Maggie's heart leapt to her throat, and abruptly, she withdrew her hand. But he reached out quickly to catch it.

"Don't stop," his voice rumbled as he turned her hand over in his. "Please."

The last word was barely audible as he bent to kiss her palm, the warmth of his mouth sending a shiver up her arm. And then the moist warmth of his mouth was traveling along her wrist to the crook of her elbow.

Maggie's eyelids were heavy. They dropped uncontrollably as her arm became limp in Mark's hands. Outside, the wind screamed and was answered by a loud crackle in the fireplace. Funny she should notice such a thing as his chin brushed against her blanket-covered breast and his tongue traced a path to her shoulder.

Her lips moved, and she heard a voice peculiarly like her own. "I don't want this," it said.

He kissed her neck, and when he spoke, his breath fanned the newly moistened skin. "Try that on someone else."

The challenge brought her to momentary consciousness. Jerking away, Maggie came quickly to her feet, the effort setting her head to reeling. Mark followed and stood towering only a foot behind her. He put his hands on her shoulders, and his voice was low and caressing. "Don't run away from me, Maggie. Look at me."

Allowing him to turn her around, she looked up slowly.

"I already told you," she said shakily. "We'll come to terms. Foxcroft is yours."

"So you said."

"There's no need for us to get . . . involved."

"No need?" Mark said in a low voice. "Maggie, you must be crazy." His fingers held the sides of her face as he stepped closer. "You make me feel . . . something," he mumbled. "I want you . . ." His voice trailed off as he bent toward her.

Maggie's shattering attraction to him was so entwined with mistrust that she no longer knew where one stopped and the other began. All she knew, as her heart began to pound deafeningly, was she longed to believe in him.

His lips were gentle as he pressed them to hers once, twice, and then raised his head to stare longingly into her eyes. Maggie was transfixed as his fingers slipped into her hair, his palms coming to rest on her cheeks. His mouth captured hers with such force that had he not been holding her steady, she would have tumbled.

A fleeting thought of resistance skittered through her mind, but it was no match for the memory of the longing in Mark's eyes or for the passion in the kiss that went on and on, breaking down the barrier of doubt until it no longer seemed important. He tasted of brandy and his own particular brand of maleness, a taste she remembered instantly from the oak grove. The practiced tongue roamed her mouth hungrily. Her arms hung limp at her sides as a devastating arousal raced through her veins like a drug. A hand slid down the side of her face, continuing along the column of her throat to her shoulder.

The blankets fell at their feet, and with unprecedented abandon, Maggie reached up to lock her wrists around the tall man's neck. Seconds later, with a swift movement that failed to interrupt his kiss, Mark swept her into his arms and knelt with her on the mound of blankets. Entwining her fingers with his, he held her hands to the floor and covered her body with his naked one.

"This was meant to be," he murmured in a thick voice, his lips against hers. "I knew it the first time I laid eyes on you."

He kissed her slowly, caressingly, until any reservations that might have lingered in Maggie's mind were vanquished.

The weight of his tall body pinned her to the floor, the rough old blanket prickling her back as the hair on his chest tantalized her scarcely covered breasts. His bronze skin was smooth against her own, particularly where his hardness extended above her panties to press like a hot shaft against her stomach.

He moved slowly, grindingly, and a well of liquid warmth gathered between her legs. Maggie's body took over. Dimly she realized that her tongue had begun to probe his mouth as she moved beneath him, with him, catching his rhythm until their bodies were as one, electrifying each other until each moment of delay became one of exquisite anticipation.

Releasing one of her hands, Mark's fingers traveled lightly along the inside of her arm, continuing until they found her breast beneath the filmy strapless bra.

Maggie's hand caressed his shoulders, strayed into the long hair that curled at the back of his neck. A dull ache began to throb where he was grinding against her, and she barely noticed the hand sliding to her back. Suddenly he tossed the bra aside. The milky skin of her breasts glowed in the firelight, and Mark's mouth descended on them.

He lifted his body briefly from hers, feathering a hand down her stomach, leaving a trail of chills behind. Warm fingers found the hip of her panties where lace held front and back together. One quick, sharp tug and the fabric ripped, and the panties slid away to join the bra. His lips moved to her ear, and above Maggie's panting, his whisper was barely audible.

"Trust me," he said.

A knee pried her thighs apart. The heat of his maleness reasserted itself, probing through the curling hair, massaging the sensitive mound until every nerve in Maggie's body seemed to scream. Her hips rose, and she moved up against him, forcing the shaft along the valley.

Mark released a long, shuddering breath as he moved just inside her enveloping warmth. He paused, absorbing the mind-blasting feeling, interrupting their fiery kiss so that he could look down on her now that they were joined in the most intimate of ways.

Maggie opened her eyes to gaze dreamily at him from dark turquoise pools. Above her, she found Mark's feverish eyes; within her, she could feel his body poised, waiting to invade her with welcome mastery. From behind his neck, her hands slid down his smooth back—rubbing, caressing.

Her lashes fluttered closed as he kissed her gently. His mouth covered hers forcefully, stifling a gasp as he pressed full-length inside her.

The storm outside the cottage was no match for the one that raged within.

Mark ran his palm down the smooth arm of the slumbering woman. Reaching her hand, he closed his long fingers about hers. She had fallen asleep in an immediate, childlike way, curled trustingly within the circle of his arm.

He glanced down at the hair spilling across his shoulder. In the glow of the dying fire, it looked like molten copper. He closed his eyes and took a deep breath of the unique scent that wafted from his own body as well as hers.

Ah, Maggie, he thought. You are one hell of a woman!

Behind closed lids, he pictured her, the slender naked form responding sensually to his touch. He'd been so swept away, he'd had a tough time containing himself. Just the memory made the hot blood stir anew, and Mark knew that when she awoke, he would make love to her again, this time more languorously.

She stirred against him, her nose brushing the hair on his chest. Suddenly the passionate image changed to one from earlier in the night, when her beautiful eyes had looked at him so tenderly. "You're the one who belongs there," she'd said. "Not me."

Maggie Hastings. She was more than the most tempting lover he'd ever come across. She was a damned fine woman. She deserved better than being lied to.

Tomorrow, he decided. Tomorrow—damn the risk, damn the family, damn Foxcroft!—he would tell Maggie the truth.

Mark reached around her with his free arm, hugging her close as he rested his cheek against her hair. His final lucid thought was of gardenias.

Chapter Eleven

A sharp knocking sound intruded on her dreams, and for a few seconds Maggie was in her bedroom in Kensing. Any moment now, Myra Hastings's voice would drift through the door: "Come along, dear. You don't want to be late for school."

The warm presence beside her moved, and Maggie became drowsily aware of Mark's hands covering her with the blanket. A fulfilled smile crept to her lips, and she snuggled deeper into the covers. From across the room came vague shuffling sounds and then a click as the bolt on the old door was removed.

"Mark, you sly old fox!" an unfamiliar voice boomed.

It shattered the sleep that held Maggie. Her eyes flew open and turned to the cottage door. A man stepped inside. He was broader than Mark, who, dressed only in trousers, backed up and seemed at a loss for words.

The soft gray light of dawn spilled into the hut through the doorway, illuminating the stranger. He wore a familiar-looking hat, and finally recognizing him as a police officer, Maggie clutched the blanket under her chin.

"Jerry!" Mark finally said and extended his hand. "What are you doing here?"

"Well, I'll tell you," the man began, pushing back his hat. "We got an anonymous call at the station this morning, along about one o'clock. The guy said he ran somebody off the road out here, but it wasn't until the storm let up that we were able to spot the car. As soon as I saw your Porsche, I knew you'd be out here. This old cottage was one hell of a clubhouse in the old days. Looks like it's still coming in handy."

The patrolman's gaze swept around the room and lit on Maggie, where she lay before the dying embers on the hearth. Above the edge of the blanket, her eyes glowed like two great blue-green saucers.

"Oh!" the policeman exclaimed.

"Uh . . . Maggie!" Mark interrupted quickly. "This is Jerry

Brown. We grew up together. Jerry, this is Maggie Hastings. She's visiting Foxcroft from New York. I'm afraid she's had a rather bad time of it."

"I can see that," the officer replied with a knowing grin that brought fire to Maggie's face.

With a brief, guilty glance in her direction, Mark retrieved his mangled shirt, and the two men stepped outside to afford her some privacy. Maggie scrambled to her feet, dragging the blanket with her, and her head was immediately attacked by the pounding residual effect of the brandy. She surveyed the room. Even in the dim light, anyone could see that the cottage had been the scene of a romantic interlude. Her panties and bra lay a few feet away. The dress hung forlornly on the chair.

For a moment, her mind raced back to the night before, remembering with a hot flush her lovemaking with Mark. Her gaze traveled from the unused bed to the rumpled blankets to the coals on the hearth. Only a few hours before, flames had blazed there in accompaniment to her own.

They had been unknown things, eerie, unexpected sensations with a life all their own, teased into being by Mark Fox, and him alone. Maggie was conquered, completely consumed by the man. It was a feeling she'd never known, and although her spirit was elated, she trembled with uncertainty.

After retrieving her undergarments, she examined the turquoise dress. It was ruined—shrunken and misshapen so there was no point in trying to put it on. I wore it only once, she thought wryly and, with a regretful sigh, bundled it up with her other things. She took a few moments to run a brush through her tangled hair and drape the blanket as best she could about her naked body. Taking a deep breath, she raised her chin and stepped outside to join the men.

The rainstorm had howled away, leaving the sky clear and the trees glistening. The trek through the forest seemed shorter than it had the night before. Jerry Brown forged ahead, leaving Mark to guide Maggie's progress, which was made slow by her odd, constricting ensemble of blanket and evening pumps.

Mark said nothing as they traipsed through the pines, but he held her hand and occasionally smiled at her. Each time, Maggie's blood raced a little faster and her cheeks glowed a little brighter. Her eyes caressed his broad shoulders, lingered on the bare arm where the bandage showed snowy white against the bronze bulge of muscle, reminding her of her careful ministrations, the smooth feel of his skin.

"Trust me," he had commanded, and shockingly she had obeyed. The birds sang cheerfully, and early light dappled the path they traveled. Maggie breathed in the clean smell of the pines and thought there had never been a more beautiful morning.

The sun had risen by the time the patrol car wheeled into the Foxcroft courtyard. No sooner had they pulled to a stop before the veranda than Rachel, clad in a housecoat and hair net, bustled out the front door. Mark sprang out of the front seat and opened the back door of the car, but before Maggie could make a move, he swept her up into his arms.

"Lord have mercy, Mr. Fox!" Rachel cried. "Is she hurt?"

"She's not hurt," Mark replied as he bounded up the steps so fast that one of Maggie's shoes fell off and clattered onto the tile.

"Hi, Rachel," she called cheerily as Mark strode with her into the house.

The old woman followed. "I been awake all night worrying about you children! I called the hospitals and the police! Y'all about scared me to death! Are you sure she's all right?"

"I'm fine, Rachel," Maggie said as she bounced along in Mark's arms.

"Nothing a hot bath and some sleep won't fix," he added.

Apparently satisfied, the old woman stopped at the foot of the stairs and watched fondly as Mark ascended with his cargo and headed for Maggie's bedroom.

As for Maggie, neither her disheveled appearance nor the fact that Mrs. Fox's door banged shut as they reached the top of the stairs made any impact. All her attention was concentrated on the man who carried her into her room and deposited her gently on the bed.

"Now," he said, leaning over her. "I want you to get some rest. I've got to meet with those businessmen I told you about, but I'll be back this afternoon."

Maggie simply nodded and looked at him with such happiness that a bright smile broke across Mark's face. She'd never seen such a boyish expression on his usually solemn features.

Brushing a fiery curl out of her eyes, he said, "You and me, Maggie. I've got a feeling . . ." He stopped in midsentence, his face subtly tensing. "We could have it all—but first, we've got to put this business of the inheritance behind us."

The reminder cast a shadow on Maggie's sunny mood. But

when Mark's mouth swooped down on hers, she forgot everything in the rocketing sensations he stirred.

She dozed for an hour or so, but found she couldn't rest. By eight o'clock she was out of bed and running a hot bath. She took a lengthy soak in the steaming water, which occasionally parted over her rosy breasts, the sight of which again reminded her of Mark's caresses. Luxuriating in the ritual of cleansing herself, she took a long time washing her hair and scenting her body.

Clad in a robe, a towel wrapped about her head, she emerged from the bathroom to find Rachel setting up coffee service at the vanity. The old woman had changed from the housecoat in which she had greeted them earlier. Now she wore a Sunday dress of pearl gray that enhanced the silver of her hair.

"You look nice this morning, Rachel," Maggie said as she walked over to the old woman.

"Thank you, Miss Hastings. I'm going to church pretty soon, but I heard you up and about and thought you might like some coffee. And—uh—I brought the morning paper."

"You're too good to be true. You're going to spoil me, you know." Maggie beamed as she surveyed the silver service and the neatly folded newspaper. As she sat down and poured coffee, Rachel made the bed.

"Y'all must have had yourselves quite a time last night," she called.

"Oh, yes. It was wonderful," Maggie replied dreamily and took a sip of the hot coffee.

"Wonderful, huh!" Rachel sniffed. "I reckon everybody around these parts is gonna know how *wonderful* it was when they read the morning paper."

"What are you talking about?" Maggie asked as her eyes strayed to the newspaper, and a sudden memory of the journalist, George Haley, burst into her mind.

"Turn to the front page of the local news section, honey," Rachel replied. "It's all there in black and white."

Maggie's eyes widened as she found the story. A bold headline dominated the top of the page: "Surprise Foxcroft Heiress Sparks Duel."

The story was accompanied by two large pictures, both of which had been taken at the Townsend party. One was a head-and-shoulders shot of her smiling brilliantly: The caption read, "'I'll throw them out into the street,' said Maggie Hastings of Dolly and Mark Fox, longtime residents and presumed owners of Foxcroft."

The other picture was of Mark and Arthur. It had been taken the instant after Mark had punched Arthur in the jaw. "Arthur Townsend receives a blow from Mark Fox after a disagreement over Miss Hastings."

Maggie's heart seemed to freeze. "Oh, no!" she breathed.

"'Oh, no' is right!" Rachel snorted. "Mr. Fox's temper is gonna be the undoing of him one of these days. Imagine behaving like that in front of all those fancy folks!"

"Does he know about this story?" Maggie asked quickly.

"Not that I know of," Rachel replied. "Right after y'all got here this morning, he showered and dressed and got Harold to take him into town."

"He's not going to like this, is he?"

"Hmph! *That's* the understatement of the year." Rachel gave the newly made bed a final pat and went to the door. "Don't worry about it, honey," she added with a sympathetic look. "Mr. Fox cares for you. I've known it from the first. Ain't nothing going to change that, including that newspaper."

I hope you're right, Maggie thought as she turned back to the story.

The tongues of Charleston would have plenty to wag about— two of the city's foremost families involved in a scandalous fistfight over a mysterious Yankee woman. Maggie took a quick sip of coffee, but kept her eyes glued to the page. What George Haley wrote was factually correct, but the way he presented it raised gossipy question after gossipy question and painted her as some sort of femme fatale. What was her relationship with Mark Fox? the story asked. What was her relationship with Arthur Townsend? And ultimately, the nagging question to which Maggie herself had no answer: Why had a stranger from New York inherited one of Charleston's treasures?

After she had read the story three times, Maggie leaned back in her chair. Anger welled up against George Haley and his stringy sidekick, then exploded to encompass Arthur. She'd been set up, manipulated like a pawn on a chessboard.

With an indignant huff, she rose, strolled out onto the balcony, and surveyed the beautiful estate that was the center of the controversy. She removed the towel and combed her damp hair. She had no idea how Mark would react to his name being splashed across the newspaper. She hoped that, after last night, he wouldn't really care. But her worries were kindled by the memory of a remark he had made about George Haley: "All you did was give him a headline!"

With a shiver, she stepped inside and began to dress. Worries laced her thoughts, eventually creating a claustrophobic feeling she longed to escape. Her gaze turned to the French doors and beyond to the bright outdoors. She decided to go horseback riding. She pulled on a comfortable T-shirt and jeans, and smiled as she donned her new riding boots. They fit perfectly, the supple black leather conforming to the calves of her legs. Her new feelings for Mark swelled, and she left the house with a light step.

The grounds and stables were deserted. Jeremy, like Mrs. Phipps and Annie MacGregor, stayed home on Sunday. Maggie strolled through the cool barn and impulsively stepped over to Gray Lady's stall. She reached into a nearby bin of oats, then stretched her arm over the rail and offered the treat to the mare.

"Good morning, girl," she said softly.

Gray Lady snorted and eyed her suspiciously, but then she moseyed over. A moment later she was contentedly munching out of Maggie's hand. Maggie watched the beautiful animal and glanced down at her bulging belly.

"Don't worry. You'll be just fine. Mark will take good care of you." The mare finished the oats and looked up with soft brown eyes. Tenderly, Maggie stroked the velvety nose.

"Lucky girl," she whispered before turning toward the tack room.

Lorelei greeted her with a whinny and seemed enthusiastic about getting out of the stall and into the morning air. Maggie slipped the bridle efficiently over her head, strapped on a saddle, and led the high-stepping mare into the sunshine. Moments later they were cantering along the wide dirt road in the direction of the river.

The sun shone brightly overhead, the wind rushed past, and Maggie's hair streamed behind her like a bright banner. They moved swiftly through green fields still sparkling with dew, and she was filled with a glorious sense of freedom. Her spirits rose higher and higher until they burst across her face in a smile.

A few days before, when Mark had led her on the tour, it had taken them a couple of hours to reach the pine forest that shielded the river. But as Lorelei cantered straight along the old dirt road, with no side trips or distractions, they reached the path through the pines in short order. Having been there only once, and with no particular direction in mind, Maggie initially raced past the break in the trees that marked the pathway. She then remembered the quiet, beautiful walk that she and Mark had taken through the pines. Impulsively, she reined in the mare and turned her off the road and into the forest.

Although Lorelei pranced on her trim hooves, eager for a run, Maggie held her back, and they wound through the trees at a leisurely pace. The mare settled into a walk, and Maggie relaxed her hold on the reins, allowing Lorelei to follow the worn path, and turning her own gaze to the tall, cool pines that stretched for acre after acre.

Just as she remembered, the path led her directly out of the forest and onto the bank of a Cooper River tributary. Once more, Maggie caught her breath at the wild beauty of the place. The sun reached through the towering cypresses to sparkle on the swiftly running water and on the tall, sun-bleached marsh grasses that waved in the breeze. The vast expanse of forest and river was quiet but for the gurgle of water and the occasional cry of a bird. It would have been a beautiful scene to paint, and for the first time in years her hand ached to hold a brush.

Lorelei shook her head and snorted impatiently. Maggie swung her leg smoothly across the pommel of the saddle and slid to the ground. It was then that her glance lit on the bridge just up the river, which Mark had said was old and rickety. Maggie took the reins and led Lorelei toward the overpass. Once there, she tethered the mare to a post that stood conveniently by the path, and Lorelei immediately lowered her head and began to graze on the lush grass at the water's edge.

Maggie walked up the short ramp and began to examine the bridge. The slatted structure was old and weathered, no doubt of that. But there were no sags, no missing boards, and when she grasped the handrail and tested it, she found that it barely swayed, surprising her with its soundness. Planting her hands on her hips, she eyed the causeway quizzically. With a glance at the grazing mare and a shrug of her shoulders, she ventured onto the bridge.

When she reached the halfway mark, she paused and took a sweeping look at the beautiful stretch of marshland. The wind whistled past, carrying a heady, salty scent, and she proceeded to the other side. Stuffing her hands into the pockets of her jeans, Maggie ambled along a path that curved away through the grasses, allowing it to take her where it would. The tall weeds reached above her head and gleamed cheerily in the sunshine, leaving her unprepared for the desolate scene she stumbled upon.

As she completed the curve of the path, she was confronted by a clearing and, in its center, a blackened structure long ago burned and deserted. With sudden realization, she recalled Arthur's revelation: "She burned down one of the outbuildings . . ."

This, then, was the destination of Dolly Fox's infamous night ride. As the knowledge registered, Maggie understood why Mark had so strenuously forbidden her to come to the place.

She walked through what once had been the front yard and approached the remains of the building. She could tell from the remnants of the walls that the frame cottage had been small—four rooms and a tall stone chimney. Peering over one of the charred partitions, she saw that there was nothing to be viewed on the inside. Nature had long since taken over, further disfiguring the burned interior with vines and weeds. She stepped back a pace, took a long look at the forlorn hut, and began to circle its blackened boundaries.

She was met with another surprise when she reached the back of the house—a simple solitary headstone marking a grave. As she moved closer, a premonitory shiver coursed along her spine.

Weeds and vines had encroached on the gravesite, too, but when Maggie crouched beside the marker, she could detect engraving on the stone. Her fingers tugged at the tenacious vines, and after working for a couple of minutes, she could read the name: Stella. No dates. No "Rest in peace." Just Stella.

After a moment of wondering about the identity of the woman who lay in such a forsaken spot, Maggie rose to her feet and brushed the dirt from her hands and knees. Thoughtfully, she circled back to the front of the cottage and, with a final look at the scarred clearing, turned toward the bridge.

Perhaps it was understandable that the woman, who could only serve as a reminder of a night of horror, would be left in anonymity in the wilderness. But Maggie rebelled against the idea that anyone who had met so tragic an end should be so utterly forgotten. The morbid subject chilled her warm, happy mood, and she found herself hurrying back to Lorelei. Once they had made their way carefully through the pines, she nudged the mare to a run, and the exhilaration of a fast ride all but obliterated the recollection of her gloomy excursion into the wilderness.

She returned to Foxcroft House with thoughts of Mark uppermost on her mind. She strode through the deserted foyer and up the stairs toward his quarters. Perhaps he had returned from his business meeting. Reaching the second story, she started toward the stairs to the third floor.

"It's true, I tell you!"

The vehement female voice that rang from the direction of Dolly Fox's rooms was an unexpected disruption in the quiet house. Maggie froze. A low-pitched murmur responded to the woman's outburst, and Maggie quickly imagined John Henry patiently trying to calm his mad cousin.

The murmur dropped away and everything was silent but for the calm ticking of the nearby grandfather clock. Maggie quickly scaled the stairs to Mark's rooms to find that he had not yet returned.

This time there was no feeling of trespassing, no John Henry to bar her way. With the license of a lover, she boldly entered Mark's rooms and sank down onto the massive king-sized bed. Stretching languidly, she smiled and soaked up the essence of Mark that pervaded the place. His ruined clothes from the night before had been carelessly tossed on a chair. The scent of his after-shave lingered in the air.

Folding her hands behind her head, she gazed around the room, taking in the sporting prints that crowded the pine walls, the horse show ribbons and trophies, the hefty books propped on the desk. She noticed the corner of a sheet-covered parcel jutting out from behind the desk. A quick frown furrowed Maggie's brow as her gaze focused on the object, which was almost completely hidden. Just as quickly, she remembered Mark running through the rain from the library, carrying a rectangular object covered with a sheet.

Suddenly the phone rang. Thinking that it might be Mark, she scrambled off the bed and across the room.

"Hello!" she said breathlessly into the phone.

"Margaret Elizabeth Hastings, please," a gruff voice answered.

"This is Maggie Hastings," she replied, puzzled by the use of her full name.

"Ah, Maggie . . . I see," the voice stumbled. "Miss Hastings, please allow me to introduce myself. I'm Captain Jack Lewis, an old friend of your father's."

"My father?"

"Yes, ma'am. Knew him years ago, and a fine man he was, too. And when I saw your picture in the paper this morning, well,

I just had to call and pay my respects. I called several times earlier this morning, but there was no answer."

"Oh, yes," she replied. "I went out for a ride."

"My, my, a horsewoman. I'm sure your father would be proud."

"Excuse me?" Maggie said. She was bewildered by the comments the stranger was making. Yet she felt no threat.

"Yes, ma'am. I remember those old times as if they were yesterday. I warrant there's many a tale I could tell you. In fact, I've got a few things here that belonged to your father."

"Things of my father's?"

"Yes, things he left behind all those years ago. Why, nothing would give me greater pleasure than to pass them along to you. I would have done so a long time ago, but I didn't know where you were, not until this morning. And to find out you're right here in Charleston, right here!"

"Yes, well, I just arrived a few days ago, Captain . . ."

"Lewis," he supplied. "But please call me Captain Jack. All my friends do."

"Okay, Captain Jack. You say you have some things that belonged to my father. What sort of things?"

"Why, there's a whole trunkful of stuff here. I've kept it safe and sound all these years. I had a feeling our paths would cross one day. And now that they have, I've got a good idea. I own a restaurant down here in the District. It's called Cap'n Jack's Queen, and it would be an honor for me to serve you lunch, compliments of the house. Why, it would be a small thing compared to everything your daddy did for me."

"That's nice of you," Maggie replied. Her typical caution was quelled by the kindliness of the man's voice. "I'd love to meet you, and have lunch. When would you like me to come?"

"No time like the present," he answered with a good-natured chuckle. "Why don't you drive on in today?"

"Today?" Maggie echoed and glanced at her watch. Eleven o'clock. Rachel was at church, and who knew when Mark would return? She still had the keys to the Mercedes.

"Sure," she answered. "How about today at twelve-thirty?"

With a last possessive glance about Mark's room, she returned to her quarters and donned a white sundress with a full skirt. Allowing her hair to hang free, she fixed gold loops in her ears and gazed at herself assessingly. Despite a lack of sleep, her turquoise eyes sparkled brightly, and the South Carolina sun had kissed her with golden highlights that gleamed from her hair and skin. She had never looked better.

Perhaps, she thought with a quick memory of Mark, it wasn't *all* due to the Carolina climate.

Noonday sun flooded the streets of Charleston. It shimmered on the white buildings and sidewalks, lighting up the azaleas that spilled through the city in bright splashes of pink, fuchsia, and snowy white.

Maggie slowed her pace and lowered the car windows, allowing a warm breeze to lift her hair as she feasted her eyes on elegant houses and flower beds. As she drove toward the Historic District, she thought that no place looked more beautiful in the springtime, not even Paris.

Turning onto Meeting Street, she moved into the heart of the District. Here time had been contained and the spirit of another age preserved.

Maggie slowed the Mercedes to a crawl, enjoying the rich feel of the place, realizing with satisfaction that she was beginning to learn her way around. As she passed Wentworth Street she flashed a quick look down the shady avenue on which Mark's town house stood. The thought of him again invaded her, followed by a tingling rush. She was beginning to accept the familiar sensations that gripped her heart and left it racing.

As Maggie drove through the peaceful Sunday streets of Charleston, she remembered a day in Kensing several years before—the day Shelley had married Nathan. With the wedding only an hour away, they had readied themselves in an anteroom of the church.

"I'm *sure*," Shelley had insisted with a radiant smile as she came to stand before her maid of honor. "One day, Maggie, you'll care more for a man than you do for yourself. His needs will matter more than your own. His wants will come first. That's when you'll know what it means to love. That's when you'll be sure, as I am."

With a start, Maggie realized she felt that way about Mark Fox. It was more than a physical connection—that had simply unlocked the door to a wealth of feeling that had been building for days. She actually *loved* him, this tall, powerful man who seemed so invincible.

Last night she had seen behind the dark curtain, had discovered a hungry lost boy who sought solace in her arms. And suddenly all her long-standing barriers had dropped away. Suddenly she had felt soft and tender, as if an unknown part of her had been born. She still felt that way—all new and shiny and full of promise.

Her thoughts turned to the agreement lying on the dresser in the green bedroom. "His needs will matter more than your own . . ." Shelley's words echoed in her mind as she remembered Mark's pain-filled eyes from the night before. "Now you can understand why I must keep Foxcroft. Without it I'm nothing."

Once again the urge to comfort him welled up. It was ironic that she, who had so recently learned to love Mark Fox, should inherit the power to hurt him so deeply. But she thought, she also had the power to undo that hurt. She decided to sign Mark's offer as soon as she got home.

Home? she thought with surprise. Foxcroft had become home. A smile broke across her face. She made her way without error to Broad Street and turned toward the harbor.

A peal of church bells rang across the peninsula as she spotted Cap'n Jack's Queen. Seeing it, she recalled the evening with Arthur, when she had cruised the streets of the Historic District in the Jaguar. She had noticed the picturesque tavern then, with its porthole windows and a ship's ramp for an entrance. Funny that several days later the place would be the site of a rendezvous with a stranger who claimed to have been a friend of her father's. On the fringe of the park across from the restaurant, she found a space and climbed out of the Mercedes.

After entering the restaurant, she paused and allowed her eyes to adjust to the dim lighting. She was unaware of the picture she made, with the bright sunlight streaming in behind her, touching her hair with fire. The eyes of the lunchtime diners turned, and among them was a pair of old ones that grew wide and then blinked in disbelief.

"God almighty," Captain Jack Lewis murmured. With quick strides that belied his years, he rounded the bar and went to meet his guest. "Miss Hastings!" he bellowed as he approached.

Maggie looked in the direction of the voice. He was a bulky, rugged man wearing casual trousers and a flannel shirt. The silvery white fringe of hair and beard suggested an age of sixty-five or seventy, and yet he moved like a younger man. His posture and gait were almost military; it was the only rigid quality about him. As he approached, his weathered face was wreathed in smiles, his blue eyes alight with merriment.

"Captain Jack?" Maggie said with a smile and extended her hand. He grasped it warmly with both brawny fists and began a handshake so vigorous that she laughed lightheartedly.

For a somewhat awkward moment, he only gazed at her in a curious manner as the welcoming smile faded. Just before he spoke, Maggie saw a sparkle of tears in his aging blue eyes.

"Captain Jack Lewis at your service," he then said in a gravelly voice. "And I'm pleased as I can be to meet you, ma'am."

The Queen, as he called his restaurant, was a roomy pub that had been made to look like the interior of an old ship. Maps and charts adorned the walls, and waiters in eighteenth-century sailor's garb scurried among tables aglow with lanternlight. Behind the long mahogany bar, a wall of mirror reflected rows of sparkling glasses.

There was a lot of talk and laughter, and Maggie thought it a good crowd for a Sunday lunch. Apparently Captain Jack had a regular clientele. Many diners called out to him as he led her through the main area and into a cozy private dining room.

"Come in, come in," he said, preceding her to the head of a banquet-sized table. "I thought we'd have lunch in here, away from all the noise. Here, now, let me take a good look at you."

Maggie submitted good-naturedly to his examination, then shrugged as he added, "You sure turned out to be a mighty pretty young lady. Yes, sir, it's downright amazing."

Captain Jack insisted on serving her lunch and postponed all talk of his unexpected invitation until after the meal. "I want you to give your full attention to the food," he said.

The old sea captain obviously took great pride in his restaurant. It was justified. The broiled seafood he served was delicious— Maggie hadn't realized how ravenous she was—and he kept her entertained all the while she dined with stories of the seafaring life he had once led.

"The Bahamas, the Indies, wild times and beautiful seas. Yes," he said, a misty look crossing his face, "those were the days."

Maggie pushed away the empty platter, propped her elbows on the table, and looked at the man affectionately. "Why did you ever leave it, Captain Jack? The sea, I mean."

"Well, I didn't leave it *all* behind. I've got this place, and some of the furnishings came from my ship, the *Indies Queen*. So in a way I feel she's still with me. But why did I leave? Well, I guess the *Queen* got old, and so did I. She was already what I'd call 'seasoned' when I bought her."

The captain paused and pulled a corncob pipe from his pocket. "And that, young lady, brings us to the subject of your daddy. He's the one who staked me out to buy the *Queen*."

"Really?" Maggie's eyes grew round. "But how . . . I mean, I didn't realize he had the money in those days."

"Excuse me," Captain Jack broke in. "But I read that story in the newspaper over and over again this morning, and I came to the conclusion there's *a lot* you don't know."

He lit his pipe, his blue eyes fastened on Maggie. Her heart began to pound, a shiver of expectation sweeping over her.

"I don't mean to butt in," the captain said soberly, smoke swirling about his head in a soft wreath. "But I thought this whole thing over long and hard. You've been out there at Foxcroft for nearly a week. If they meant to tell you anything, they would have by now. So I can only figure they don't intend to. That means they probably plan to pay you off and get you out of the picture without giving you the chance to know what it is you'd be leaving behind. At the least, they mean to hoodwink you out of something that should belong to you. At the worst . . . well, I just don't like the thought of you being out there in that nest of vipers."

The dull sense of alarm that had nagged Maggie for days became acute. Suddenly she felt like a small child watching powerlessly as a huge storm rolled toward her. A dry lump rose in her throat.

"What are you staying, Captain Jack?"

"I'm saying that the man I admired most in this world, the man who staked me for the *Queen* . . . he wasn't Mr. Hastings. He was your natural father, William Fox."

As soon as she heard the captain's words, Maggie knew he spoke the truth. It was as if a shadow that had danced in the wings of her mind had leapt suddenly into the spotlight. A faint ringing noise began to hum in her ears, making the old man's voice sound dim and far away.

"Now, I gather this is a big surprise for you, but I sure hope it's a happy one. Mr. Fox would have been mighty proud of you, young lady, and you can be mighty proud of him. The shame in all of this is that you never had a chance to know him—him and your mother both."

"My . . . mother?"

"Stella," he said, and Maggie blinked as he spoke the name she had read on the forlorn headstone only that morning.

"She was a mighty pretty lady, and you're the spittin' image of her. When I saw that picture of you in the paper, I recognized you right off. And when you walked in here today . . . why, it was like seein' your mama all over again. Anyone who ever saw Stella would know who you are, and that includes the people out at that estate. If they haven't told you, it can only mean they plan to keep the truth to themselves. That ain't right. Not when your daddy meant for you to know and to have the home that was his and his alone to give."

Maggie stared at him vacantly as her brain received shock after shock. She was the illegitimate daughter of William Fox. *That* was why she had inherited Foxcroft.

"Margaret Elizabeth," Captain Jack continued. "That's what your daddy called you. Named you after his own mother. Didn't the Hastingses ever tell you about *any* of this?"

Maggie shook her head.

"Well, I guess it's understandable, the way things happened and all. But now you're here, you have a right to know. . . . It's a long story. Why don't we have a glass of something to wash it down with?"

He poured himself a whiskey and her a glass of wine. With a quick tip of his head, he did away with the contents of the shot glass and began an incredible story.

"It was near forty years ago, not long after the war, when Mr. Fox backed me for the *Queen*. 'You sail her, Jack,' he said, 'and I'll take a percentage of the profits.' He was a good man. He didn't know when, or if, he'd get that money back. But it seemed to give him a bit of pleasure, being in business with me and the *Queen*. Used to bring his paints down to the docks and spend the whole day many a time. He'd say something now and again that let me know he didn't have much holding him at home. His wife was in love with somebody else, he said. She was in the family way when he married her, and she told Mr. Fox the child was his. Wasn't until years later he found out she had lied. Still, he cared a lot for the boy, Mark. Loved him like his own son."

At the mention of Mark, a shudder flashed through Maggie. Surely, he must have known. Why hadn't Mark told her any of this? With quick, agonizing logic, she knew there could be only one reason: He feared she wouldn't part with Foxcroft if she knew the truth. With sudden clarity she saw that her mere existence threatened him. Mark, the tormented bastard son who must surely despise William Fox's daughter. Mark, who had *lied* as he made love to her, had plotted all the while to safeguard his beloved Foxcroft.

A dull ache beat rhythmically with Maggie's heart as Captain Jack's story unfolded.

The *Queen* had made regular voyages to Kingston, Jamaica, in those days, he said. It was there that he had met Stella Matthews. Her father was an American who had failed to return to Jamaica, and Stella had scrimped and saved to earn passage to the States. Captain Jack had thought it foolhardy of her to search for him, but Stella was set on coming to America. Finally, against his better judgment, he had brought her to Charleston.

"I'll never forget that day. We pulled into port under blue skies that hadn't a cloud, and Mr. Fox, as usual, was there to meet us. I told him about Stella, that she had no money and no place to go. I knew he'd take her in. I watched them drive off in his long black car and didn't see them again for a year.

"By that time," he said, "it was obvious to me that Stella worshiped Mr. Fox. Every time she had cause to come near him, she would blush and turn all thumbs. I mentioned it to Mr. Fox, and a funny kind of light came on his face. 'Isn't she beautiful, Jack?' he said. And then I knew how he felt about her. But he was a man of honor, and he made no advances until he talked to Mrs. Fox, told her he wanted to leave her.

"At first, Dolly Fox was shocked by the idea of divorce. But in time she agreed, especially when William offered to buy her a town house in the District. Perhaps she thought she would have more freedom to be with the man she had always loved, Art Townsend.

"William and Stella planned their future. They would marry and raise their children at Foxcroft, the place Dolly spurned as a 'country barn.' But then Art Townsend was killed in an automobile crash, and Dolly seemed to go mad. She clung to William with a vengeance. She would go into a swoon at the mention of divorce, and she ranted and railed so at Stella that William eventually moved her out of the house and into a cottage by the river.

"At first Mr. Fox thought it was just a phase, that Mrs. Fox would come around and everything could go on as planned. But time went by, and she only got worse. Then you came along, and you and your mama were the light of his life. You were only a few months old when he called me out to Foxcroft that last time. We went up to his workshop, and he sat me down and told me his plan.

" 'Jack,' he said. 'Something strange is going on. Stella says she's heard noises at the cottage, and yesterday we found our dog poisoned. I'm worried about her and Margaret Elizabeth. I want to take them away from here and get them settled in Kingston,' he said. 'Then I'll come back and straighten things out with Dolly.'

"He booked passage on the *Queen* for the next voyage. But I never saw him again."

Captain Jack's voice echoed dramatically in the quiet room, the silence adding to the weight of his words. "He sent me a trunk he had packed . . . and this letter. I got 'em the day the story of his death hit the papers."

He handed Maggie a faded envelope. She withdrew its contents and began to read the precise handwriting of her father.

Dear Jack,

I scarcely know what will happen next. Two days ago, as Stella went about an errand in the barn, a bale of hay fell from the loft, missing her by inches. Now she has developed an odd sickness to the stomach that has made me come to doubt the safety of the food at Foxcroft House. The doctor has said she must stay in bed a few days, and after much discussion, I've persuaded her to part with Margaret Elizabeth until we sail.

I know not what mischief is afoot here, but I'll be damned if I'll leave my little girl in a position of risk. I called my good friends David and Myra Hastings, and they came out to Foxcroft today. When they left, unbeknownst to all but us, they took a small bundle with them. I tell you this as added insurance, for I have an eerie feeling that we've not seen the end of strange events at Foxcroft.

I shall stay by Stella's side every moment until I bring her and my little Margaret Elizabeth to you on Thursday. And then what a bright crossing awaits us all! Until then, I remain your friend,

                                                            William

Maggie raised her eyes to Captain Jack's concerned face. The old letter fluttered from her fingers. The glass of wine remained untouched. After a moment she forced a question through stiff lips. "Why didn't they tell me?"

"The Hastingses?" Captain Jack queried. "I've got a hunch about that."

The old man bent to pull an ancient trunk from under the table. "I imagine it was because of these." Lifting the trunk lid, he produced a packet of newspaper clippings bound with cord. He whipped a jackknife from his pocket, quickly cut the string, and spread the yellowed newsprint before her. "After a look at these, I guess they wanted to protect you."

Maggie's eyes moved from one clipping to the next. "Arson at Foxcroft!" the first announced. It explained that two people had died when an estate building was burned. "The deceased," the story read, "were land baron William Fox and his alleged mistress, Stella Matthews."

The next clipping was dominated by a picture of Mrs. Fox. Her dark hair streamed across one side of her face, and the gaze she turned on the photographer was venomous. "Dolly Fox Arrested for Murder!" the headline cried.

On the last clipping in the group, another picture of Mrs. Fox appeared. Her hair was combed neatly, and the dark eyes that stared from the page leered triumphantly. "Dolly Goes Free!" read the bold headline at the top.

"You can see why the Hastingses didn't come forward," Captain Jack said. "The lawyers and doctors got Dolly Fox out of it. She went scot-free. I remember what it was like. The whole city was up in arms. 'Dolly' was a household name. The Hastingses probably thought there was no better place for you to be than with them. Certainly they were not about to take you back to Foxcroft!

"By the time I tracked down their address in Charleston, they had moved and left no forwarding address. As the years went by, I came to think you'd never be seen around these parts. Mr. Fox didn't tell me about the will. Guess he never told anybody but your folks. . . ."

The old man's voice trailed away, leaving the room once again in silence. Maggie rose to her feet, her eyes fastened on a distant spot beyond the walls of the room.

"Margaret Elizabeth," the old man said pleadingly and jumped from his chair. "Please say something."

"Do I really look so much like her?" came a brittle voice.

"Stella? Yes, you sure do. Why, I wish you could have seen

her. What am I saying? You *can* see her likeness. Mr. Fox painted a lot of pictures of her. They used to be up there in his studio. Unless somebody moved 'em, I guess they're still there. I remember one in particular he had hanging up there on the wall. It was of you and your mama both. He called it his Madonna. And that picture of Stella could just as easily be of you. You go to his studio. You'll see it."

Maggie began to move toward the door.

"Wait a minute, young lady," Captain Jack commanded gruffly. "Are you feeling all right?"

"I'm all right, Captain Jack. Thank you . . . thank you for all you've done."

"But . . ." he sputtered as he followed her through the deserted restaurant. "Don't you want to take the trunk with you?"

"You've kept it safe for me all these years. What difference will a few weeks make? I'll be back for it, Captain Jack. You can count on it."

Maggie's last words drifted through the now deserted restaurant, and the doors swung closed behind her.

Late afternoon sun poured through the rear window of the Mercedes, but she felt as if the blood had frozen in her veins. Thoughts and faces and fragmented conversations raced in frenzied circles around her mind: William Fox's daughter . . . Captain Jack's weathered face . . . "the spittin' image of your mother . . . his Madonna" . . . the rain pouring down as she watched Mark running from the studio, carrying a parcel wrapped in a sheet . . . the clean space on the wall in the dusty studio . . . the hidden parcel in Mark's bedroom . . . Arthur Townsend's warning: "Don't be taken in. . . ."

Maggie refused to blink as stinging tears gathered in her eyes. A sharp pain shot through her. She clutched her chest as, deep within her, something new and shining shattered, the pieces twisting and falling, landing like heavy rubble on her heart.

Chapter Twelve

Mark finished filling the numerous troughs with fresh water, then let himself into Gray Lady's stall and began to comb the mare's long mane and tail. The day had gone well, the New Yorkers having been properly impressed with the sweeping beauty of Canadys Isle's tropical beaches and rolling hills. The three men had even begun to point out various sites for buildings outlined in the development plan. Yet Mark knew that it would be months before they reached a final decision. For now it was enough that they had seemed impressed with the site.

After seeing them off at the airport, he had hurried home only to find Maggie gone. He was both irritated and disappointed.

Maggie. Her image had crept into his mind even during his business meeting on the island. Twice, one investor had found it necessary to repeat himself. The second time he had remarked irritably, "Sorry to break in on your time, Fox, when you obviously have more important matters to think about!"

But even that had failed to deter Mark's train of thought. By two o'clock, when he ushered the men out onto Wentworth Street, he had called his cleaning woman and offered her double pay to have the town house in order by seven that evening. By the time he directed Harold to stop at the florist's shop, his plan had taken shape: First, a nice dinner somewhere in the city, then a night on Wentworth Street. Later, tucked away in the cozy bedroom on the second floor, he and Maggie would sip wine by candlelight. He would fill his arms with her and hold her close as he whispered the facts of her past—a story, in some ways, more bitter than the one he'd told her the night before. Who better to tell Maggie she was the daughter of William Fox than the man who had been raised as his son?

A quizzical expression crossed Mark's face as he began to rub down Gray Lady's withers with a soft cloth. He had never talked to anyone about his parentage. Not until Maggie. Something about the tender way she had bandaged his arm, the soft look in her eyes, had drawn him out, and he found himself saying things that were so deeply repressed he had nearly forgotten they were there. All of his confusion, hurt, loss—emotions he hadn't allowed himself to feel in years—had come rolling out like a long-dammed tide.

How, he wondered, would she take the news about herself? Would she be furious that he'd kept the truth from her so long? If so, he could only hold her—take the lashing and keep on holding her until the tears fell or the smiles came. He could only explain that at first he had refused to believe she was who they said, and that, yes, he was ashamed to say, he had felt threatened. Now he wondered, threatened by what? That Maggie might stay on?

She'd only been at Foxcroft a few days, and yet he couldn't imagine the place without her. What would it be like without the sound of her bouncing down the stairs or laughing with Rachel? Without the sight of her swinging backside as she sashayed away in a huff? Without the exhilarating knowledge that he could round a corner and run into her unexpectedly any time he was home? What would Foxcroft be without her? Damned boring and quiet and empty. Just as it was before she came.

Mark had no idea how long his fiery feelings for Maggie would last, but of one thing he was sure: He didn't want her flying out of his life, not yet.

His arms stilled on the mare's back, and he lowered his head to rest his chin where they crossed. He would have to handle Maggie carefully. Eventually, he hoped, she would draw comfort from him as he had from her last night, allowing their bodies to know once again that shattering closeness, that obliterating catharsis that wiped away everything but the feeling of their being joined.

Damn, but it had been good between them! Hell, it had been earthshaking! No other woman had ever had such an effect on him.

How many women have you been with anyway? Forget it, he told himself. Don't even count. Then here comes this Yankee woman who slams the breath out of you so hard you feel as if it's your first time.

What he experienced with Maggie *had* been a first-time thing. She made him think and feel and do the most remarkable things—like buying her flowers. They were nearly past the florist's when he shouted at Harold to turn in. Now the corsage of gardenias waited in the refrigerator. Gardenias. He had associated the scent with Maggie since the first time he held her in the oak grove. He knew without a doubt that for the rest of his life, whenever he caught the fragrance of gardenias, it would bring the thought of her.

The corner of his mouth lifted in a faint grin. He had told Rachel to deliver the flowers while Maggie was getting dressed for dinner. He wondered what she would think of his message. "Last night was only the beginning," the card said.

The grin deepened.

A corsage? A romantic note? Damn, Fox! You're acting like a schoolboy out to impress his date for the prom!

The shadows in the barn had deepened considerably since he came in. Mark let himself out of Gray Lady's stall, then reached over to stroke the mare's face. His gaze drifted to the toes of his boots. Absently, he tugged the brim of the old cowboy hat low on his forehead, then lifted puzzled eyes to stare along the darkened corridor to the barn entrance where the afternoon sun made a square of light.

He had asked Rachel to let him know as soon as Maggie returned. Now the afternoon was drawing to a close.

Where the hell was she?

The sun hung low in the west as Maggie brought the Mercedes to a screeching halt before the veranda. The long drive had passed in a blur as her stunned thoughts distilled into one plan of action. Mindless of anything other than that notion, she stalked into the shadowy hall, leaving the front doors of Foxcroft standing wide open.

She looked neither right nor left as she glided noiselessly through the house. She climbed the stairs, her sandaled feet making no sound on the carpet. Without hesitation she entered Mark's rooms and went directly to his desk. As if from outside her own body, she watched a hand reach for the parcel he had concealed.

She drew the heavy object from its hiding place. Through the sheet, Maggie could feel the shape of a heavy wooden frame. She held the shrouded portrait in front of her and swept aside the covering sheet.

Suddenly she was staring at herself. The same heart-shaped face. The same flaming hair. The same brilliant eyes. Even the same smile, but this smile was directed to the baby cradled at the woman's breast.

A keening wail split the twilight and rang through the halls of

Foxcroft. After a moment, Maggie realized the sound had issued from her own throat, and at the same instant the wall of shock that surrounded her crumbled. As if glued to her fingers, the painting remained in her hands as she ran mindlessly from Mark's rooms and down the flights of stairs.

In the foyer, her frantic gaze lit on the telephone. She let the painting slide to the floor as she grabbed the phone book and tore through the pages.

"Air . . . air freight . . . airlines!" she muttered and hurriedly dialed the number of a carrier. As a reservation clerk answered, Maggie became dimly aware that the overhead light in the foyer came on, followed by the sound of Rachel descending the stairs.

"New York!" she shouted into the mouthpiece. "I want to go to New York!" Her eyes flashed briefly to Rachel, who was halfway down the stairs, a horrified expression on her face.

"Tonight!" Maggie cried into the phone. "As soon as possible. . . . Two hours? Yes, I can make it. . . . Hastings. Maggie Hastings. Yes, I'll be there."

With a rush, she slammed down the receiver, bent to retrieve the painting, and turned to confront Rachel. "Have you seen William Fox's latest?" she asked as she strode toward the old woman. "Quite a masterpiece, don't you think?"

"Lord have mercy," Rachel murmured as she turned her wide eyes from the painting to Maggie's angry face.

Maggie glared at the woman, but when she spotted tears behind the thick spectacles, her temper faded.

"Yes . . . have mercy," she repeated. "Rachel, why didn't you tell me?"

"Mr. Fox wanted to do that himself," the old woman replied with a sniffle. "When the time was right, he said."

"I'll bet," Maggie cut in harshly. "Right after he got my name on his papers and ran me out of Foxcroft!"

"No, honey, no! Mr. Fox cares for you. Why, just this afternoon he said things have been happening so fast he hasn't had time to fit it all in!"

"Rachel . . ." Maggie said in a voice dripping sarcasm. "You'd be *surprised* at the things he's had time to fit in!" She swept up the staircase, leaving the old woman to stare after her.

A moment later Rachel waddled rapidly down the stairs. "I'm gonna get Mr. Fox, that's what I'm gonna do!" She said the words to herself, but they didn't escape Maggie. "He's out there tendin' that mare."

"No!" Maggie cried so loud that the old woman spun around in alarm. "Don't get him! I don't want to see him!" She turned and walked stiffly into the green bedroom. "I don't ever want to see him again."

After taking a last shocked look at the painting, Maggie placed it on the divan, piled her luggage on the bed, and raced through the room gathering her things. She saw the file of papers that would give Mark title to Foxcroft. With a sneer, she grabbed them, ripped them to shreds, and pitched the scraps into the air to fall like confetti.

She had just returned from the bathroom, her arms full of toiletries, when something drew her attention to the doorway. She stopped in midstride as her eyes focused on Mrs. Fox. Behind her, trying to draw her back, was the agitated figure of John Henry.

"But, Dolly, you can't be sure of this!"

"Let go of me," the woman ordered, snatching her arm from John Henry and stepping into the room. "I'm sure! For the first time in years I'm sure! I *know* what I saw."

She turned, her gaze rising to meet Maggie's. Dolly Fox cut a somber figure, dressed in black and carrying her cane, but holding herself erect, seeming statuesque despite her slight size. A streak of gray sliced through the dark hair, but the eyes were as black as those in the portrait painted thirty years before. They traveled wildly over Maggie's face.

"Where are you going?" she demanded.

"Back to New York, you'll be happy to hear," Maggie snapped. Now that she knew the truth, she was no longer frightened by Mrs. Fox. In fact, she felt a flare of vengefulness toward the woman who had tormented Maggie's own flesh and blood. A cold smile touched her lips at the irony. After all these years, Dolly Fox would finally be ousted from Foxcroft by the daughter of William and Stella. The madwoman could rave all she liked, but she couldn't undo the decision Maggie had made. She crossed to the bed and began to pack.

"There's something I must say to you," came Mrs. Fox's dry voice. As Maggie glanced up, the mistress of Foxcroft limped slowly toward her.

"I've heard enough for one day," Maggie replied curtly. The woman surprised her by lunging forward and grabbing her arm.

"You must listen!" she cried. "Please!"

Maggie turned her gaze from the bony fingers on her arm to the pleading face of Dolly Fox.

"All right," she heard herself say. "What is it?"

"The first night you came here," the dark-haired woman began, "when you walked into the dining room, it was like seeing Stella. For years I had been unable to picture her. In my dreams she would appear in a white dress like the one you're wearing, with her hair falling loose over her shoulders. But in the center, where her face should have been, there was only blackness. Then you walked into the room, and suddenly there was Stella! I thought, My God! She's come back to haunt me!"

Maggie broke into the woman's ravings and began closing up her suitcases. "I've got a plane to catch."

"No, wait!" Dolly Fox cried. "Hear me out! Something very important began to happen!"

Impatiently, Maggie placed her luggage on the floor, folded her arms across her chest, and turned to the older woman.

"At first I thought it was just a dream," Mrs. Fox continued. "But then it began to come to me in the daylight, taking on more color and more life until I knew it was real. It was the memory of that night long ago, a memory I had buried so deep that it took the sight of your face to bring it back!"

A glazed look came over the woman's black eyes. "I had been drinking; I drank a lot in those days. It was late, and I was lonely. I went up to William's studio, but he wasn't there. And I knew . . . I *knew* he was out there with her. I was furious. My Art had been killed, and I couldn't bear the thought of William with Stella. I ran to the stables, saddled my horse, and raced toward the river cottage.

"I remember the clatter of hooves as my horse cantered across the bridge. I rounded the curve and galloped into the clearing. But the cottage was on fire. I reined in as quickly as I could. The heat was searing, and the noise of the fire was deafening. Suddenly I heard a cry, and something—someone—ran toward me all aflame. My horse reared, and I was thrown!"

Her voice had begun to rise, and a look of panic crossed her face. "Later, no matter how I tried, I couldn't remember what happened that night. But since I first saw you, little by little, things have begun to come to me. Now I know the truth, thank God.

"*I* didn't do it! *I* didn't hurt anyone. The fiery figure that ran toward me was your mother, and the cry that I heard was hers. 'Harold!' she screamed. 'Harold!' And then . . . the fire—"

Mrs. Fox's voice broke, and tears began to spill from her dark eyes as she buried her face in her hands.

A moment later, when she looked up, she found Maggie's stricken gaze still on her. But Maggie was seeing the image of the smiling woman in the portrait, her newfound mother, going up in flames.

"You have no idea what's it was like," Mrs. Fox was saying. "To be put on trial. To have friends turn against you. To wonder yourself what you're capable of. Life has been living hell for me."

"No more," came a thin voice Maggie recognized as her own. "Please, no more."

"I may be many things," Dolly went on, "but it wasn't *I* who caused the fire. It was Harold!" She bit the name off as if it had a bitter taste.

Suddenly the image of Stella vanished from Maggie's mind, and she was staring into the tear-streaked face of Dolly Fox. Once again she was standing in the elegant guest room at Foxcroft, realizing what hurt most in all of this bizarre revelation. A knife twisted in her heart, and the blade was Mark's deceit. She turned a swift, bleak look on Mrs. Fox.

"I must go," she said simply and swept away, borne forward by a sense of betrayal so dark it clouded her vision.

She hurried past the silent, gaping face of John Henry and ran down the stairs, oblivious of Mrs. Fox, who followed her to the staircase. Behind her, at the top of the stairs, the woman in black dropped her cane and, with considerable effort, held the Madonna portrait high above her head so the two people waiting below could easily see it.

Maggie reached the bottom of the staircase where Rachel and Mark stood quietly in the foyer. All of them were too preoccupied to notice the stealthy retreat of the man who had been listening from the dining room. His thick face contorted with rage, Harold slipped quietly through the kitchen and out the back door.

"What's going on?" Mark's voice boomed.

With a brief accusatory glance in Rachel's direction, Maggie walked up to him.

"Go back to your mare!" she spat.

Oh God! Mark thought as he searched her face. It was the most beautiful face he'd ever seen. But now it wore a look of frigid detachment. During the past few days he'd seen many emotions in those turquoise eyes—the glitter of outrage, the twinkle of merriment, even the soft, liquid look of desire. But never had he seen such utter opacity, as if there were nothing behind those eyes but an empty shell. An unfamiliar pang of dread shot through him.

"Wait just a minute!" he commanded, grabbing her arm so that she dropped a bag.

He continued to hold her wrist until she wrenched it free and looked up at him furiously. Later she would recall each detail of his face—the burning eyes, the tense expression. But at that moment she was blind to everything except that he had deceived her.

"You're *good*, Mark," she said coldly. "*Very* good. I can see where your reputation comes from. No wonder you figured you could talk me into just about anything. You could have, you know."

"Maggie," he said tenderly, "you don't understand—"

"I understand perfectly. How long did it take you to hatch your little plot? Keep the secret. Romance her. Get her to sign the agreement—quickly now, before she finds out! Then we'll get rid of her, and if she objects, it'll be too late!"

"It wasn't like that, Miss Hastings," Rachel spoke up, taking a hesitant step toward the angry couple.

Maggie never glanced in her direction. "Arthur Townsend is right about you. He may be a pompous ass, but he's got *you* pegged. Last night you made me believe in you. I fell for your little scheme; I actually believed you had every right to Foxcroft and I had none! I actually felt guilty for wanting it! Of course, that was before I knew that my own father meant for me to have this place!"

Mark's blood pounded at his temples. "Maggie—" he tried again.

"You lied to me," she interrupted. "I asked you what was going on, and you looked straight at me and lied!"

Mark swallowed with some difficulty. "I was going to tell you the truth. Believe me."

Like a whip, Maggie's hand landed with a resounding crack across his cheek. Rachel gasped in the background, but Mark took the blow quietly. Slowly, as if the slap had sapped his energy, he turned back to face her. His handsome face was scarlet, but he only looked at her mutely.

Maggie stared back for a strained moment, then retrieved her bag and walked down the hall. She was nearly to the door when she whirled around to face the four people who watched her, dumbfounded.

"I'm going to New York to settle my affairs, but I'll be back! I expect you to be out of here within the month!"

She ran down the front steps, threw her luggage into the Mercedes, and roared away from the house. When she glanced into the rearview mirror, her dry eyes clearly beheld Mark's tall frame in the doorway.

"I simply cannot endorse this course of action," Morely bellowed, his shrewd conservatism giving way to indignation.

"You've made that perfectly clear," Maggie responded.

"The inheritance taxes are staggering. Operating costs are high. And come January you'll be looking at property taxes. Also, I might point out, you're completely inexperienced at running a place like Foxcroft. In six months your expenses will have obliterated your insurance settlement. And the only income you'll have is a monthly rental on your parents' house in Kensing."

"I'll think of something," she said. It couldn't be as impossible as Morely said. Foxcroft was *hers*, dammit! She'd fight for it if necessary.

"You could live luxuriously, without a financial worry, on the proceeds from Mark Fox's offer," Morely went on. "It's eminently fair, even generous. Why in God's name do you insist on refusing it?"

"I simply must," Maggie returned stubbornly. "Now, will you process this will, or are you going to force me to turn to one of your less celebrated associates?"

She left Albert Morely to shake his head and cluck scoldingly. But he had agreed to do her bidding, and she knew that although he disagreed with her decision, he would serve her interests impeccably.

At first, the days passed slowly, but once she started preparing to depart, Maggie found that time began to race. She sold her car, rented the house, and stored many of the furnishings. She took her time in choosing the belongings and mementos she would take to her new life. Luggage and boxes filled the barren living room.

The evening before she was to leave, she and Shelley lounged comfortably on the sofa while a fire crackled on the familiar hearth. It was the last of the firewood that David and Myra

Hastings had stacked, and as she stoked the flames, Maggie felt that something never to be recovered was going up in smoke.

"Maggie," Shelley said, "are you sure you want to do this?"

"I'm sure," came the short reply.

"But what are you going to do down there?"

"Live."

"All alone?" Shelley reached out to touch Maggie's shoulder. "This doesn't have anything to do with getting away from Nathan, does it?"

Maggie's gaze jumped to her friend. She hadn't heard from Nathan since her return to Kensing. She was hoping she never would again.

"I'm aware of what's been going on, Maggie. Nathan has carried a torch for you for a long time."

"Not a torch—"

"A *torch*, Maggie! But apparently a dose of flour was all it took to kill the flame!"

With mounting surprise, Maggie took in Shelley's calm smile. "Nathan and I have talked things through. I knew all along that when the time was right, we would. He cares about me and about our marriage. We're working things out, and I'm very happy. So don't run away. Please!"

Maggie breathed a sigh of relief. "I'm not running away, Shelley; I'm running *to* something. To Foxcroft! It's like nothing you've ever seen. It's where my life is now."

"You sound as if your mind is made up."

"It is."

"Won't you be awfully lonely?"

"I won't be alone. Rachel has agreed to stay. She took charge of the moving and settled Mrs. Fox in the Charleston town house. By now she's back at Foxcroft waiting for me. Rachel said Foxcroft has been her home for many years, and it's been her life to serve the Fox family. She says that I'm Mr. William's child and that she considers it an honor to stay."

"She sounds like quite a person," Shelley said softly.

"She is," Maggie agreed. "She's even building me a household. She got Annie MacGregor to help her with the moving, and now, I'm told, Annie is to move into Foxcroft House. The apartment house she was living in turned condominium, so . . ."

"So Rachel took her in," Shelley supplied with a chuckle.

"Right. She wrote me a long letter that brought me up on everything that's been happening, and she sent some clippings. It seems the Fox name is making headlines again. The story is in all the papers. Harold has disappeared, and everyone is taking that as evidence to support Dolly Fox's claim—that it was Harold who set that fire so many years ago. People are saying he should be charged with murder."

"Murder!" Shelley breathed. "I can't believe this. It's too bizarre."

Maggie looked at her friend solemnly. "I know. But now that I think of it, Harold is the one person I've known in my life who seems capable of murder. Dolly Fox reported it was just like her husband to have taken in a crazy man. 'He took in people the way some folks take in stray cats,' she says. She told her story to anyone who would listen, and George Haley, the reporter, was happy to write down everything she had to say. She told him all about me."

"What do you mean—all about you?"

Maggie stood and wandered restlessly to the fire. "That I am her husband's illegitimate daughter. That I was spirited away when I was a baby. That no one knew where I was or even if I was alive. She told Haley that I had come to Foxcroft without knowing anything and that the sight of me had made her remember . . . because I look so much like my mother."

Maggie's voice trailed off, and she stared a moment longer into the flames. Then she turned and tossed Shelley a bitter smile. "The story made very good reading. I'm sure George Haley's readership is soaring!"

Shelley regarded her compassionately. "Are you sure you want to walk back into all that?"

"I'm sure," Maggie replied, taking on a brighter look. "When you see Foxcroft, you'll understand."

Shelley decided to broach the forbidden subject. "And what about Mark Fox?" she asked. "Have you heard from him?"

"No," Maggie snapped.

That wasn't quite true. He had called the night she arrived in Kensing, but she had hung up on him. Since then—nothing. During the past weeks, she'd reviewed their love affair scathingly, seeing it more and more clearly for what it was, something tawdry and cheap.

"Did Rachel have anything to say about Mark?" Shelley asked stubbornly.

Maggie looked at her friend. Though she would have denied it to anyone who asked, the very sound of his name still caused her blood to race.

"Rachel says he's gone crazy. She says he moved all his furniture out into the courtyard and then just drove off. The next day he was out in the pasture, just outside the line between my property and his. He had a crew of men with him, and they started constructing a building. John Henry, of all people, helped him. Mark told Rachel that he intends not only to move his horses there but also to live there himself!"

"Aha!" Shelley exclaimed. "I knew it. And all this time you've been trying to convince me that he doesn't care for you, that he only used you."

"It's true! Don't you see?" Maggie didn't realize how hard her expression had turned, how harsh her tone. "That night in the cottage I told him that if I thought I had any right to Foxcroft, I'd fight him for it. So what did he do? He made love to me, won me over. It was disgusting the way I fell for his scheme. The next morning I was ready to sign his damned papers! I had been warned. I should have known better. Mark Fox seduced me, and the whole time he was making a fool of me!"

"So that's it," Shelley pointed out softly. "It's your *pride* that's hurt."

"Not just my pride," Maggie admitted abruptly. "I thought . . . He made me think . . . Forget it. I don't want to talk about it."

"But maybe you should, Maggie. At least *think* about it. A man who didn't care for you wouldn't choose to live in the middle of a field just to be near you."

"More likely to be near Foxcroft!"

"I don't believe that," Shelley insisted. "Don't you think it's possible you've misjudged Mark?"

Memories flashed through Maggie's mind. "Just put your name on the dotted line so I can have my house back!" he had shouted angrily. "You're better off leaving," he had said with a dark look. Every time she thought of such things, she felt an ache in her throat.

"It's quite simple, really," Maggie said finally. "The man can be charming, but he's a con artist, and I was very nearly another of his marks. As soon as he romanced me into signing his papers, he would have dropped me from his life. There's no lesson to be learned here."

"I disagree. I think you've learned something very important, Maggie. All these years you waltzed along—here in town, in

Paris, in New York—and men fell at your feet so readily, so easily. Too easily. You never had to give anything or even feel anything. Whether you admit it or not, Mark Fox taught you something. You finally learned how it feels to care."

Tears welled up in Maggie's eyes, but she tossed her head and looked at Shelley defiantly until the tears receded, leaving only a feral sparkle. "If that's true, then I've also learned how it feels to be betrayed!"

A sympathetic expression crept to Shelley's face. "Maggie, you're so quick to condemn anyone who falls from grace. I'm afraid you're condemning the one man in your life who's made you care."

A passionate image of Mark swept through Maggie's mind, dark hair falling across his brow, green eyes glittering between nearly closed lids. "Trust me," he had whispered before his lips crushed hers. It had been so easy for him. He had kissed her, and she had yielded. Proud Maggie Hastings, brought low by a drawling Don Juan.

"Can't you give Mark Fox the benefit of the doubt?" Shelley persisted.

Maggie turned away from her friend. "No, I can't," she replied coldly.

But even Maggie's bitterness toward Mark had failed to diminish the urge she felt to return to Foxcroft. She had been gone a month, and now the place seemed curiously unreal, as if she had conjured it up on a warm, fragrant night. Yet there had not been an hour left unconsumed by her memories. Her dreams swam with images of Mrs. Fox and Rachel, Captain Jack and John Henry. And several times she had wakened with a start, the memory of Mark's lips still burning on her own. The thought of him haunted her. But she had made a promise to herself—to exorcise him from every part of her, to return to Foxcroft with the clear head and unencumbered heart she would need to begin anew.

The next morning she would fly south to claim the home and the life that were her birthright.

PART TWO

Pride goeth before destruction,
And an haughty spirit before a fall.
—Proverbs 16:18

Chapter Thirteen

Sunlight streamed through the restaurant window, illuminating the white hair that fringed the old man's head, so that he looked quite angelic.

"They were to have been yours," he said in a raspy voice.

Maggie had directed the cabbie at the airport to take her straight to the Queen, and as she expected, Captain Jack was pleased to see her. He had hustled her into the private dining room and produced the contents of the trunk. She turned from his kindly face and took a last look at the fine-stitched embroidery on the small garments. With a feeling of wonder, she returned the baby dresses to the chest.

"Stella did that with her own hands," the captain ventured. "You were a very much loved little girl."

A lump rose to Maggie's throat. "I *was* loved, by two very fine people who gave me a wonderful home and life. I just never knew about this other love." A wistful look crossed her face. "But I always felt there was *something* . . . something that called to me. Now I've found it."

She closed the trunk and studied the captain with misty eyes. "Thank you for everything, Captain Jack. You've been a real friend to me. If ever there's anything I can do for you . . ."

She let the words trail off as the old captain tipped back his cap and grinned.

"Now that you mention it, how about a date?"

She chuckled lightly.

"The mayor gave me a couple of box tickets to the last Spoleto concert, the finale of the festival. It'll be out at Middleton Place next Saturday. They're going to have fireworks. I wasn't going, but it occurs to me that it might be something a young lady like you would enjoy. Would you like to be my guest?"

Maggie smiled, a special fondness glowing in her eyes. "Captain Jack, I'd love to go."

Together they loaded the trunk into a taxi, and during the long

211

ride to the plantation, Maggie's eyes often strayed to the old chest with the leather bindings and brass lock. It had yielded treasure after treasure—her own lacy christening gown, her mother's sewing supplies, her father's leather-bound journals, which she intended to read, and even a small tortoiseshell box containing the gold fox-head ring she had seen in his portrait. The memorabilia and dreams of parents she had never known.

David and Myra Hastings would always hold a place in her heart. But as Maggie had looked through the possessions of William Fox and Stella Matthews, she had felt a new bond form. When she returned to Foxcroft, it was as their daughter.

Mark Alexander Fox—owner of thousands of acres of rich Carolina property, real estate developer *extraordinaire*, chairman of a multimillion dollar corporation—hung his hammer on a rough-hewn board and wiped running sweat from his brow with the back of a grimy hand.

Squinting up at the sky, he saw that it was still clear and pale, seemingly bleached by the high sun that beat down mercilessly upon his bare back and shoulders. It had been so for days, the golden sphere burning away even the wisp of a cloud as it blazed down on the half-dozen shirtless workmen, leaving their limbs and faces roasted.

Mark's skin had blistered several times over, but he refused to surrender to the pain. His skin had simply turned ever darker so that now he resembled the Indians who had roamed the low country centuries before.

He stepped back and, resting his hands on his hips, took a critical look at the partially completed wall jutting away from the house. Due largely to his own energy, the new structure had risen from the ground like a weed. He had called in favors from carpenters, electricians, and plumbers to get the two-story house constructed in just a few weeks. It was a simple building with open rooms and rough cedar walls. But it was perfectly adequate to shelter him and his uninvited house guest, John Henry, who had refused to move to the city, insisting on residing as close as possible to Foxcroft House.

All that remained to be built was a complex of horse stalls that would extend from either side of the house. They were barely begun. It would be weeks before Mark could move his animals from Foxcroft stables.

He walked to the cooler that stood beneath the single nearby oak and withdrew a cold beer, then leaned against the tree trunk and took a long swig. His eyes turned across the expansive green field to where the white chimneys of Foxcroft towered beyond the red-roofed barn. Rachel had said that Maggie was due to arrive that day. For all he knew, she was already there, settling into the spacious rooms of the grand old house.

He turned back to the workmen who labored at one of the stalls. Who would have thought he'd ever be reduced to living in a hastily built house in the middle of a field?

But you don't *have* to live here, an inner voice challenged.

It was true. He could have bought, or built, nearly anywhere. When Mark had been questioned about his odd choice of residence, he'd announced glibly that he wanted to be nearby when the new mistress of Foxcroft House came to her senses and vacated. The truth was that he was driven to remain near Foxcroft by the same resentment that motivated John Henry.

Taking another gulp of beer, he recalled the day Maggie had raged away. "I expect you to be out of here within the month!" she had shouted. After that, he'd lost his mind for a while. He had hauled his belongings out of the house and thrown himself maniacally into the building of his odd-looking new home.

The thing he'd feared most had come to pass: Foxcroft was lost—at least for a while. Maggie didn't know what she was getting herself into. She'd be broke in six months! Hot-headed, stubborn, self-righteous . . . Ah, hell!

As the long days and nights passed and his anger abated, Mark had discovered that the loss of Foxcroft was not the only one he regretted. In retrospect, Maggie seemed a rare kind of jewel—a gem he had handled so carelessly that it had slipped right through his fingers.

He missed her challenging wit and flashing smile. Most nights he had lain awake as a misty vision materialized in the darkness— a rosy face with startling blue-green eyes that had turned as pale as ice when she struck him. But then the angry visage would dissolve into an earlier memory, when those eyes were like dark, shimmering pools as she pulled him down to her.

She had made her feelings clear—resoundingly so when she slapped him, emphatically so when she hung up on him after he called her in New York.

No woman had ever rejected him, and Mark had just about convinced himself that was why Maggie stayed so irritatingly on his mind. He simply hadn't had his fill of her. That was all. In time, his passion for her would have cooled, just as it had with all the others.

He glanced again across the field, a hard look in his eyes. Maggie. He craved her as a thirsty man craved water, but it would be a cold day in hell when he admitted it to her again.

With a few swift gulps, Mark drained the beer can, tossed it on a nearby trash pile, and went back to work.

A high sun pierced the trees, dappling the sandy road as the taxi turned between the markers and onto the avenue lined with oaks. Once again, the grandeur of the place made Maggie catch her breath. The driver seemed as impressed as she. The auto crept along, giving her time to devour the sight of the rolling green lawns and, ahead, the circular courtyard. Beyond, the white walls of Foxcroft reached high against the clear sky.

As they turned into the courtyard, Maggie spotted Annie and Rachel standing on the veranda, waving vigorously. The taxi had barely stopped when the two women descended and helped Maggie out of the backseat, smiling and chattering like a couple of happy magpies. Maggie laughed lightheartedly as they went up the steps and across the porch. When they reached the entrance, Rachel pushed the double doors open wide and turned to Maggie with a warm look.

"Welcome home, honey," she said. "Welcome home."

Maggie stepped inside and fell silent. Rachel and Annie sensed her need for privacy. They held back, allowing Maggie to enter alone, her eyes taking in the great hall, the split staircase, and the mammoth chandelier where rays of sunlight danced off the crystal shafts.

Coming to a stop near the foot of the staircase, she turned, her eyes retracing her steps. The same dark atmosphere lingered in the house, but she fancied it reached out to her, tugging at her heart like a dear friend. "I'm yours," it whispered. "Make of me what you will." With a bright smile, Maggie bounded up the stairs.

William Fox's letter had been specific in regard to the furnishings, and very little was missing. The masculine chambers on the third floor, however, were empty. The major surprise was in the opulent rooms of Mrs. Fox. She'd taken nothing with her but a few clothes, and piles of books were everywhere. Apparently she had filled her life with fiction rather than face reality.

Maggie immediately seized on the cleaning and airing of Mrs.

Fox's long-cloistered rooms as her first task as new mistress of Foxcroft. With a vague sense of desperation she was determined to remove all traces of the old.

As she carted stacks of books back to the library, Rachel and Annie took down the heavy velvet drapes from the windows, leaving behind translucent sheers that invited a flood of light into the peach-colored rooms. The dark russet bedspread was replaced by a frilly white coverlet, and by late afternoon the rooms were shining and cherry, a bright contrast to the dull cells that had harbored Dolly Fox.

When they were finished, Annie went downstairs to brew a pot of tea and Rachel accompanied Maggie on a brief inspection of the upstairs rooms. As when she had first toured the house, Maggie was struck by the seemingly endless stretch of bedrooms and baths, which Rachel had kept in perfect order over the years. Foxcroft House was capable of hosting a small army of guests, and as Maggie led the way back to her own green room, she couldn't help comparing the grandiose spaciousness of the house to the diminutive architecture that had become the modern standard.

Flopping comfortably across the foot of the bed, she looked at Rachel thoughtfully. "This place is huge," she murmured.

"It's big, all right. And it's far away from everybody. I been thinking we need a man or a dog around here."

An expression of worry flirted across Rachel's round face, and Maggie grinned reassuringly. "Maybe . . ." she hedged. "About the dog, I mean."

Propping herself up on an elbow, she returned to her earlier train of thought. "You know, this house reminds me of a castle. I can't imagine why anyone would build something this size."

Rachel came to stand by the bed and looked down fondly on the fiery-haired girl, an heiress to a way of life she knew nothing about.

"It's big because it was built for another age," the old woman began softly, "another lifetime, when places like this were owned by planters who lived like lords and ladies. The plantations were miles apart, and when the families got together, it was a grand affair. They'd come from miles around, from up the Ashley and the Cooper and from down Savannah way. They'd come in their carriages and stay for days at a time. All these rooms were full in those days."

Maggie looked at Rachel dreamily, her head filled with images of ladies in ringlets and hoop skirts, strolling about the Foxcroft grounds. "Tell me more," she prodded. "Tell me about when Foxcroft was a plantation."

A look of resignation came over the old woman's face. "In a lot of ways I guess those times were grand. In some ways, ugly. There was a love of good horses and fine food and beautiful houses and good manners. Honor, that was the big thing with the planters. Why, they might duel over an insult to the family honor. And there would be parties and balls, and when the ladies retired, the gentlemen would get together in the smoking room. They'd drink mint juleps and talk about politics and crops . . . and slaves. I know about these things because my grandmother used to tell me stories. She was a slave once, and she never got over feeling like one."

"But that was another lifetime, Rachel, just as you said. Surely no one thinks in racial terms anymore."

The old woman shrugged her shoulders as if she doubted Maggie's naive remark. "You're in the South now, honey. We've got our share of prejudiced folks. My nephew, Jonas, is having a hard time. Smart as a whip, he got a scholarship to the university, and now he's an accountant. But he just isn't getting much work. The folks he knows can't afford to pay him. And the rest? Well, seems like they want a white man to keep up with their money."

Suddenly Rachel's face took on a brighter expression. "But just like everywhere, the good folks in Charleston outnumber the bad. Mr. Fox, he's one of the best. I've had me a good life and a good home."

Maggie reached out to squeeze the old woman's plump hand. "You'll *always* have a good home," she said.

That night, as Maggie settled into bed, the soft sounds of the estate stole into her room. It was like a dream come true, being back. She lay still for a while, absorbing the feel of the place.

A little later she got out of bed and walked to the open French doors. A cool flower-scented breeze caressed her; the katydids and crickets soothed her ears with their peaceful songs. It was so different from New York, with its noise of cars and sirens and people passing on the street. Here there was an air of fantasy.

She stood by the doors a full half-hour before succumbing to the same urge that had struck her on a sleepless night a month before. Donning a light robe, she made her way down to the kitchen to heat some milk.

Opening the refrigerator door, she noticed a white box on the second shelf. A note was tucked just inside the cover, and the envelope bore her name. Maggie retrieved the box and opened the card. The handwriting was bold and masculine. "Last night was just the beginning," it said.

Her head began to throb as it all came back—her ecstatic night with Mark, her bright happiness the morning after, her despair when she discovered the truth. She swallowed hard when she opened the box and found a corsage of gardenias.

The blossoms, once white and fragrant, were brown and wilted, steeped in the cloying scent of dead, decaying things. Her gaze drifted back to the note she still held in her left hand. "Last night was just the beginning." The beginning of *what*, Mark? she wondered. Your treachery?

She dropped the note atop the withered flowers. With all thoughts of warm milk wiped from her mind, she tossed the box into a wastebasket and left the room.

Days slipped by, and life at Foxcroft assumed a routine. Another woman might have been lonely so far from the bustle and companionship of a town, but not Maggie. Except for the long string of meaningless relationships, she had always been alone. For as long as she could remember, there had been only a few close friends, a few loved ones. Now she had Annie and Rachel to lean on, and between their friendship and her own special feelings for Foxcroft, she was creating a new kind of happiness for herself.

She set herself the task of learning everything about the place. There was not a closet left uninvestigated, not a curve of the land unstudied. She drove herself hard, rising early and staying up most nights beyond midnight as she made her way through the household records Mark had kept over the years.

She admitted to no one that Mark was the cause of her frenzied pace. When she slowed enough to entertain leisurely thoughts, memories of him sneaked cruelly into her mind. But Maggie was more determined than ever to forget Mark Fox and his Machiavellian ways. With his deceitful silence, he'd told her more than a thousand words could. When Rachel occasionally brought him up and insisted on defending him, Maggie cut her short.

A week flew by, and the day of the Spoleto concert arrived. It was the first Saturday in June, a clear day that dissolved into a clear, mild night.

Maggie knew something of the famed festival named after its

predecessor in Spoleto, Italy. A week-and-a-half-long celebration of the arts, it featured special presentations of music, drama, dance, and the visual arts.

Captain Jack had advised her to dress casually, and Maggie decided on tailored forest green slacks and a cream blouse with a ruffle at the throat. She pulled her hair back sedately with a clasp, but the style only served to accent the appealing shape of her face and the color of her eyes. Donning a light jacket against the cool evening air, she stood back to survey herself. She had the look of gentry, she thought, and with a satisfied smile she went down to meet Captain Jack. She climbed into a dark sedan with bold lettering on the door: "Captain Jack Lewis. Catering."

"You're full of surprises," she teased as they drove along the highway. "Catering now, is it?"

The old captain glanced over and grinned. He wore gray trousers, a navy blue jacket, and a worn, misshapen cap.

"Sure, I cater. Started doing that when I was in the navy, assigned to the Officers Club. It's easy. Put fancy names on fish eggs and liver, and the fine folks lap it up. That's how I know the mayor. I catered his daughter's wedding."

After a moment the captain looked over again to find his young companion staring. "You're something else," she said admiringly.

The drive to Middleton Place was a long one. After traversing both the Cooper River and the Ashley, they turned north. As they cruised through the twilight, Captain Jack told her about the historic site. It sounded beautiful, and Maggie found herself trying to take it all in at once as they turned into the plantation.

The place was ablaze with lamplight. Royal palms and magnolias shielded the front of the massive plantation house. Sheep and ducks roamed the sprawling stable yard, and on the lawn strutted a number of peacocks. At the top of the drive, an attendant flagged them down and gave them directions to the back of the house before racing away with the car.

As Maggie and the captain passed through a gate and along a path between the house and a hedge maze, the sound of the orchestra drifted invitingly on the evening air.

An usher asked to see their tickets, then led them around the crowded lawn. Ahead, the white orchestra shell glowed luminously against the darkening sky. Crowded benches stretched up to the stage, which was flanked by a half-dozen elevated boxes draped with red-white-and-blue bunting. It was to these prestigious seats the usher led them.

About the time Maggie and Captain Jack were seated in the mayor's front box, the orchestra completed its selection, and a round of applause swept through the crowd. Maggie joined them enthusiastically, then glanced at the captain with a bright smile as the musicians began another selection.

An hour flowed by on the cool June breeze. Maggie didn't realize how absorbed she'd become in the music until intermission. It was only then that she leaned back in her chair and turned to Captain Jack, who was busily packing his pipe. She laughed lightheartedly at the old man's grumblings about "classical stuff" and then turned her gaze to the lanternlit boxes across the way.

She didn't expect to see anyone she knew, but her eyes fell immediately on Arthur Townsend and his mother, Isabel. Their heads were close together as if they were engaged in a heated conversation. The sight of them triggered a sour memory, and Maggie's gaze slid hurriedly to the next box, occupied by an unknown couple, and then continued to the third box, where it froze on the face of Alicia Townsend. The dark-haired woman was staring directly at her, and as Maggie watched, she tossed her hair over the shoulder of her red blouse and turned to her escort, Mark Fox.

At the sight of him, all the cold indifference Maggie had cultivated in herself vanished. An ache flared in the pit of her stomach as her heart lurched into a thunderous pace. She noted the casual slouch of his body, the camel-colored jacket, the open-throated white shirt. His head was turned away from Alicia and toward her, and although Maggie couldn't make out his features, she sensed a hard expression on his face, a hate-filled look that leapt the distance between them, damning her from across the crowd.

She tore her eyes away and mumbled a quick excuse to Captain Jack. "I'll be back," she assured him and, stepping out of the box, descended into the milling intermission crowd.

She found herself walking toward the maze. Leaving the crowd behind as she turned onto the path by the house, she reached a recess in the maze hedge and sank onto a solitary bench.

The night was cool and clear, but her thoughts were fevered and cloudy. It was the first time she had seen Mark since her return. For a month she had obliterated each thought of him with bitterness. Yet the mere sight of him across a crowded lawn had made her quiver. In Kensing it had been so natural, so easy, to feel contempt for the man, to step once more behind the barrier of aloofness that had always shut her off from any feeling. But now, with Mark nearby, Maggie suddenly realized it would not be so simple.

Her gaze lingered on the dirt path. She noticed immediately when a pair of black spike heels stepped quietly into view. With a sense of dread, Maggie looked past the shapely legs and snug red skirt to Alicia's face. There was no denying the woman was beautiful, though her face was marred by an expression of superiority.

"So you came back," Alicia drawled.

Perhaps it was the red ensemble; as Maggie looked at the woman, she thought suddenly of a rose, a cultivated American Beauty bred over generations to produce the most refined flower—and the deadliest thorns.

"Did you doubt that I would?" Maggie asked.

"I hoped," Alicia returned, taking a casual step closer. "At any rate, I didn't expect to see you *here,* and with a tradesman no less. You *do* test the limits of propriety, Maggie. A caterer for heaven's sake."

She was looking down her nose as she had probably done for a lifetime. "Just who do you think you are?" Maggie flashed.

"There's no question of who I am," came the polished voice. "Alicia Townsend Harward, wife of a powerful politician, daughter of one of the first families of Charleston. My ancestors helped build this city, and I cut my teeth on social functions like this one. Let me tell you something of the standards governing these concerts: Box seats are reserved for the city's leaders, not for caterers and Yankee riffraff!"

Maggie came quickly to her feet. "Apparently not everyone in Charleston upholds standards as high as yours, Alicia. The mayor gave Captain Jack tickets to tonight's performance!"

Alicia sneered. "I wouldn't care if the President himself gave you tickets! You still don't belong at this concert *or* in Charleston. Why don't you just leave?"

Maggie gave her a hard, level look. "I wouldn't give you the satisfaction." She started to leave, but Alicia blocked her.

"It was quite obvious you made note of my escort. My husband is out of town quite often, so you'd better get used to seeing Mark with me. Really, it's too ridiculous the way you languish over him."

"I'm not languishing over anyone," Maggie snapped. "You're perfectly welcome to Mark Fox."

Alicia raised a brow. "Good," she replied, placing a hand at her breast so that her diamond rings sparkled brilliantly against the red blouse. "Because *I'm* the one woman who can be exactly what Mark wants. From me he can have unending love with no strings. That's where women make their big mistake with Mark. They don't know him. He's like a wild stallion; he can't be roped in like a calf. The harder they try, the farther he drifts away. And then he comes back to Alicia."

Perhaps it was true. He was here with her, wasn't he? Maggie stepped around the shorter, curvaceous woman. "If you're really as confident as you pretend to be, Alicia, why do you find it necessary to seek me out and ply me with your incestuous fantasies? As far as I'm concerned, you and Mark deserve each other! You're both sick!"

She hurried along the pathway as Alicia's taunting laughter rang across the crest of the hedge.

The evening was ruined. Maggie turned her chair so she would have no opportunity to glance toward Alicia and Mark. Still, she felt Mark's morose stare boring into her. When the orchestra began its final selection, and the quick rhythms of the *William Tell* Overture filled the air, she leaned over to Captain Jack.

"Would you mind getting the car?" she asked, her eyes straying cautiously in Mark's direction. He was staring at her, as she had suspected all along.

"Sure, young lady," the captain replied. "But don't you want to see the fireworks?"

"I'm sorry. I'm just not feeling very well." The excuse was partly true. Ever since her encounter with Alicia, she'd felt ill.

She told the captain she would meet him at the entrance, and after the old man walked away, she glanced again in the direction of Mark's seat. This time he was leaving the box as Alicia attempted to hold on to his sleeve. He snatched his arm free, and as Maggie watched his tall shape stalk out of view, she knew with certainty he was on his way over.

Without stopping to think of anything but her reluctance to confront him, she darted out of the box and ran into the fringe of trees that stretched to the front of Middleton House. A night wind whistled through the limbs, rustling leaves and muffling the sound of her steps. She felt a bit cowardly as she moved through the copse, leaving the woodsy cover only when she reached the path by the hedge. Ahead was the gate where Captain Jack would be waiting with the car. She walked briskly along the path, and had reached the gate when she heard Mark's voice.

"Maggie!"

With a start she turned and beheld him. At first his tall body was motionless as he watched her from fifty yards away. Then he took long strides toward her.

As if in slow motion, Maggie turned to the drive. Captain Jack waited in the car, regarding her curiously. Once again she turned toward Mark. He was halfway up the dimly lit path, the handsome lines of his face barely discernible. She stepped over to the car and climbed inside. Just before the door slammed shut, she heard her name called out again—furiously.

Captain Jack pulled away from the curb, and from her safe position, Maggie turned to look through the rear window. She saw Mark pass swiftly through the gate and come to stand in the driveway, his lanky legs planted firmly apart as he watched them drive away. Suddenly he was outlined dramatically against the night as an explosion of fireworks burst into colorful light behind him.

It was nearly eleven when Captain Jack dropped her off. Annie and Rachel were long abed, and the halls were silent. The new mistress of Foxcroft turned out the lights left on for her return, beset by loneliness as she climbed the stairs to her beautiful bedroom.

Mark, she thought with irritation. *He* was the cause of her despondency. She thought she'd put him behind her, but she was still haunted by the way his masculine presence filled a room, the way his dark air of power could turn into a sexuality that stopped her breath. It was her curse that of all the men she'd known, the one who held the power to melt her, body and soul, was a cad. Perhaps, more than anything, she hated Mark for that.

Stripping off her clothes, Maggie left them in a heap and drew a comforting old nightgown over her head. She crossed the room and flipped on the FM radio. The moody sound of violins filled the air, and she was reminded of the night Mark gave it to her. He had knelt and examined the bruises on her calves. The memory was so vivid—the sight of his dark head bent over her, the long hair curling over his collar, the feel of his hands on her leg.

Maggie sat down at the vanity and took a long look in the mirror. The face in the reflection was serene, giving no inkling of the confusion it concealed.

Her gaze left her own image and began to travel about the room through the looking glass. Everything was in its place and showed Rachel's thoughtful touch: the coverlets carefully turned down on the four-poster bed, the chocolate milk sitting on the bedside table, the Madonna portrait propped up on the divan, where Maggie had instructed it to remain until she could decide where to hang it.

As she looked at her mother's image, an idea was born. Her gaze darted to the hefty old trunk she had deposited at the foot of her bed. It took only moments to retrieve her father's journals.

There were four in all—each bound in gold-tooled black leather, each with a brass clasp. Removing the top one, she set the other three aside and climbed under the covers. She released the clasp and turned to the first page, on which was inscribed in gold leaf the single word, "Records."

She began to turn through the old book and was disappointed to find only neat records of household accounts, running columns of cost figures, notes about salaries of employees, a ruled-off section listing prices of art supplies. About ten pages into the volume, she came upon a different-looking page.

January 2. It's the beginning of a new year—for people like me, a sad time. I suddenly feel a need to write, to record my feelings somewhere other than on canvas. If I cannot find some way of communicating how utterly empty I feel, I think I shall go mad.

I completed the winter landscape today and took it to show Dolly. As usual, she tried to admire it, but as usual I could see through her false enthusiasm. She has no care for my paintings, or for me, and after I showed her the canvas, I decided to destroy it.

John Henry ran out of the house and tried to stop me. Poor soul, he's so devoted to Foxcroft. He's forever trying to patch things up between Dolly and me. Perhaps he feels a sense of responsibility, since it was he who first brought Dolly to me as a model.

I remember his nervous hesitancy when he made the suggestion so long ago. He has changed greatly. Back then he was the quaking son of an old but penniless family, someone I hired to help me manage the estate because I sensed his hopeless pride. Now he is the dignified cousin of the mistress of Foxcroft. He clings to the place as if it were his salvation.

Maggie turned ten or fifteen pages and found a similar entry, this one dated February 15.

Dolly insisted that we go to the Valentine dance last night. I suppose I shouldn't be surprised that of all the affairs to which we have been invited, this would be the rare one she would wish to attend. There must have been a hundred people at the Townsend house—or should I say the DeGruy house, since the old Battery mansion came down through Isabel's family, not Art's.

Dolly wore red satin and looked radiant, as she always does when Townsend is around. I can't help but wonder if Isabel is blind to the obvious passion between her husband and my wife or if she simply doesn't care about it. I am a fool. I've been a fool for seven long years, hoping I could make the woman I married fall in love with me.

Time has passed, and we've all grown up. But nothing has changed. I'm still the outsider who adores the prettiest girl in school. She's still the freshman in love with the captain of the football team. She refuses to see that he deserted her in a time of need. For Dolly, it has always been Townsend. I guess it always will be.

Maggie's tired eyes were stinging. What a lonely heartbroken man her newfound father had been. She decided to rest for a while before she read on, but only moments after she settled her head comfortably against the pillows, the journal fluttered closed within her loosened grasp.

Awhile later a dream took her to the library. All alone she stood before the portrait of her father. All alone she watched a tear slide down the painted face of William Fox.

Bam! Bam! Bam! The sound was sharp and loud. *Bam! Bam! Bam!* It pierced the shroud of peaceful slumber that had enveloped Maggie.

"Yes. What is it?" she called, sitting up groggily.

The bedroom door flew open, and Annie hurried into the room. "Saints preserve us, miss! They've driven off with the car!"

"What?"

"Yes'm! The man gave me this letter for ya. Said it would explain everything!" With a quick, nervous movement, the

Scotswoman dropped an envelope in Maggie's lap and fled the room.

Slowly Annie's hurried words made their impact. Maggie grasped the letter and held it up before her. She immediately recognized the handwriting on the envelope as Mark's. Now she was awake, and her fingers hastily extracted the note.

"After last night, it's obvious you want no peacemaking between us. Fine. Then I see no reason why I should lend you the Mercedes. If you check the records, you'll find that titles to all Foxcroft vehicles, except the old truck, is held by Foxcroft, Inc., which I own. Maybe a few rides in a stick-shift pickup will improve your mood. If so, feel free to give me a call. Yours truly, Mark."

With a frustrated roll of her eyes, Maggie plopped back on the pillows and snatched the covers over her head.

"Great!" came the single muffled word.

It was midmorning, a bright sun already warming the streets of the District, when Arthur Townsend stepped briskly into the florist shop.

"A dozen long-stemmed American Beauties," he drawled. "And if you'd be so good as to humor me, Jonathan, I'll ask you to be quick about putting an arrangement together. I'd like to take a look at it before it's sent out."

"Yes, sir, Mr. Townsend," Jonathan Briggs said and bustled away to the back of the shop.

Arthur leaned against the counter, a grim smile on his lips. He had failed to perceive two salient characteristics of Maggie Hastings: She was not easily dominated, and she was often headstrong and rash.

When she rejected his suggestion of turning Foxcroft into a tourist spot, he had scrambled together another scheme—a sort of shill arrangement in which he would send a front man to approach her with the kind of preposterous story that would appeal to her. Perhaps that of a fine old southern gentleman who, through a quirk of fate, had lost his own property and saw in Foxcroft a chance to regain the likeness of his home. She might fall for something like that. All Arthur had needed was a little time to make the knowledge of Maggie's inheritance public so that it seemed reasonable that a stranger should approach her. Time to turn her fully against Mark so that she would be ripe for an alternative offer.

But then his plans had been shattered. Maggie, the daughter of William Fox? Yes, his mother had assured him. She knew she had seen that face somewhere. She recalled that it was on a day long ago, before she had ever imagined the truth about Art and Dolly, when she had visited Foxcroft. It was there in the parlor that she had seen a woman—a servant, to all appearances—who was the very image of the flame-haired heiress.

Arthur had been amazed. Maggie had further amazed him by moving in to claim the estate and insist on living there herself! Who could have foreseen the woman doing such a thing?

Perhaps it was not yet too late for him to make up for his earlier misappraisal. Though Maggie seemed oblivious to the fact, Foxcroft would prove an insurmountable financial burden. All he had to do was wait and, in the meantime, ease himself back into her good graces.

It was clear to see she was on the outs with Mark. Only last night at the Spoleto concert, Arthur had hidden in the maze as he heard Mark approach. Unseen in the shadows, he had stifled a laugh as he witnessed the scene—Mark chasing the bright-haired woman who rode away and left him furiously calling her name.

It was obvious Mark wanted her, and as Arthur stood concealed in the hedge, an idea had crystallized in his mind. Perhaps now he finally had a chance to defeat the rival who had tormented him as long as he could remember.

His thoughts raced back to his childhood, and to his father's rare show of interest or encouragement.

"Good, Arthur. You're improving!" he had called as Arthur cantered a thoroughbred around the ring. "Maybe one day you'll be good enough to ride head-to-head with Mark."

Always, it seemed, his father's comments had been attended by references to Mark. It had only inflamed Arthur's hatred to learn in later years that this thorn in his side was his half brother, the bastard son of his own aloof father.

It didn't matter that Mark had listed Alicia second in line to inherit Foxcroft after his death. Arthur had no desire for such generosity. Nothing Mark would freely give had any value. Only those things that could be taken away gave Arthur any satisfaction. And of those there were precious few.

But now the opportunity he had sought for a lifetime shone before him like a bright star. Not even snatching the Canadys Isle contract could match the impact of taking Mark's home *and* his woman!

Jonathan Briggs hurried over to the counter bearing a vase of dark red buds nestled among fresh greenery.

"Yes, they'll do," Arthur said to Briggs, who smiled proudly.

"Nothing but the best for you, Mr. Townsend," the older man chortled. "And what, may I ask, is the destination?"

"Foxcroft House," Arthur returned.

Chapter Fourteen

There was no note on the roses, but Maggie recognized Arthur Townsend's calling card. With a grimace at the memory of his treacherous alliance with George Haley, she placed the flowers on the dining table and went upstairs to clean Mark's deserted quarters. An hour later Arthur was ringing the bell.

"I'll get it!" Maggie called, but she wasn't quick enough to beat Rachel to the door.

"Rachel. How good to see you," she heard Arthur say as she approached.

"Hmph!" the old woman snorted. "Ain't no need to be spending that charm on me, boy, or sending any flowers out here either. I saw *your* true colors a long time ago!"

"Rachel," Maggie interrupted with a firm tone. "I'll take care of this. Come in, Arthur," she added as the old woman huffed away.

He was an impressive man; the dark European-tailored suit perfectly fit his tall, slender frame. Yet he lacked the sensual impact of his sister, or of Mark.

"It's been a long time since I last saw you," he said as he stepped inside. His look raked her from head to toe. "You're still as beautiful as ever."

With a glance at her old shirt and shorts, Maggie looked up at him with amusement. "Come, now, Arthur. I admit you're unsurpassed when it comes to flattery, but even *you* can't convince me of *that*! Come into my parlor," she added wryly and, leading him into the rose-colored salon, pointed briefly to the doors that opened into the dining room. "Thanks for the flowers."

"I'm glad you like them."

She sank onto the settee. "Sit down. What's on your mind?" Maggie took a hard look at Arthur. For the first time she noticed a hooded, serpentine quality about his eyes.

"I wanted to welcome you back, Maggie," he began smoothly. "And I guess I wanted to make sure there are no hard feelings."

"Hard feelings?" she repeated.

"Yes. Alicia's party. It was so embarrassing—that bizarre scene with Mark, and then the story all over the newspapers the next day."

"Ah . . . And that was a complete surprise to you, I suppose?"

"Why, y-yes. Of course it was!"

Maggie looked at him challengingly. "Let's drop the pretense, Arthur. I know you set me up with that reporter. I just don't know why!"

Arthur looked away and ran his fingers absently through his hair. The gesture reminded her immediately of Mark.

"I didn't know how things were going to turn out," he said, looking at her earnestly. "I was only trying to open things up a little. Mark had hidden you away, and he was pressuring you to sell Foxcroft, I could tell. I only wanted to throw a wrench into his plans. Believe me, I've seen what he can do—"

"I'm beginning to understand," Maggie broke in. "What you did had nothing to do with me. You were only trying to get at Mark."

The supplicating expression faded. "What's wrong with that?" Arthur demanded. "He's an arrogant, ruthless bastard. Just once I wanted to get the better of him. Just once I wanted to come out on top."

"Even if you had to step on me to do it."

"I didn't look at it that way, Maggie. I didn't think talking to Haley would hurt you in any way. It was only later, when I read the sensationalistic story he put together, that I realized I had put you in a bad position. I didn't intend to alienate you, I only want to be your friend."

A sly smile spread across her lips. "After seeing the 'friendly' way people behave around here, maybe I'd do better without any friends at all."

A cold look settled on Arthur's hawklike features, and Maggie sensed that she was getting her first look at the real man behind the gallant facade.

"That's where you're wrong, Maggie. Charleston is a closely knit place. You'll find yourself out in the cold without powerful friends. You've already pitted yourself against Mark Fox and his circle of influence. Don't do the same with the Townsends."

"I haven't pitted myself against anyone, Arthur."

"Oh, no?" he said with a laugh. "What do you call evicting the Fox family?"

"Justice," she replied.

Arthur's brows arched in surprise. "Aha, I detect a note of vindictiveness in your voice. Could it be you're out for revenge? Revenge against the man who almost sweet-talked you out of Foxcroft during a night spent in a gamekeeper's cottage?"

Maggie's gaze hardened.

"You seem surprised that I know your secret," he continued brutally. "I don't know why you should be. Charleston is a small place. The story of your night in the forest with Mark is all over town. Why, you've even achieved a modicum of notoriety; you're being called 'the one who got away'!"

Fire rushed to Maggie's cheeks. "I don't want to discuss this any further," she said. "I don't care what the town thinks, and I'm not out for revenge. All I want is to be left alone here at Foxcroft."

"Left alone? For how long, Maggie? Just how long do you think you can actually hold this place together?"

"As long as it takes!" she snapped. "Don't make the same mistake as Mark. Don't assume I'm unable to run Foxcroft. I'll do quite all right!"

Maggie's angry expression pricked at Arthur's resolve to maintain a calm front.

"Oh, sure, you'll do all right! What will happen when that paltry little insurance bonus is gone? Let's see, that should take a few months, and then you'll be down to the meager rental from the New York house. Surely you don't think that will be enough to run this estate—unless you plan to break it up and sell it off piece by piece! A painting here, a chair there, until there's nothing left! There you go with those big eyes and that startled look. You're so naive, Maggie. Sure, I know all about your finances. And you can bet your life that if I do, so does Mark!"

Maggie opened her mouth to object, but Arthur rushed on.

"Surely no one's ever needed an ally more than you do, Maggie. Your money's going to run out. You're going to have to part with this place for a song, and everyone in real estate knows it. All we have to do is wait. Why do you think Mark is hovering around here like a vulture? Don't forget, I warned you about him."

It took all her willpower to appear unflustered. In a smooth, fluid movement Maggie rose from the settee.

"Yes, you did warn me about Mark," she began in a deceptively sweet voice. "You pointed out every despicable trait, right down to claiming he would stop at nothing to get Foxcroft. Conveniently enough, you never compared your own motives to Mark's. There isn't much difference as far as I can see. Now, why don't you get out of here?"

She had caught him off guard. It took Arthur a moment to leap to his feet. "Wait a minute—"

"No! *You* wait! I wouldn't trust you as far as I could throw you!" She walked out of the room, then waited for him to follow.

"Don't you think I know what you're after?" Maggie asked as he caught up to her. "All this talk boils down to one thing: You want to snake your way into Foxcroft. Well, let me tell you something, Arthur. I *don't* like being set up. I *don't* like your snobbish, two-faced ways. And I *don't* like your Hollywood dreams for this place!"

She yanked the front door open and, with a flourish, extended her palm toward the courtyard where his Jaguar awaited.

A pleading look came over Arthur's flushed face as he reached for her hand. "Please . . . Calm down, Maggie. I came here to make amends, and it seems I've only made things worse."

"Get out!" she insisted, her eyes glistening as she snatched her hand away.

"You'll regret this, Maggie," he announced.

"I doubt it. I'm telling you here and now, Arthur. Don't ever darken my doorway again!" As he stepped outside, she slammed the door behind him, thankful that she had gotten rid of him before the burning in her eyes could shame her. Mark had spread the story of their rendezvous. It was the final betrayal.

Maggie balled her hand into a fist and pounded once against the door. Her instinct had been right from the beginning—Mark's bleak demeanor rose from a heart that was cold and dark. She'd once told Shelley she could imagine him doing something terrible and walking away without a thought. Now she could see him sitting in some smoky bar, relating the story of his conquest of her to his leering buddies! "I admit she took off on me," he would say in conclusion, "but at least I got some pleasure for my trouble."

Tears distorted her vision as she peered through the side panes and watched the Jaguar race away.

A titter came from the parlor, and she turned in time to see Rachel hurry toward her. Unaware of Maggie's distress, the old woman wore a gleeful smile.

"I been waiting a long time to see that snippety youngun get his comeuppance," she called before she disappeared, her mirthful laughter trailing behind her.

Arthur was right about one thing. As the weeks slipped by and Maggie plowed through tax forms and records and bills, she discovered the staggering expense of running an estate the size of Foxcroft. Like a grand old lady, it demanded special care. The cost of supplies, services, and utilities was immense, and Maggie was beginning to understand Morely's outraged objections when she'd insisted on claiming her inheritance.

"I'll think of something," she had insisted to the attorney, but she was no closer to a solution now than when she had first arrived.

Each morning she woke with the intention of spending the day locked away in the library, analyzing her financial position and devising a course of action. Each day she put it off. There was plenty of time, she assured herself as she succumbed to the lure of being mistress of Foxcroft. There were the grounds, the stables, and the house to tend to. Resisting the urge to cut corners and conserve her limited funds, Maggie stubbornly envisioned a new era of grandeur—the opening of the ballroom, the restoration of William Fox's studio, a new bridge and landscaping at the river where a cottage had once stood and where her mother now lay. She'd never been so busy.

Thoughts of New York were few; memories of her previous life grew hazy. Dimly she realized just how much Foxcroft was beginning to mean to her, and just as vaguely she was aware of a metamorphosis in herself. She had assumed a new identity. She was no longer the carelessly rootless Maggie Hastings, but Maggie, the daughter of William Fox. Illegitimate, yes, but nonetheless the last of a long line.

Occasionally the significance of her responsibility struck her. And at times when she looked at herself—as she did now in the expansive mirror-filled ballroom—she thought she could see a physical difference. Dressed in faded cutoff jeans and a T-shirt, her hair pulled back in a red bandanna, she looked as young as ever from a distance. But up close she detected a determined expression that gave her heart-shaped face a new maturity.

She turned away from the mirror she had just finished cleaning. She and Annie had scoured the vast dusty room, stripped away the furniture coverings, polished the mirrors, and waxed the hardwood floors. Now all that remained to be cleaned was the giant crystal chandelier.

Maggie tossed her cloth into a nearby bucket and glanced around the ballroom with satisfaction. The French doors to the terrace stood open, admitting a fresh breeze to the long-closed room and allowing a shaft of sunlight to gleam across the newly polished surfaces. Her gaze lit on Annie, who was giving the floor a final sweep with the dust mop.

"Why don't you take a break, Annie? I think I'll step outside for a breath of fresh air."

"Yes'm. It'll soon be sundown, and glad I am to see ya take a bit of a rest, Miss Maggie," came the Scottish burr.

Maggie stepped onto the terrace. The screen of pear trees had lost the white blossoms of springtime and now shimmered with the tender green of early summer. Honeybees hummed comfortingly around the veil of honeysuckle that hung over the terrace wall. Unmindful of the grime on her hands, Maggie brushed a curl from her forehead, leaving behind a streak of dirt. Her attention was on the beautiful place that was now her home, and with a sigh, she walked to the edge of the terrace and perched on top of the wall.

The rolling emerald green lawns were carefully groomed, for she had enlisted the help of Jeremy's father. Mr. Thompson came twice a week, and although his fee took a chunk from her small budget, Maggie deemed the expense worthwhile. His efforts showed proudly in the well-tended grounds. The brick-lined paths were painstakingly trimmed, the hedges immaculately pruned. And beyond the freshly painted white gazebo, the bright reds and yellows of the rose gardens blazed where azaleas had earlier bloomed.

Over the past weeks, Maggie had begun to accept the pace of life in the South. Like an ancient river, life flowed slowly, leaving her time enough to enjoy vivid scenes and rich moments. This was such a scene, such a moment, and Maggie savored it greedily. A voice came from behind her as she surveyed her beautiful land.

"This place has always been mighty nice," Rachel said. "But seems like you're putting the *pure* life back into it. It never looked prettier, honey."

As Maggie turned to face her, the old woman added scoldingly, "Wish I could say the same for *you*."

"Oh, Rachel," Maggie pouted. "You don't expect me to parade around here in a party dress, do you?"

"You know better than that, but you could sure do with a little more sleep and food. Why, the weight's dropping off you, and look there! You've got circles under your eyes. You drink this glass of lemonade I just made. And tonight, after you have a good supper, it's off to bed with you!"

"Yes, ma'am!" Maggie replied with a grin and took a sip of the cool drink.

Rachel wandered to the patio couch and began to plump the dark green cushions. After completing the small task, she continued to hover nearby.

"Is there something else?" Maggie asked.

The old woman hesitated a moment. "You told me never to bring him up, but I thought you might want to know that Mr. Fox called while you were cleaning the ballroom. He's in Charleston, and he wanted to let us know that a crew of men will be taking his horses out of the stables and moving 'em to the new stalls he built out in the meadow."

"Wait just a minute." Maggie hadn't heard from Mark since the short note and his repossession of the Mercedes. After the initial shock of hearing his name, she grasped what Rachel was saying and her instincts sprang to defend her possessions. "The will . . . Two of those horses are mine. You don't suppose he's instructed his men to take all of them, do you?"

"Why, I don't know, Miss Maggie," Rachel answered with wide eyes. "I'll bet they've already gotten started out at the stables. Maybe you ought to go and take a look."

"I think you're right." Maggie bounded down the terrace steps, sprinted across the lawns to the oak thicket, and made her way quickly to the stables.

Rachel was right. The workmen were there, and the place buzzed with activity under the late afternoon sun. A half-dozen trucks crowded the crude roadway Mark had cut across the property line, and as Maggie watched, she saw a man in overalls leading a prancing steed toward a waiting van.

With long strides, she stalked toward him. It wasn't until she came closer that she recognized him as John Henry Alexander. The sight of him in anything other than formal attire was unexpected, but the harsh look he turned her way was exceedingly familiar. Maggie looked from his scolding face to the beautiful bay he was leading away from the stables.

"What do you think you're doing?" she demanded.

Somehow, even in workmen's clothes, the man managed to look like an aristocrat.

"I'm leading these animals to our *temporary* home. But I assure you, Miss Hastings, I'll soon be leading them back across this nonsensical property line. One of these days, those who *belong* here will again be lodged at Foxcroft!"

He jerked on the lead rope. The bay lurched responsively as John Henry strode away.

Maggie watched his retreating back for a moment, then scanned the stable yard. She spotted Jeremy and called out to him.

He turned and waved. A shy smile lit his freckled face as he waited for her at the entrance.

"Hey, Miss Maggie."

"What's going on here?" she said with a sweep of her hand.

At the far end of the barn, hidden in the shadows of Gray Lady's stall, a man's head snapped up.

"Maggie!" The name was uttered on a soft whoosh of breath, as if someone had socked him in the diaphragm. Mark had been examining one of the mare's hooves. He replaced it gently on the floor as his heart began to hammer. Absently settling his hat low on his head, he straightened and moved to the gate.

"Mr. Fox is moving the horses over to his new barn," the boy said. "Guess that means I won't be coming over here no more."

"We'll see about that," Maggie returned. "A couple of the horses are supposed to stay here, and I'd like you to take care of them. After all," she added, "you're one of the best horsemen in these parts."

He beamed at the compliment. "Sure, Miss Maggie. I'd be proud. 'Course you know I'll be working for Mr. Fox most of the time."

"That's okay. I'm sure we can work something out. Tell me something. Who'll be in charge here?"

"I am!" came a deep voice from the far end of the barn.

A tall figure stepped out of Gray Lady's stall and into the long hallway. The door behind him was open, admitting a flood of sunlight so that Mark was but a dark, forbidding silhouette. As he walked slowly toward her, Maggie found she couldn't move.

Dressed in boots and jeans and a dark polo shirt, he was as she remembered him. The brim of the worn cowboy hat dipped across his forehead. The green eyes burned in a face turned a deep bronze by the sun.

Mark stopped but a foot away and slouched in a seemingly casual pose. Yet his devouring look was anything but casual as it traveled up Maggie's long legs and slender curves, flickered to the bright hair that had escaped the bandanna, then settled on her face.

The face he had conjured from the darkness so many nights. Only now, its sun-kissed color made the blue-green eyes even more startling.

There was something else, something solemn and grown-up that belied the childlike streak of dirt across her forehead. Even with a dirty face, she was more riveting than he had remembered.

"Hello, Maggie."

The sound of his voice triggered an infuriating thrill inside her. How could the mere *sight* of him reduce her knees to jelly?

"Rachel told me you were in Charleston," she said guardedly.

"I told her I'd be here to move the horses."

Maggie recognized Rachel's handiwork. "I see. Apparently, Rachel is still playing matchmaker. She doesn't realize the game is over."

To her surprise, Mark grinned rather dismally and reached toward her face. With a quick, instinctive movement, she slapped at his hand.

So this is how it's to be, he thought. His arm dropped to his side. "There's some dirt on your forehead," he said flatly. He stepped back a pace, folded his arms across his chest, and regarded her coldly. "What's your problem?" he asked.

"I don't have a problem. I just wanted to make sure your men weren't taking all the horses." Glancing around, she saw that Lorelei and a roan gelding named Prince were still comfortably ensconced in their stalls.

"Your horses are still here," Mark said. "But I wasn't talking about them. Why did you run away from me at the concert? I don't know why you're so damned mad. *I'm* the one who has a right to be angry!"

Maggie laughed harshly. "You?"

"Yes, *me*! *I'm* the one who's been thrown out of his house. *I'm* the one you walked out on. *I'm* the one you left standing in the drive at Middleton Place like a fool!"

"Fool!" Maggie hurled the word at him, not believing she had heard him use it. From the corner of her eye she noticed Jeremy melt away toward the far end of the barn.

"You don't know the meaning of the word, Mark," she continued in a low voice. "Please don't complain because I left. Your goal all along was to make a complete fool of *me*!"

"That was *not* my goal! What would you have done in my place? Some stranger appeared out of the North, swooped down here, and claimed my house! No one realized who you were."

"Nice explanation," Maggie cut in. "But it doesn't quite work. One look at that portrait and you knew who I was! Anyone would!"

"All right, I knew!" Mark boomed. "I intended to tell you, but I was too late. I'm *sorry!* Are you satisfied?"

"No, I'm not," Maggie replied in a lethal tone. "I don't believe you. And I don't want your apology. If you apologize, then I have to be gracious and accept, don't I? Well, I don't *want* to be gracious. Let's just leave things the way they are!"

Mark's cheeks had turned scarlet by the time she finished. But he had glared at her for only seconds when Jeremy's voice rang through the barn.

"Mr. Fox, come quick! It's Gray Lady!"

Mark whirled, his long legs taking him swiftly to the mare's stall. Maggie arrived just behind him.

"You told me to watch her, Mr. Fox. You said that if she started pacing or pawing, I was to call you," Jeremy hastily explained.

True to the boy's word, Gray Lady was pacing nervously to and fro, her wild eyes turning rapidly to Mark as he began to talk to her soothingly. "Easy now, girl. Easy there, Lady. It's okay. You're going to be all right."

Clearly rejecting that idea, the mare snorted loudly.

"She's about to foal," Mark muttered. "Jeremy, get the iodine and some clean sheets out of the tack room. Maggie, put the water to boil on that hot plate in there. Easy, girl," he continued to the mare.

Jeremy hopped to his duty, and almost as quickly, Maggie followed. By the time she returned to the stall, Gray Lady's water had broken.

"It's only a matter of time," Mark murmured, his eyes on the mare, his face a peculiar ashen color. Gray Lady began to paw frantically at the floor of the stall.

Jeremy looked up at Maggie with eyes as round as her own. She stretched a protective arm about the boy's shoulders. "Shouldn't you go in there and help her?" she asked Mark.

"Not until after she foals," he answered softly.

Ten minutes later the mare lay clumsily down on her side. Her white-rimmed brown eyes were locked on Mark as his voice droned on in a stream of comforting words. From a spot a few feet from Mark, Maggie's eyes strained through the lengthening shadows to focus on the prone mare. Suddenly a white, balloonish membrane appeared and then a small foot, and another! A nose came into view, and then, miraculously, the remainder of a baby horse emerged! In awe, Maggie found her eyes turning to Mark. He seemed to be restraining himself from rushing into the stall.

"Can't you go in now?" she whispered.

"Not until the amnion breaks and the foal breathes. Not until Gray Lady stands." In a frustrated gesture, Mark whipped the hat from his head and sent it sailing along the corridor. "Come on, baby," he urged quietly. "Breathe!"

As if on cue, the white amnion sack broke and the small dark foal was free—free and obviously breathing. It was then that Gray Lady struggled to her feet, breaking the umbilical cord in the process. Mark was inside the stall like a shot, bending over the foal, and applying iodine to its navel.

Maggie and Jeremy were mesmerized. Together they watched as Mark stood and began stroking Gray Lady affectionately.

"Good girl," he crooned. "You've given us a pretty little filly, haven't you?" As if in understanding, the mare rubbed her nose against Mark's chest and snorted proudly. "Yes, sir, a pretty little filly," he repeated softly.

"Is she all right?" Maggie asked.

"She seems to be." Mark glanced briefly in Maggie's direction. "But I have to make sure the foal nurses." He turned back to the mare.

Eventually Maggie and Jeremy found a comfortable spot in the nearby haystack. Her own maternal instinct flared as the boy settled his head against her shoulder and proceeded to fall peacefully asleep.

An hour passed, and the sun slowly set, the last gray shafts of light stealing quietly out of the barn. It was dark by the time Annie hurried into the stables, a thin sweater clasped about her narrow shoulders.

When Maggie quickly held a finger to her lips, the Scotswoman whispered worriedly, "I've been lookin' all over for ya, Miss Maggie. Rachel didn't know where in the world ya might be. We've been warming your supper."

It was only then that Mark emerged from Gray Lady's stall. "Most of the danger has passed, Maggie. Hey, Jeremy! Time to wake up and head on home."

As the boy got up, rubbing sleep from his eyes, Maggie's gaze turned to where Mark towered in the darkness. "Will you need any help with Gray Lady?"

He ran a hand through his hair. "Well, I could use a little help cleaning her up when the placenta drops."

"I'll stay," Maggie said firmly as Annie left the barn with Jeremy in tow.

Mark reached up, turned on a lantern, and looked at her piercingly in the new light. "Thanks," he mumbled and let himself back into the stall.

The waiting began. Outside, the crickets and katydids sang in the cool night air. Inside, Mark remained with Gray Lady, and Maggie became uncomfortably stiff, sitting on a chair just outside the tack room. She rose to her feet and stretched languidly before coming over to the stall.

Just as she arrived, Mark ordered, "Get the water and some rags."

She was suddenly energized. Bolting to the tack room, she hurried back, spilling only a small portion of the water in her haste. Mark held the gate open, and she slipped inside the stall. There it was—the bright red placenta. Dropping to her knees, Maggie dipped a clean rag in the hot water and began bathing Gray Lady's legs, murmuring soothingly as she had heard Mark do.

He was silent, standing out of her way, stroking the mare's nose as Maggie worked. When she finished with Gray Lady, she turned to the foal and began to carefully wash away the stains of birth. The small animal looked at her trustingly, and Maggie became so absorbed in her task that she forgot Mark's presence. It wasn't until she finished and came to her feet that he spoke.

"You've done a hell of a job," he said quietly.

Her only reply was a quick look in his direction. Her attention was seized again by the foal as it scrambled to its feet and wobbled awkwardly to Gray Lady. Seconds later it was contentedly nursing.

Mark and Maggie let themselves out of the stall and stood just outside, watching the mother and newborn in the age-old ritual. There was a unique feeling in the air. The miracle of birth made everything else mundane.

It was Mark who broke the silence. "They're going to be all right now. If it's okay with you, I'd like to leave them here a week or so before I try to move them."

"Fine," Maggie replied, her eyes dreamily focused on the animals, for whom she now felt a special fondness.

"That will mean I'll have to come over here every day to look after them. Can I assume we've put the unpleasantness behind us? There's no reason for us to be at odds with each other."

Maggie turned to him then, a sarcastic look forming on her face. "No reason?" Like a flood, the resentment she felt toward this man washed over her again. "Forgive and forget, huh? I don't think so, Mark!"

When she began to walk away, she felt his strong hand on her arm. She twirled, an angry sparkle in her eyes. "How you must despise me!" she accused.

Mark's hand fell away. "Why would you say something like that? Because I took back the Mercedes?"

"No! That's the first straightforward thing you've done! I'm talking about the fact that I've inherited the estate. Why can't you be honest for once, Mark? You hate me for taking Foxcroft from you, and you'd do *anything* to get it back!"

"I don't hate you," he blazed, "although maybe I *should*!"

He glared at her, and Maggie returned the look with fervor. Seconds ticked by as they faced off in tense silence.

"There's nothing else I can do," Mark finally stated. "I offered you an apology, and you trampled on it. All I can say is that I didn't expect you to be what you are. I pictured some greedy Yankee who cared only about money. As I got to know you, I realized a couple of things. One, that you had a right to know everything."

Maggie folded her arms across her breast and looked at him sharply. "And the other?"

Mark hesitated, and when he spoke, his voice was barely audible. "That I wanted you to stay."

"Oh, *please*, Mark," she sneered. "I'm not the wide-eyed girl who stumbled into this a few months back. You can drop that routine. It's not going to get you Foxcroft."

"Never mind Foxcroft," he said sternly. "Will it get me you?"

The bold question left her speechless.

His gaze bored into her as he added, "I seem to recall one stormy night when you weren't so indifferent to me."

"You've got nerve to bring up that night!"

Mark's expression turned to stone. "Why shouldn't I bring it up? At least I remember it! You seem to have blocked it from your mind."

"If you really planned to tell me about my mother and father, you could have told me then, that night in the cottage!"

For a moment, Mark halted. When he spoke, the deep voice

rumbled. "If you'll recall, Maggie, reciting history wasn't the foremost thing on my mind. I'd discovered something I thought was more important." Bright color came to his cheekbones. "I'd discovered how I felt about you. I told you, and then I showed you."

To Maggie's dismay, tears burned at the back of her eyes. She raised her chin and lashed out at him. "Yes, you told me, Mark. As I recall, it went something like this: 'I *want* you.' Very effective! Unfortunately, it doesn't seem to have meant very much. Otherwise you wouldn't have spread the story of your conquest all over Charleston!"

She watched the color drain from his face to be replaced by the dark mask she remembered from long ago.

"You've got everything figured out, haven't you?" Mark asked quietly. "Did it ever occur to you that I *didn't* spread any story about us? You're so quick to name me the villain, you never even thought there could be another explanation!"

As if spellbound, Maggie stared at Mark. Even now she felt an urge to believe in him.

"It must be wonderful to be so damned perfect you can set yourself up as a judge!" he went on. "But this is one defendant who won't be begging you for a pardon, ma'am. Maybe one of these days when you stop dwelling on all the wrongs that have been done to you, you'll see some of the ones *you've* inflicted. That day, maybe you'll come to me without accusations!"

Maggie backed haughtily away, her limbs trembling. "That day will never come!" she declared angrily.

Mark gave her a derisive look. "Fine!" he thundered. "I can live with that!"

Maggie spun and swiftly retreated. Mark watched as she stormed out of the barn. Then he turned and leveled a violent kick at a bale of hay.

When he got home, he took a fast shower, dressed in casual slacks and shirt, and thumbed through his address book. When he came to the name Carol Conrad, he paused. He hadn't seen Carol in months. It was damned late to be calling, but Carol had never cared how late he was. Mark stepped over to the phone, and ten minutes later the Porsche was roaring toward Charleston.

That night Foxcroft slept in darkness but for a single light that burned in the green bedroom. Maggie paced restlessly from one end of the room to the other as the memory of Mark taunted her.

It was past midnight when, in exasperation, she stepped out

onto the balcony. The summer night was clear, brightened by the faraway glow of a full yellow moon. A mild breeze tugged at her hair, pressed the filmy nightgown against her body, and brought the heady aroma of honeysuckle from the terrace below.

The ache was back, the wrenching sensation she thought she'd put to rest. She'd let anger and bitterness take hold until she'd almost convinced herself the hurt never existed. But one look at Mark had brought it rushing back, the feeling that her very insides were being torn apart within her.

Tears came to her eyes, but after a moment she wiped them irritably away. It was then that a shuffling noise caught her attention. With a start Maggie looked below to the dark terrace. The noise had come from among the pear trees. She waited, her eyes straining through the darkness, but the noise didn't repeat itself. All was quiet but for the peaceful night sounds with which she'd grown familiar. With a last look across the moonlit grounds, she stepped inside and drew the French doors closed.

Miles away, in a sleek apartment building, Mark shifted in the double bed that was far too short for his tall frame. Carol had fallen asleep with her head on his shoulder. He glanced down at the short-cropped hair that was as dark as his own. She was a good lover; her sinewy body had never failed to excite him. But tonight things had been different. Tonight he'd barely made it through.

Mark stared up at the ceiling. Maggie had stayed on his mind the whole time.

Withdrawing his arm from around Carol, he placed his palms behind his head and closed his eyes. Once again Maggie's face materialized—the soft curling hair, the vivid eyes.

"Dammit!" he said aloud, his eyes flying open.

"What?" Carol murmured groggily.

Mark looked down as she settled herself more intimately against him.

"Nothing," he muttered and turned away from the sleeping woman.

Chapter Fifteen

Thunder rumbled across the estate, the sound seeking entrance through the ancient brick walls of the house and finding it at the open balcony doors on the second floor. Maggie glanced up from the journal as a breeze swept into the green bedroom, followed by the eerie yellow glow of faraway lightning.

"Heat lightnin'," Rachel had commented the night before. "Ain't good for nothin'. Just summertime showing off."

No rain would come. The only shower the heavens would release had already fallen hours before. That was how it had been for the past week or so. In the late afternoon, clouds began to race across the clear sky, swiftly gathering in a dark mass. The wind rose to near-hurricane force, whipping the treetops into green waves, snatching branches away from trunks to toss them about like feathery debris. Then the rain descended in dense, heavy sheets, accompanied by blinding shafts of lightning and cracking thunder.

Once, a few evenings earlier, a bolt had struck particularly close, and Foxcroft's electric power had flickered and died, leaving Maggie, Rachel, and Annie to huddle with candles by the windows and watch as the tempest raged.

Unlike the springtime rains that lingered for a day or two at a time, the summer storms were short-lived evening phenomena. The rain poured mercilessly for an hour or two, pounding at the dry soil whose depths it failed to penetrate, swelling rivers and streams to floodlike proportions as runoff from the parched ground surged into gulleys and riverbeds. As darkness fell, the rain stopped, but thunder and lightning continued to roll across the night sky.

The next morning the heavens would be clear. A hot sun would rise, begin its daily baking of the moistened topsoil, and the process would start anew.

Another peal of thunder. Another mild rush of air. This time

Maggie didn't even bother to look up as her attention was drawn to the slender volume in her hands.

April 10. I have begun a new portrait, and the subject gives me joy. It is Mark. I am painting him astride one of his beloved horses. My biggest challenge is to entice him to sit still long enough for me to complete my sketch. He is so full of energy, so full of life. That is what I shall seek to capture in oil.

Today, when I asked for the tenth time that he keep the horse still, he replied, "I can't hold him much longer, Dad." The sound of his young voice calling me Dad never fails to touch my heart. It is bittersweet because it reminds me that I am not, in truth, his father. I cannot change the past, but I have given him my name, and I can give him the fatherly care I never had, the kind of care Art Townsend seems loath to give his legitimate children, much less his unknown one.

Dolly swears no one knows. I remember when she confessed she was already carrying Mark when first I lay with her. It was, I believe, the bleakest day of my life, my pain granting me the strength to give her an ultimatum. If ever she makes public Mark's parentage, she will be turned out of Foxcroft and away from Mark. This I could do; for although I am not his blood father, I am his legal one.

I believe Dolly will always keep our secret. Fear will make her hold her tongue. And I pray to God Mark never learns the truth, for I couldn't love the boy more if he were my own son.

Reading her father's journals had become Maggie's nightly bedtime custom. By and large, the entries were simply thoughts that had spilled out of his mind and onto the page, explanations of his art, comments upon the estate and its people. This entry touched her more deeply than most.

Pensively she closed the volume and turned out the light, the subsequent blackness adding a dramatic contrast to the glimmering lightning that continued to steal into the room. In the shifting darkness, she imagined Mark's face. Earlier that day she had watched from the terrace as he led Gray Lady and her gangly foal toward their new home in the sprawling modern structure that looked so incongruous against the ancient fields of Foxcroft. As their shapes faded into the distance, Maggie had felt that the last fragile bond between her and Mark Fox was broken.

Now, as she reflected on the journal entry, she knew how much it would mean to Mark to read it. He seemed to think that William Fox had merely tolerated him, had raised him as a son only out of a sense of pride or duty. The journal negated such notions.

If she and Mark had been on better terms, she would have shown him the poignant words her father had written. But Mark had known so much about her and had kept cruelly silent. Now it was her turn to do the same. The poetic justice gave her no pleasure.

The next morning Maggie returned to William Fox's studio. She hadn't been there since that rainy spring day months before.

As if inviting her entrance, the old lock offered no resistance and the studio door swung wide. Maggie stepped inside, and for a moment the musty smell of the air took her back to that rainy day when she had stolen into the forbidden sanctuary only to find that someone had already trespassed there. Her eyes strayed to the blank spot on the far wall, and her fingers tightened on the heavy frame of the portrait in her hands. She had kept it in her room until it had gradually dawned on her that there was only one place for the Madonna, and that was where her father had hung it.

She replaced the picture and turned to survey the studio. It was more like an apartment than a workroom, and she wondered if her father had actually lived here among his paints and canvases rather than in the main house with Dolly.

She struggled with a rusty latch until she managed to unfasten it and raise the heavy window. A warm breeze rushed in, lifting her hair and leaving behind the scent of newly mown grass. She found a feather duster and brushed away the dirt that had settled on the canvases propped up along the walls.

She spent the next couple of hours sifting through oils and watercolors, landscapes and still lifes. There were portraits and figures in an impressionistic style, and she recognized the subject of some of them as her mother.

Toward the back of one of the stacks she found three nudes, and with a gasp realized the subject to be Dolly Fox. Of the three, the best was one in which the subject reclined on a velvet couch against a background of scarlet drapery. William Fox had used bold color and strokes to capture the dark-eyed woman's earthy beauty. With a nod of admiration, Maggie judged it one of his finest works.

It wasn't until she had nearly finished looking through the vast collection that she came across a group of canvases depicting the Carolina coast. Among them were several paintings of a ship, and on close inspection she was able to make out the name, *Indies Queen*. As she studied the painting, an idea formed. She selected a large canvas in which the old ship loomed majestically against a stormy sky and fled the studio with the painting in hand.

After shedding her jeans in favor of a cool sundress, Maggie hurried out to the garage, slowing her pace when her eyes lit on the only means of transportation left to her, the old pickup. How long had it been since anyone had driven the antiquated thing? The old door creaked mightily as she opened it, and as she climbed behind the wheel, she felt her resolve weaken. Maybe it wouldn't even run.

After a few wheezing chugs, the engine finally kicked in. Everything seemed to be in order except that the fuel level was low. Maggie depressed the clutch, shifted into low gear, and lurched comically out of the garage and up the oak-lined drive.

Charleston was as beautiful as ever, its buildings sparkling white in the afternoon sun, its gardens lush with the colors of summer. An exhilarating breeze picked up as soon as she drove onto the peninsula, and she surrendered herself to the beauty of the place. When she spotted an art supply store, she parked and went in to pick up canvas and oils. Her new life was under way, and painting would be part of it.

After parking across from Cap'n Jack's Queen, she retrieved the canvas and was about to carry it inside when the doors swung open, startling her so that she stumbled back a few steps. Looking up, she recognized Patrolman Jerry Brown. The memory of their inauspicious first meeting flashed through her mind as she took in the man's battered face. He had a black eye, and his nose was taped as if it had been broken.

A blush rose to Maggie's cheeks, but it didn't match the red color that flooded Jerry Brown's face and neck. Without even an excuse-me, he hurried past her, down the entrance ramp, and along the street. Before he darted around the corner, he cast a hasty look in her direction, as if in fear she might be following. With a puzzled shrug, Maggie proceeded into the Queen.

The restaurant area was empty, having been closed after lunch and not yet opened for supper. A few people lounged around the dimly lit bar. They looked at her curiously as she approached, and she caught the attention of a young bartender, dressed like a sailor and looking her over appreciatively.

"Hi there," she said brightly. "Is Captain Jack around?"

The young man grinned and was about to reply when the captain came lumbering through the kitchen door. His old eyes fastened quickly on Maggie.

"Well, well, well. Come to see your old friend Jack at last, have you, young lady?" He ended with a ho-ho-ho that reminded her of Saint Nicholas and ushered her to the end of the bar.

"What have you got there, Margaret Elizabeth?" he asked, gesturing to the canvas.

"I'll let you have a look if you promise to call me Maggie," she teased.

The old man seemed overwhelmed by the gift of the painting. Holding it reverently before him, he studied the image of the *Indies Queen* and then looked at Maggie with such gratitude that he didn't need to say a word of thanks.

He poured tall glasses of iced tea, and they admired the painting together. Maggie gently pointed out a few of the elements that made the oil a work of substance—its composition, rich color, and skillful use of light and shadow. Also, she noted, William Fox was masterful in his treatment of the sea.

"Water is one of the most difficult things to paint, and he executed it beautifully," she concluded. "He was a true artist."

They whiled away the rest of the afternoon together, Captain Jack deciding he would hang the painting in a prominent spot in the restaurant foyer. When a couple came in and sat down at one of the dining tables, she realized the dinner hour was upon them.

"By the way," she said, as Captain Jack walked her to the door, "do you know a police officer named Jerry Brown?"

"Jerry? Sure I do. Known him since he was a fresh-faced kid. He eats most of his meals here, why?"

"I met him a couple of months ago. Today, as I came in here, I ran into him. He acted as if he'd never met me. He hurried away without saying a word."

"Now, that don't sound like Jerry," Captain Jack remarked, rubbing his bristly chin. "If there's two things Jerry likes, it's ladies and talking."

"He certainly looked the worse for wear today. Was he in an accident?"

The old captain chuckled. "I guess you could call it that. Happened right out in front of the Queen a few nights ago. Jerry's mouth finally got him in trouble. He came here for supper like usual. He was just getting ready to leave when someone showed up looking for him. Guess who it was."

"Who?"

"Your friend, Mark Fox."

Maggie's eyes widened as Captain Jack went on with grudging admiration in his voice.

"That boy meant business, I'm here to tell you. He said something about Jerry shooting off his big mouth and that he was never to let the lady's name cross his lips again. Then he took poor old Jerry outside and whipped the daylights out of him!"

The story stunned Maggie. It wasn't Mark who had broadcast the story of their rendezvous, but Jerry Brown, the patrolman who had rescued them from the gamekeeper's cabin!

A smile broke across her face. "Thank you, Captain Jack!" she blurted, throwing her arms around the old man and surprising him with a hug. "I'll see you later. Thank you!"

She leapt into the pickup and wheeled away from the park as if she'd been driving the old truck for years. Mark hadn't betrayed their night together, as Arthur implied. On the contrary, he had defended her honor!

It didn't mean anything really—just that one of the more recent wounds to her ego ceased to throb. She spotted the sign for Wentworth and impulsively veered onto the picturesque street lined with gingerbread-trimmed houses.

She chided herself that it was a high-schoolish thing to do, but then grinned and thought, Who cares? She didn't know the address, and realized that it was Dolly Fox, not Mark, who lived in the city residence. But for the moment it was enough just to drive along and look, relishing the idea of Mark's connection with the place, glorying in the notion of his championing her.

Late afternoon sun filtered through the palms and Spanish moss, painting the narrow thoroughfare with a golden glow. She didn't notice the silver Porsche until she was almost upon it, nor did she recognize the couple standing next to it until they turned to stare at the solitary truck cruising slowly toward them. Mark lounged casually against the sports car, and the dark-haired woman who hung on his arm was Alicia. They looked for all the world like a happy couple out to enjoy the tranquillity of a summer sunset.

Maggie's ebullience was shattered—first by a pang of jealousy, then a surge of panic. There was no exit from the cloistered street except straight ahead. They had spotted her, and there was nothing she could do but drive past the two people whose attention was focused on her.

Reaching inside herself, she drew from a well of bravado and returned their gaze levelly, forcing herself to maintain a steady pace. As she chugged past in the ridiculous truck, she nodded to them in cool acknowledgment. Mark's expression changed from surprise to amusement, and she got the impression he knew exactly what she was doing on Wentworth Street. Alicia's arched brow and faint smile implied contempt.

Once past them, Maggie kept her eyes straight ahead to deprive them of the satisfaction of seeing her look into the rearview mirror. The narrow street seemed to stretch out endlessly, but finally she was able to turn off Wentworth Street.

Her pulse was racing, her palms had gone moist, and a familiar heaviness weighed on her chest. She pictured Mark standing there, with Alicia hanging all over him, and it struck Maggie how little she truly knew of Mark Fox. She remembered his towering rages, when she'd wondered just what he might be capable of. As she turned her thoughts to Alicia, a shudder ran through her.

Until now she'd disregarded Alicia's ravings. But something about the way the couple had looked together chilled Maggie to the bone. Mark was a lusty man, and—here in the sultry southern climate where lust seemed to breed like a fungus—who could tell what he might do? Perhaps he *was* having an affair with his half sister, who made no secret of her incestuous desire.

The thought was sickening. In one fell swoop, it obliterated any earlier joy at the foolish notion of Mark as a shining knight.

The sun was nearly down and lights were blinking on as Maggie left the city behind.

Because of her preoccupation with Mark she had forgotten to stop for gasoline. The truck had gone only a mile beyond the Cooper when the engine coughed a few times and died.

Maggie managed to steer safely to the shoulder of the highway. She had stood by the truck in the dusky light only a few minutes when a long red Cadillac convertible approached. It flashed its parking lights and pulled over. As it came to a halt, Maggie noticed the car was an older model, and that three men were in it.

It wasn't until they climbed out of the Cadillac and sauntered toward her that her welcoming smile faded. There was something threatening about the three stringy men wearing sloppy jeans and

baseball hats. There was a resemblance among them, all three
looking to be in their forties and leering unattractively. Anxiously,
Maggie scanned the highway behind them. It was deserted. Too
soon, they were upon her.

"Evenin', ma'am," one of them said, then spit a long stream of
tobacco juice neatly over his shoulder.

"Howdy," said another, pushing his cap back on his head and
giving her the once-over. The third hung back behind the other
two, grinning.

"Good afternoon," Maggie said firmly. As the men's eyes
lingered on her bare shoulders and legs, she wished she were
wearing something more modest than the flimsy sundress.

"Having a little trouble?" said the one with the tobacco, his
smirk disclosing badly stained teeth.

"Oh, not much trouble." She would prefer waiting by the
roadside for hours to dealing with these undesirables. "My—
uh—my boyfriend has gone to get some gas." She laughed. "We
were silly enough to run out."

One man stroked his bristling beard. "Funny, we didn't pass
nobody on the road."

"He must have gotten picked up," Maggie explained.

"You're not from around here, are ya?" asked the tobacco
chewer, who lounged back against the pickup and leaned brazenly
toward her.

Maggie backed away. The twilight was fading. Soon it would
be dark, and here she was, alone on a country highway with three
dangerous-looking strangers. Her pulse began to race, and when
her voice came, she stammered. "No . . . I—uh—I'm from
New York. I just moved down here."

"And already had time to find yourself a boyfriend," sneered
the tobacco chewer's companion. "Well, we oughtn't to let a
young Yankee girl wait for her boyfriend all by herself. Maybe we
should keep ya company until he gets back." He pulled a flask
from his back pocket as, behind him, the third man snickered
ominously.

"How about a drink?" the man added, offering the flask.

"No . . . no, thank you," Maggie returned.

"Aw, come on!" he pressed. "One little drink."

He waved the flask in her face, and Maggie began to feel
desperate. At that moment the sound of an approaching vehicle
drew their eyes to the road. It was an old flatbed truck with coops
of madly clucking chickens in the back. Maggie's mind screamed

for it to stop as she ran out to flag it down. The truck rumbled past, then veered off the road and began to back up toward them.

"There he is now!" Maggie announced with relief as the three rednecks shuffled their feet and began to mosey toward their car.

Maggie turned gratefully toward the old flatbed and watched a tall black man about her own age climb out. It wasn't until he came near that she recognized Rachel's nephew, Jonas.

As Jonas approached, the Cadillac roared off the shoulder of the road, one of the men calling out a racial insult as the car sped onto the highway.

Coarse laughter followed, and in a flash, Maggie's fist went up in a universal gesture. When she turned indignantly to Jonas, she found a smile on his face.

"I thought I recognized you, Miss Maggie," he said in a throaty voice.

"Boy, am I glad to see you!" she breathed. She explained her situation as she followed Jonas to his beat-up truck.

They had to cross back over the Cooper to reach a gas station, and when they arrived, Jonas suggested she stay in the truck.

"Why?" she asked curiously.

Jonas pulled the truck to a neat stop by the pumps and regarded her with big brown eyes. "This isn't New York, Miss Maggie. This is a well-to-do area of Charleston, South Carolina. Not everyone around here is agreeable to the idea of seeing a white woman in the company of a black man."

Maggie's eyes flashed as she answered. "The South hasn't cornered the market on prejudice, you know. It exists in different forms everywhere I've traveled. In whatever form, it's ugly. I'm not about to let it influence anything I do!"

She got out of the truck and walked into the bright lights of the gas station. When Jonas procured a can for the gas, she stood with him as he filled it. It wasn't until two elderly ladies came out of the convenience store and stopped their chatting to stare that she saw firsthand the kind of reaction Jonas had predicted. She stared back rebelliously until the two women bustled away, their heads bent to each other in hurried whispering.

As Jonas drove back toward the forsaken truck, the summer night grew black, leaving the familiar landscape cloaked in a cool, quiet disguise. Occasionally the chickens in the back erupted into a chorus of clucks.

"Rachel said you're an accountant," Maggie began with a nod in the direction of the chickens. "Do you farm as well?"

Jonas grinned ruefully. "No, although you might think it if you saw my place—chickens, goats, baskets of homegrown vegetables. The cream of Charleston society isn't exactly beating down my door to become part of my clientele. Most of my clients don't have any cash to spare, so they pay me in crops or livestock."

They sighted the pickup, and Maggie let the subject drop. In short order, Jonas had the truck running again.

"Let me pay you," she urged, and for the first time detected a vague look of animosity in Jonas's eyes.

"Would you have paid that white trash in the Cadillac?" he demanded.

Maggie climbed into the pickup and regarded the proud man. "No, I wouldn't have offered to pay them," she admitted. "I would have considered putting up with their obnoxious behavior payment enough."

Slowly a smile broke across Jonas's face. Maggie met it with one of her own.

"Are you any good as an accountant?" she asked.

"Damned good!"

"I've got my hands full trying to manage Foxcroft. Would you be interested in handling my accounts?"

"Would I be interested?" Jonas grinned. "Was Antony interested in Cleopatra?"

Maggie chuckled. "Good. Why don't you come out to the estate next week and have a look at the books? And, Jonas," she added as he stepped away, "I may not be able to pay you a lot, but I can promise you it won't be in chickens."

The summer waxed on, and a blanket of sweltering heat wrapped itself around the Carolina low country. Maggie wore as little as possible as she worked around the estate, and many were the days when she was reminded of Arthur's remarks about the coveted breezes of the Battery. Now she understood the torrid heat of the countryside that planters of old had longed to escape.

She adopted the southern custom of going barefoot, and she donned footwear only when she went riding—making an unconventional picture in tall black boots, a pair of shorts, and a halter top. Through the countryside she would race, her fiery hair streaming out behind her, her skin gleaming a rich caramel brown in the hot sun.

Riding had become a daily activity. Jeremy did the best he could, in the time he could allot, at keeping the stables in order.

But he often had to leave tasks undone. Those and the exercising of the mounts fell to Maggie. She alternated days between the mare and the gelding, and discovered that Lorelei had the smoother gait while Prince had the speed. She gloried in the fact that her horsemanship had risen to a certain standard of excellence and that both her steeds were in superior condition.

On her daily treks to the stables she sometimes caught a glimpse of Mark across the field at his newly built facility, a barnlike house with horse stalls extending like arms from either side. Most of the time he was putting his black horse, Sonny, through the paces on the steeplechase course he had erected. Occasionally he worked Gray Lady's filly on a long line in the white-railed ring. He never gave any sign of having noticed Maggie as she went about her duties, and since leading Gray Lady away, he had not strayed across the property line that divided them.

Rachel, however, was a constant source of unsolicited information and advice. "Mr. Fox has done turned himself into a hermit," she would say. "His mama says he doesn't ever go into town anymore." Or: "That Mr. Fox is one in a million. He won that horse show the other day and gave his prize to the hospital."

On one such occasion, the old woman managed to elicit a response. "Mr. Fox is a proud man," she said. "If you want him back, you're gonna have to do something, Miss Maggie!"

"I never *had* him in the first place," Maggie snapped. "Why would I want him back?"

Rachel mutely rolled her eyes.

Rachel had no way of knowing how bitter the taste of pride had become. Maggie was plagued by dreams of Mark—the way he smiled, the way he kissed, the way he felt. It helped to remind herself that the man she longed for didn't really exist that Mark Fox was *not* the tender character she had fabricated in the gamekeeper's cottage. But just when she thought she'd pushed him from her mind, another dream would come and she would wake with a start, feverish and aching.

One night she caught herself murmuring, "I love you." She sat up abruptly, and as the words echoed in her mind, tears sprang to her eyes. Once again it was necessary to dredge up all the memories—Mark's cold rages, his lies, maybe even a sordid affair with Alicia! Sitting alone in bed, in the quiet early hours, Maggie steeped herself in such thoughts until she was properly disgusted by her longings.

The next morning Rachel and Annie entered the kitchen to find

Maggie already up and about, a grim expression on her face. They'd seen the look before, and kept their distance until their mistress's cheerful mood returned.

The second week in July, Maggie had a long meeting with Jonas. His immaculate figures and columns had enforced a strict order on the wild mess she had presented him. Unfortunately he echoed what Morely and Arthur and Mark had predicted. Come the first of the year, tax season, she was going to be in trouble.

"I don't mean to scare you, Maggie, but you're investing a pretty penny in upkeep and renovations on this place. And nothing's coming in. At this rate, it's just a matter of months."

Maggie quavered, but she managed to give Jonas a smile. "Well, then, I'll just have to bring something in. I'll start looking for a job."

Jonas shook his head regretfully. "It will have to be one hell of a job."

"I can always sell the New York house."

"I wouldn't advise that. It's a sound investment property, and the sum you'd gain would only stave off the inevitable for a short while. As your accountant, I have to tell you what you don't want to hear: You should consider selling Foxcroft now, before your position worsens."

Maggie looked at him solemnly. "I can't do that, Jonas. I'll have to think of a way. That's all."

So far she hadn't thought of anything, and something close to panic was swelling within her. Day after day she tried to reassure herself as she plunged into some project at the estate, laboring well into the night and then climbing the stairs and collapsing on the bed, leaving little time for nagging worries before the sleep of exhaustion overtook her.

Her reward was that her efforts showed. Foxcroft responded to her like a thoroughbred to a trainer. The grounds and gardens flourished, the house sparkled with new light and life. As Maggie stripped away the heavy draperies from all the windows, the house lost its dark cast. Sunlight poured in through sparkling panes, lighting up the rooms, dancing across the polished wood and silver.

Rachel declared the place had never looked so bright and inviting. With a sense of pride, Maggie agreed. The darkness of Foxcroft had vanished.

By the end of July, she had refurbished the studio above the library, stored many of her father's paintings in racks, and distributed a few favorites throughout the house. She planned to bring the studio back to life with her own work and had even gone so far as to mix a few watercolors and test them on her father's old papers. Long before, she'd decided on her first subject—the unspoiled marshes out by the river that had captured her artist's eye the first time she saw them.

The riverbank now looked quite appealing. She had hired Mr. Thompson and his brothers to rebuild the bridge and reclaim the peninsula that lay beyond. Now a graceful white arch spanned the tributary. Maggie often rode out to the spot and allowed Lorelei or Prince to graze by the water while she wandered along the path through the tall grasses.

The blackened rubble of the burned cottage had been carted away from the clearing in the marsh. Maggie had pulled away the vines and weeds from the headstone so that the marker no longer appeared forlorn and forgotten. Surrounded by a new white fence, it rested in a tranquil, well-tended spot that was often brightened by a rose or a spray of wildflowers, which Maggie would deposit while taking a break from her morning ride.

It was on such a clear morning that she lingered in the marsh, allowing Lorelei to roam freely and munch the lush grass by the cypresses. Part of the cottage's brick hearth still stood four feet tall, and she climbed on top, raised a hand to shield her eyes and took a sweeping look at the expansive wildlife sanctuary.

The white shapes of gulls and egrets and herons flashed against the electric blue of the sky, then plunged into the deeper blue channels of water that streaked the marshland. Sunlight glistened on the golden grasses that danced in the breeze, and Maggie was sizing up the spot as a possible vantage point from which to paint when a rustling noise caught her attention. The sound had come from behind her, within the tall screen of wheat-colored weeds that ringed the clearing.

She turned and studied the now silent area. "Lorelei?" she called, but there was no sign of the animal. No whinny, no answer of any sort. An eerie feeling that she was being watched swept over her. Feeling suddenly isolated and vulnerable, Maggie kept her eyes on the spot in the grasses and scrambled down from the chimney.

She told herself that it was the wind, that it was silly to be spooked on such a bright summer morning. Nonetheless, she left the clearing and marched as rapidly as her boots would allow along the path to the bridge. But Lorelei was nowhere to be seen.

Maggie's heart began to thud as she trotted to the pinnacle of the arching bridge and looked up and down the deserted riverbank.

"Lorelei!" she called. Her voice echoed from one gray cypress to the next. The only answer was a familiar rustle in the grasses on the riverbank. Like a shot, Maggie was off the bridge and dashing into the forest toward Foxcroft House.

On horseback, the path through the pines was just long enough to be a pleasant ride. But on foot it seemed to stretch out and double in length. By the time she reached the broken tree that marked the midway point, she was out of breath, and her initial alarm had receded.

"It was the wind," she mumbled, "and Lorelei must have wandered home." With a weary laugh at herself, she slumped against the broken tree and cast a glance behind her. It was then that she saw a figure dart behind one of the pines.

A quick scream tore from Maggie's throat, and she began to run in earnest. The heavy boots seemed to weigh her down, occasionally tripping her and pitching her into scratchy pine branches. But she recovered quickly and continued through the trees at breakneck speed.

Her throat was dry and aching when she emerged from the shadowy forest and began to stumble along the sunny dirt road leading to the back lawns of Foxcroft. She wouldn't chance slowing her pace by looking back to see if anyone was there. Although her legs felt like rubber, panic drove her on. It didn't occur to her that the person, whoever it was, might have meant her no harm. The stealthy presence had managed to exert a menacing intent in only seconds. Maggie raced on, the blood pounding so loud in her ears that she didn't hear the clatter of hooves galloping toward her from around the bend.

Suddenly Mark's giant black steed thundered into view. The sight of the familiar horse and rider flooded her body with relief and stemmed the wild flow of adrenaline that had kept her going. Her knees promptly folded, and she collapsed in the middle of the road.

Mark reined in so quickly that his horse kicked up a cloud of dust. In an instant, he was by her side, pulling her to her feet. His hands grasped her arms roughly.

"Are you hurt?" he demanded.

"Mark!" she gasped hoarsely. Her face was streaked with tears, and her chest heaved as she fought for breath.

"What's wrong? Did you take a fall?" He asked the questions hurriedly, searching her face for bruises or cuts.

"No," she managed. "Lorelei . . . she's gone."

"I know," he replied shortly. "Jeremy said Lorelei came tearing into the stableyard without you. That's when he ran over to get me. What happened?"

"I . . . I don't know. I was in the clearing . . . and when I got to the bridge, she was gone. Someone chased me through the woods!" Maggie's voice cracked on the last word, and she cast a frightened glance up the road.

Mark regarded her skeptically. "*Chased* you? Are you sure?"

"I'm sure," she replied a little more calmly. "I saw him."

"Him? What did he look like?"

"I couldn't tell. He hid behind a tree."

"Are you sure it wasn't just a shadow?"

"I *saw* him, Mark," she said firmly.

The terror in her eyes convinced him. "Come on!" he commanded, leading her to Sonny.

"Where?"

"To find him!"

Maggie twisted out of his grasp. "No!" she shouted with wide eyes.

Mark studied her for a moment. "I'm going to check this out. Now," he added smoothly, "are you coming with me, or do you prefer to stay here?"

"All right, then," she said, glancing briskly over her shoulder. "May I have a leg up, please?"

A grin pulled at the corner of Mark's mouth as he helped her mount, then vaulted up behind her and slid brazenly forward until he was molded against her back. Reaching around her, he took the reins, allowing his arms to graze the bare skin of her midriff between her shorts and top. Maggie straightened rigidly, and behind her, Mark grinned as they took off at a fast clip for the path through the pines.

They saw no one in the forest. When they reached the riverbank, he paused to check the moist earth for tracks, but found nothing. They circled the clearing, which was also deserted. Then Mark turned Sonny toward the tall marsh grasses. As they approached the tall golden grasses Maggie spotted a break, the beginning of an animal trail leading through the marsh in the direction of the river.

They were nearly swallowed up by the whispering reeds closing and waving behind them as they passed. Eventually, the grass thinned and they came upon a stand of cypresses. Mark reined in as they spotted a campsite at the edge of the trees.

"Come on," he said and, after helping her down, went over to examine the spot.

Kneeling at the blackened remains of a fire, he began to sift through the coals and ashes. He came to his feet, dusted his palms on his jeans, and walked the perimeter of the site.

Maggie stood with the towering horse. She had no desire to go any closer to the camp. How long? she wondered with a shiver, recalling the many times she'd ridden out to the clearing alone. How long had the man been here watching her?

Mark rejoined her. "Can't tell much from the site. Looks as if it was only used for one night, maybe a week or so ago. Probably just a bum traveling through. There's a railroad a few miles from here. Or maybe it was a poacher; occasionally we find evidence of them here in the sanctuary."

"A week ago?" Maggie questioned. "But that doesn't explain the man I saw just now."

"No, I guess it doesn't." Mark turned to peer through the cypress that stretched like a tall army toward the river. "Let's keep looking."

They spent another hour zigzagging through the marsh, then crossed the river and dismounted. Mark led Sonny to the water's edge, and as the horse bent to drink, Maggie knelt to fill her palms with the cold water. Letting most of it run between her fingers, she pressed cool, wet palms against her hot face.

Mark stood on the bank and watched, his gaze drawn to the feminine spectacle in the near-nothing shorts and top and the tall black boots. The sun shifted through the trees, lighting her hair like a bright flame against the water.

Damn! he thought as the familiar heat stirred inside him.

Maggie left the river and scaled the bank to join him, and Mark's senses zeroed on the woman before him. He'd sworn off her after the encounter in the stables. But now, in the privacy of the river glen, all that mattered was the way she set him on fire. He sensed that once he touched her, he could break down the barrier between them.

Maggie caught the change in him. No longer the distant lord of long ago, Mark had become the hot-blooded male of the game-keeper's cottage. The air turned electric.

"I suppose I should thank you," she said.

Mark crossed his arms across his chest. "For what?"

"For coming after me."

He gave her one of his cocky, teasing looks. "What do I get for my trouble?"

Maggie raised a brow. "I wasn't aware that you took tips!"

"Oh, yes." He stepped over and took her in his arms as smoothly as if they embraced every day. "The tips are the best part."

Maggie pushed at his hands and backed away. "Mark! You can't just put your hands on me like that!"

"Oh, really?" he said, taking a step toward her.

"Yes, *really*! I'd like to be treated with a little respect."

"I recall what you like," he drawled.

Maggie glared at him as he took another step. "You reduce everything to such a base level!"

Mark looked down at her steadily. "What I feel for you isn't base. Neither is what you feel for me."

"I don't feel anything for you!"

His gaze held hers. "That's a lie. I'd say that makes us just about even—a lie for a lie, and so on."

He reached for her. She backed away, and they began a slow, sinuous chase in the direction of the pines.

"Listen to me, Mark. You came after me today, and I appreciate it. But after all that's happened, the best we can hope for is a civil relationship. I'm willing if you are."

He grinned. "Oh, I'm *willing* all right."

"Will you be serious?" Maggie demanded. "I'd like to get this settled once and for all!"

She came to a defiant halt, and he advanced until their bodies nearly touched.

"No more than I," he said quietly.

Maggie stared up at him, and she was caught. She had sworn to herself that the love she once felt for the man had turned to hate, but she couldn't take her eyes from his face. They moved from the square jaw where yesterday's beard made a shadow to the high cheekbones streaked with sunburn, to the vivid green eyes that regarded her searchingly from under the brim of his hat.

Mark watched her soften and leaned toward her, his heart ramming at his rib cage. "Don't tell me you feel nothing for me," he murmured.

Maggie stood as if she were made of stone. He kissed her gently at first, and when he gathered her close, a moan gushed from his mouth into hers.

For an instant she was shocked into stillness; then her body responded with a hunger that resurrected itself from the deep recesses where she had buried it. The feel of him took her back to the night when they had shared themselves fully. As her hands played over the rough material of his clothing, her mind's eye saw a tall, naked form gleaming in the firelight.

Mark's hand was on the back of her head, slanting her face forcefully against him, his mouth hard and possessive, as if he would brand her with its mark. A dull ache flared in her stomach and pounded through her body. It was only when he swept her up into his arms and began to walk toward the pines that Maggie's eyelids drifted open, and she awoke as if from a dream.

"What are you doing?" she murmured.

"What I've been wanting to do for months," came the gruff reply.

A picture of his plan burst into her mind—she saw herself sprawled on the pine needles making wild, uninhibited love, giving herself once again to the man she couldn't resist but didn't trust. At the thought, her body stiffened. "Put me down," she said.

Mark's gaze snapped to her face. He stopped walking, but continued to hold her, his eyes narrowing as he assessed her change of mood.

Maggie looked away. God, but she hated herself for having surrendered to his kiss! She hated him for making her want to!

"Put me down," she repeated firmly.

He complied, but continued to hold her against him.

"I need to get back," she said and tried to move away. Mark didn't allow her to budge. Finally she met the fierce look in his eyes.

"That's not fair, Maggie," he growled.

"*Fair?*"

"That's right! You never should've kissed me like that if you intended to stop!"

She stared up at him, the familiar anger bursting through her. "A kiss is just a kiss, Mark. It's not an open invitation. And besides, you're one to be talking about fairness! You of all people!"

Exasperated, Mark dropped his arms and stepped back a pace. "So we're back to that, are we? Okay. Listen, and listen well,

Maggie. This is the last apology you'll hear from me. I was wrong before. I'm sorry. Now why don't you just forgive me?"

Maggie looked at him blankly. She'd never cared enough about a man to learn how to forgive.

"I can't," she said simply. "I don't trust you, Mark."

A muscle twitched along his jaw as his brows drew together in a dark line. "Somebody must have hurt you badly."

Maggie's chin lifted. "Somebody did."

He regarded her intently. "You mean me."

She only looked at him.

"Well, I'm glad I made *some* impression!" Mark fired. He shifted his weight from one foot to the other. "I'm finally getting the picture. It doesn't matter *what* I say or do until this estate thing is settled. Why don't you just sell Foxcroft? You're going to have to sooner or later!"

"No!" Maggie blazed. "That's what you'd like, isn't it? You don't care that Foxcroft is all I have from a father I never knew! Do you think it means nothing to me?"

Mark studied her ferocious expression. "Fine," he muttered. "Apparently Foxcroft means more to you than anything or anyone!"

"That should come as no surprise!" Maggie retorted. "You feel the same exact way!"

Mark stalked over to Sonny and vaulted onto the back of the animal. Without a word he pulled her onto the towering steed, settled her in front of him, and nudged the horse into a brisk walk.

The trip back to the stableyard was long and tense. The sun beat down upon them, the smell of honeysuckle mingled with the faint aroma of masculine cologne, and Maggie's attention was unswervingly focused on Mark. One strong bare arm encircled her, the hand casually cradling the reins against the stallion's black mane. Occasionally Mark's chest brushed against her bare back, making her long to relax against him. But the silence between them was heavy. Maggie held herself erect and did her best to wrench her thoughts from the man who rode behind her.

Chapter Sixteen

Mark perched on the corner of Todd Williams's desk and began to shuffle through the copies of his competitor's drawings. There were eight in all, each of which defiled the natural beauty of Canadys Isle.

The development that Townsend & Company proposed comprised rows of white high-rise condominiums with seaward-facing balconies stacked one on the other like so many building blocks. The complex, with its regimented shopping areas and recreational facilities, was like any other one might see in Atlantic City or along Miami Beach. No consideration whatever had been given to the unique, unspoiled terrain of the island. If Townsend won the contract, the beauty of Canadys would be lost forever.

Still, it had been three months since Mark had put the three investors on a plane to New York. Three months of silence. Perhaps this was why.

He tossed the copies on the desk and looked up at Todd. "Why didn't you tell me about these sooner?"

Todd Williams snatched the pipe from his mouth. "I tried to tell you. I called you more than a week ago to let you know I had sweet-talked my free-lance friend out of these copies. You were out riding, John Henry said. I left a message and never heard a word, so I called again four days ago. You were out in the ring working your new foal, John Henry said. So this time I told him it was urgent. You never got back to me! And now you show up without any warning after a week and a half and ask me why I didn't tell you any sooner?"

With a grimace, Mark turned away from Todd's accusing stare and strode to the wall of windows. Below, the street was ablaze with sun, but the heat seemed to have frightened no one into staying indoors. The sidewalks were bustling with colorfully dressed pedestrians.

Todd came to stand nearby. "Friend to friend, Mark, what the hell has gotten into you? I used to have to run you out of here in the evenings and even on weekends. Now I hardly see you. You can't run a successful business this way. What's wrong?"

"Nothing," Mark rumbled. "Nothing's wrong. I've just got a lot on my mind."

Mark buzzed Sally Ann. "Please get the New York investors on the line for me," he said.

Todd Williams's eyes twinkled as he reached for the phone. "Now you're talkin'!"

Moments later the chief investor's crisp voice was crackling through the receiver. "It's never been a question of whose plan is the most aesthetically appealing, Fox. Yours is, by a long shot. But we're in business. We've got to be realistic. Townsend's outline offers fifty more residences. At about a hundred grand apiece, that's a half million dollars."

"Not quite," Mark said. "Townsend's condos would have to sell more cheaply than the units I'm proposing. And besides, those additional fifty units are located on the southern tip of the island, right in the middle of the Gullah village I took you to see."

"Okay, okay. I admit I like your idea about upgrading the village but leaving it basically intact. It's quaint, interesting. It would make Canadys Isle unique. But that feature is not worth five hundred thousand dollars! Townsend says some of the finest property around Charleston was once inhabited by clusters of blacks who were relocated to make way for profitable development. I'm not a sentimentalist, Fox. The bottom line with me is profit, and Townsend says those villagers don't have any documents registered in the office of deeds and records—no proof of ownership whatsoever."

Mark raked his fingers through his hair. "He's wrong. Either he hasn't done his homework or he's trying to sell you a bill of goods. Those people and their ancestors have lived on that island for more than a century. They hardly ever leave the island, and they don't trust banks and government offices. But right after the Civil War, when the slaves were freed, Mr. Canady gave a map of the island to his favorite house servants. It clearly specifies that the southern tip of that island was his gift to them. That map has been guarded and passed down from generation to generation. The matriarch of the village keeps it in her Bible, for God's sake! If your men show up in that village with bulldozers, you'll get slapped with an injunction so fast it will make your head spin!"

With that, Mark finally elicited a sputter from the New Yorker. "If what you say is true, then Townsend is misinformed and his plan is not viable. I'm glad you called, Fox. We'll get to the bottom of this. I'll be getting back to you."

Mark replaced the receiver, a look of relief spreading across his features.

He grinned as he turned to Todd Williams. "We just won a very important round."

It was still twilight when Maggie and Rachel and Annie squeezed into the old pick-up and drove over to the Thompson farm. The barn was lit with Chinese lanterns, and a crowd was square-dancing to a lively blue-grass band. When they moved closer to the flatbed truck being used as a stage, Maggie saw with surprise that the leader of the band was none other than Jeremy's father, her groundskeeper. The hands of the slow-spoken man were fairly flying on his fiddle!

Maggie smiled and began to clap her hands with the rest of the crowd while Rachel and Annie moved off to mingle about the long, food-laden table. After a while, Jeremy stepped up and began introducing Maggie through the crowd.

She met *all* the Thompsons, three brothers' families with "kinfolk" numbering in the twenties. Ida and Jake Campbell, a smiling, elderly couple with a small farm beyond the Thompson orchards. The Miller family, with seven children, the oldest of which was a teenaged boy who gazed at Maggie with lovesick eyes. Prune-faced Widow Larkin who shook Maggie's hand and then hurried to a group of wide-eyed ladies who stared from a distance—agog, it seemed, that the mistress of Foxcroft should attend a dance in the Thompsons' barn!

Before long, Maggie was drawn into the gaiety and ended up square-dancing the night away. It was one of the best times she'd ever had.

After that night, Maggie felt accepted. Neighbors occasionally stopped by, or waved when she passed them on the road. Foxcroft had always held a revered place in the community, and now *she* was regarded as the "lady of the manor." She acquired the code of gentry graciousness—certain offers or favors were expected to be politely overlooked, while others must be gratefully accepted, lest the neighbor be offended. Instinctively, Maggie seemed to know the difference.

As the long summer days crept by, the "ladies of Foxcroft" became the pet favorites of the scattered residents of the Carolina countryside. Many was the Sunday Rachel's church circle sent baskets of goodies or fresh-baked bread, and on a regular basis, the Thompsons' flatbed truck wheeled into the courtyard laden with surplus fruit and vegetables from their orchards and gardens.

"They're lookin' out for us," Rachel would often say, the sparkle of a tear shining behind her bifocals.

Maggie's heart swelled with love for the land, the people, the life of Foxcroft. She was bound to it in a thousand ways.

May 1. Today is May Day, a time for streamers around the maypole, bright flowers, picnics, and romance. I haven't thought of the spring holiday in years. Perhaps my memory of it has something to do with the young woman I met today at the harbor. She came over from Jamaica on Jack Lewis's *Queen*, and I swear I've never seen such a colorful girl, with her golden skin, fiery hair, and turquoise eyes.

Stella, her name is, and she's a sad story, having come from Kingston to search for a father who long ago deserted her. She had nowhere to go, Jack said. She seemed so fragile, standing alone on the docks like a solitary flower. And yet when I spoke with her, I found such strength, such fire, that I was compelled to bring her home.

I would pay her to be my model, I told her. She could earn her keep by posing and by doing light housework. But in truth, my reasons for bringing Stella here are so complex that I dare not dwell on them. Perhaps I hope that her spirit will brighten the darkness that has so long enshrouded Foxcroft.

It was the final entry in her father's second volume. Maggie kicked the coverlet off her legs and climbed out of bed. A glance at the night table told her it was after midnight. Her hand strayed to lift the mass of hair off her hot neck as she moved languidly toward the French doors. Each night she opened them with the hope of feeling a breeze. Each night they delivered only muggy heat. As she looked across the back lawns, she saw only the darkness of the summer night, the occasional blinks of fireflies, and the outlines of the familiar trees, motionless in the still air, and she heard only the singing of the crickets.

The quiet darkness was oppressive. She stepped back inside and turned on some music before wandering to the chest where she kept her father's journals. She traded the second leather-bound volume for the third. Her hours were growing ever later, she thought, as she crawled back into bed and began to turn the slim pages. Her practiced eye quickly found the first of her father's personal notes.

May 22. All is as it has always been, I suppose. The household runs. Dolly keeps to herself. I paint. Then what is the difference, I ask myself? Yet I know without asking.

It has been only three weeks since Stella arrived. But she has managed to bring tremendous change. Where once there was only darkness, now there is light. Where only hopelessness dwelt, there is now hope. She does it naturally, quietly. Yet each peal of laughter, each illuminating comment, plants a new seed of life in a household long dead. Or perhaps it is not in the household that these miracles occur, but in me.

Today as I sketched her in a wide, straw hat, shadows fell across those vivid eyes, giving them a solemn depth that once again reminded me of the strange circumstances of her life. Deserted, penniless, she sailed to a new world on the long chance of finding a father. I commented on her courage, and she gave me a puzzled look. "But you would have done the same," she said innocently.

I could only chuckle at the time, but later I wondered: Am I capable of the same courage I see in this artless woman? "Valor in adversity"—the phrase comes to mind when I look into Stella's clear eyes.

Several ensuing entries were along the same lines—the way his painting was progressing, Stella's unique virtues as a model, comments about her as a woman that were made in such a respectful, self-denying way that Maggie found them ever more touching. Even if she hadn't known the outcome of the story, she would have been able to see that the sad, wealthy master of Foxcroft was falling in love with a mystery woman from the poor side of Kingston, Jamaica.

At odd times, Maggie felt a strong bond with her unknown mother. This was one of those times. Aside from their obvious physical resemblance, there was the fact that their lives seemed to be parallel. Both had lost their parents, had been left all alone, and had come to Foxcroft as strangers.

As she turned out the bedside light, a vision of Stella formed in the darkness. Little by little, through her father's journals, Maggie was learning to know this strong, brave woman who had been her mother. The vision lingered long after her eyes closed, its presence like a guardian angel. From across the room came the comforting sound of music as Maggie fell peacefully asleep.

Both Rachel's birthday and Annie's fell in the third week of August. Maggie overheard them discussing it one day in the kitchen, and an idea was born.

Rachel and Annie had willingly taken on additional duties without question; neither had expressed a sour thought at being paid no more for shouldering the extra responsibilities. Both women seemed to enjoy playing a more important role at the estate. It was no longer just a place to work; in a sense it was now their home.

Rachel carefully pickled and canned a vast amount of fresh produce the Thompsons brought to Foxcroft, until the cellar shelves were filled with carefully labeled jars to be retrieved in the fall and winter.

Annie had made a deal with the Thompsons to buy all the firewood they produced from a strip of timberland they were clearing. Already two cords were stacked behind the house and covered with a tarpaulin.

"There's no sense running up a big heating bill the way Mrs. Fox did," the Scotswoman had said, "when every room in this house has a perfectly good fireplace."

As time passed, Maggie realized she couldn't manage without Rachel and Annie. And so, with warm feelings of affection and excitement, she began to plan their birthday party.

She asked Mr. Thompson if his group was available on the third Saturday of August. His answer was a wide, gap-tooth smile and a pleased "Why, me and the boys would be proud to play, Miss Maggie."

She arranged with Captain Jack to do the catering, and together they decided on an old-fashioned southern picnic. Maggie would set up long tables on the back lawns, and the captain would supply barbecued ribs and chicken, corn on the cob, coleslaw, potato salad, corn bread, and watermelons. The coup de grace would be a giant chocolate birthday cake.

A week before the party, Maggie walked into the kitchen and bade Rachel and Annie to stop their work. "I would love to surprise you two," she began, "but there's no way I can do that and be sure to include everyone you want to invite. I'm going to throw a birthday picnic for you next Saturday afternoon! There will be badminton and horseshoes and horse rides for the children, and music and good food for everyone. So I want you to get busy and invite whomever you please!"

Never before had she seen the two chatty women speechless, but their silence lasted only a moment. With beaming smiles and a telltale sparkle in their eyes, they took an instant to embrace their benefactress, then bustled off to invite friends and family. With the arrangements made and a continually growing guest list, Maggie sat back and prayed for a sunny day.

The Saturday of the party dawned cloudless and hot, and from the break of day on, Maggie was in a frenzy. The badminton net was strung between two oaks near the path to the stables. Horseshoe pegs were driven near the library, and long tables, courtesy of Captain Jack, were set up at the base of the terrace and covered with red-and-white-checked cloths.

Captain Jack and an assistant named Bart brought a massive grill, ice chests brimming with chicken and ribs, a keg of beer, and a vast supply of iced tea and lemonade. The two men set up the grill in a makeshift workstation on the spacious terrace.

By two-thirty a stream of cars and trucks lined the avenue of oaks. Maggie greeted the guests at the door and led them through the house to the back lawns. At first, the guests who were strangers seemed so overwhelmed by the grandeur of the estate that they retreated into awed silence, but as soon as Mr. Thompson's band settled on the gazebo and struck up a lively tune, everyone seemed to loosen up. As the crowd grew and the music got louder, it became clear the gathering was on its way to being a huge success.

Maggie walked up to the terrace and checked in with Captain Jack and Bart, who were busily preparing a vat of spicy-smelling barbecue sauce.

"Everything's fine, just fine," Captain Jack assured her swiftly before turning back to his chore.

With a smile at the giant white chef's hats bobbing on the two men's heads, Maggie stepped up onto the terrace wall and surveyed her milling guests. In the spirit of the picnic, she wore a denim skirt, sandals, and a white off-the-shoulder blouse. As she stood on the elevated wall, a mild breeze flirted with the deep eyelet ruffle adorning her blouse.

She was pleased by what she saw. Old, young, black, white— everyone seemed to be having a good time.

The party was in full, raucous swing, and Rachel and Annie

seemed to be having the time of their lives. As Maggie smiled with satisfaction, Annie spotted her and beckoned her down from the terrace. For the next hour she was led good-naturedly from one group to another as Annie and Rachel tried to outdo each other in introducing her to the guests.

It was a little past five when Captain Jack rang a large dinner chime and the crowd lined up beside the food-laden tables. The captain, Bart, and Maggie ladled healthy portions onto an endless stream of paper plates while Rachel and Annie filled cups with tea and lemonade and beer. Mr. Thompson and his wife, Flora, were among the first in line, and after quickly consuming their fill, they returned to the gazebo. To the accompaniment of her husband's fiddle, Flora kept the feasting crowd entertained by singing country ballads in a sweet, clear voice.

Maggie had just finished a plateful of the delicious fare when Rachel hurried up to her.

"One of my guests just got here," she told Maggie. "She says she can't stay. But she wants a word with you."

"Who is it?" Maggie asked.

Rachel drew in a deep breath. "It's Mrs. Fox."

"Mrs. *Fox*?"

"Well, you *did* say to invite anybody we wanted to," Rachel reminded her. "She's up on the terrace."

Maggie wound her way through the crowd and started up the stairs to the terrace. The memory of the night she fled Foxcroft came rushing back, and with it came the image of Dolly Fox's stricken face. But as she approached, she found that the woman who awaited her bore no resemblance to the debilitated creature she had confronted months before.

Dolly Fox now wore her hair clipped flatteringly short about her face. The gray was gone, apparently rinsed away. She wore a rose-colored summer dress that enhanced her slim figure, and the cane seemed like a stylish accessory rather than a crutch. A few paces behind her, a handsome young man in chauffeur's livery bent to sniff the few pieces of chicken that still sizzled on the grill.

As Maggie drew near, she noticed a lively sparkle in Dolly's black eyes. The woman looked twenty years younger, an impression that was heightened when she smiled and extended her hand.

"Hello, Maggie," she said in a strong voice only vaguely reminiscent of the dry one Maggie remembered.

"Mrs. Fox," she said, briefly shaking the woman's slender hand.

"I gather it's a surprise to you that I'm here. Don't worry—I'm aware of how you must feel toward me, and I don't plan to linger. But I did want to wish Rachel a happy birthday, and I hoped to have a few words with you as well."

Dolly Fox's dark eyes swept the grounds. "My, my . . . Rachel said you had done wonderful things out here, and she was right. This place has never looked so good."

"Thank you," Maggie said.

"Let me start by saying that you have given me back my life, Maggie, and I can't think of any way to repay you."

Maggie blinked in astonishment.

Dolly Fox, despite her cane, strolled smoothly across the patio. Maggie followed in bewilderment. "I never liked being stuck out here in the country," the older woman said. "For more than twenty-five years, Foxcroft was my prison."

She paused and looked at Maggie intently. "And then you came along and changed all that. What's the old saying? 'You shall know the truth, and the truth shall make you free'? You gave me the truth, Maggie. You gave me the strength that comes with knowing. Now I can live in the city and hold my head high. And if notoriety surrounds me," she added with a crooked grin similar to Mark's, "I don't really mind. In fact, I rather enjoy it."

When Maggie only stared, the woman continued brusquely. "But I'm digressing, I came here not to gloat over my belated good fortune but to make you aware that you have an ally. You see, I behaved contemptibly toward your father. It may shock you to learn that I came here as his model and then tricked him into marrying me when I was pregnant with another man's child. And I was unkind to your mother, who gave William the love and commitment I never could. At a time when they could have been completely happy together, I used my grief to cause them misery."

She made an impatient gesture with her hands. "This is beginning to sound like a pointless confession. I can't change the tragedy of the past. I can't make amends to people who are long dead and gone, but perhaps I can with you. I somehow feel that fate brought you here to give me a new life, a second chance. I don't intend to botch it. Just know and remember that when you need a friend, you have one in Dolly Fox."

The woman regarded her with such sincerity that, to her surprise, Maggie felt a lump rise to her throat. Mrs. Fox had no way of knowing how much Maggie had been able to learn about the past through her father's journals. The dark-eyed woman couldn't have known that Maggie was well acquainted with Fox family secrets that hadn't seen the light of day for twenty-five years. Dolly was offering these unflattering revelations without whitewashing them as many would have done. She tendered them like a peace offering, and as Maggie looked into the proud midnight-black eyes, she understood for the first time how a man like her father could have loved Dolly Alexander Fox for much of his life.

Suddenly the band struck up the familiar chords of "Happy Birthday," and Maggie glanced around in time to see Captain Jack and Bart carry the mountainous candlelit cake to the center table. With shining eyes she turned back to Mrs. Fox.

"Come," she said huskily. "Join the party."

"Really?" Dolly Fox questioned hesitantly.

"Really," came the reply, and with a brief exchange of smiles, the two women descended the stairs together.

After the cake was served, the guests gathered around Rachel and Annie, who delightedly began to select packages from the pile of birthday presents. Nimble fingers unwrapped treasure after treasure to the admiring roar of the crowd. There were embroidered aprons, homemade preserves, and hand-quilted pot holders. But at no time were the exclamations louder than when Rachel and Annie unwrapped the large flat presents from Maggie.

She had done a full-figure charcoal sketch of each woman, and she was pleased with the results. The lines were clean and spare, but each portrait captured unquestionably the appearance and personality of the subject. Framed simply and identically in wormwood, the sketches were signed "Happy Birthday. Love, Maggie."

Annie embraced Maggie and began to circulate through the crowd and show off her new work of art. Rachel perused her likeness reverently, then reached over to squeeze Maggie's hand before passing the sketch to Mrs. Fox. "I just want you to look at what this child has gone and done," Rachel said, wiping a tear from her round face.

Mrs. Fox studied the sketch and turned to Maggie in surprise. "I knew you had your mother's looks," she said, "but I didn't realize you had your father's talent."

"I'm afraid I can't aspire to *that*," Maggie murmured modestly, but she was pleased nonetheless.

The remaining presents were opened, and as the summer sun dipped toward the horizon, guests began to take their leave.

"Thank you, Miss Maggie" . . . "Great party, Miss Maggie," came the calls as Maggie smiled and waved farewell to the departing crowd. It was then that Jonas's tall, svelte fiancée approached.

"It was a lovely party," Naomi offered.

"Thank you. I'm glad you could come. Jonas has spoken of you so often, I feel as if I've known you for a long time."

"And I, you," the dark woman returned with a smile.

Maggie tilted her head and looked up at Naomi curiously. She was so tall and slender, quite regal actually, like an African queen, with her smooth dark complexion, beneficent eyes, and the longest neck Maggie had ever seen. But the two young women had no chance to continue their conversation as more of the guests stopped by to thank Maggie for her hospitality.

Finally, Rachel and Annie moved with the last of their friends and family toward the front of the house. With a tired sigh, Maggie slumped into the chair next to the one where Mrs. Fox was still quietly observing the goings-on of the "common folk" as if from a throne.

"Seems you're a big hit, *Miss* Maggie," she said with an amused glance. "I must point out how unusual and admirable I think it is for you to have given a party for these . . . working people."

Maggie gave her a somewhat defensive look, but Dolly Fox continued briskly, "Don't get me wrong. My father was a farmer. I come from this class. I rode into the aristocracy on a wave of good luck—your father. He was a fine man, an excellent man. But I'll tell you honestly, I wouldn't give two shakes for many of the so-called elite. In most cases, it would take ten of them to measure up to the honor in one Rachel or Annie MacGregor."

Maggie smiled and realized quite suddenly that she had come to like Dolly Fox more than any woman she'd met in a long time. It was at that moment that a yawn stole over her.

"Long day?" Mrs. Fox said with a smile. She turned her gaze across the lawns, past the tables where Captain Jack and Bart were packing up, to the thicket of oaks near the stables. "And it looks as if it's not over yet," she added.

"What do you mean?" Maggie asked tiredly.

"Unless my eyes deceive me," Mrs. Fox replied, "that's my son over there. And he has John Henry in tow."

As Maggie looked quickly in the direction Dolly indicated, she saw Mark's tall form turn to a smaller man who began to gesture emphatically. John Henry.

"Looks as if my cousin is on another rampage," Dolly said, shaking her head. "He wouldn't think of moving into the city with me. Had to stay near the estate. Poor crazed man. I think the loss of Foxcroft affected him more than anyone."

At that moment John Henry strode into the oaks and out of view. After a moment Mark started across the lawns. He was leading a tall Irish setter whose red coat gleamed brightly in the light of the setting sun.

Mrs. Fox chuckled. "Mark was never punctual, but he always knew how to make a grand entrance."

"Oh, yes," Maggie replied caustically. "He's a born actor, that one."

She rose to her feet and regarded the approaching man as if she were sizing up an adversary. He was hatless, the light gleaming on his dark hair. As his tall form moved across the lawn, she focused on the familiar, confident gait—more a swagger than a walk. She knew it so well.

Mark put distance between himself and John Henry. The man had insisted on coming along—lured by Foxcroft, Mark thought, like metal to a magnet. But as soon as he spotted Dolly, he had stopped in his tracks, got that look of angry vengefulness about him, and refused to go any farther. Somehow, John Henry blamed his cousin for all his troubles—Dolly and the bright-haired woman who stood beside her.

As Mark crossed the yard, the setter trotting a step or two ahead, he was able to study the two women. What a surprise to find them together, his mother sitting demurely in a patio chair and Maggie standing beside her like an avenging angel, her gaze leveled at him as if she was ready to do battle.

Standing straight and tall like that, the sun setting fire to her hair, the little spitfire looked sensational. Bare suntanned shoulders glistening above a white flounce of a blouse, tiny belted waist, short denim skirt that stopped above the knee, and long slender legs that seemed to go on forever.

He was just close enough to discern the daring point at which her décolletage clung. The ruffle of her blouse rested just along the crests of her breasts in a way that would whet any man's appetite, make him long to pull the blouse just a little lower. Yet, Mark imagined, if his own hand reached out to do just that, it would be smartly smacked away.

His brows drew together. More and more, he was beginning to think Maggie used her feminine attractiveness purposefully—that she actually enjoyed the feeling of power. He remembered the last time she had kissed him so invitingly, then pushed him disdainfully away. More and more, he was beginning to feel like her toy.

Dolly Fox gazed for a moment at the slim young woman who stood so proudly against the glowing backdrop of sunset. She had impatiently tossed the flaming hair behind her shoulders and lifted her chin high. It was easy to see the animosity that seethed through Maggie. "A born actor," she had called Mark. For the first time Dolly suspected there were strong feelings between her son and the Foxcroft heiress. Maggie was fairly bristling with defiance. And Mark had been an absolute boor for months. Perhaps this was why.

The dark-haired woman rose to her feet. "Mark is headstrong and hot-tempered," she said. "But he's a good man."

"Sorry," Maggie answered shortly. "I forgot for a moment that you're his mother."

"Mother or not, I'm not blind to his faults or his virtues." Dolly Fox's voice tightened a bit. "Don't be so hard-hearted."

Maggie's head swung around. "If anyone's been hard-hearted, it's your son!"

"Come, now, Maggie. Something totally unexpected has happened to all of us, not just to you. Something we wouldn't have expected in a hundred years has slapped us in the face, changed our lives. People aren't always at their best when they're caught off guard. You and I have made peace with each other. Why not try it with Mark?"

Maggie's look turned bleak as Mark drew near. "Even if I wanted to," she said levelly, "I wouldn't know how to begin."

"Hello, Mother," came his deep voice. "Maggie," he added, as if including her in his greeting were an afterthought.

She hadn't seen him since the day in the forest. His hair had grown long, almost to his shoulders in back, although the front, which curled around his sculptured forehead and jaw, was relatively short. In a sleeveless white T-shirt and gray gym shorts that bared his long muscular legs, he was sloppily, unnervingly sexy.

Maggie raged at him silently. As he leaned over to give Dolly Fox a peck on the cheek, she knelt and began to pet the beautiful dog.

"I didn't expect to see you here," he continued to his mother.

"I'll bet you didn't."

"Where's Rachel?"

"Up front," Dolly answered. "Saying good-bye to the guests." With a nod to the setter, she added, "Is this her birthday present?"

"Yes. She mentioned awhile back she'd like to have a dog. This is Margaret."

"Margaret?" Maggie repeated icily and came to her feet.

"Yeah. I named her myself." Mark's eyes came to rest on her. "She's very well trained. Watch this. Margaret, sit!" he commanded, and the setter obediently sank to her haunches. "See how well she obeys?"

"Very impressive," Maggie muttered, folding her arms across her chest and turning up her nose.

A spark sprang to Mark's eye, an edge to his voice. "Pity the bitches I come across don't have Margaret's temperament and intelligence. Perhaps," he added with a raised brow, "it has something to do with breeding."

Maggie shot him a glare.

He returned it.

"Perhaps you'd be more successful," she suggested with mock courtesy, "if you confined yourself to dogs and left the other bitches to someone more qualified."

Mr. Thompson and his wife Flora chose that moment to approach the small group, and with a sense of satisfaction at the angry flush her barb had yielded, Maggie turned her back on Mark. Her face took on a bright smile as she addressed the Thompsons.

"All packed up?" she asked. "I must compliment you two. Both of you were wonderful today."

With downcast eyes and colorful blushes, the Thompsons thanked her, and then Mr. Thompson spoke up. "Miss Maggie, before I leave, I want to tell you something. And maybe you'd be interested too, Mr. Fox. Some of the kids were playing out by the old slave cabins this afternoon. Seems one of 'em has been broken into."

"Which one?" Mark demanded.

"One of the last cabins on the row. I'll show you if you like," Mr. Thompson offered.

"Yes, I'd like to have a look," Maggie said.

Mark turned to her, a firm look on his bronzed face. "I'll go," he announced authoritatively. "The huts back up to my property."

"I *said* I'll have a look," Maggie repeated with a flash of her eyes that Mark swiftly met with a look of equal determination.

Dolly stood silently, watching the two of them battle it out. Finally her hot-tempered son had met his match. With a bemused shake of her head, she interrupted. "Okay, you two. I think it's time for me to get going. Mark, don't forget, lunch at my house tomorrow. And, Maggie, if ever you should want to visit an infamous old lady in the city, you know where to find me."

The chauffeur materialized from somewhere. As Maggie watched Dolly Fox walk away on the young man's arm, she couldn't help but compare the woman's surprising charm and flair to the occasional surfacing of those same qualities in her son. Her eyes turned back to find his green ones leveled on her. In silence, they followed Mr. Thompson to one of the old brick huts beyond the stables.

As Mr. Thompson had said, the lock on the door had been jimmied. The Irish setter wandered into the shadowy cabin where boarded windows shut out all but small shafts of dusky light. The dog sniffed the earthen floor and, passing the stone hearth, moved to investigate a mound of blankets in the corner. The memory of the forest chase flashed through Maggie's mind, and a shiver ran up her spine.

"Someone's been crashing here, all right," Mark said, his head bowed to accommodate the low ceiling of the hut. "Look at the ashes on the hearth."

"That's what I thought," Mr. Thompson agreed. "Should I nail the door shut?"

Looking around the small room, Mark paused for a moment. "No. I think a stakeout might be in order."

"Whatever you say, Mr. Fox." Mr. Thompson pushed the floppy hat back on his head and scratched his forehead thoughtfully.

"Yes, whatever you say," Maggie repeated and drew a look of surprise from Mark. Perhaps it was the lengthening shadows or the grim atmosphere of the old slave cabin, but she suddenly felt that her home was being threatened. Grudgingly she welcomed Mark's support.

They stepped outside into the welcome open air. The light was soft and fading, but Maggie could have sworn there was a fleeting look of the old warmth in Mark's eyes.

"I have to get a few things together if I'm going to stay out here tonight," he said, his deep voice rumbling. Handing her Margaret's leash, he added, "Will you take the dog to Rachel and wish her a happy birthday from me?"

Mr. Thompson accompanied Maggie back to Foxcroft house, and Mark sprinted off in the opposite direction.

Night was falling by the time Maggie reached the main house and turned the dog over to Rachel and Maggie amid squeals of delight. Captain Jack was putting together the last of his equipment, and after Maggie had helped him load it into the truck, she leaned casually against the cab.

"Didn't I see you with Dolly and Mark Fox?" the captain asked.

"Yes," Maggie replied.

Captain Jack's old eyes took on a feral gleam. "If those folks give you a hard time, young lady, I want to hear about it."

Maggie rested a hand on the man's shoulder as she smiled at him fondly. "Thanks, but they're not giving me any trouble. In fact, if you can believe it, Dolly offered me her friendship. As for Mark, I've already had all the trouble I'm going to take from him."

"Okay," Captain Jack relented. "As long as they didn't spoil your day."

"Everything was perfect," she assured him as he climbed nimbly into the driver's seat. "I couldn't have done it without you. And when you send me the bill, I don't want you to skimp."

A pleased expression settled on his face. "Cost," he said. "Everything at cost."

"Captain Jack! I expect to be treated just like any other customer."

"But you aren't just any other customer, young lady, especially after what you've given me."

Maggie gave him a curious look. "What have I given you?"

"That painting of the *Queen*. The other day one of the art dealers from down in the district had lunch at my place. Some Frenchman—Bouchard, that's his name—noticed the picture right off, said a lot of nice things about it, and offered to buy it on the spot. When I told him it wasn't for sale, he said to let him know if I changed my mind. Said it was worth a couple of thousand bucks, Maggie," the captain added soberly. "Now that we know how valuable it is, I'll understand if you want it back."

"Don't be silly," Maggie replied with a smile. "It's your painting."

But as she lingered on the front steps and watched the captain's truck disappear through the oaks, his comments about the painting echoed over and over again in her brain.

It was nearly nine o'clock when the long summer day finally submitted to darkness. Maggie joined Rachel and Annie on the rocking chairs on the veranda, and together they rocked back and forth and discussed the day's events.

With the Irish setter curled comfortingly at their feet, it was a peaceful time—the night still gently kissed with gray light, the yellow glow of fireflies dotting the lawn, the clean smell of cooling air. Above the splash of the fountain, Maggie could hear the rhythmic, soothing song of crickets. But every now and then, when an unexpected sound pricked her ears, her attention flashed to the violated slave hut at the end of the row.

Rachel and Annie went on and on about the party—how beautiful the day was, how delicious the food, how proud they were to have invited their friends and families to the estate. Why, such a thing had never happened before!

"It was the most wonderful time I ever had," Rachel concluded.

"Me, too," Annie chimed in.

At their insistence, Maggie helped them hang their birthday sketches on the walls of their rooms before climbing the stairs to retire.

She left the French doors open to admit whatever cool air the night offered. When she turned out the light and settled her head on the pillow, the image of the slave cabin formed in her mind's eye. The intruder was probably just a poor harmless vagrant, she told herself, but the thought failed to comfort her. Somehow the hut had become linked with her frightening experience in the pine forest. The thought of the cabin conjured up the same terror she had felt as she fled from the unknown shadow that stalked her. A long time passed before she was able to sleep, and then only because she knew that somewhere in the darkness Mark was keeping watch.

Early the next morning, without so much as splashing her face or running a brush through her hair, she put on a worn housecoat and went down to the sunny kitchen in search of coffee. She found Margaret ahead of her. The well-behaved dog was sitting patiently in a spot by the window, as if she already knew her place.

"Good morning, girl," Maggie greeted, dropping to her knees. The dog padded over, wagging her fringed tail vigorously. Maggie refilled her big bowl with fresh water, and Margaret lapped it up gratefully, if somewhat sloppily.

Maggie made coffee and sipped half a cup, contented with watching the beautiful animal. Mark's gift. Margaret was obviously pure-bred, her graceful body moving smoothly as she pranced about the kitchen, stopping occasionally to look up at Maggie with friendly, intelligent eyes. Maggie was musing that she would have to go out and buy dog food when Margaret began to yip at the back door.

"Oh!" Maggie mumbled as she grasped the dog's message. Retrieving the leash from the window seat, she fastened the clasp on Margaret's collar and was awarded a fierce wagging of the tail. Apparently, walking the dog was to be a new daily duty.

The fresh air of the morning, having not yet grown heavy with humid heat, was the best of the summer day. Everything was quiet but for the cheerful songs of birds. There was no need for Maggie to worry about her appearance. She was at Foxcroft, on her own land. It was a wonderful feeling to stroll along the bricklaid paths, stopping occasionally as the setter demanded. She was unaware of the picture she and Margaret made walking along together, the morning sun glistening on the dog's red coat much as it did on her own hair.

They took their time, taking a leisurely tour of the grounds, and it wasn't until they climbed the steps to the terrace that Maggie realized someone was watching. As she looked ahead toward the back door, she saw with a start that Mark was standing on the terrace only a few yards away, a large sack of kibbled dog food slung over his shoulder.

"I forgot to bring this last night," he said.

Margaret began to wag her tail furiously at the sight of him, and Maggie allowed the leash to fall from her fingers as the dog lunged in Mark's direction. Putting down the sack, Mark crouched and began to pet the setter affectionately, talking to her much as he had to Gray Lady.

He was as disheveled as she, Maggie thought as she came closer, quickly closing the neck of her robe. He now wore jeans instead of shorts, but he hadn't changed his shirt since the night before. His beard was thick. She gathered he hadn't slept all night.

After a moment, he straightened. "Where do you want this?" he asked with a nod to the sack of kibble.

"In the kitchen." Stepping around him, she led the way inside. Margaret bounded in, and after hoisting the large sack, Mark followed and let the screen door bang shut behind him. Maggie absently backed away, her hand climbing to the throat of her robe as he deposited his burden by the kitchen table.

"Rachel loved her present," she ventured as his eyes came to rest on her.

"Good," he muttered and fell into his characteristic stance, shifting his weight to one leg. "By the way, I didn't see anyone last night. I'll keep an eye out tonight, and if no one shows, I'll board up the cabin tomorrow."

Maggie's immediate impulse was to rebel against his proprietary attitude toward *her* property. But as she studied his tired face, she realized he didn't deserve a shrewish reaction.

"Okay . . . Thank you."

"Sure," he replied.

Mark stepped briskly to the door, then halted, his hand on the knob. He turned to look over his shoulder, his gaze searching her face. They stood there for a moment, he scrutinizing her silently, and she becoming transfixed as always. He seemed about to say something when he apparently changed his mind. With a muttered oath he stomped out and pulled the door closed with a bang.

Maggie drew a long breath and wandered to the bay window to watch his tall form stalk out of view. When Mark was about, he still managed to make her feel all fluttery, and she hated him for it. But after he had gone, more and more often the ice of her bitterness became a pool of sadness that washed through her until she forced her attention to something else.

Maggie turned from the window and went about feeding the setter, but her mind remained fixed on Mark Fox. She was beginning to wonder if she would never be able to stamp out the secret yearning that flared inside her whenever he was near.

Chapter Seventeen

The salty air was warm, the morning sun drenching the weathered dock as Maggie and Naomi—Jonas's fiancée—boarded the ferry. They were the only passengers, and after a fruitless call of "All aboard!" the rough-mannered captain sent the old vessel lurching into the sea, each rise and fall bringing a welcome cool spray across the foredeck.

Maggie shielded her eyes from the glaring sunlight and peered ahead. She had been invited by Naomi to visit Canadys Island. Gradually, the island took on color and character. Azure water lapped at a white strip of beach. A forest of palms, oaks, and palmettos blanketed a rolling stretch of land seemingly devoid of human interference but for the rickety wooden landing the ferry was steadily approaching. The noisy engine was cut, and in short order the captain threw a line to a solitary black man on the landing, who secured the launch. Maggie and Naomi had barely stepped off the ramp when the ferry captain called out.

"Be back here at three o'clock unless you plan to stay the night!" he ordered brusquely. The old ferry shuddered into motion and began the short voyage back to the mainland.

Shrugging at the man's gruffness, Naomi turned to the elderly black man who stood nearby. "Mornin', Mingo," she offered cheerily.

"Yessum," the old man replied, whipping a wide-brimmed straw hat from his silvery head and nodding to Naomi. From beneath lowered lids, he looked in Maggie's direction. With a quickness that mocked his obvious years, he plopped the hat onto his head, fled the landing, and disappeared behind a curtain of twisted oaks draped with Spanish moss, the outer fringe of a seemingly endless forest.

Naomi smiled reassuringly as they strolled across the landing. "The people here are very friendly, I promise you. They're just shy, that's all. They don't see many strangers, and remember, many of them have never been off the island. I imagine you look a little strange to them, with that bright hair of yours."

With a self-conscious gesture, Maggie smoothed the wavy tresses away from her face as she followed Naomi along a dirt path leading through the trees. Here the dense branches formed an umbrella against the penetrating sun, and Maggie luxuriated in the momentary coolness. She wore a sleeveless blouse and light skirt, but the summer day was already warm, and the close tropical moisture of the island seemed to intensify the heat. All around the path crowded a confusion of palms and oaks linked by Spanish moss, its lacy gray fingers seeming to reach for the bright wildflowers clustered on the sandy ground below. Overhead the palm fronds rustled with a breeze bearing the muted calls of seabirds. The place was enchantingly pristine.

Quite suddenly the forest ended and the path led them into a clearing flooded with sunlight and striped by a rutted road of crushed shell. From the left came a creaking sound, and Maggie turned to behold an ox-drawn cart, the likes of which she had seen only in old photographs. The cart plodded toward them, and as it passed, the two black men on the buckboard tipped their hats before calling and whistling to the oxen to quicken their pace. To the right were a couple of wooden shanties and, beyond them, a crudely built village.

A noisy commotion drew their attention to the road. A small boy raced over to Maggie and Naomi, followed by six other children.

"It's here!" the boy cried jubilantly. "De white fox done brought Juba's privy in a truck!"

"That's 'has brought,' Ben!" Naomi corrected. She taught these children school several days a week. As the children ran out into the yard, she called, "And it's not 'de white fox,' it's Mr. Fox!"

Maggie's heart skipped as her head snapped in Naomi's direction. "Mr. Fox?"

"Mark Fox," Naomi replied blandly. "He's been out here fairly often during the past few months. The children love him. He always brings them candy. And tonight, I hear, he's planned a town meeting to be followed by a cookout."

"What is he doing here?"

"You might say he has a vested interest in Canadys Isle. He's trying to get the contract to develop it."

Suddenly Maggie remembered where she had heard of Canadys Isle. The night Mark took her to the Atlantic House, he'd mentioned the island and the development he planned there. Maggie had blocked the night from her memory; no wonder she'd failed to recall the mention of Canadys Isle.

"The Canady family sold the island recently," Naomi explained. "Mark Fox is negotiating with the investors who bought it. They want to turn the island into an expensive resort. Can you imagine?"

It *was* hard to imagine. There was a captivatingly unspoiled air about the island and its people. What would be their fate when their home was turned into a resort?

"What will happen to the people?" she asked.

"*Nothing's* going to happen to them, that's what!" Naomi returned. "The developers can do whatever they like with most of the island, but all this land on the southern end of the island belongs to the Gullahs—the descendants of the freed Canady slaves who have lived here for more than a century—and they have a document to prove it. The developers will have to leave them alone!"

Naomi's brown eyes narrowed. "Mark Fox has been talking to the villagers about how to adjust to the changes that are going to happen when the building starts. At first I thought he was just a fast talker looking to get something out of these folks, but now I don't know. He seems to be on the level, talking about improvements they can make around town, how they can sell their crafts at the new shops that will be built. Today he brought Juba an indoor toilet, first one in the village," Naomi concluded, her gaze resting on Maggie. "Jonas's aunt Rachel thinks an awful lot of Mark Fox. What do you think?"

"I don't know what to think," Maggie replied, looking across the road to the shanty that seemed to be the largest in the village. Outside it was a truck with several workmen moving around it. A dark-haired man clothed only in gym shorts straightened away from the vehicle, and she caught her breath in recognition. She watched a moment longer as the men lifted a large crate and disappeared behind the hut.

It was in her mind to get away without running into Mark, but one of the children—a pretty young girl who looked to be in her teens—led them directly toward the hut that was the center of activity.

"Where are we going?" Maggie asked in bewilderment.

"Juba is rather the queen of the village," Naomi replied. "And Pheby, this child is her granddaughter. She has paintings at Juba's I'd like you to see."

The sun poured down on them like a molten shower as they crossed the crushed-oyster-shell road. Maggie's feet began to drag as she saw herself being drawn into a confrontation with Mark. Too soon they were mounting the stone steps to the shanty's porch, where an elderly black woman sat. Silvery hair peeked out from the red bandanna coiled about her head, and gnarled fingers flew at their task of weaving an intricate basket from the long reeds lying in a pile across her ample lap. Beside her, along the full length of the porch, stood an array of beautiful handwoven baskets. Beyond her, from within the house, came the shouts and clatter of men at work.

Maggie looked to Naomi and Pheby, but they only stood silent. It wasn't until Juba looked up and acknowledged them that either of them spoke or moved, and Maggie realized they had been waiting to be recognized, like suitors in a royal court.

"Hello, Juba," Naomi said with a smile. "I'd like you to meet my friend, Maggie Hastings. I've brought her to look at Pheby's paintings."

"Hello," Maggie offered as the woman turned to her. The dark eyes were yellowed and bloodshot with age, but they looked out piercingly from the deeply lined face.

"Excuse me, Grandmother," Pheby softly interrupted, then bowed her head to the old woman before sweeping into the house, the swinging screen door making no sound as it closed behind her.

"Pheby speaks and moves so beautifully," Maggie murmured, her eyes returning to Juba. "She's a lovely girl."

"Talented, too," Naomi supplied with a proud look in Juba's direction. "I wouldn't be surprised if Pheby got her artistic talent from her grandmother. Basket-weaving is quite an art, you know, and Juba's baskets are among the finest."

Juba straightened with pride. "Why, it don't take nothin' to make a basket, except the time to sit down and work this here bone through the grass. The menfolk go out and git all the sweet grass and pine and bulrush I want."

Juba put down her weaving and regarded Maggie steadily. "But Pheby—she's different. She's special. Not like Naomi said—she don't git nothin' special from me. She gits it from her grandpa. And she was learned by a white man teacher when she was nothin' but a chile, jest like her mama before her. Readin'. Writin'. The man come out here every week before her grandpa passed on. Now the teacher don't come no more, and I reckon Pheby's grandpa been turnin' over in his grave. He was always lookin' out for us, Mr. Canady was. Yessum, my Pheby's grandpa was a real gentleman, and that's why *she's* a lady!" The old woman's voice rang as her bony finger pointed to the door where Pheby had passed.

Maggie was so absorbed in Juba's story that it took her a moment to catch the gist. Juba and Mr. Canady. That was where Pheby got her honey-colored skin and light eyes.

"Yessum, Pheby's their kin, but the Canady family done forgot that," she muttered, her voice dry and brittle. "They forgot all the rest of us, too."

"I'm sure they haven't forgotten," Naomi offered.

"They sold the island," Juba accused. "Sold our home, right out from under us!"

"No one's sold your home," Naomi assured her. "No one can ever sell your land as long as you keep your map safe."

At that moment Pheby called out, "Miss Naomi? Miss Hastings? I've got the paintings."

"Bring 'em out here in the sun, chile!" Juba called firmly. "Bring 'em out where I can see!"

A swell of hammering and clanking rose from the back of the house as Pheby opened the screen door and crossed the porch, laden with a half-dozen canvases stretched over crude frames. With downcast eyes, she passed Maggie and Naomi on her way down the steps into the sunlight.

When the girl hesitantly extended the first of her efforts, Maggie directed a critical eye over the scene. Among heavy tropical foliage a clear brook sparkled in shafts of sunlight where a black woman bent to fill a pail. In the foreground was a single pure white wild orchid. Such color!

"Give me the others!" Maggie ordered, and when Pheby complied, Maggie propped them up against the porch and began walking slowly back and forth, her eyes moving from one canvas to the next. The island forest. The wooden shanties. The people on the beach. Pheby painted what she knew and somehow managed to make it take on universal implications. The bright color was sensational. The technique? A pure primitive style that would have made even Gauguin envious!

"They're magnificent," Maggie announced and missed seeing Pheby clap her hands over her mouth with excitement, although she heard Juba's triumphant cackle.

"Pheby, how many more have you done?" Maggie asked.

Pheby turned suddenly doleful. "No more, Miss Hastings."

" 'Tain't so!" Juba cried. "Go on over to the church, chile, and fetch that one you drawed up a long time ago! And you, Naomi, go inside and bring my Bible. It's settin' on the table. Go on, now! And you, you with the hair afire, you come on up here with Juba. I'll show you somethin'. I'll show you what the girl drawed up for her grandma."

Within minutes Naomi had appeared on the porch with a large black Bible, followed closely by Pheby who returned from the church with another canvas.

"Now I'll show you somethin'," Juba said as Maggie joined them on the porch. The old woman withdrew an often-folded piece of paper from the middle of the Bible and presented to Maggie an old and faded, but carefully drawn map of Canadys Isle. A heavy line of demarcation bounded the southern portion of the island which was clearly labeled as the property of Juba's ancestors. The signature of Thomas S. Canady was inscribed on the map along with the date—1866.

"Now, look at what this chile done," Juba insisted as Pheby held up a large, colorful copy of the map. The proportions were exact, the lines of the island identical, although Pheby had enlarged them and added colorful trees and flowers and water to the original black-and-white drawing. The Canady signature was perfect; no forger could have done better. Pheby not only had her own artistic style but also was blessed with an instinctive eye for reproduction.

The noise and commotion that had been issuing from the rear of Juba's hut suddenly ended in a resounding cheer. Maggie paid no heed. Her attention was on the shy, hazel-eyed face of Pheby.

"You're an extremely gifted artist," Maggie said. "This map is incredibly accurate. No photograph could be more exact; certainly it couldn't bring to life the original as you've done. But the works I most admire are your paintings of the island. They're exquisite! Can you do more?"

"Why, yes, Miss Hastings," the girl replied as Maggie turned swiftly to Naomi.

"When you asked me to come here, Naomi, I had no idea I would see such talent. I wouldn't even recommend a good school where Pheby could train. Her style is too original, too pure, to be tampered with. If she can produce another dozen paintings, I'll try to arrange a showing for her at a gallery in Charleston. Would you like that?" she asked, turning back to Pheby with an intense look.

Tears sparkled in the hazel eyes. "Oh *yes*, Miss Hastings!"

* * *

Mark stood just inside the screen door. He had finished installing Juba's blasted toilet in the scorching heat only to stride through the hut and be stopped dead in his tracks by the sound of Maggie's voice.

What was *she* doing on Canadys Isle? And why had his heart lurched at the sound of her voice when he'd sworn off the stubborn woman and intended to stick by his vow?

Yet Maggie's presence immobilized him as he stood inside the stifling shack, his eyes racing over the slim form in the pale yellow skirt and blouse. She sat on the porch with her back to him, the canvas balanced on her knees. Rays of sun lit her hair and bathed her suntanned arms in a golden glow. Like a man possessed he watched her, a tightness springing to his loins as the heat of desire swept through him. Perhaps his uncontrollable heat reached out to her, for at that moment, for no apparent reason, she turned to look directly at him as if she'd known all along that he was there behind the screen.

Mark stepped quickly onto the porch. "Afternoon, ladies," he offered with a casual grin that settled on Maggie.

Something had told her he was behind the door even before she turned. Now his bare chest and legs seemed to fill the airy porch. Maggie willed her heart to beat calmly.

"Hello, Mark," she said as the other women extended greetings.

"So you think Pheby's a pretty good painter?"

"She's better than good," Maggie replied, turning from the tall man to bestow a smile on the girl. "And before long, everyone's going to know it. Here, Pheby," she added, handing the canvas to the girl. "You may take this back to the church."

As Pheby sprinted away, Mark said, "Why don't you three come inside and take a look at the magnificent— uh—convenience we've just put in for Juba?"

They filed through the small house to a rear room where a number of villagers had poked their heads through open windows to ooh and aah over the gleaming white porcelain fixture Mark and his crew had installed. After several gleeful flushes brought cheers from workmen and islanders alike, Juba hobbled over to Mark.

"Tell me," she said with an impish grin, "what will I do with all the spare time I'm gonna have, now that I won't be hiking outdoors every time nature comes callin'?"

Mark chuckled along with the crowd until the old woman

extended her hand. "Thank you, son," the queen of the village murmured.

Mark took her hand and looked down on the bent old woman. "You're welcome, Juba. It's only the first of many new things you'll be getting. I promise you that. Now, everyone," he added, raising his voice, "how about a little lunch? We brought over a truckload of fried chicken and beer. Sure would hate to cart it all back to the mainland!"

Again everyone cheered, and there was a mad rush toward the truck. In the confusion, Maggie retreated unnoticed into the front room. The floor and walls were rough pine, the furnishings few. The room was spotless. Walking to a single table standing in the corner, she reached for the treasured Bible that lay in a place of honor on a handwoven mat. Absently she caressed the old book, running her fingers lightly across its black leather cover.

As she had watched Mark's kind behavior with Juba, he had once again managed to touch her, to trigger a sense of pride in him even as she reminded herself she had no connection to him, no tie at all but a stormy night long ago. Still, Mark continued to exert an inescapable hold on her. Time, the great healer, had done no more to erase that bond than it had to salve her hidden wounds.

The air in the small room was hot and still, the heat of the August day washing over her to send rivulets of perspiration running between her breasts and along her back. She jumped when the screen door swung open with a loud creak.

"Lord, it's hot!" Naomi exclaimed. "Mr. Fox has invited us to lunch, and chicken sure sounds a lot tastier than the peanut butter sandwiches I brought. Come on, Maggie," she urged.

Maggie walked out to the truck to find that the villagers and work crew had already picked up beer and chicken and found shady spots in which to settle. Only Mark waited for her at the flatbed. As she approached, he held out a box of chicken.

A devious grin pulled at Mark's mouth. He was in a dangerous mood. He'd searched the crowd, waiting for Maggie to appear. The longer she had remained inside, the more determined he'd become that she would not escape him.

"Miss Hastings." He greeted her with a raised brow. She grasped the box, but he continued to hold on to it. "It seems everyone has found a place to picnic," he said. "I have my heart set on a spot nearby. Care to join me?"

Maggie hesitated.

"In the spirit of a civil relationship?" Mark added mockingly.

She looked into the emerald eyes. They seemed much brighter now that his face was so deeply bronzed.

"Go ahead, Maggie," Naomi suggested from nearby. "See a little of the island."

"Yes, come on, Maggie," Mark added quietly. "What's the matter? Afraid?"

Maggie snatched the box of chicken from his hand and followed his swaggering lead into the forest.

They traveled along a narrow trail that was hardly a path, so overgrown was it with the roots of oaks and the stubby branches of palmettos. She refused to ask him to slow down, even though Mark's long legs carried him much more speedily than she could manage through the undergrowth. Gritting her teeth, she only eyed him defiantly each time he grinned at her.

"This is a deer path," he mentioned on one such occasion, and just as Maggie was beginning to think he was leading her into the very heart of the island, they came out of the forest and into a clearing. Mark stopped, surveying the scene with obvious pleasure as she looked about with wide eyes.

After the wild, junglelike thicket, it was as if they'd stumbled upon an oasis. Lush grass rolled up to a pond lined by a few palm trees. To the north, a hill rose steeply, its rocky crest split by a sparkling waterfall that plunged into the pond below. Fifty yards to the south, the ground sloped down; Maggie saw that they stood on a sort of plateau.

"It's beautiful," she said softly.

Mark's eyes briefly met hers. "I thought you'd like it." He strode to the edge of the pond, sat down, and removed his sneakers.

Maggie glanced around the tropical paradise, her gaze eventually returning to Mark, as he excitedly swung his feet around and plunged them into the water.

Maggie caught the spirit. Feeling suddenly adventurous and free of the usual caution Mark triggered, she sat down beside him and stripped off her sandals to dangle her feet in the cold, clear water. Leaning on outstretched arms, she threw her head back and closed her eyes against the sun, a faint smile curving her lips.

Mark studied her, deciding she'd grown even more beautiful in the past week. Then he caught himself. He had said he was through trying to win her over, trying to make up for the terrible wrong he was supposed to have committed. He had made himself a promise: If things between them were ever to be straightened out, it would be Maggie Hastings who did the straightening.

But as Mark watched her and remembered the accusing anger that could blast forth from those peacefully closed eyes, he thought it doubtful that hot-tempered Maggie would ever forget the past and come to him once more as a warm, willing woman. He grabbed a beer and took a long swig, but his eyes eventually returned to the spot where her ankles dangled in the pool.

"That stream comes from a natural spring," he said in an effort to turn his thoughts elsewhere. "The islanders have used it as their water source for a hundred years." He paused, but there was no reply. "How did you happen to come to Canadys Isle?"

The gurgling roar of the waterfall was enchanting; the heat of the sun, intoxicating. "Naomi brought me," Maggie replied lazily.

"Why?"

"To see the island and to look at Pheby's artwork. I think that was her ulterior motive. Pheby's paintings are incredible! This whole island is incredible. It's as if the clock had been turned back a hundred years. There's something so appealing about the people. They have innocence and dignity at the same time."

Maggie cocked her head and opened an eye. "They don't quite know what to make of you, you know. What exactly are you doing here, Mark? Your eagerness to commercialize this island seems inconsistent with the protectiveness you've showed toward Fox-croft."

Mark's gaze flashed to her face. "There's no inconsistency. The South is one of the last desirable underdeveloped regions in the nation. Investors and manufacturers from all over are descending on the place. It doesn't please me to see landmarks and natural resources being swallowed up or to see tourist traps springing up on what was once a forested countryside or a clean beach. But what am I supposed to do, bury my head in the sand? Real estate development is my business. And I can control some of the inevitable changes, try to make them happen in the best possible way."

"But how can you even think of taking the land away from these people?" Maggie pursued.

"I'm *not* taking their land!" he thundered. "*I* didn't buy the island; some of your fellow New Yorkers did! And they're a hell of a lot less concerned about what happens on this island than I am. They'd just as soon rob the islanders of their land and be done with it. And there are developers here in the South who feel the same way. If I get the contract, I'll try to build up this island so the Gullahs can get along with all the changes that will come. I'm not the capitalistic monster you're making me out to be, Maggie!"

Slowly, like a sleepy feline, she shifted her position to lean on one elbow. With a perverse sense of enjoyment she had deliberately baited him into anger. Now Mark's green eyes glittered beneath the darkly knit brow, and his sunburned cheeks glowed. It gave her pleasure to manipulate *him* for a change.

"I never said you were a monster, Mark. A devil, maybe . . ."

She added the last with a sudden, teasing smile that made Mark's mouth ache to kiss her. She had angered him purposely, tested her power over him, only to taunt him with a mocking smile. Mark was unaccustomed to being put on the defensive by a woman, irritated that he was unable to master the fiery-haired vixen who had dropped into his life.

"Here!" he said, abruptly thrusting a cardboard box upon her. "Eat your chicken!"

Alicia Townsend Harward picked her way daintily along the narrow path, occasionally glaring at the backs of the two black children who led the way, cursing the roots and vines that grabbed at the high heels of her sandals.

When Mark had casually mentioned the cookout he was planning on Canadys Isle, she had insisted on arranging the food for the event.

So far, the little liaisons she'd been able to contrive had failed to bring Mark around. But one day, when the time was right, Alicia knew he'd give in. Alicia always got what she wanted, and she would have Mark one day—if not as a husband, then as a lover.

She saw nothing incestuous about desiring the male she had idolized since childhood. The elite of bygone eras had often married within their own families, and Alicia saw herself and Mark as modern-day aristocrats who were not subject to the social laws and prejudices of the common people.

Enticed by the idea of strolling alone with Mark under a balmy starlit sky on an isolated island beach, Alicia had failed to realize just how primitive Canadys Isle was. The caterer had arrived late at the dock, and she had been forced to pay that pirate of a ferry captain to prevent him from launching his decrepit vessel and leaving her behind on the shore. Then she'd had to endure that shabby little village where all those strange people stood around, their dark eyes boring into her.

The only saving grace had been the unexpected presence of John Henry Alexander, who had brought the stacks of documents Mark wanted for the town meeting that would precede the cookout. Alicia had known John Henry most of her life and didn't much like him, particularly since he was cousin to Dolly Fox. But at least he was civilized. After learning that Mark was having lunch in the forest with Maggie Hastings, and setting off on a hot, dismal hike to find them, she was glad that John Henry trod only a few paces behind.

The image of what Mark and that Hastings woman might be doing irritated her more than the prickly palmetto branches snatching at her skirt. With each uncomfortable step, she grew angrier.

John Henry was no less irritated as he struggled along behind Alicia, the intense heat making him perspire beneath the summer jacket he stubbornly wore. But then, he thought, what else should he expect? His life the past few months had been miserable. His home had been invaded by that piece of baggage from up north, and then he had been turned out of Foxcroft! As if *she* had the right to evict the family from the estate!

"How much farther?" he called irritably.

A small black boy turned to flash him a smile. "We ain't even halfway there yit!" He giggled and darted ahead.

Alicia Harward gave the boy an angry look. John Henry loosened his collar, complaining under his breath as he followed the woman through the torrid, junglelike forest.

Mark had stretched out by the pool while Maggie went off to admire the lilies and orchids that grew in clusters at the edge of the wood.

Gradually she had surrendered herself to the seductive charm of this place that seemed to exist apart from everything else. Time was suspended. Her life at Foxcroft, even her ambivalent feelings for Mark, seemed hazy and far away. The only realities were the hot sun, the rhythmic splash of the waterfall, and the sweet fragrance of the flowers. She felt a oneness with the wild beauty and freedom of nature.

When she returned to the pond, Mark seemed to be dozing. For a moment she looked down admiringly on his tall muscular form, so carelessly attractive in the brief gym shorts hanging low on his hips. In her suggestible state, Maggie fancied him a sun-bronzed immortal—perhaps Narcissus, come to drink from the clear pool. A dreamy smile softened her lips, then twisted into a mischievous grin.

"Sure is hot," she tested with a whisper.

Mark's reply was a muffled grunt. She went quietly to the pool and bent to collect some cold water in her cupped palms. She approached Mark on bare feet and, with a quick movement, tossed the water in a freezing splash on his bare chest. A ringing bellow thundered over her giggle as he leapt to his feet and whirled to see Maggie backing away, shaking with laughter.

"Think that's funny, do you?" he blazed. In an instant his look of surprised outrage became a menacing smile.

"Come here, little girl," he crooned, taking slow, deliberate steps in her direction. "It's awfully hot out here today. I think it's about time we took a dip!"

On the last word he lunged for her, and Maggie shrieked as she bolted toward the forest path. But her legs were no match for Mark's. She reached the trees only to have a long, muscular arm encircle her and snatch her back into the clearing.

"Leaving so soon?" his deep voice teased above her ragged laughter. He swept her effortlessly into his arms and swung around in the direction of the pool. "Why, I wouldn't *hear* of it!"

"Mark, no!" she managed as he carried her closer to the cold water. "I was only having a little fun."

"Well, if you thought *that* was fun," he rumbled with a wild smile, "you're gonna love *this*!"

She had time for one last, disbelieving look at his profile before he quickened his pace and jumped into the pool. There was an instant of flight during which Maggie barely heard her own scream, and then the icy water rushed up around her as she and Mark plummeted beneath the surface. The cold depths closed above their heads for only a second before Mark found his footing and propelled them back to the surface. Sputtering and struggling to wipe clinging hair from her face as she hung in his arms, Maggie was speechless before she became aware of Mark's hearty laughter.

"Put me down!" she gasped.

"If you insist," he replied nonchalantly and, to her horror, tossed her, bottom first, into the five-foot-deep pool.

Again Maggie came up sputtering, but the initial shock of the cold water had receded and it now felt quite pleasant. She looked at Mark, who stood only a few feet away.

"Of all the—" she began, but something about his happy, boyish expression made her hold her tongue.

She had seen that look on the face of Mark Fox only a few times, and in each instance it had captured her heart. In spite of herself, she laughed along with him so that their carefree voices filled the glen—only to fade moments later as their eyes locked in silent communication.

The icy water had shocked her out of her daydreams, but the hypnotic effects of the tropical glade lingered. With rare abandon, Maggie returned Mark's look with a dangerously long one of her own before dipping below the water's surface. She emerged with her hair slicked back from her face, her eyes leveled on Mark's. Then she swam slowly to the bank and stepped gracefully out of the pool.

She glanced down at herself before turning twinkling eyes to Mark. "I'm a mess," she announced.

Having followed her to the edge where the water was but a foot deep, Mark surveyed her slender form. Her clothing was molded to her body, the light fabric no more than a veil over her skin, clearly showing her rosy nipples, the brief outline of a single undergarment, even the lines of her suntan.

"I don't see anything messy about you," he replied in a thick voice. "Quite the opposite, in fact." When his eyes met hers, there was no doubt of the message. "The water's great. Why don't you come back in?"

"I don't think so." Maggie stepped away from the pool and watched him follow her out of the water, his tall, masculine form enhanced by the meager cover of clinging shorts.

She realized what was happening. The moment was charged. Soon it would be too late to stop the current that was crackling between them. As in a dream, her thoughts and limbs moved sluggishly in the weight of the electrified atmosphere. She was surprised when a stubborn, level-headed voice issued from her lips.

"I can't go back on the ferry like this," she said, the words sounding prudish to her ears. "I've got to get dry."

Mark's eyes burned the length of her body. "Take your clothes off, wring them out, and spread them on that flat rock over there. They'll be dry in a few minutes."

Folding her arms across her breasts, Maggie tossed him a

challenging look. "You seem forever to be suggesting that I remove my clothes after you've seen to it that they're soaking wet."

"Why not?" he responded, raising a dark brow. "It's not as if we were strangers."

She looked at him quietly, her eyes communicating her thoughts, and Mark lost the last thread of his resolve to keep his distance. Taking a quick step forward, he grabbed her shoulders.

"Let bygones be bygones, Maggie. Why do you insist on punishing yourself and me for something that happened months ago?"

His touch generated shivers along her arms as the intense look in his eyes held her captive, breaking down the fragile barrier she had built against him. He was not a devil or a monster, just a man. And at that moment, in the privacy of the hidden, spellbinding glade, the only feeling that seemed important was that she wanted him—that she had wanted him, and no other, for a long time.

"I'm not punishing anyone, Mark," she said breathlessly. "Not now."

His eyes widened as if he doubted what he'd just heard. Then slowly, as if he feared she might break away, he lowered his head and kissed her.

The taste of his mouth was so familiar, the unnerving pressure of his tongue so instantly remembered. The expected flood of warmth rushed through her. This feels so right, Maggie thought before the will to think deserted her. She became once again that stranger, that unknown temptress who lived only in Mark's arms. Her mouth opened, her arms crept around his neck.

Mark's hands roamed over her, reminding him that the actual feel of her body was no less exciting than what he had remembered. Grasping her hips, he pulled her to him. Her hands slipped along his arms and around his waist as she pressed herself wantonly against him so that only their wet clothing was a barrier.

Mark's blood thundered through his veins. The pressure of his hardness strained below the waistband of his shorts. And when her tongue prodded his mouth to fill it with slow, searching lunges, he lost control.

His hands tore at her skirt until he could reach beneath to the filmy undergarment, and then he was somewhere on a plane of ecstasy. Never in his life had he felt as this redheaded woman made him feel. A unique emotion rushed through him, but his every hungry sense was focused on the taste, the smell, the long-awaited feel of Maggie.

He sank to his knees, taking her with him. Only then did he free his mouth and raise his head to look down at her dazedly. The eyes that returned his look were dark turquoise with passion. Mark knew then that his desire would not go unrequited, that the moment for which he had hungered had finally arrived.

"Maggie," he said, a hand rising to her cheek. "Don't you see? None of it matters. Not the past. Not Foxcroft."

The last was nearly lost as Mark's mouth closed again on hers. Maggie heard something about Foxcroft, but the blood was rushing too loud in her ears for her to make sense of it. Unbridled desire had taken over, and it paid no heed to mumbled words.

Twigs and stones were imprinting themselves on the skin of Mark's knees, but he paid them no heed. Under her skirt, his hand traced the line of Maggie's flimsy panties. They were barely there, and his fingers reached easily inside the sheer fabric. He began to stroke her and was electrified by her body's quivering response. His mouth trembled on hers, and he felt as though his heart would burst.

Maggie's senses were drugged by the feel of the man who held her, possessing her in a way she would have permitted from no other. With Mark, she had no choice. When he touched her, she was his. The primitive instinct to have him overpowered all logic, all thought. There was a drumming in her ears, a pounding ache between her thighs. The hot August sun poured down, but it was not the cause of the pulsing heat within her.

The first sound that pierced the glade was that of childlike giggling. It made no lasting impression, blending easily into the shrill bird calls that occasionally rang through the forest. But the giggling was followed by a voice that was impossible to ignore.

"My, my," Alicia whined. "Animal instincts gone wild in the forest, it would seem."

"So it would seem," her male companion agreed.

"God in heaven!" Mark gasped. Coming abruptly, unpleasantly to his senses, he lurched to his feet, pulling Maggie with him and encircling her shoulders in an iron grasp.

Maggie's startled gaze caught a glimpse of two gleeful faces as the children darted into the trees. Still in shock, she looked on the two people in the world she wanted least to see. Clothed in a light blue sundress that complemented her dark looks, Alicia stood regally by the path. Beside her was John Henry, an unlikely comrade but for the sneering hatred Maggie knew they both felt toward her.

"What the hell are you two doing here?" Mark demanded.

"Why, John Henry is here to help you with your town meeting," Alicia answered coolly, her polished manner and appearance making Maggie all too aware of her own disheveled state. "And I'm here to act as hostess at the quaint little picnic you're throwing tonight. Remember?"

Mark rubbed his forehead. He did, in fact, remember. He had asked John Henry to bring pictures and brochures for the meeting. Alicia had volunteered to bring the food for the cookout, as she seemed to volunteer for everything he was involved in nowadays. He had simply forgotten about the two of them in the heat of discovering Maggie here on the island.

Maggie stood frozen. So! Mark had invited his voluptuous half sister to his tropical frolic!

"*I* was invited," Alicia confirmed. Taking a few steps toward them, she looked insultingly at Maggie. "What's *her* excuse?"

"Her excuse is that she's with me!" Mark fired back.

"We can see that," Alicia returned smoothly.

"Have you finally found a way of doing business with this lady?" John Henry asked bitingly. "Dare I hope the two of you have reached an agreement about the sale of Foxcroft?"

"Shut your mouth, cousin!" Mark thundered as Maggie leapt out of his grasp. A hurt expression swept over her upturned face as the liquid eyes that had engulfed him only moments before turned hard as flint. "You know better than to believe that, Maggie," he said. "That's not how it is."

Her eyes impaled him. "Isn't it, Mark?" she snapped before turning stiffly to face her archenemies.

The wanton wood nymph of the glade had fled, leaving a fully alert Maggie at the mercy of stark daylight and two pairs of mocking eyes. She raised her chin and stepped disdainfully toward the intruders.

"I'm happy to disappoint you, John Henry," she announced. "There will be *no sale* of Foxcroft. You put too much stock in Mark Fox's charms. It seems they have far more impact on Mrs. Harward."

Mark came up behind her and reached for her arm. Maggie snatched it free as Alicia's airy laughter rang out.

"Really, Maggie," the woman sneered. "*I'm* not the one who just got caught on her knees with her skirt up!"

"Perhaps not this time, Alicia, but don't despair," Maggie retaliated with a swift glare at Mark. "Who knows what the night may bring?"

She stalked past Alicia and John Henry, a slight breeze making her wet clothes settle coldly on her skin.

Mark took a few steps after her. "Maggie!" he bellowed. When she ignored him, he came to a halt, his hands making fists at his sides.

"You don't need to run away like a schoolgirl!" his voice thundered after her.

"You're right! I don't *need* to!" she hurled over her shoulder. "I just *want* to!"

When Maggie closed the front door of Foxcroft House behind her some hours later, she surrendered to her gloomy mood. Slumping against the wall, she closed her eyes as visions of Mark passed through her mind. Once again her foolish spirit had soared like a wild bird, only to plunge back to earth with a numbing thud. When would she learn?

Leaving the doorway, she walked listlessly to the receiving table. Rachel had not yet made her way through the house to light the lamps, and in the late afternoon shadows, Maggie struggled to read the mail left for her on the silver tray. A letter from Shelley. A businesslike manila envelope bearing the official seal of the county.

With a sense of foreboding, Maggie withdrew the contents of the manila envelope. It was a property tax assessment. The exorbitant figure swam before her eyes as she stared unseeingly down the vacant hall.

Chapter Eighteen

Two days later Naomi called to tell Maggie that Juba's hut had been ransacked on the night of Mark's cookout. The old woman had been attacked and knocked down when she surprised the interlopers.

"She wasn't seriously injured," Naomi assured Maggie over the phone. "Just a bump on the head. Her assailants had already found what they were looking for—Juba's Bible, or more specifically, the map inside it. They made off in a speedboat Mingo didn't recognize. I don't know what will happen now. That map was the only proof the villagers had of their claim on the island."

"But who would *do* such a thing?" Maggie cried.

"Two white men Juba had never seen before," Naomi replied. "She was able to give the police a fairly good description of one of them, but everyone knows the assailants were only hired hands. The theft occurred when Mark Fox had called all of the islanders away from the village. They're all saying the theft was Mark's idea. And after all, Maggie, who would have more to gain? All he had to do is hire a couple of thugs to make away with the map while he kept the villagers occupied at the party.

"It will be interesting to see the course that the development of Canadys Isle takes," Naomi concluded bitterly, "now that the villagers are at the mercy of Mark Fox."

A few minutes later Maggie said good-bye and replaced the receiver. Mark might have a streak of deceptiveness, and she certainly held plenty against him, but she found it difficult to believe he'd masterminded a raid on Juba's home, especially when she recalled his kindness to the old woman and his excitement over his plans for the village.

"Of course he didn't do it!" Rachel huffed indignantly when Maggie told her the story. "That boy wouldn't pull anything underhanded like that!"

Maggie wouldn't have expected the old woman to say anything else.

The news of the burglary was shocking; the ramifications of it could be tragic. Why hadn't Juba registered her map with the proper authorities and filed it in a government office where it would have been safe?

As soon as she asked herself the question, Maggie knew the answer. The Gullahs had no faith in the modern judicial system and codes. They kept to themselves, reverently handed down customs and treasures from one generation to the next for safekeeping within their own homeland, among their own people. Many of them, as Naomi said, had never been off the island. What would happen to them now?

In the short time Maggie had been on the island, she had fallen under its spell. She was appalled to think of its unique spirit being devoured in the name of progress. And she was even more appalled at the notion that Mark might be behind it all.

Naomi assured her there was nothing she could do, but Maggie sent a basket of fruit to Juba and an encouraging note to Pheby, urging her not to allow the incident to deter her from painting, reminding her of the tantalizing possibility of a gallery showing. Only then could Maggie turn her thoughts back to her own dilemma. If she couldn't come up with a successful course of action, she would lose Foxcroft.

Many a day she paced the house, drawing concerned looks from Rachel and Annie and nervous yips from the Irish setter before she bolted to the stables and saddled up Prince or Lorelei. The rides were settling, and Maggie found she could think better with the wind in her face.

It was so hot, and had been for a remarkably long sequence of days. Each morning the sun dawned bright and yellow in a clear sky to pour down a shimmering wave that would hang in the still air, scorch the fields to a dusty brown, and leave Mr. Thompson shaking his head as he applied all his ingenuity to preventing the Foxcroft lawns from burning up altogether. Even twilight failed to bring the cool of darkness, the day's heat only lingering in the hollows, steaming with a humid mist the next sunrise would burn away.

Only a walk through the shadowy pines brought relief from the suffocating heat and allowed Maggie to concentrate. The taxes weren't due until January. She had a few months to raise the money.

She could sell the New York house, but that offered only a temporary solution. The money, Jonas said, would quickly be gobbled up, and then what would she do—sell the estate piece by. piece, as Arthur suggested?

All of them—Arthur, Albert Morely, John Henry, Mark—all those men expected her to fail. Each had denounced her intention of holding on to Foxcroft, had called her crazy for even trying. Maggie was beginning to think they were right.

She was fully aware that the sale of Foxcroft would make her a rich woman, but wealth held no appeal compared with her feelings for the estate. She belonged here, had set down roots just as deep and strong as those of the oaks. She had learned the story of her beginnings, had come to know of a mother and father long lost. She had grown to love her life and the people who shared it.

If she had to leave, where would she go? Back to New York? To the meaningless existence she'd had before? The thought terrified her.

Perhaps it was the recent brush with Pheby's artistic talent that turned Maggie's thoughts to her father's paintings. Pheby's style was the raw, brazen technique of a natural; her father's was the carefully controlled skill of a longtime student. Yet they shared something: Both were talented in their own right.

Art. It was Maggie's field, after all, the subject she knew best in the world. Her thoughts lingered on something Captain Jack had said weeks before: An art dealer had offered to buy the painting of the *Indies Queen*.

Each time the idea crossed her mind, Maggie vehemently dismissed it. She refused to part with her father's paintings. In a way they meant as much to her as Foxcroft itself. Still, the thought kept returning, hovering in the back of her mind as night after sleepless night crept by.

Finally, one midnight in late August, a wisp of a notion was born. It took most of the night and the next day to congeal into a solid idea—an idea that just might work! As quickly as it unveiled itself to her, Maggie sprang into action. She flew up the stairs to change her clothes, drawing surprised glances from Rachel and Annie at this sudden burst of energy.

Minutes later she charged back down the stairway, the keys to the old truck in her hand, her destination—Cap'n Jack's Queen. But as she reached the foyer, she halted abruptly at the unexpected sight of Mark standing just inside the double doors with Rachel, Annie, and a gangly young man.

"Hello, Maggie," Mark rumbled. "This is a friend of mine,

Edwin McCoy. Forgive us for intruding, but I was hoping for a minute of your time."

Mark didn't look well. His face was unshaven and gaunt; his long hair hung into bloodshot eyes.

"What is it?" she asked.

"It's about the theft of Juba's map," Mark began. "I've racked my brain for days, trying to think of a way to help the Gullahs. Maggie, when I saw you at Juba's that day, you were admiring a painting Pheby had done. You said it was an exact copy of old Tom Canady's map, remember?"

A light dawned in Maggie's eyes as she grasped the idea that Mark had come up with.

"Absolutely," she said. "I studied it very carefully. Even the most discriminating critic would agree that Pheby's work is true to the original in every detail."

"Would you be willing to make a statement to that effect?" Mark asked. "If you write down what you just said and I swear that I heard you say it that day on the island, Edwin here will notarize it. Then we'll take Pheby's painting straight to the office of deeds, and there shouldn't be any more question as to who owns the southern tip of Canadys Isle."

Rachel's round face broke into a beaming smile. "I told you, Miss Maggie. I *told* you that boy didn't have anything to do with stealing that map!"

Maggie realized suddenly that she hadn't been so sure. She breathed a sigh of relief as the group moved into the parlor. Within a half-hour, Edwin McCoy had drawn up an official-looking document, which she signed. Rachel and Annie withdrew to the kitchen, and Mark allowed the notary public to precede him as Maggie showed the two men to the door.

"Who do you think hired those men to break into Juba's house?" she asked as Mark halted in the doorway, fixing her with an unfathomable look.

"I have an idea," he answered. "But unless the two men are caught, there's no way of proving it. More than likely, we'll never know who was behind the burglary at Canadys Isle. The important thing is that the attempt to rob the islanders of their land has been thwarted. Thanks for your help."

"You're welcome." Maggie looked away from the emerald eyes that hypnotized her too easily.

Mark hesitated for a moment. "How about going out with me tonight to celebrate?"

A host of painful memories flashed through Maggie's mind, culminating in the recent one of Alicia and John Henry's embarrassing intrusion on Canadys Isle. She lifted her chin.

"I was happy to do anything I could to help the villagers, Mark. That doesn't mean anything has changed between us."

The chiseled lines of his face turned to stone. "And it never will. Right, Maggie?"

He glared down at her, but she refused to flinch, returning his look in stern silence.

Mark shook his head, his grim look intensified by the scraggly growth of beard. "You make me out to be the worst, the *lowest* culprit in the world. I'm not, Maggie. I made a mistake long ago. That's all. And I'm getting damned tired of being treated like a liar!"

A strange feeling swelled within Maggie. As she looked at Mark, a seductive voice seemed to question all the rigid rules that had governed her adult life.

"Dammit, woman!" he barked. "Do you think you're the only one with any pride?"

A lump rose to Maggie's throat. She opened her mouth to say . . . what? No words came, and after a moment Mark whirled and vaulted down the veranda steps.

An hour or so after he left, Maggie was able to push the thought of him out of her mind. It was only then that she recalled the plan of action that had burst upon her just before the men arrived. It was too late to drive into Charleston, but a phone call would do.

"Captain Jack? Hi, it's Maggie. I had a thought today. Remember the painting I gave you? What? No, I don't want it back! But you told me that one of your customers, an art dealer, expressed interest in it. Do you remember his name?"

La Galerie Bouchard was a converted town house on Meeting Street. Dripping with wisteria and antebellum charm, its street-level dormers now served as display windows. Shaded by scalloped awnings, framed with lacy wrought iron the color of pewter, each display a colorful abstract painting by a contemporary artist. Palms curved gracefully toward the windows from a diminutive courtyard surrounded by a cast-iron fence. Maggie hesitated, her hand coming to rest on the gate.

The morning was so cheerfully bright, the early September sun shifting in and out of shadows on the street. It wouldn't do to be pessimistic. Yet as she paused outside the posh gallery, her fingers gripped her parcel nervously. It's a good idea, she told herself. I only need a partner.

She returned her attention to the gallery. The sight of it took her back to another life, another place, where the aroma of freshly baked bread wafted along a street lined with outdoor cafés, where students gathered to discuss the merits of the latest gallery exhibit, where she had dined one night at the flat of a penniless artist and the next evening at a nobleman's château.

The one consistent theme of her life in Paris had been art—the study of it, the quest of it, the love of it. This love came sweeping back as Maggie stared at La Galerie Bouchard. The place had a decidedly Parisian flavor, and on a wave of nostalgia she passed through the iron gate.

A tinkling doorbell sounded as she stepped into the deserted showroom, but her focus was drawn immediately to the paintings—ornately framed oils, delicate watercolors, bold acrylics. With a sigh she realized how much she had missed the beauty of the art world.

"*Bonjour,*" came the French greeting from behind her. Maggie turned to find an elegant man of perhaps fifty, dressed in a European-tailored suit. With his black mustache and the distinguished-looking silver streaks at his temples, he had the look of a man one might expect to meet on the Champs-Élysées rather than in a Charleston shop.

He studied her, then said, "*Très belle!*"

"*Merci, monsieur,*" Maggie returned smoothly.

A look of surprise dawned in his blue eyes. "Aha! *Parlez-vous français?*"

"*Un peu,*" she replied. "I studied at the University of Paris."

"*Bon,*" he pronounced with an approving nod. With a glance at the canvas Maggie carried under her arm, he added, "*Etes-vous une artiste?*"

"No, I'm not an artist," she answered quickly. "More an art lover. My name is Maggie Hastings." She extended her hand, and the Frenchman bent to kiss its back. "Are you Monsieur Bouchard?"

"Claude Bouchard at your service, *mademoiselle.*" He straightened, his gaze returning to her face. "Call me Claude, *s'il vous plaît.* And your name is somehow familiar, but I am sure I would remember had I met someone so lovely."

"Thank you again, *monsieur,*" Maggie replied, remembering with a smile the romantic flattery of the French. "We have not met, but I believe you heard my name from Captain Jack Lewis. I'm the one who gave him the painting you admired in his restaurant, the oil of the *Indies Queen*."

"Ah, *oui*! The painting of the ship. Such talent, this artist called Fox."

Maggie was heartened by his enthusiasm. "Yes, William Fox. He was my father."

"Ah, then you are a *madame* rather than a *mademoiselle*."

"What?" Maggie murmured, and then understood. "Oh, you mean because my name isn't Fox. No, I'm a *mademoiselle*. My name is different— It's a long story."

"There is no need to explain," Claude Bouchard assured her. "I understand. Now, what may I do for you?"

"I have a proposition for you," Maggie answered in a confident manner designed to hide her desperation. She turned a steady look on the suave art dealer.

"Monsieur Bouchard, the painting you saw is only one of a series of oils that my father painted of the *Indies Queen*. Apparently that's how he worked, in series. There are landscapes, still lifes, portraits—all of them at least as good as the painting you saw. How would you like to be the exclusive publisher of my father's work?"

"Publisher? *Je ne comprends pas.*"

"Reproductions," Maggie explained. "I would like to publish limited edition prints of my father's work."

"*Lithography?* You are speaking of *lithography?*" The Frenchman's eyes seemed about to bulge from his head. "*That* is not art! That is a camera taking pictures of art!"

Maggie's heart sank. She had forgotten how contemptuous purists could be about reproductions.

"I was thinking more of hand-screened serigraphs," she ventured.

"Slightly better," Monsieur Bouchard reported. "But the painting I saw doesn't lend itself to serigraphic reproduction."

"Some of the still lifes and portraits do," Maggie insisted.

"*C'est impossible!*" he exploded. "Never have I exhibited anything but original works! The original carries the very soul of the artist. Reproductions are empty, meaningless!"

He raised a hand with conviction, the gesture reminding Maggie immediately of one of her Parisian instructors. Claude Bouchard's eyes were blazing, but as he noticed Maggie's dismay, his expression softened.

"*Mademoiselle, permettez-moi* . . . Let me be frank with you. Your father's work is good, *n'est-ce pas?* But it would be difficult to sell his work—even the originals."

"Why?" Maggie asked in confusion.

"*Parce qu'il est mort,*" the Frenchman replied bluntly. "He has been dead for many years. And he is unknown. Someone such as I, who loves and studies art, can easily see the merit in your father's painting. But the public is another matter. The rich patrons who can afford to pay what your father's work is worth—they want recognizable names or rising young artists about whom they can boast. They want excitement!

"In short, your father's work offers only art for art's sake. And today, that is not enough. To launch an unknown artist, the work must offer more than beauty. It must offer excitement, intrigue, better yet, notoriety!"

Maggie's hopes plummeted as she listened to him, and her disappointment showed clearly on her face.

Monsieur Bouchard regarded her sympathetically. "Better that you hear the truth. Other dealers would probably take no time to explain. They would just say no."

"Very well, then," Maggie said with a spirited lift of her chin. "Before I go, would you tell me what you think of this?"

She produced the canvas and revealed a realistic oil study of the marsh. With the company of the Irish setter, she had swallowed her fears and returned to the isolated clearing beyond the cypresses with easel and palette. It was her first visit to her mother's grave since the frightful day she was chased through the forest. This time no shadowy figure or unexpected sound had alarmed her, and once she decided on perspective, the scene had taken only a week to paint.

The cottage's crumbling chimney was set against a vibrant, sunny background of golden grasses and swooping birds, suggesting that human creations fall prey to time, while the living marsh goes on forever. Perhaps she had been inspired by her father's work or by her strong feelings for the beautiful marshland where tragedy had struck so many years before. Whatever the reason, Maggie knew the painting stood head and shoulders above anything she'd ever done.

Claude Bouchard's expert eyes flew over the painting. "*Oui,*" he murmured. "It has substance. But this is not your father's work, although the richness of color is similar."

Maggie watched his gaze sweep to the bottom right corner where the painting was signed "M.E.H."

"Would you be interested in displaying it?" she asked. "On consignment, perhaps?"

Monsieur Bouchard looked at the painting again, this time with the assessing eye of a dealer. "*Oui,*" he said ultimately. "I would agree to do that. Who is the artist?"

"The work is mine," Maggie admitted, eliciting a look of shock from the Frenchman. "You may attach to it whatever price you think fair."

"*Mademoiselle!*" he exclaimed. "I thought you said you were not an artist! Of course I will display your painting, here in the window. And we will see if it sells, *n'est-ce pas?*"

Maggie watched as he replaced one of the window display paintings with her own. "Abstracts do not do well in Charleston anyway," he muttered as he rejoined her.

"*Merci, monsieur,*" she said and prepared to take her leave, offering her hand.

The gallant Frenchman brushed her fingers with his lips. When he looked up, a new light of understanding shone in his eyes. "*Mademoiselle,* if you should change your mind about selling your father's originals, perhaps I could arrange to invest in them myself."

"I appreciate your offer, Monsieur Bouchard. But I don't intend to part with my father's work."

He gave her a searching look. "Forgive me, but if I may be so bold, it struck me that you might be in need . . ."

Maggie regarded him with fire in her eyes. "You're right. I need money. But I haven't given up on the idea of serigraphs."

"But . . . who will purchase the equipment? Who will do the work?"

"*I* will," Maggie returned firmly and left the gallery.

As she had listened to Claude Bouchard, Maggie's strength of purpose had momentarily flagged. But then a resilient, if daring, idea had reared its head. She didn't have the funds to pay the exorbitant taxes levied against Foxcroft, but she did have enough to purchase equipment and produce prints of her father's paintings.

Granted, she had hoped for the support of a gallery, but she couldn't abandon her plans because of one setback, not when she knew that dozens of companies did a good business by merchandising limited editions. Usually the major costs were artists' royalties and printing expenses. Maggie had an edge. Not only did she own the paintings, but also she had the ability to print them herself. The overhead would be negligible compared to the profits from a successful edition.

Selling reproductions of her father's work was the only promising idea she'd come up with. She couldn't let it die without a fight.

As she drove back to Foxcroft, she realized she was making a big decision. She had a deadline: The taxes were due in January. If she followed through with her plan, it would be best to make the Christmas gift season the target. She would have to work night and day to have the reproductions ready.

What if they didn't sell? What if she sank the last of her funds into a failure? If that happened, she would be forced to accept the fact that Foxcroft was beyond her means. She would have to do what everyone expected—sell.

A call to Jonas yielded nothing but dire warnings. "How can I agree with an idea that requires the investment of nearly all your remaining assets?" he cried.

"Jonas, calm down. Look at it this way: I can't pay the tax. I've got to do something! I admit this is a gamble. But at this point I have no *choice* but to gamble."

With a new sense of purpose, Maggie returned to the studio and began reviewing her father's work. Pulling a variety of canvases and papers from the storage racks into the sunlight, she spread the paintings around her and began to size them up from a new vantage point—marketability. Claude Bouchard at least had made her see that selling art was not an exercise in aesthetics, but a business.

Suddenly her searching eyes lit on the perfect painting. Lifting a watercolor study out of the way, she retrieved an oil that suddenly shouted at her with its suitability. Its lines were clean, it colors pure enough to be easily screened. The technique was impeccable, the subject, breathtaking. But most of all, the work offered the notoriety that Claude Bouchard had mentioned.

Maggie took the canvas over to the worktable and propped it up before her. There was no question. This was it—her chance, her hope. Like a hidden treasure, it had been locked away in the long-deserted studio, waiting t   nerge years later with the promise of her salvation.

Her trembling fingers strayed to the signature of William Fox as her gaze slid to the midnight-black eyes of the subject. Before she invested in a frame and silks and a host of other supplies, she had to talk to Dolly Fox.

A few mornings later she parked the old pickup on Wentworth Street in front of the Fox town house. She had blocked the canvas on a wood frame and wrapped it in brown paper. Now, with determination, she picked it up and climbed out of the truck.

The sun was golden in the sky, continuing to shower summer heat on the white Charleston streets. Maggie glanced up the narrow palm-lined avenue and remembered the day she had passed Mark and Alicia in this very spot. Irritably, she returned her attention to the parcel she carried and, with a brisk step, approached the garden gate.

The stylish town house was the perfect setting for the newly fashionable Dolly Fox. The garden was lush with magnolias and flower beds; the house sparkled with a new coat of blue paint. As Maggie climbed the steps to the small front porch, the door swung open and Mark looked down on her imperiously.

"Come in," he said solemnly, holding open the door so that she had to press by him.

It seemed to take an interminable time as her breasts brushed against his jacket. Her eyes flickered up, and she discovered that his green ones were on her. She detected no warmth there, however, only cold curiosity

"Maggie! Do come in." Mrs. Fox's voice drew her attention beyond Mark and into the foyer, a circular room capped with a chandelier and serviced by a gilded elevator from which Dolly Fox emerged. She looked lovely and refined in a lemon dress, an image that made Maggie's request seem utterly tasteless and insulting.

"Good morning, Mrs. Fox." She went to meet the older woman and added, "You look very pretty today."

Dolly Fox's face lit up with coquettish pleasure. "Thank you, my dear. Such a compliment demands that you drop the 'Mrs. Fox' and call me by my given name. I'm glad you called. Come, let's go into the parlor. I've asked Mark to join us for coffee and scones. I see him so rarely. I hope you don't mind."

Maggie smiled brightly at her hostess, but inwardly she cringed. She hadn't planned on making this pitch in front of Mark. Swiftly she reminded herself of the importance of her mission. Following Dolly Fox into a sunny parlor, she deposited the wrapped painting on a Duncan Phyfe sofa and took a seat by a tea table set with silver service.

Mark swaggered in and sprawled in the chair across from her. Folding his arms across his chest, he cocked his head to one side and regarded her suspiciously.

Dolly Fox proceeded to impress Maggie anew with her savoir faire. She led an exchange of pleasantries about Rachel and Annie's birthday party, then described an opera she had seen. But for replenishing his coffee cup, she all but ignored her sullen son. There was no denying the antagonism he exuded.

"Now then, Maggie," Dolly said. "What is it you wanted to talk to me about? And what is that mysterious package you've brought?"

The time had come, and not wishing to show any hesitancy, Maggie plunged in. "Dolly, I have a favor to ask. I'm planning to undertake a business venture. It has to do with art. That's my field. I'd like to take a beautiful work of art and create reproductions of it . . . to sell."

"It sounds like a good idea to me," Dolly commented with a puzzled look.

"This is one of my father's paintings," Maggie continued. "I'd like to hold a reception at Foxcroft before Christmas. That's where I'll unveil the painting and offer the prints."

"Why are you doing this?" Mark broke in.

Maggie turned her eyes to his dark, aristocratic face. "I have my reasons."

"Of course you have," Dolly spoke up and, with a disapproving glance in her son's direction, added, "Mark, don't be rude. So, Maggie, you want to reproduce William's painting and sell the prints at Foxcroft. Very enterprising. But what has this to do with me? What is the favor?"

Maggie took a quick breath. "Actually, I need a model's release for reproduction. But even if I didn't need the release, I would want your permission because of the—uh—nature of the painting. I'll come straight to the point with you, Mrs. . . . Dolly. It will be *your* name as much as the beauty of the painting that will sell the reproductions. If you give permission to produce the prints, I'm prepared to offer you a percentage of the profits."

Dolly Fox's dark eyes were gleaming. "Now you've really piqued my curiosity. Let's see it."

As Maggie began to unwrap the package, she noticed that Mark straightened in his chair while his mother leaned forward expectantly. With a flourish, she pulled away the paper and stepped

aside. Nestled against the crimson velvet of the sofa, the magnificent nude shone with the glow of a jewel.

Dolly's eyes grew wide. "Oh, my word!" she exclaimed, her
hand straying to the string of pearls at her throat.

"You've got to be kidding!" Mark snapped, his stormy gaze
turning to Maggie. "Why have you come up with this scheme?
Are you broke?"

"If she is, it's her business," Dolly retorted. Her eyes traveled
over the likeness of her that had been painted many years
before—a dazzling, raven-haired temptress, reclining on a Cleopatra chaise and regarding her viewer proudly. A slow, self-
satisfied smile spread across her face.

"I haven't thought of those paintings in years," she breathed.
"William did the series when I first went to Foxcroft as a model."

Maggie glanced from her to Mark and found that he was staring
at his mother with shocked admonishment.

"It's a masterpiece," Maggie said hurriedly. "And you were a
beautiful subject. I assure you, if I produce the prints, I'll do my
utmost to preserve the high quality of the work."

"This is the most outlandish thing I've ever heard!" Mark
bellowed.

"It's not outlandish," Maggie replied succinctly. "I know what
I'm doing. I've produced hand-screened serigraphs before, and
I'm good at it."

Mark came to his feet and glared at her. "You told me
point-blank you're not an artist!"

"Well, apparently Claude Bouchard disagreed with me," she
returned heatedly. "One of my paintings is hanging in his gallery
right now!"

"All right, you two. That's enough," Dolly interrupted. "Let's
just consider this calmly, shall we? Whatever Maggie's reasons
are for coming up with this idea, I can see why it could be a sound
business opportunity."

"What do you need with a business opportunity?" Mark
demanded. "You've got more money than you know what to do
with."

"Perhaps," his mother replied thoughtfully. "But this idea
intrigues me."

"Mother," Mark began in a tone of horror, "surely you won't
allow a nude painting of yourself to be gawked at by the public?"

Dolly's eyes snapped as she turned to her son. "Why not? It's
not pornography; it's a work of art. And if I say so myself, I look

wonderful. Why shouldn't the Fox family make a little money off a public that has stuck its nose into our affairs all these years? They're so eager to whisper about that scandalous Dolly Fox, why not give them something to talk about?"

A mischievous smile curved her lips. "Can't you just *see* Isabel Townsend's face?"

Mark had raised his arms in supplication. Now he allowed them to fall, slapping against the legs of his trousers. "I don't believe it! You want to go along with this half-baked scheme!"

"It's not half-baked," Maggie stated. "I've considered everything very carefully."

"And *you*!" Mark's eyes darted to her. "You must be pretty damned desperate to come up with something like this. I was hoping we could finally get this Foxcroft thing settled and put it behind us. Why do you have to be so stubborn? Why can't you just let things take their course?"

A cold mantle settled about her heart as Maggie heard him once again imply that sooner or later, he intended to reclaim the estate.

"I don't consider it stubborn to want to hold on to my home, Mark," she announced in a deadly tone. "That's what I consider Foxcroft to be . . . my *home*. And if you resent my fighting for it, that's just too damned bad!"

Mark stared at her intently before grinding out his parting words. "What I resent is that Foxcroft stands between us. You've put it there, Maggie, and maybe one of these days I'll realize you intend to *keep* it there!"

He exited the room with long strides, and after a moment the slam of the front door split the air. Maggie's gaze turned warily to Dolly Fox and found, surprisingly enough, a hint of admiration on the woman's face.

"You have an uncanny effect on my son," she said, and watched the determined young woman's chin rise another notch. "Let me tell you something about him, Maggie. Until you came along, women fell into Mark's hands like ripe fruit. Don't be too hard on him. He's a proud man, and he's not accustomed to having to fight for a woman."

"Your son hasn't had to fight for anything as far as I know," Maggie returned firmly.

Willing herself to forget him, refusing to allow him to spoil her precious opportunity, Maggie focused earnestly on the woman before her. "Enough about Mark. I want to know what you think of my proposition."

Dolly Fox hesitated, her black eyes locked on Maggie. "All right, I'll agree," she began. "But on one condition. I have no idea what's in store for you and my son—for all of us. All I know is that things can't go on like this indefinitely. This Foxcroft business has brought you two to a boiling point, and I don't know who burns hotter, you or my son."

"Mrs. Fox—"

"Hear me out. I like you, Maggie. I hope everything works out for you, and I'll help if I can. But I love my son. I want him to be happy. At times I think *you* could make him happy, but both of you are so proud. Both of you have violent passions and tempers. Who can say if you'll ever learn to control them?

"You must make me a promise, Maggie. If something goes wrong, if you decide to part with the estate, don't sell it to the Townsends or to some stranger. Lord knows, I'm happy here in the city. But Mark loves Foxcroft as much as you do. Promise me that if you ever leave, you'll sell the estate back to him."

Dolly's dark eyes were bright with conviction. Maggie had no choice.

"I promise," she said in a low voice.

Dolly grinned, a corner of her mouth dipping crookedly as her son's was wont to do. "Then we're in business."

"Thank you, Dolly. I won't forget this. And by the way, the reception at Foxcroft will be an unveiling. I hope you will be there as a sort of co-hostess."

"Who will attend?" Dolly asked.

"Everyone who's anyone, I hope. I've heard that Claude Bouchard has a most impressive clientele. If you agree, I'll ask him to help me compile a guest list."

"Fine." Dolly raised a mischievous brow. "Just make sure the Townsends are on it."

It was nearly noon when Maggie stepped into Claude Bouchard's gallery. He was chatting over a painting with an elderly couple, but when he saw her, he disengaged himself and hurried over.

"Maggie . . . *bonjour!*" The debonair Frenchman was as handsome and impeccably groomed as before.

"*Bonjour,*" she returned with a wide smile. "Claude," she said when he came to greet her, "I've brought a painting to show you. I'm going to produce the serigraphs I told you about. I'll introduce them at a reception at Foxcroft!" Her words tumbled out enthusiastically, eliciting a smile from Claude Bouchard. "I hope you'll help me draw up a guest list," Maggie concluded.

"But of course, *mademoiselle!* I will help you. And I have good news. I sold your painting not a half-hour ago. A tall, brusque young man came in and demanded to buy it. He so readily agreed to pay five hundred dollars that I thought perhaps I should have asked for more.

"He studied the painting very carefully as I rang up the sale. In trying to make conversation, I asked him quite innocently what he liked about the work. He glowered at me and gave a curious answer before stomping out of the gallery. 'It bears the mark of a Fox,' he said, 'the mark of a Fox.'"

Chapter Nineteen

It was "devilish hot" for October, Rachel complained. Every day Maggie repeated her grumblings as she toiled and perspired in the studio. In the lingering heat of an Indian summer, she found it difficult to believe her reception was barely two months away. She had set the date for the second Saturday in December.

Claude Bouchard's help was invaluable. He introduced her to a supplier and arranged for her to purchase supplies at a discount. He suggested she limit her edition to two prints and therefore justify the price of five hundred dollars each. Already he was spreading the word of the reception to his clients. To hear him tell the story, the Historic District was buzzing with the news that a nude portrait of Dolly Fox was to be published and that the unveiling ceremony would take place at Foxcroft.

Perhaps that was why Maggie had begun getting calls from reporters, among them, George Haley. Nothing had given her greater pleasure than to refuse the pushy man an interview while dangling a carrot of hope that she might be talked into giving him an exclusive the week before the reception.

Jonas told her how to apply for the business license she would need to sell the prints, and Maggie filled out the necessary papers. She drove into Charleston, ventured into the municipal building, found her way to the proper office, and filed her application. As Maggie passed the mayor's rooms on her way out of the building she was annoyed to see Alicia and Grover Harward chatting cozily with the city's foremost official.

She hesitated only a moment, but it was long enough for Alicia to catch sight of her. Before their eyes could make contact, Maggie continued briskly along the echoing corridor toward the staircase. She was halfway down when she glanced over her shoulder and saw Alicia steal into the licensing office she had just visited.

"Nosy bitch," Maggie muttered under her breath, and promptly dismissed the thought of the woman.

Everything was under way and all that remained was to produce the serigraphs. But as Maggie looked around the cluttered studio and examined the empty drying racks, she wondered with a sinking feeling if that would ever happen.

The background of the painting, a large block of graduating burgundy color, would be easy enough to reproduce. Like most serigraphers, she would begin with light and work her way to dark in separating the colors. And it was the light areas, the flesh tones of the subject in the foreground, that were giving her trouble.

She had purchased twenty cans of ink and mixed them fifty different ways in her quest to match the rich oils her father had used. He'd created a luminous Dolly Fox with mysterious eyes and glistening flesh. Subtle highlighting and vivid pigments had been meshed and bred to yield a mesmerizing depth. When Maggie finally realized what she would have to do to reproduce that luminescence, she began to appreciate the magnitude of the project she had undertaken. It would take the blending of twelve colors—twelve separate screenings of each print—to achieve a richness faithful to that of the original.

She cast an uneasy glance at the hinged serigraphy board on the worktable, already set up with its first frame. The mitered frame was of the finest quality, as was the organdylike white silk Maggie had stretched tightly over it. But the frames would remain unused until the first time-consuming steps of reproduction had been accomplished.

Her task, unlike the creative artistry of her father, was based on a painstaking procedure which, though it did not call for the vision of an artist, required the technical skill and close attention to detail. After preparing her inks, she would lay thin paper over the painting and carefully trace the areas in which the color would appear. She would repeat the process twelve times—one oddly marked paper for each color she would use. The tracing papers would then serve as models as she cut lacquered film that would adhere to the underside of the silk, creating a screen.

When all twelve screens were ready, Maggie would secure a sheet of expensive bond paper to the printing board and attach a frame and screen. The first color would be ivory, and with a flat knife, she would spread the puddinglike ink in a band across the top of the screen. Using a squeegee the same width as the frame, she would make one—and only one—pass over the silk. Then she would scrape the excess ink back into the pot, remove the paper, check for coverage and blots, and store it on a drying rack.

She would then load another sheet of paper and repeat the process until she had screened the first color of the entire edition. That process would be repeated twelve times, a different screen for each color, until the final indigo black was laid, kissing the serigraph with the depth Maggie longed for.

The hinged frame would have to be carefully lined up with the paper; the screens, perfectly aligned; the hues, true so as not to suffer when they were hung next to the original.

But then, Maggie thought, those tasks were concerns of the future. All she had accomplished in three weeks was to mix her inks. Ominously acknowledging the amount of work that remained to be done, she taped a sheet of tracing paper over the painting and began to mark the areas for her first color.

She was halfway through the tracing a week later when Claude Bouchard visited her at the studio. His tailored suit and polished grooming made Maggie take a regretful look at herself. She hadn't paid much attention to her appearance lately. In deference to the lingering heat, she wore shorts and had pulled her hair into a ponytail. Colorful splotches of ink streaked her arms.

But Claude didn't seem to mind. "You look as if you've been finger-painting," he teased, an affectionate twinkle lighting his blue eyes.

They spent most of his visit looking over her work. He complimented her progress and raved over the color samples she proudly dabbed onto printing paper. All in all, he seemed quite impressed, and Maggie's ego devoured the praise. She hadn't realized how hungry for approval she was until Claude Bouchard so willingly gave it. It wasn't until she walked him out to his car that he broached another subject

"I nearly forgot! On Saturday I want you to accompany me to Mannering Hall for the last polo match of the season and the party afterward. The proceeds of the event will go to the Historic Society."

"But, Claude," she said in dismay, "I was planning to work every day. I don't have time to go to a polo match."

The look on the Frenchman's face was kind but firm. "Ah, but you must *make* time, *chérie*. Some of my best customers—and *your* best customers—are members of the Historic Society. The party is one of the few galas of the fall. Everyone will be there. What better time to mingle with the crowd and give people a chance to look at you? What better way to promote the sale of your work? *N'est-ce pas?*"

* * *

After lunch on Saturday, Maggie reluctantly ceased her work and went to her rooms to get ready for the polo match. She chose her attire carefully—a soft ivory angora dress with a scoop neck and clinging skirt. The waist was cinched tightly with a burnished gold belt, the effect of which Maggie repeated with choker and earrings. As a final touch, she pulled back one side of her hair with a gold comb, so that the shining mass dipped provocatively over one shoulder. The overall effect was precisely what she wanted—understated enough that she could talk business, feminine enough to draw a man's eye.

Mark was a polo player. She hadn't seen him in weeks, and the thought of him nagged at her, though she sought to crush it at every turn. Even now, as she took a final look in the mirror, she saw her eyes sparkle at the prospect of running into him at the match. When Claude Bouchard picked her up in a long black Cadillac, his admiring comments brought roses to her cheeks.

The drive to Mannering Hall was beautiful. The picturesque Carolina countryside rolled past, ribbed by split-rail fences, dappled with timberland. Maggie lowered her window and took a deep breath. The trees were red and gold against the rich blue sky. The afternoon sun was warm, but the fresh air held a welcome crispness that smacked of autumn.

Mannering Hall had a history similar to that of Foxcroft. Built in the 1700s, the brick mansion had acquired the antebellum columns and veranda in later years.

Claude wheeled past the wrought-iron gate, continued through some fenced pastureland, and approached an open field crowded with people. He parked a fair distance from the polo field, but Maggie didn't mind the walk, since it gave her a chance to study the gathering. Colorful flags marked the playing field, their triangular shapes flapping in the breeze. Bleachers and dark green cabanas lined the boundaries, and on close inspection, Maggie discovered the cabanas sheltered refreshment tables. As she and Claude walked onto the field, the crowd ebbed and flowed about them. Maggie had never seen so many floral-print dresses and wide-brimmed hats. So many gentlemen in white linen suits. Southern gentility on parade.

Claude began pointing out people he recognized and introducing her to art patrons. It didn't take long for word to spread that she was here, and soon a small crowd clustered about them.

"Monsieur Bouchard, where did you find this charming young woman?" an elderly man asked.

"It was she who found me," Claude laughingly replied.

"I hear, Miss Hastings, that you're quite an artist!" came a comment from a younger man. Maggie said thank you and turned to answer a question about art reproduction.

It was then that she noticed Arthur Townsend standing beyond the fringe of the crowd. His eyes met hers for the first time since she had ordered him off her property, and she expected to find hostility on his face. Instead, she detected a look of amusement. Raising a brow, he nodded to her and moved away. She had only a moment to wonder what he might be up to before she was drawn back into the crowd.

Claude seemed to be glorying in the attention, but Maggie found it stifling. Above them a breeze ran through the massive limbs of live oaks, but around them the air was still, heated by the people who pressed so closely, heavy with conflicting scents of expensive perfumes. Maggie began to find it difficult to respond courteously to the clawing crowd that hemmed her in.

"Miss Hastings." A plump woman in a garish purple dress gained her attention by fastening sausagelike fingers on her arm. "Is it true what they say about the painting? Is Dolly Fox *nude*? Not even a stitch?"

The woman's southern accent was oppressively thick, and her giggle was even more irritating. Before she could catch herself, Maggie answered sarcastically. "Why, yes, ma'am," she mimicked, smoothly drawing her arm out of the woman's grasp. "Isn't it just *too* awful?" Her remark drew a puzzled smile from the overbearing woman, as if she thought she might have been insulted, but wasn't sure.

Claude quickly excused them from the crowd, and as he led Maggie away on his arm, he looked at her scoldingly. "Maggie, that woman, Mrs. Crenshaw, is one of the matriarchs of the Historic Society. She will *definitely* be on your guest list!"

"I don't care," Maggie said. "She descended on me like a big purple bird!"

Claude laughed appreciatively, and as he led her to a cabana and procured glasses of wine, his good humor reasserted itself. So did her own as they strolled toward the playing field in relative anonymity and managed to find good seats on the second row of bleachers next to the field.

She had been closeted in the studio for too long. Now, with the

clear, brilliant sky overhead and the green field before her,
Maggie put the prints behind her and surrendered herself to the
carefree enjoyment of the afternoon. She reveled in the fresh air,
and Claude's company. He was one of the most charming and
intelligent men she'd ever known. Without fearing that he would
misconstrue her friendliness, she was able to relax and laugh with
him lightheartedly as she wasn't with most men.

Eventually, eyes began to turn to the dashing Frenchman and
fiery-haired woman who seemed to be enjoying each other's
company so much. Whispers began to fly around the bleachers,
but they were interrupted when the brassy call of a bugle filled the
air.

The applause rumbled heartily, and from the double cabanas at
the far end of the field emerged a stream of horses and riders. In
gladiator fashion, the players circled the field, occasionally
saluting the cheering crowd. All were attired in white helmets and
jodhpurs of their sport; one team wore red shirts while the other
wore forest green.

"There are four players on each team," Claude explained. "The
captain of the team leads each color, followed by his three
teammates, and then four seconds. The ponies are trained thor-
oughbreds."

Maggie nodded as the parade reached the bleachers where they
sat. She had just spotted the tall rider leading the green team when
a familiar female voice rang out from a short distance away.

"Yoo-hoo, Mark! Here I am, honey! Mark!"

Maggie looked down the row and spotted Alicia vigorously
waving a white scarf. Mark turned at the sound of his name, and
Alicia jumped to her feet. With the theatrical flair of an actress,
she blew him a kiss over the heads of the crowd. A wave of nausea
swept through Maggie when she saw Mark respond with a
dazzling smile.

A muscle tightened in the arm that was linked with Claude's,
but Maggie kept her eyes on Mark's face. She saw his smiling
gaze sweep over the crowd and then freeze upon her. As he slowly
rode past her, the smile was replaced by a hard look that became
accusing as it turned from her to Claude and back to her again.
Within a moment he was gone, but the coldness in his eyes had
managed to chill her.

Maggie glanced down the row and picked up the conversation
of Alicia and her companion.

"That Mark Fox is absolutely dreamy," said a fair-haired

female. She appeared thin and mousy next to Alicia's dark beauty.

"You might as well stop purring over Mark," Alicia retorted, her sneering eyes turning to Maggie, "unless you want to see *this* pussycat bare her claws."

With a defiant toss of her head, Maggie turned to watch the match.

Polo was an exciting sport, she decided. The ponies raced across the green field, the players swatted the wooden ball with long, flashing mallets. Throughout the afternoon, no one played more daringly or successfully than the tall rider on whom Maggie's attention was centered. Her heart swelled as Mark made one magnificent move after another.

When the match was over, Mark stood inside the players' tent and peered around the flap and across the field. A constricting feeling clutched his chest as he watched Maggie leave the bleachers and stroll away toward the main house, her hand intimately linked in the arm of the Frenchman.

Mannering Hall's great banquet room could have accommodated King Arthur's court, and it certainly suggested all the majesty of Camelot. Scarlet-trimmed tapestries hung on the walls, and at the head of the hall, a giant family crest hung above a bandstand where a nine-piece orchestra was tuning up.

Arranged on the black and white tile floor, mahogany tables were set with candelabra, flowers, steaming platters of food, and silver trays of delicacies. Behind the tables waiters in tuxedos stood ready to serve the fashionable guests who filed by, filled their plates, and then clustered about the cavernous hall or wandered out into the gardens. As Maggie stepped up to the table, the musicians began a nineteenth-century melody that heightened the impression of an aristocratic celebration.

Arthur stood a discreet distance from the refreshment area, his attention centered on the shapely woman in ivory whose flaming hair outshone the gold at her waist and throat. He watched as Claude Bouchard invited several ladies to precede him in the refreshment line, allowing them to separate him from his attractive guest. Arthur studied Maggie's graceful figure and recalled the night months before when he'd held her briefly in his arms. The remembered tantalizing feel and scent of her body brought a warm stirring beneath the fabric of his tailored trousers.

He had considered courting Maggie, then dismissed the idea almost as soon as it came. She was too surprising, too unpredictable. Her stubborn stance on the issue of Foxcroft had chilled his ardor, and now she was going to ridiculous lengths to hold on to the estate!

When she had ordered him off the grounds in a fit of temper, Arthur had realized that he could not use Maggie to acquire the property he had long coveted. Still, she retained one redeeming quality: Mark wanted her. The Foxcroft stallion, who had dallied with any mare of his choosing ever since coming to manhood, had finally met a filly who had ensnared him. Anyone with eyes could see it. Why, the inescapable truth of it had thrown Alicia into an absolute tizzy!

In Arthur's eyes, Maggie Hastings had ceased to be a woman. As he came up behind her, he saw not the shapely legs and curving back but simply an instrument for his obsession—a means of getting at the archenemy who was his half brother.

Her eyes on the tempting contents of her plate, Maggie turned away from the table and nearly collided with Arthur. Apparently, he'd been waiting for her. Dressed in a dark suit, he looked taller and older than she recalled. But the air of superiority was the same.

"Allow me," he said and, before she could object, whisked the plate out of her hands and led her away from the noisy bandstand. He found a spot to his liking and turned to her with a bow, offering a tray of delicacies as if he were a waiter. "And what would milady relish this evening? Some caviar perhaps?"

Maggie made a selection from the plate and looked up at him warily. "What do you want, Arthur?"

"Come now, Maggie. Why so curt? Haven't I done as you demanded? Haven't I kept my distance from Foxcroft . . . and from you?"

"So far, so good. Don't spoil a perfectly good record."

Her testy manner reminded him unpleasantly of Mark, but Arthur swallowed the impulse to snap a retort. "Really, Maggie," he said in a placating tone. "There's no need to be insulting. I simply thought this misunderstanding between us had gone on long enough."

"Misunderstanding?" The turquoise eyes narrowed. "I want nothing from you, but I know exactly what you want from me. There's no misunderstanding."

"I think there is. I simply offered you a business deal that you rejected. That doesn't mean there has to be animosity between us. Believe me, Maggie, I've come to accept your position on

Foxcroft. Obviously you're determined to hold on to it at any cost. Why else would you be planning this—how shall I say—rather *odd* unveiling at the estate?"

Maggie chuckled lightly. "Odd or not, the idea seems to be causing quite a stir. I hope you'll attend. Your name is on the invitation list."

"Really?" Arthur raised a brow and smiled. "In that case I wouldn't miss it for the world. In fact, I'll go you one better. Not only will I accept your invitation, but I'll extend one of my own. How about having dinner with me tomorrow night?"

"No, thanks," she replied coolly. "I plan to work tomorrow night."

"Monday night, then."

Maggie gave him an irritated look. "I'll be working every night until the reception."

Arthur's smile faded. He paused a moment. "Working?" he snapped. "The truth is you're enamored of Mark Fox, and no one else is good enough for you!"

His outburst surprised him as much as Maggie.

"That's not true—" she began, but Arthur broke in, his hazel eyes glittering.

"Alicia told me how she found you and Mark on Canadys Isle."

A hot flush rose to Maggie's face. "That's none of your business! I'm well aware of your feelings toward Mark, and I won't be used as a pawn in your game against him!"

"Loyal to the end, eh, Maggie?" He thrust the hors d'oeuvre tray into her hands and stalked away.

Maggie's eyes followed him as he joined his mother. In an electric blue knit that stretched to cover her round shape, Isabel Townsend looked rather like a robin's egg nested in jewels.

Arthur leaned over and whispered something in her ear, and she threw back her head and laughed heartily, her gaze sliding in Maggie's direction. When she found Maggie's eyes on her, the smile left her face. Tilting her nose in the air, she turned her back in contempt.

Alicia was bored. Her husband was out of town on yet another political matter and Mark was nowhere to be seen. She looked restlessly over the heads of the aristocratic guests at Mannering Hall, halting on the figure of Maggie as she approached the group surrounding Dolly Fox. Undetected, Alicia moved close enough to pick up their conversation.

The sound of their gay chatter turned her stomach. It was unbelievable. The two women she loathed most in the world had formed an alliance. Who would have thought that the mad southern recluse and the sluttish newcomer from New York would strike up a friendship?

But then, Alicia's life had been strewn with ironies. Just when she had reached the age when she could properly adore her tall, handsome father, he'd been taken from her. Just when she had in her clutches the only man she'd ever loved, she had lost him to a despicable revelation from Dolly Fox.

Although Mark had withdrawn from her, Alicia had never given up hope. She'd waited, overlooking his dalliances with a long stream of paramours, secure in the belief that he would eventually succumb to the eternal love she offered. His interludes with other women had been short-lived, meaningless. Alicia had been certain that she alone was the one constant woman in Mark's heart—certain, that is, until the appearance of Maggie Hastings.

Alicia could no longer ignore Mark's passion for the redhead, not after the episode on Canadys Isle. The obsessive, hungry way in which he'd held her, the wild look on his face as he refrained from running after the hot-headed bitch. And then he had turned on her and John Henry, his voice hard and cold as he berated them for their "insulting intrusion."

It never occurred to Alicia that her biting remarks might have warranted Mark's outburst. She was too accustomed to doing and saying exactly as she pleased. Behind her back, many called her a spoiled brat—she who had never learned the meaning of the word no, who did not know how to curb her impulses. Some said she was too rich, that she had too much idle time to get mixed up in other people's lives, to harbor shameful, taboo thoughts.

Whatever they said, it had taken thirty years of pampering to create Alicia Townsend Harward. She simply was what she was. As she approached Maggie and Dolly, it was with the outrage of one who had been heartwrenchingly wronged.

"I know the reception will be a success," Maggie was saying, "if it rests solely on the merit of the painting and the beauty of the subject. I'm only worried about the serigraphs themselves. If only I can finish them in time!"

"Oh, I'm sure you will," Dolly assured her. "After seeing your work at Rachel's party, I'm convinced that when it comes to art, you're your father's daughter. Not only will you finish your prints in time, but they'll be absolute masterpieces!"

"I'm sure they'll be marvelous!" came a voice filled with sarcasm.

Dolly and Maggie turned to find Alicia behind them. As usual, she made a striking impact, wearing a black dress with a neckline that dipped brazenly between her breasts.

"I couldn't believe my ears when I heard," Alicia continued, her eyes on Dolly. "For twenty-five years you hide yourself away in the countryside, emerging only once that I know of—to spread that sordid little story about you and my father. Leave it to you to come up with an outrageous reentry into the land of the living. I suppose I shouldn't be surprised, but a *nude painting*!" The almond-shaped eyes swept haughtily over the older woman. "Dolly Fox, it's hard to believe *even you* have so little taste."

"Taste?" Dolly repeated. "That's an odd subject for you to bring up, dear. Why, for all your finishing schools and European travels, it's always been quite impossible for you to grasp the basic concept of common decency *or* taste."

Alicia raised a dark brow and struck back. "Such a quick tongue. You're so self-centered, Dolly. Do you ever stop to think what this lewd painting fiasco might be doing to your son? Do you *ever* think of Mark?"

"Not as often as you do, I'm sure," Dolly replied.

An uncharacteristic blush raced to Alicia's cheeks. With a look of hatred that encompassed both women, she whirled away without another word.

"I've never been able to tolerate that girl," Dolly said as she watched Alicia's curvy shape blend into the crowd. "*She's* the reason I had to tell Mark about his father."

Maggie noticed that her companion glanced self-consciously into her champagne glass before continuing. "I haven't given Mark an easy life, I'm afraid. He's had money and a name, but he's had to stand up to a lot of guff, first about the fire, and then about his father. I would never have told Mark about that except for Alicia. She made it impossible for me *not* to intervene, the way she chased after him. It was shameful. Even after I made her and Mark believe me, she *still* panted after him like a hungry bitch. Thank heaven Mark had the decency to fight her off!"

Maggie remembered the times she'd seen Mark and Alicia together, the taunt that "he always comes back to Alicia," the fact that they seemed to turn up together at the oddest times. She bit her tongue to keep from voicing her doubts about Mark's integrity.

"It sickens me that Mark has remained firm about naming her in his will," Dolly muttered absently.

"His *will*?"

"Yes. If I die before Mark does, everything he owns will go to Alicia. He insists that she cares for him, and she'll be his only flesh-and-blood relative, except for Arthur, whom he regards as an enemy. But whether she's my own son's flesh and blood or not, I can't *stand* that woman!"

Dolly delivered the last in a murderous tone. Her eyes were fixed across the room where Alicia stood with her mother in a small group of admirers. "She inherited all of her father's shortcomings and none of his good qualities."

Maggie studied Dolly pensively. "You loved him?" she asked softly.

"Art? Oh, yes, I loved him. Even with all his faults. Even when he left me to marry Isabel's money." Dolly looked at Maggie quickly. "But every cloud has its silver lining. That was when I started modeling for your father. And if I hadn't done that, we wouldn't have this lovely nude that's causing such a stir, would we?"

Her joie de vivre apparently restored, Dolly looked about the crowd mischievously. "This really *is* fun. I wish I'd gotten here earlier. I didn't arrive until after the match, just in time to see my son stomp off the field and into the bar. God, he's in a black mood!"

Maggie chose not to pursue the subject of Mark. "I didn't even know you were here, Dolly," she said and took a sip of the bubbly champagne.

Dolly fastened her black eyes on Maggie's rosy face. "Well, my dear, I certainly knew you were here. The whole place is talking about you and that Frenchman, and Mark is positively in a rage! Speak of the devil, here he comes now."

"Mark?" Maggie asked quickly.

"No, the Frenchman!" Dolly replied with an interested look at Claude. "Introduce me," she added in a whisper.

With a pleased grin, Maggie began, "Claude, I'd like to present—"

"Merci, my dear Maggie, but there is no need for an introduction," Claude broke in, training his blue eyes on Dolly. "I would recognize the beautiful Dolly Fox anywhere." He bent his sleek, dark head over Dolly's hand.

With a light, flirtatious laugh, Dolly returned, "And *I* would recognize the flattery of a Frenchman!"

The two became absorbed in each other so quickly that Maggie slipped away without their even noticing. A few couples had begun to dance, the crowd forming a ring about the floor. Maggie wound her way among the elegantly dressed guests and found a deserted spot by the terrace doors. Her eyes lit again on Claude and Dolly. Now that she saw them together she realized they were perfect for each other. She watched them laughing and talking at the edge of the dance floor and wondered why she hadn't thought of it before. Too caught up in her own affairs, she supposed.

A cool breeze rushed in through the terrace doors, and the music swelled as the orchestra began a new number. Maggie's thoughts returned to the stunning image of Mark galloping across the polo field.

She had immersed herself so thoroughly in her work that she had managed to keep him off her mind most of the time. Yet she was unable to forget him, to return to her old carefree way of toying with a host of men as she had done for most of her life. She hadn't been out with a man, except Claude, in months. The old footloose Maggie was gone, as if, somehow, she had lost herself months ago in Mark's arms. She looked again at Dolly and Claude. The sight of them together made her feel suddenly alone.

Her reverie was interrupted by a feminine southern voice that had become far too familiar. "Where's your honey, *honey*?"

Alicia seemed to slither around like a snake, waiting until just the right moment to rear her head and strike. As Maggie turned to face her, she found that Alicia was searching the crowd.

"Ah, there he is," she drawled, her eyes turning languidly to Maggie. "Looks like you've lost him to the lady in red. But don't fret. A gentleman like Claude Bouchard would never hang around a tramp like Dolly Fox for very long."

Maggie studied Alicia's beautiful, vicious face for a moment. "I don't need this," she muttered and started to move away.

Alicia's claw-tipped fingers flashed out to grip her arm. "Maybe not," she whispered as Maggie spun around with flashing eyes. "But you sure as hell need a business license to pull off your little artistic coup, now, don't you?"

The flash in Maggie's eyes died, her feet becoming suddenly immobile.

"I thought that might get your attention," Alicia continued. "I can't get over how naive you still are. You should have sold the estate a long time ago. Do you really think you can fight the powerful people who want Foxcroft? You and your stupid scheme!"

Maggie's eyes widened. "All this time," she said, "I thought you were obsessed with Mark. But you're not, are you? It's Foxcroft you want!"

Recalling what Dolly said about Mark's will, Maggie thought ahead to the terrible possibility that the Townsends could one day own all of the Fox family holdings, everything that had been built and passed down through generations.

"As long as I'm in possession of Foxcroft," Maggie added with heated conviction, "you and your family have no chance of getting your hands on it!"

"Believe what you will," Alicia said with a scornful lift of her brow. "All that matters to me is getting you out of Charleston, Maggie Hastings. I understand this business ploy of yours is meant to enable you to hold on to Foxcroft. But," she added with a mocking smile, "everything depends on that little old license. My husband says it sometimes takes months and months to process an application. Sometimes they even get lost! And Grover should know. Why, just the other day he was discussing the matter with the chief of police."

Alicia lowered her voice menacingly. "Let me warn you, Maggie. If you attempt to sell that art without a license, I'll have my husband close you down on the spot. Believe me, he'll do anything I say!"

Satisfied with the stricken look on Maggie's face, Alicia gave a musical laugh and moved away.

With a sinking feeling, Maggie watched her dark, shapely form glide toward the exit where Arthur and Isabel waited. Suddenly three pairs of mocking eyes were leveled on Maggie. As she returned their gaze helplessly, a sudden image of David and Goliath popped into her mind. And then, en masse, the Townsend family turned and strolled out of the place as if they owned it.

There was no mistaking Alicia's earnestness, and a feeling of vulnerability settled in Maggie's stomach. The party dragged on, and she hung miserably on the sidelines, hiding behind a smiling mask as different groups stopped by to chat. Every now and then her eyes flickered to Claude and Dolly, who seemed caught up in a budding romance. Claude had persuaded her to part momentarily with her cane, and now they swayed tenderly to the soft music.

When the orchestra began "April in Paris," Maggie's thoughts raced back to the night of the Townsends' party when Mark had held her close as they danced to the same melody. Bitterly, she scanned the crowd for him, her search once again yielding no sign. He had not so much as set foot in the banquet hall and, for all she knew, had long ago left the premises.

It was nearly ten when the chauffeur came to collect Dolly. She seemed to be floating as she made her exit, and a brief look at Claude's smiling countenance told Maggie that their happy evening would be the first of many.

Then, with the diplomatic assertiveness of a true businessman, Claude made the rounds of the dwindling crowd with Maggie at his side.

A half-hour passed as they said their good-byes and walked through the great house to the front veranda. Once they stepped into the bracing night air, Claude turned to her with a rush, as though he could contain himself no longer.

"Ah, Maggie, *chérie*," he said, impulsively grasping her by the shoulders and kissing her smack on the mouth. "Tonight you have made me the happiest man in the world. Tonight I found the woman of my dreams!"

Maggie chuckled at his exhilaration over Dolly. "And she, I believe, has found the man of her dreams!"

"I pray that it is so," Claude returned, his blue eyes shining.

It was during that brief moment of silence that the faint sound of a female voice intruded.

"Mark, what is it?" Sally Ann asked, her voice low and sultry. "What's wrong?"

With a start, Maggie turned and peered into the shadows where two people were leaning against the veranda railing a short distance away. Even in the meager light that spilled from the windows, she recognized Mark. He was with a blond in a short blue dress.

The woman was looking up at Mark, but his eyes were on Maggie, and they were filled with such loathing that the message burned true and clear through the darkness.

"What's wrong?" the blonde repeated with a furtive glance over her shoulder.

Mark's glare was unfaltering as he pulled the woman to him and covered her mouth with his.

Maggie's sharp intake of breath was like a hiss. Her eyes froze on the two people as the blonde's arms reached around Mark's neck so that the blue dress climbed up her thighs. Mark's hand slid down her back, below the brief skirt. Maggie hardly realized she was holding her breath, but when she released it, she was once again capable of motion. Quickly she linked her arm in Claude's.

"Let's go," she mumbled.

Claude leaned back to take a better look as Maggie pulled him toward the steps. "You know, *chérie,* I believe that amorous young man is the one who bought your painting."

"I said let's go!" she commanded in a harsh tone that drew a startled look from the Frenchman.

Chapter Twenty

As they cruised along the highway in the Cadillac, Claude glanced occasionally at Maggie. He sensed she didn't wish to be disturbed and kept quiet.

Lost in thought, Maggie stared out the window where the velvety black countryside raced past. The cool, uncaring Maggie Hastings of the past had tramped carelessly on a hundred hearts. Now she knew how it felt to be the trampled one. It was a devastating feeling, cutting deep where no comforting touch could reach.

She had denied her feelings for so long, occasionally managing to convince herself that she had cut Mark out of her heart. But there was no denying the ache she felt. Numb with the hurt of seeing him embrace another woman, she had forgotten about Alicia. It wasn't until Claude stopped the car in front of Foxcroft House that she suddenly remembered, and in a hollow voice repeated Alicia's threats about withholding the license.

A rare sneer crossed Claude's distinguished face. "It is of no consequence. Alicia Harward has overlooked the fact that you have friends. Maggie, weeks ago you came to me looking for a partner. I refused you. But now I would like to change that. I would like to help you and Dolly. But it's more than that. I haven't felt so alive, so inspired, in years! I wish to be more than an adviser.

"So here's what we'll do. If Alicia should manage to delay your license, we will simply take orders for the serigraphs at the reception, but we will do the actual selling through La Galerie Bouchard. If you operate under the protection of my business license, she can do *nothing*!"

Tears of gratitude welled up in Maggie's eyes, and she hugged her friend long and hard before leaving him. She stood on the veranda in the cool autumn darkness and watched the red taillights disappear up the avenue of oaks before turning and letting herself into the house.

She snapped off lights as she walked through the elegant foyer, and as she climbed the stairs, she found herself wishing Claude Bouchard could solve the other problems in her life as easily. Even if she hadn't been deep within the house, she was too preoccupied to have noticed the distant scream of tires as a solitary car careened through the Foxcroft markers and screeched onto the sandy road between the oaks.

As had become her habit late at night, Maggie turned on the radio. Mellow jazz filtered through the room as she shrugged out of the angora dress, draped it over the divan, and slipped on a translucent white negligee. After sitting down at the gilded vanity, she removed the gold comb, shook her hair free, and stared into the mirror. But she didn't see the flawless face. She saw a tall, dark man kissing a blond.

Finally anger overcame the hurt. "He's a liar and a cheat! Forget him!" she said aloud, then grabbed the hairbrush and began to thrash the fiery mane with a vengeance.

She halted in mid-stroke when the sound of a commotion came from downstairs. First there was a loud bang as if the front door had been slammed, and then Margaret's shrill barking. Fearfully, Maggie dropped the brush and flew from the bedroom into the dark hall, feeling her way along the wall. Her fingers found a switch, and the chandelier flooded the foyer with light.

In disbelief, she beheld Mark at the foot of the stairs. At that moment, Margaret came tearing around the corner, barking at the top of her lungs.

"Quiet!" Mark said. The setter immediately recognized her former master, greeted him happily, and then curled up on the floor. Mark turned to Maggie, tilting his head so he could study her at the top of the stairs. A wild look coursed through his eyes.

"Not too late for a social call, I hope," came the deep voice.

Maggie's blood pounded like a hammer in her temples. "How did you get in here?" she demanded.

He grasped the banister and stared at her, a crooked grin sliding across his face. "If you don't want me to come calling," he slurred, "you should change the locks." As he started up the stairs, his foot missed the first step and he stumbled.

"You're drunk!" she accused.

"Not *that* drunk," he replied and demonstrated by quickly scaling the steps to the landing.

The wide-eyed faces of Rachel and Annie appeared at the foot of the stairs. They were in their nightdresses, but Rachel was armed with a rolling pin and Annie carried a canister of mace.

"Rachel, he's drunk! Help me get him out of here!" Maggie cried, her alarm building.

"Mr. Fox—" Rachel began.

"Go back to bed!" he interrupted. "I have business with your mistress."

Rachel tried again. "Mr. Fox, why don't you come back tomorrow when everything's settled down?"

Mark turned to the two women and pointed his index finger threateningly. "If you two know what's good for you," he growled, "you'll get the hell out of here!"

Maggie dashed into her bedroom and locked the door on the sound of Mark's harsh laughter.

Backing away from the door, she stared helplessly at the knob. It turned as the intruder tested the lock. Bam! The portal shudderingly withstood the first blow. But when the second came, Maggie jumped as the lock splintered and the door swung open.

Mark stepped inside, folded his arms across his chest, and regarded her menacingly. From where she stood in the center of the room, Maggie directed her eyes swiftly over his tall form. Black boots. Mud-streaked, white jodhpurs. Rumpled shirt. Windblown hair. Flushed face and angry eyes.

She had longed for him, even as logic scolded her for doing so. But not this way. The man before her was the dark, threatening male she remembered from the beginning, the one who seemed capable of horrendous deeds.

"What do you want?" she demanded bravely, her gaze lighting on the intimidating biceps that bulged beneath the sleeves of his shirt.

His reply was the white flash of a jagged grin, a forbidding parody of goodwill. Even that imitation of a smile disappeared as his mouth clamped shut.

In that instant, Maggie sensed that he was enjoying the scene he was creating. Once again he was forcing her to be on the defensive, and once again her ire blossomed. Like the lord of the manor, he had burst into Foxcroft and sent her comrades scurrying in fright. If he thought he could so easily threaten *her*, he was mistaken.

"What's the matter, Mark?" she asked challengingly. "Couldn't your little blond friend keep you entertained?"

A hint of surprise crossed his stern features. As he took a few steps forward, Maggie backed away.

"That sounds like a jealous woman talking," he rumbled as he pulled a boot off his foot and tossed it toward her. "And here I thought you only had eyes for the Frenchman."

Maggie easily sidestepped the sailing boot. "I won't even dignify that remark by addressing it!" she said. "You've got nerve to question me about anyone *I* might spend time with, the way you pal around with your half sister!"

The lines around Mark's eyes and mouth deepened. He tugged off the other riding boot and tossed it toward its mate.

"*Mademoiselle*," he muttered. "*Chérie!*" As he seemed to become suddenly aware of the radio, he quickly turned the volume up full-blast. The blaring of brass and guitar flooded the room as he turned back to Maggie with a dangerous look.

"Is that all I had to do all these months?" he yelled. "Talk French? Okay: *Voulez-vous coucher avec moi?*"

He peeled the polo shirt off and threw it on the floor. "Bouchard is welcome to you, *mademoiselle*. Just as soon as I get you out of my system!"

Maggie's startled gaze left the broad expanse of his bare chest and traveled to his burning eyes. Instinctively her hands flew to shield her breasts, where her nipples showed rosily through the translucent gown.

"Don't bother to cover yourself," Mark commanded as he swaggered toward her. "You seem to have forgotten. I've seen everything you have to offer!"

Maggie backed blindly away. "Mark—" she began warningly, but he paid no heed. She bumped against the bedside table and groped behind her back until she felt her hand closing on a crystal ashtray. In a fierce gesture, she raised it above her head.

"Mark, I'm warning you. Don't come any closer!"

She hadn't gotten the last word out of her mouth when he lunged for her, knocking the ashtray out of her grasp and catching her arm before it could move in his strong hand. She swung the other limb and managed to land a blow against his ribs before he captured that as well, and pulled her against him.

"Come here," he mumbled. "You may not have any love in that heart of yours, but you have desire. I know. I've seen it!"

"Let me go!" she cried. Drawing back her bare foot as far as she could, she drove the ball of her foot into his shin.

His response was to wrench her sideways and push her across

the bed, with him following. His muscular body pinned her down as efficiently as his hands held her wrists. Hair cascaded across her face, and with a swift movement, Mark transferred both wrists into one hand and brushed away the hair with another.

"Kiss me!"

"You're crazy!" she spat. "Get off me! Get out of my house!"

His face was only an inch away, his hand securing her head so she couldn't move. "Kiss me once, and *then* tell me to go," he challenged.

His lips were gentle as he lowered them to her cheek. Slowly his mouth slid to her ear, where it sent warm breath coursing into the shaft. Chills danced along her spine.

"Mark! Stop it!" she ordered.

His lips remained at her ear. "You want me to stop?" he whispered. "Then kiss me."

A few seconds elapsed, and he raised his head enough to look down at her. Maggie stared back. He read her indecision as acquiescence and lowered his mouth to hers. Gently, his lips grazed her closed mouth. His tongue traced her trembling lips, reaching just inside to the tender pinkness where the nerve endings became electrified.

He carried on patiently with his teasing, seductive caresses, sucking her upper lip into his mouth, repeating the process with her lower lip until her mouth opened of its own accord.

His hand glided to the side of her face, his fingers playing over the fine texture of her skin. And then, as if he would stretch out the moment, his lips met hers, his tongue sliding into her mouth to travel languidly over its entirety.

On and on, his mouth made love to hers, his hand skimming down her face to stroke her neck, his thumb settling lightly in the hollow of her throat where her pulse beat wildly. He caressed her in a way that said she was the most precious thing in life, something to be cherished, and without being able to help herself, Maggie began to slip. After what seemed an eternity, he withdrew his tongue and planted several tender kisses on her parted lips.

Her eyelids fluttered open, and she returned from the warm, dreamy land in which he had placed her. His green eyes regarded her assessingly, and still he held her captive. After a moment, she tried her voice.

"One kiss," she murmured, her pride welling up valiantly. "You said you'd leave after one kiss."

From only inches away, he studied her, the ghost of a smile

playing at the corners of his mouth. "I lied," he whispered and launched a fresh attack.

His mouth swooped down on hers, his tongue plunging forcefully into her mouth, stifling any protest.

No! her mind cried silently, but even as her brain made the feeble effort, her rebellious mouth began to respond.

With one finger he traced her collarbone until he reached the delicate shoulder strap of her negligee, his touch becoming firm as it followed the silky fabric around the curve of her breast.

She'd fought him for so long, but now she realized it had been useless. Whatever he was, she was in love with the man, obsessed by him. There would never be anyone else. When his fingers strayed beneath the negligee to fondle the softness of her breasts, she was lost.

His mouth remained on hers, drawing her into himself, and it was only when she began to kiss him passionately in return that Mark released her wrists. Her traitorous arms went around his neck, the fingers reaching into the thick hair at the nape of his neck.

Mark's hand caressed her breast, then traveled along her body to her knee and back up, under the filmy negligee. His hand was warm as it slid up her thigh, his kiss driving as the hand reached her smooth hip and pushed the gown up to her waist.

No matter that the door hung strangely open or that the loud music was shaking the room. No matter that she didn't trust the man who held her. His lips possessed hers several quick times before he backed away. As Maggie's eyes came lazily open, Mark pulled the gown swiftly over her head. Just as swiftly, his mouth returned to hers, one hand stroking her hair, the other quickly removing his jodhpurs. He rolled onto her, his naked hardness pressing into her stomach.

They lay sprawled crosswise on the mattress. Mark tightened his grasp around her body and drew her with him to the center of the bed. For a moment he raised the upper portion of his torso above her and looked down with crazed eyes.

She couldn't read those eyes. She was tired of trying. At this moment, all she longed to do was surrender. Her hands ran up the rippling muscles of his arms until they locked behind his neck. She pulled him down to her, and he crushed her mouth beneath his. His hand tangled again in her hair as his glistening body pressed her deep into the silk comforter.

Mark pressed his knees between her thighs, prying her legs

invitingly apart. The feel of his body was warm against her inner thighs, and then his fierce hardness pressed between her soft lips, sliding up and down with a pressure that drove her mad. He touched her teasingly then, entering and withdrawing until she could endure it no longer. With a muffled moan, she thrust her hips upward and enveloped him.

His movements were those of an expert, now slow and gentle, now swift and demanding. His mouth ravaged hers as his hands roved every inch of her, as if he would memorize her body. Time passed unheeded as his lovemaking became ever more urgent.

With a flash of surprise, Maggie felt a warm tremor spark into existence as Mark moved against her. She would have torn her lips away from his, but he captured her face in his hands and submerged his tongue deep within her mouth. Her breath came and went in quick gasps through her nostrils.

Rhythmically, the tremor began to bristle with intensity, each wave a little brighter and hotter. And suddenly it had a life of its own, building to a brilliant throbbing she thought she couldn't stand, until it exploded, rocking her body with the sensation.

After the first earthshaking waves subsided, she grew aware that Mark was still deep within her. He shuddered, his mouth coming to a standstill on hers, and she clasped him to her, holding him tightly until he expelled a long, shaky breath.

She began to stroke the taut muscles of his back and eventually felt them relax beneath her fingers. After a moment he kissed her tenderly and laid his head next to hers. Still joined, they rested for a long time.

Nothing seemed to matter. The loud music was assaulting her. The weight of Mark's body was upon her. Slowly Maggie opened her eyes and looked beyond the dark shape of his head. The room was hazy in the glow of the bedside lamp that continued to burn.

"Mark . . ." she began, but his immediate answer was to place a finger against her lips. Gently, then, he withdrew from her and climbed out of bed. Her eyes barely open, Maggie watched him cross the room and turn off the radio, deciding he had the most magnificent body she'd ever seen. She smiled faintly as he returned.

"Come here," he said and crawled with her beneath the covers. He turned out the lamp, and then his arm encircled her. With ecstasy still coursing through her veins, Maggie snuggled her naked body against his.

"Sleep," his deep voice commanded as he secured her head against his neck.

Her nostrils were filled with the smell of him; her arms, with the feel of him. Her hand strayed through the dark hair on his chest, then grew still as he began to stroke her hair soothingly. Almost instantly she fell into the peaceful rest that had eluded her for months.

The sun was not yet up, but a curtain of gray light stole into the room, falling across Maggie's face. She came slowly awake, as if she'd been drugged. The strange feel of her body reminded her of the night before. A groggy smile curved her mouth as her hand strayed under the covers in search of Mark's warm body. When she realized she was alone, her eyes flew open and she sat up in the bed with a start.

Her gaze swept the room. The crystal ashtray lay on the floor next to her crumpled negligee, but the boots and jodhpurs and polo shirt were gone. Mark's words flooded back to her with cruel clarity: "Bouchard is welcome to you, just as soon as I get you out of my system!"

Maggie sank back against the headboard as if the wind had been knocked out of her. He had done it. He had gotten her out of his system, and now he was gone.

What could she have been thinking? She hadn't been thinking at all! As always, when Mark touched her, her brain went on hold, as if she were some wide-eyed innocent, as if she hadn't learned long ago what it was that men wanted from her. But nothing in Maggie's past had prepared her for the way she now felt, as if a callused hand had pulled her heart out. With a muffled sob, she buried her face in the pillow where Mark's head had rested.

It was sunrise when Rachel and Annie crept fearfully up to the room, their faces displaying shock at the sight of the splintered door that hung from its hinges. Annie clutched her housecoat nervously about her throat, and Rachel planted her plump hands on her hips in disapproval.

Together they ventured inside toward the bed where Maggie sat so woodenly propped against the headboard. Her hair was wildly tousled, and bare shoulders gleamed above the comforter that had been pulled up to cover her breasts. Annie and Rachel looked at each other in silent understanding of what had occurred.

"Oh, Miss Maggie!" Annie whimpered as she searched her pocket for a hanky.

Maggie turned her head toward the two women, looking not at them, but through them. The coldness she felt inside had frozen in her eyes. It was clear to her now that the night had meant nothing more to Mark than the challenge of a conquest, something he needed to get out of his system. She, fool that she was, had slipped once again into the fantasy of loving him. Now that she was awake, she saw that he'd used her and left her like a one-night stand.

"Mr. Fox is hot-headed, I know," Rachel began thoughtfully, "but he cares about you, Miss Maggie. I've known it from the first."

Maggie's eyes flashed to Rachel's round face. "I want you to promise me something, Rachel. You, too, Annie. I want you both to remember this always, and never let me down. Will you promise?"

Both women nodded vigorously. "Ya know we will, Miss Maggie," Annie's accented voice purred.

Maggie focused on them intently. "This night is never to be mentioned again. And as for Mark Fox, I don't want to see him, I don't even want to hear his name. Do you understand?"

"But—" Rachel began in distress, apparently still wanting to defend the man she had raised as a child.

"No 'buts,' Rachel!" Maggie snapped. "Mark Fox no longer exists!"

Rachel and Annie cringed at her ferocity, and when she was satisfied that both of them were properly impressed with her decision, Maggie swung her legs out from under the covers and left the bed. Uncaring of her slender nudity before her trusted friends, she headed toward the bath. It was suddenly important that she take a scalding shower.

"But, Miss Maggie," Annie sniffed, "what are you going to do?"

"Do?" Maggie repeated with a hard glance over her shoulder. "I'm going to work, that's what I'm going to do."

Across the adjacent dawn-lit field, Mark sat in the window seat of his new bedroom and stared in the direction of Foxcroft. Clad only in a towel wrapped around his hips, he ran a hand over his newly washed hair, then rested an arm on his upraised knee. His expression was as dark as his thoughts.

He had behaved like a savage, bursting in like that, using force against a fragile woman. His self-reproving gaze dropped to his hand, where it rested on his bare knee. Only hours before, that hand had knotted itself in Maggie's hair, subduing her, imprisoning her until he could work his seduction, using every trick, pushing in every way he knew until she was beyond the point of resistance.

He hadn't wanted it to be that way. He had wanted her to come to him willingly. Now that would never happen. He knew Maggie. Already she would be in the midst of self-contempt, regrets, and vengeful denunciations of him. It was all too easy to picture the cold look in her eyes when she announced, "Nothing has changed between us, Mark"—as she so often had.

After she fell asleep in his arms, he had stayed soberly awake, imagining her dismissal, remembering her obvious infatuation with the Frenchman. It was that recurrent thought that had finally catapulted him out of Maggie's bed and off her property. Hadn't he watched her using her charms on Bouchard all yesterday afternoon? Hadn't he heard her say she'd met the man of her dreams?

Maggie was a beautiful woman. Why had he never considered the fact that she would attract a great many men and perhaps be attracted in return? It was something to be expected, but it had caught Mark completely off guard. That was part of the reason he'd broken into her bedroom—to blot out the image of Bouchard.

Mark straightened his shoulders rebelliously. But beneath the tough-guy veneer a feeling of emptiness stole over him. The real reason he'd gone to Maggie had nothing to do with the Frenchman. The feelings that erupted last night had been brewing for months.

Maybe, he'd thought, maybe if he made love to Maggie one more time, felt her body encasing him just once more, maybe *then* he could be free of her.

Mark lifted his eyes again to stare out the window toward Foxcroft, trying absently to remember which of the distant chimneys led to the fireplace in the green bedroom.

It hadn't worked. He wanted her more than ever.

Weeks sped by as Maggie secluded herself in the library studio. She worked long hours and tried not to panic. The work was going too slowly, she worried. Too damned slowly!

Claude often managed to calm her nerves. "Don't think of your deadline," he would say. "Think only of your work."

He was in constant touch by phone. Having embraced the

project with a zest Maggie suspected had something to do with Dolly, he'd offered to arrange the packaging for the prints as well as the formal invitations to the reception. Trusting his judgment, Maggie accepted his help gratefully.

The reception was less than a month away when he came by to check the guest list a final time. He also brought one of the invitations.

Maggie held up the sample.

"It's lovely, Claude," Maggie managed. She'd been living in the isolated, dreamlike world of the studio, but the invitation she held made everything suddenly real. Soon two hundred guests would receive the invitations. In only a few weeks those people would pull up to Foxcroft in their expensive cars to see the serigraphs that were still four colors away from being finished.

With a surge of panic, Maggie pulled one of the prints from a drying rack. With only eight colors applied in various shapes across its surface, it resembled an elementary paint-by-number picture.

"Patience," Claude advised as he took his leave. "You're doing an excellent job. Don't think about the reception. Think only of your work."

"Think only of your work," Maggie repeated to herself and, with a deep, steadying breath, began preparations for the screening of the ninth color.

It was late in the day when Rachel tapped on the studio door and entered bearing a vase of gardenias. It was a surprise to see the summer flowers on such a brisk autumn day.

Although Maggie kept the old potbellied stove burning, the studio had grown cold with the chill of November. The shift in the weather had been sudden, warm humid days changing almost overnight into crisp, sparkling autumn. Only a few weeks ago, the hot sun had poured through the north-facing wall of windows, heating the studio like an oven. Now the same windows invited the chill of the outdoors as the temperature dropped day by day.

She smiled at Rachel, glancing at the flowers as she scraped blue ink off the squeegee with a swift, practiced swipe. "Thank you, Rachel. They're beautiful."

"I can't take credit for them," the old woman said, turning an affectionate look on the gardenias. She came into the room and placed the sweet-smelling flowers on William Fox's desk. "They're from Mr. Fox," she said.

"Put them in the trash!"

As was her habit when she became vexed, Rachel plopped her fists on her ample waist. "Mr. Fox is just not as bad as you make him out to be, Miss Maggie. You two got off on the wrong foot. That's all."

"Wrong foot!" Maggie exploded. "Rachel, when are you going to stop defending him? He's made a fool of me for the last time!"

"Pooh!" Rachel shot back. "That pride of yours is gonna do you in, Miss Maggie. In the past few weeks Mr. Fox has called on the phone four times, and I hung up, like you said. He came by the house twice, and I turned him away. But if you want these flowers thrown in the trash, you're gonna have to do it yourself!"

Rachel delivered the last with an emphatic nod of her silver head and waddled self-righteously out of the room. Maggie hurried after her, watching the broad expanse of her back until she was safely at the bottom of the spiral stairwell.

"Ornery old woman," she muttered as she went back into the studio and cast a suspicious glance at the gardenias.

Their rich scent brought back a memory, and her mind re-created the scene: the Atlantic House, Mark in a white dinner jacket, leaning across the table to place a gardenia in her hair.

A card was nestled in the greenery. Maggie stared at it accusingly before removing it.

"We need to talk," the note said. Not a supplication. Not an apology. Just a statement of fact: "We need to talk."

She crossed the room to the stove, tossed the note into the flames, and watched its edges blacken and curl.

It was midnight, only a week before the reception, when Maggie applied the final screen of black to the first of the prints. As usual, she was alone in the studio but for her faithful companion, Margaret, who seemed to have adopted Maggie and her night-owlish ways.

"Well, girl," she said to the setter. "Let's have a look."

With trembling hands she pulled the paper from the board and held it up before her. Her breath caught as her gaze fell upon the vivid color and glowing subject of the first completed print.

"Beautiful," she whispered with a sense of awe. And then she squealed so that Margaret jumped to her feet and commenced barking.

"It's beautiful!" she cried and laughed with relief as she turned in a circle under the bright studio lights. Margaret trotted over, continuing to yip joyfully. As Maggie rushed to the easel on which the original oil was displayed, the dog followed closely at her heels.

Pride swept through her as she held her work next to her father's. She had done it: She had reproduced the depth, the feeling, *all* of it! No one else could have done it, she realized with satisfaction. No one would have had the drive, but then no one had so much riding on the result.

The soft pink light of sunrise spilled through the north windows as she placed the last print on a shelf. She bent over to touch her toes, then stretched her arms toward the ceiling. She was tired and stiff, but her gaze hovered contentedly on the tall, full drying racks that crowded the room. After the edition dried, she would sign and number each print in pencil. That, she thought with a confident smile, would be child's play.

She had decided to display only one of the proofs and one of the finished edition next to the original at the reception. The buyers could examine those, and each reservation would be recorded— the number of the print and the party to whom it was being sold. Then the entire edition would be packed and transported to Claude's gallery.

She'd failed to receive a business license for the sale of the prints. A call to the license bureau had yielded effusive apologies and excuses, but Maggie was sure Alicia was behind the act of sabotage. She smiled as she imagined Alicia's false certainty of having thwarted her. The treacherous woman had no way of knowing Claude had provided a detour around the roadblock she had so cleverly erected. And she would not know until the night of the reception, when Claude introduced himself as the purveyor of the serigraphs.

Maggie glanced again at the shelves. Each represented a payment that would ensure her ownership of Foxcroft. A percent-age of the profits would go to Dolly and Claude, of course. But even if only half of the prints were sold, Maggie would be able to pay the property tax. Even Jonas had to approve of those numbers.

She turned to the madonna portrait. For a moment she studied it and was uplifted by the expression of love on the face of the mother she'd never known. She sensed that she was redeeming that unknown woman—that penniless, tragic woman whose daughter had become mistress of the estate where she had worked as a servant.

"Come on, girl," Maggie said to the setter as she turned out the lights and exited the studio. "Nothing can stop us now."

Outside the library, the newly risen sun was devoid of warmth, and a brisk wintry breeze rustled the barren vines and swirled through the walkway. Shivering, Maggie began to run gaily along the corridor with Margaret at her side.

Exhilaration replaced her weariness as she crossed the lawn to the front of the house. The clear, invigorating morning air had planted a notion in her head. She raced up the stairs to get jacket and boots and was on her way to the stables before Rachel and Annie had emerged from their quarters.

Prince fairly danced as she led him out of the stall and under the pure blue of the sky. Once she was on his back, the roan bolted toward the dirt road to the river, and Maggie let him have his head, enjoying the wild rush of wind as much as he did.

They slowed only when they reached the pines, and with a decisive tug on the reins, Maggie directed Prince through the forest to the river. The graceful new bridge sparkled white in the sun, and after a nudge to his ribs, the gelding pranced across, continuing to the clearing in the marsh.

Not since she had finished the oil study of the chimney in the marsh had Maggie visited her mother's grave. She dismounted and led Prince to the well-tended little spot surrounded by the white picket fence. But she gasped as her gaze lit on the headstone. Under the solitary name of Stella, someone had scrawled a single word: "whore."

Maggie swallowed hard and, after wrapping Prince's reins securely around a fence post, stepped inside the gate to kneel by the marker. The coldness of the morning wasn't the reason behind her tearing eyes as she reached out to touch the stone. On close examination, she discovered that the word had been written with charcoal, perhaps even the charred end of a stick. She rubbed at the coarse graffiti, but succeeded only in smearing the letters. They would have to be removed with cleaner.

She came angrily to her feet and surveyed the clearing as if to find and seize the culprit who had vandalized her mother's resting place. But beyond Prince there was only the desolate stone chimney, the sunlit grasses, and the endless expanse of marsh.

A sinister feeling of danger crawled over her, bringing with it the memory of that terror-stricken day when she had been chased through the forest. Once again, the tall weeds had eyes that watched her, following her every move as she ran out of the fenced plot and snatched up the reins. Seating her boot hurriedly in the stirrup, she vaulted into the saddle and wheeled the gelding around. She felt a little less vulnerable sitting atop Prince, poised for flight. Still, it was at a smart clip that she directed the roan out of the clearing and through the pines.

Prince cantered at a brisk pace, and Maggie rocked smoothly with his gait. The wind whistled through the tweed of her jacket and chafed at her hands and face, but she was oblivious to the chill. No longer was she mindful of her success with the serigraphs, her lack of sleep, or the exhilaration of the morning. Her thoughts were on the desecration of the headstone and on who might be responsible.

A plan formed as she rode along. She would scrub the stone clean, but she would not return to the clearing alone. She would get Mr. Thompson and his brothers and their hunting dogs. If some vagrant was using the marsh, they would find him. They would comb every inch of the peninsula if necessary.

Thus was Maggie preoccupied as she raced along the dirt road and through the open fields that stretched to Foxcroft's back lawns. She failed to notice a man some distance away mounted on a steed that came to a halt as its rider spotted her. It was a vague sound, like approaching thunder, that eventually intruded on her thoughts and drew her eye. By then Sonny was closing in.

Mark leaned forward, his face nearly hidden behind the steed's pointed ears as he urged the animal to greater speed. In answer, Maggie pressed her heels against Prince's sides and bent low over his neck as the gelding tore into a full gallop.

Behind her, Mark directed his steed out of the meadow and onto the hard-packed road. Wind coursed deafeningly past Maggie's reddening ears, all but drowning out the fearful clatter of the stallion's churning hooves. Speeding through the countryside, she and her roan were a red streak, Mark and his midnight steed, a dark blur.

Mark scowled into the fierce wind. He had felt like a fool when his mother started seeing Claude Bouchard. *She* was the woman of the art dealer's dreams, not Maggie! But the foolishness he felt then didn't come close to the frustration that had mounted within him as Maggie consistently refused to see him or even talk to him. His scowl deepened.

Within moments Mark had closed the gap between them. He pulled up, adjusting the stallion's pace to that of the gelding, and simply rode beside her. When Maggie chanced a look in his direction, she saw that her nemesis, clothed all in black, looked like an extension of his powerful horse. With a flash of her tearing eyes, she turned away and leaned into the roan's lathering neck, burying her chin in his coarse mane and planting the reins just behind his ears as a reminder that he had total freedom in his breakneck speed.

"Come on, Prince," she urged through numbing lips. "Come on!"

The back lawns were just ahead when Mark called out to her, "Pull over!"

Their horses were flying along the road together, only a foot apart.

"Pull over!" he repeated, and when she ignored him, his arm shot out across the roan's neck, his hand closing forcefully around the fists that were frozen on her reins. In a smooth, steady motion, he reined in her mount while matching the maneuver with his own.

The horses slowed, snorting and tossing their heads at the sudden change of pace. Maggie stared straight ahead as the steeds settled into a walk. Mark's hand was still possessively clenched around her own.

"Thanks for pulling up," he said sarcastically.

Her only answer was a straightening of her spine.

"Will you walk along here for a minute?"

Still she gave no reply.

"Dammit, Maggie!" he exploded. "I've been trying to talk to you for weeks!"

She turned toward him, a look of contempt on her face. Even so, she devoured the sight of him, the dark hair swept back by the wind, the ruddy cheeks framed by the upturned collar of a black leather jacket, the parted lips, the feel of which she longed to forget but stubbornly remembered. His fingers gripped hers tightly, and as always, Mark's touch electrified her. Yet all that showed in her eyes was a spiteful gleam.

Mark's hand fell from hers.

"Listen to me, Maggie," he began. "After the match, I thought you and Bouchard . . . You seemed to be wild about each other. But it didn't take Mother long to straighten me out about Claude Bouchard."

"So?" Maggie voiced coolly.

"So that's why I left your room the night of the match. And that's the reason I came to Foxcroft in the first place!"

"And forced your way into my bedroom!"

The lines in Mark's face deepened, the green eyes glittered. "I forced my way in, Maggie, but I didn't force everything that happened, and you know it!"

"How kind of you to remind me," she returned icily.

The memory of that shocking, hurtful morning came back— waking up alone, feeling used and deserted. She looked at Mark steadily, the coldness in her heart showing in her eyes.

"That night meant nothing," she lied. "Don't pretend it did."

Mark's jaws clamped shut, making the cheekbones stand out rigidly beneath windburned skin. "Just a casual encounter, huh? You never cease to surprise me, Maggie. I had no idea I was making love to such an inconstant woman. Love 'em and leave 'em. Is that it?"

"Something like that," she answered tightly.

His expression was a mixture of bewilderment and anger. "Damn, how did you get to be so tough?"

The wind whipped Maggie's fiery hair about her head, making it seem alive above her burning eyes. "You made me this way, Mark. You and the rest of the people who always take and never give!"

He stared at her stonily. "What I've given, or tried to give, you've thrown away without a thought."

"Without a thought!" she cried. "If you had any idea how many times I've thought of you! I've never felt for anyone what I feel for you, and I've never been so used!"

An expression of sudden comprehension broke through Mark's grim expression. "What are you saying?"

Horrified at the words that had tumbled from her mouth, Maggie turned away. When she didn't answer, Mark reached for her reins, but she jerked them out of his reach, causing Prince to skitter away a few paces.

"Are you saying that you care for me?" he demanded.

She spun in the saddle to face him. "If I was fool enough to care for you once, I know better now!"

Mark's jaw twitched. "The way we are together, Maggie . . . you *know* it's something special. And yet you keep denying it out of some perverse sense of pride."

"I don't need you to judge me," she retorted. "In fact, I don't need you at all!"

A hurt look flitted across Mark's features. "You know," he said. "I'm just about ready to believe you."

"Please do! I don't lie, Mark. Unlike you, I always mean what I say."

A freezing wind swept by as Mark's frown deepened. "You never forget, do you? You never let anyone else forget! Tell me something, Maggie. Have you been this way with everyone in your life? The slightest failure, the slightest disappointment, and they're out? If so, then you must be pretty damned lonely!"

His stinging words reminded her abruptly of Shelley: "You're so proud and so quick to condemn anyone who falls from grace." Suddenly, Shelley's comment seemed all too true. Maggie lifted her chin.

"Why don't we forgo the psychoanalysis, Mark?" she asked curtly. "I don't believe *you'd* fare too well under close examination, do you?"

She nudged Prince and began to move away. She didn't have to see the fury on his face; she heard it in his voice.

"Turn and run, Maggie!" he thundered. "Run away, just as you always do!"

Her reply was to kick Prince into a trot, and Mark didn't try to follow. When she was thirty yards up the road, he called out to her crossly.

"You'd better walk your mount in! He deserves it!"

She was in the shelter of the oaks when she chanced a look over her shoulder. The tall horse and rider were moving resolutely toward the invisible line that divided Mark's territory from her own.

Chapter Twenty-one

Mr. Thompson and his brothers devoted most of the afternoon to searching the marsh for the vandal. They found no one, but at least Maggie had the opportunity to clean her mother's headstone without the fear of being terrorized.

Claude Bouchard showed up late in the day, and if possible, his exuberance over the finished prints outstripped her own. He kissed his fingertips in the Continental pronouncement of excellence, then kissed Maggie squarely on the mouth. With a feeling of triumph she retired early in the evening.

As she dressed for bed, Mark's comments haunted her: "You must be pretty damned lonely!" he'd said. He was right. She *had* been lonely for most of her life.

Lately, Mark's stormy eyes had managed to make her question herself. The doubts had been vague, fleeting feelings, and she'd dismissed them as the result of the man's uncanny effect on her.

Now for the first time Maggie experienced a real flash of misgiving about her proud nature. She'd always thought it one of her greatest strengths, a sort of street-smart quality that lifted her beyond the clutches of scoundrels. Now she realized that it had separated her from everyone close as well.

She climbed into bed wishing she were more like Cholley— forgiving, understanding, trusting. But when her head met the pillow, the troublesome thoughts vanished. Maggie hadn't slept in nearly forty-eight hours, and even a final memory of Mark didn't prevent her quick surrender to slumber.

The next day was Monday, and she awoke in midmorning to a quiet household. Rachel and Annie had gone off together to do the household shopping, but they had left a silver coffee service in Maggie's room. The pot was still warm when Maggie poured herself a cup and began to dress. It was nearly noon when she pulled on her boots and coat and strolled out of the house in the direction of the stables, leaving the Irish setter to yip disappointedly at being left behind.

December. The limbs of the oaks danced naked in the wind, but the sky was dazzling. Cold air bit Maggie's face as she walked across the lawns, but she enjoyed looking over her property in its somber dress of early winter. Like spring and summer, this season at Foxcroft had its own unique, stately beauty.

As she entered the stable yard, she glanced across the expansive brown field and paused. Mark was in the white-railed ring across the meadow, working Gray Lady's filly on a long line. The cowboy hat sat low on his head, and he wore a heavy sheepskin jacket. She could almost hear him crooning to the filly, "Easy there, girl. Easy, now."

As she watched, he led the foal to a post, exited the ring and started across the few hundred yards between his property and the Foxcroft stables. Maggie was aware that he occasionally walked over to retrieve livery or equipment he'd left behind. But she didn't want to run into him, not today. She picked up speed as she moved into the shadowy barn. She would be away on Lorelei before he arrived.

She walked quickly past the vacant stalls and was reaching for the latch on the tack room door when she heard a shuffling sound behind her. Before she could turn, a massive hand clamped itself across her mouth as an arm enclosed her in a steely grip.

"I been wanting to get to you for a long time, missy," came the gruff voice from just behind her ear.

Maggie's mouth was completely covered, her teeth embedded in a coarse workman's glove. A scream ripped from her throat only to die before it reached beyond the gloved fingers.

"Keep quiet, I tell ya!" the familiar voice ordered.

Her breath came in rapid gasps through her nostrils.

"Are you gonna keep quiet?" Harold demanded.

The dirty stench of him was overpowering. Maggie nodded her head. It was a constricted move, as the man's body hunched oppressively over her, pinning her arms to her sides, lifting her feet nearly off the ground. Gradually, the hand over her mouth relaxed.

"Been watching you," he said in a low voice. "Riding them horses all summer with hardly a stitch on. You and your mama, reckon you're two peas in a pod, the both of you nothing more than a couple of whores!"

Maggie blinked in sudden understanding as her lips moved against the glove. "You . . . you . . ."

"Yes, *me*!" he interrupted. "It's been me all along. The stupid police have been combing the whole state, and I've been right here the whole time, watching and waiting."

Harold. Maggie's thoughts careened in terror.

"Yeah, I been waiting for the right time, 'cause I ain't gonna end up with the short end of the stick, ya hear me?" he yelled in her ear. "I got something to say and you might as well be the one to hear it!"

Governed by instinct alone, Maggie's right leg flew out and back, the hard heel of her boot connecting with his shin. There was a muttered oath as the arms about her loosened their grip. Maggie wrenched her body and nearly broke free before she was recaptured. Then the arms were around her more tightly, and the hand crushed her face so that she could barely breathe.

"That wasn't very smart, missy," the hoarse voice crooned. "You're gonna listen to what I got to say whether you like it or not! I'm tired of hidin' out in the cold. I'm *tired* of waitin' for a ship that's never gonna come in."

At that moment, a small sound came from outside. Harold's arm clenched her like a vice. "Shut up!" he ordered.

They heard approaching footsteps.

"You'll keep quiet if you know what's good for you," he whispered, and then the gloved hand left her bruised mouth. She saw from the corner of her eye that it reached for something hanging from his belt. It wasn't until Mark strode into the barn that she remembered the machete.

"Mark!" she cried.

He stopped in mid-stride, whirling toward the sound of her cry. As his eyes found her in the shadows, Harold raised the machete threateningly.

"Ain't no reason to come any closer, Mr. Fox," Harold challenged. "Not if you value the red hair on this one's head!"

Mark's heart skipped as he saw Maggie in Harold's clutches, then seemed to stop altogether as he took in the terrified look on her face. He raised a hand in a calming gesture.

"Come on now, Harold," he said after a moment. "You know you don't want to hurt her."

"Hmph! You and the others have been mighty quick to think I've done murder. What makes you think I won't do it now?" Harold hesitated before rushing on. "I'm tired of taking all the blame. I got something to say, and if somebody has to die for me to get it said, then so be it!"

Mark tipped his hat back on his head. His face took on a

sympathetic look as he stepped toward them. "You got something to say? I'll listen. You don't have to hold the woman."

Harold's fist was still raised, clutching the machete so that the blade pointed in Maggie's direction. She hung silently in his grasp, her fear having risen in her throat so that it was choking her.

"Stop right there!" he yelled, the sound piercing Maggie's ear as she watched Mark came to an abrupt stop six feet away. He folded his arms across his chest and regarded them calmly.

"Come on, Harold," he said in a low voice. "We've known each other a long time. I'll listen to whatever you have to say. Just let her go."

There was a silent, tense moment. Harold chuckled, then tipped his head back and roared, the laughter sounding harsh in Maggie's ears.

"She's gotten to you!" his voice came finally. "This nameless little hussy has got you hog-tied!"

Mark's carefully friendly expression turned grim. "I'll make it simple for you, Harold. You let her go and tell me what's on your mind, or I'll get you. However long it takes, I'll hunt you down. And you won't be happy about it when I find you."

Harold paused for a second and then began to laugh again. As he did so, he loosened his hold on Maggie so that she slid to her feet, her knees nearly buckling as she took a tentative step.

"Makes no difference to me," Harold said to Mark as she crept away, still unable to voice a word. The machete remained poised in the air as he continued. "I'll tell you or her or both of ya. Just as long as it gets told."

As soon as Maggie was several feet away, Mark sprang into action. As she watched in horrified silence, he lunged through the air toward Harold, his hands outstretched, grasping for the brawny fist that brandished the machete.

But Harold was too quick. The bulky arm raised itself with startling speed only to fall swiftly toward Mark, the hilt of the machete connecting with the side of his head with a loud crack. Mark fell to his knees as Maggie screamed.

Only then did Harold turn his bloodshot eyes to her. "I'll be back," he swore. And then he turned and lumbered out of the barn as Mark rolled to the floor, clasping his head.

She rushed to his side, bending over him and reaching out to touch his hair. "Mark—" she said in a tight voice.

"I'm all right," he grumbled. "Watch where he goes! Go on!"

It seemed her feet were weighted with lead, but Maggie hurried as best she could to the barn door, arriving in time to see Harold making quick progress across the field in the direction of the pines. She watched until he disappeared beyond the horizon; then she returned to Mark. He had stood, and as she approached, he retrieved his hat, dusted it off on his pants, and irritably put it on. It failed to hide the small red gash above his left temple.

"Harold went toward the pine forest," Maggie reported. "Are you all right?"

The eyes he turned on her were angry but clear. "He gave me a headache, that's all. How about you?"

She regarded him with wide eyes. "I'm fine . . . thanks to you."

In a sheepish manner, Mark glanced at the floor, shifting his weight to one leg before returning his eyes to her. "Yesterday you said you didn't need me. I guess having me around comes in handy after all."

Maggie's terror began to recede. She brushed a curl from her eyes and smiled in relief. "Guess so," she agreed.

In an instant of silence, she found her eyes locking with his. "Hadn't we better phone the police?" she asked. "Shouldn't they look for him?"

"We'll let them know he was here, all right," Mark replied. "I'll call them as soon as I get back to the house, but it won't do any good. Harold knows this land better than anyone alive. If he doesn't want to be found, he won't be. And another thing, I don't know what he was so worked up about, but chances are he won't stop here, now that he's shown himself. I don't believe for a minute that he's a murderer, but he sure as hell could scare the daylights out of you, Rachel, and Annie. Warn them. And until he's caught, keep your doors locked and your wits about you."

Maggie nodded, looking at Mark's forehead, where it was swelling beneath the small gash. "You're certain you don't need a doctor?"

"All I need is a drink," he drawled. "But I appreciate your concern. Can I take it to be genuine?"

The green eyes sparkled down at her. The atmosphere between them was suddenly charged, and Maggie began to back away.

"It's genuine," she said quietly. "I—uh—I've changed my mind about taking a ride." She fled before the familiar swell of emotion could take root.

Mark watched thoughtfully as she nearly flew out of the barn.

She had said her concern for him was genuine. It was a very small admission; yet it gave him hope that one day she'd admit the full scope of the feelings he suspected were there.

He was now convinced that Maggie's passion was real, but that she had locked it behind a door he couldn't open; he had tried every key he knew, with only fleeting success. He was gun shy at this point. Trying to corner Maggie was like trying to lasso a beautiful mustang—a tempting prize, but when you tried to close in on it, you were likely to get painfully kicked.

Mark waited until he saw her clear the oak grove and start across the lawns to the house. Then, resignedly, he left the barn and turned in the opposite direction.

That night, for the first time in weeks, Maggie reached for her father's journal and opened it to the final entry in the third volume. She read it once, her pace slowing as she reached the end of the passage. Her eyes strayed to the old chest at the foot of the bed, then returned to the page as she read the entry once more.

March 12. I've made up my mind to take Stella and Margaret Elizabeth away from here. We'll sail with Jack Lewis to Jamaica, and I'll settle them safely in Kingston until I can work out the arrangements with Dolly. Who can say how long we'll be gone from Foxcroft? But what does it matter? My bride-to-be and my daughter will be with me.

All I shall hate to leave behind is Mark. I wonder how much he'll grow while I'm gone, how many special moments I'll miss. The boy grows dearer to me every day. As I write, my eyes fall on the fox-head ring, the rubies glittering in the lamplight. Now, as I face separation from my son, I vow that he will have this ring on his eighteenth birthday. As God is my witness, on that day he will wear this ultimate symbol of Fox authority. And it will sit proudly on his hand.

Maggie closed the volume and turned out the light. Images of Mark tumbled through her head, culminating in the vision of him lunging bravely at Harold as the wildman swung the flashing machete toward his head. She knew what she had to do.

The next day passed in a frenzy of preparations for the reception. The mirrors and floors of the ballroom were freshly polished, the velvet drapes taken outside where Annie vigorously beat them.

In the afternoon, two police officers came out to look around the barn where Harold had appeared. They didn't stay long, and Maggie got the feeling they were responding reluctantly, purely because the request had come from Mark Fox.

It wasn't until evening that she picked up the journals and the tortoiseshell box containing the fox ring, put them in a bag, and headed for the stables. The ride would be short. She wouldn't bother with a saddle. She pulled a bridle over Lorelei's head, climbed on the mare's bare back and started toward Mark's new home.

Stars twinkled high overhead, and a half-moon shed light against the black December night. The air was crisp and still, the quiet broken only by the sound of Lorelei's hooves as they crunched along the frosty turf. A moment of fright swept over Maggie at a sudden memory of Harold, and she pressed her heels to the mare's sides and moved quickly toward the household lights glimmering ahead.

In only minutes she reached the sprawling structure and tethered Lorelei to the hitching rail out front. Glancing briefly at the barnlike house with its rows of stalls extending right and left, she crossed the dirt yard and knocked on the door. Moments later, an overhead porch light came on as the door swung open.

Mark seemed shocked to see her. For a moment he simply stared, standing in his stocking feet, dressed comfortably in jeans and a sweat shirt, a newspaper in his hand, a flesh-toned Band-Aid over the colorful bump on his forehead. Behind him, Maggie glimpsed a rustic room with a fire burning cheerily on a brick hearth.

"May I come in?" she asked finally.

At that, he seemed to come to life. "Of course," he murmured as he opened the door wider and watched her step inside.

"May I take your jacket?"

"No!" she replied too hurriedly, and pulled the collar close. "I can't stay long."

The room she entered was at once cozy and masculine. The heavy furniture was rustic and comfortable-looking, the cedar walls bestowing a clean scent on the air. Familiar furnishings were clustered about, and as Maggie's eyes made a quick tour, they lit on her painting of the chimney in the marsh, which hung above the mantel.

A noise drew her eye from the fireplace to a balcony that overlooked the room. John Henry stepped out of a doorway and came to the railing to glare down at her.

Maggie turned swiftly to Mark. "I have something for you," she said and thrust the paper sack into his hands.

He pulled the books and the small box out of the sack. Glancing at them, he looked back at Maggie with a puzzled expression.

"What's this?" he asked.

"The box and its contents belong to you," she replied. "William Fox wanted it that way. You'll find out for yourself when you read his journals, which I'm only lending you. He wrote quite a bit about you on those pages."

Her eyes turned upward to John Henry. "There are even a few passages in there about you," she said.

The older man pursed his lips as Maggie had seen him do many a time. "I'm not interested in anything *you* bring into this house," he announced and stalked imperiously out of view. Yet as Maggie continued, she had the distinct feeling that he lingered just out of sight, devouring every word she uttered.

"He kept those journals religiously, Mark. It's obvious he cared for you very much."

Turning abruptly away, Mark walked to a table where he deposited Maggie's offerings. "I don't understand," he said in a thick voice.

Maggie came up quietly behind him. "I thought you ought to know. And the box, as I said, is yours."

Mark removed the tortoiseshell lid and withdrew the golden ornament. "His ring!" he murmured, his eyes turning to Maggie, filled with an emotion she had never seen.

"He wanted you to have it," she said. "He wrote about it in the journals."

At that moment Mark's face looked so open, so surprisingly dear, she longed to touch it. She looked briskly away and focused on the stack of slender books.

"I'll keep the fourth one," she added, stepping over to take the bottom volume from the stack. "I'll get started on it tonight, after I finish some work in the studio." Her eyes drifted back to Mark and found him studying her.

"So you're going through with it," he said. "This painting scheme of yours?"

"Of course I'm going through with it. The reception is only four days away—no matter how ridiculous you think the idea is!"

Mark's brow furrowed. "Calm down! I haven't said anything was ridiculous. My God, do you always have to shoot off like a rocket?"

Maggie's fingers played nervously on the brass lock of the journal. She couldn't help it. Her relationship with Mark was fraught with ambiguities, and she felt defensive whenever he was near.

Suddenly, beneath her fidgeting fingers, the brass clasp sprang open, startling her so that the volume slipped from her hands and fell to the floor. As she and Mark bent to retrieve it, they both noticed that an odd scrap of cloth had slipped from between the pages.

"What's that?" he asked as she picked up the fabric.

"I don't know. A scrap of velvet, crimson velvet. Maybe the journal will explain it," she said as they came to their feet.

"Yeah, the journal," Mark repeated, again looking at her solemnly. "What's this all about, Maggie? The books? The ring? Why, after all this time, have you brought them to me?"

She paused for a moment. "I have an old trunk full of things that belonged to them. The journals and the ring were in it. After reading some of William Fox's diary entries I realized you should see them, too. He would want you to read for yourself that he loved you as a son."

Mark's eyes were riveted on her. The warmth of the fire was suddenly oppressive, and its crackling seemed intrusive. She took a quick, deep breath and plunged into her speech before she lost her nerve.

"Mark, I did some thinking last night. You could have been seriously hurt yesterday when you lunged at Harold, and that's only one of the times you've come to my rescue since I've been here."

She glanced self-consciously at the floor before again meeting his eyes. "There's been a lot of trouble between us, Mark, but there have also been times, like yesterday, when you've come through for me. Those are the times the ring and journals are meant to repay."

Mark's expression turned dark. "Repay? I don't want payment for saving you! Not in the way you mean."

Impatiently, Maggie tossed her hair over her shoulder. "Can't you just accept these things as a peace offering? As long as we're going to be neighbors, maybe we ought to try being neighborly!"

Mark folded his arms across his chest and eyed her coolly. "And just how long do you suppose we'll remain neighbors?"

"If the prints are successful," she said, "it could be a very long time."

"And if they're not?"

She stared at him defiantly. "As Rachel would say, I'll just have to cross that bridge when I come to it."

Mark's face was grim, the lines around his mouth creasing deeply.

"Maybe this was a mistake," she added hurriedly. "I've got to get going. I have a lot of work to do tonight."

"You didn't walk over here, did you?" Mark demanded as he followed her to the door.

"No. I rode over on Lorelei."

"Is Jeremy there? At the stables?"

Maggie turned at the doorway. "Tonight? Of course not, why?"

His face took on the look of a thundercloud. "Why? One day you're assaulted in the barn, and the next night you go riding in there alone? In the dark?"

"If I remember correctly," she said with a taunting glance at his bandage, "it was *you* who was assaulted."

"Be that as it may," he replied gruffly, "you're not riding over there alone."

The night air was biting as they crossed the field toward Foxcroft—Maggie on the mare, Mark towering beside her on the black stallion. She clutched her father's journal in one hand and the reins in the other as she watched clouds of steam rise from Lorelei's nostrils. Mark was a formless bundle in his sheepskin jacket, the ever-present hat pulled low on his head.

When they reached Foxcroft, he directed the prancing stallion from one end of the barn to the other as he inspected the entire structure. He brought Sonny to a halt outside the stall in which Maggie settled Lorelei. As she began to walk through the barn, she chanced a look in his direction. If he saw it, he made no sign as the stallion walked sedately beside her.

"Thanks for coming with me," she said as they reached the stable yard.

"I'll see you through the thicket," he rumbled, then slid off his horse and took the lead toward the oaks. The three of them picked their way quietly through the trees. It wasn't until they reached the edge of the grove that Mark halted his horse and turned to Maggie.

"That was nice of you . . . bringing me those things." His voice floated on the darkness.

"It was the right thing to do."

"I don't understand you, Maggie. I think I've got you all figured out and then you pull something like this."

"I'm not *pulling* anything, Mark," she said sharply. "The journals are yours to read. And the ring is yours to keep. You deserve to have it."

"So you said."

"Is that so hard to understand?"

He gazed down at her. Moon shadows shifted across her face as the wind rustled the limbs of the oaks. Frosty clouds of warm breath puffed from her open lips. She was so close. He wanted to reach out and take her, hold her until the barrier between them crumbled. Instead, he clenched his hands within the sheepskin pockets of his jacket.

"Everything these days is hard to understand," he said quietly. "Before you came along, things used to be fairly simple."

His statement hung in the air, reaching out with hidden, tantalizing meanings. Maggie blinked several times, her eyes straining to see his dark silhouette, her heart lunging into the ragged tattoo that only Mark provoked.

"Maggie," he began and took a step closer.

Like a frightened rabbit, she backed off. He halted. Behind them, Sonny began to stamp and snort, expressing his displeasure at being forced to stand still in the cold.

"That night, Maggie . . . the night we were together in your room. I'm sorry—"

"There's no need to be sorry, Mark. I've already told you. What happened, happened."

"I'm not sorry for what happened between us. How could I regret the fact that we were as close as two people can get? But I'm sorry for the way I left. There's nothing I would have liked better than to stay with you—"

"Mark, don't." The old magnetism was pulling at her. "It doesn't matter. Don't you see? There's too much standing between us. I can't just *forget* it."

He looked at her sternly. "You don't seem to have any trouble forgetting it when we're making love. You know as well as I how hot we are together."

Maggie's eyes began to sting. "And how long would that last? Until someone else turned your head? A few more tumbles, a few more hot rendezvous. That's not what I want, Mark. I told you long ago I wouldn't be one of your conquests, and I meant it."

"Dammit, woman!" he exploded. "I care—"

She surprised him by springing forward and pressing a hand across his mouth. Mark's voice stilled behind her gloved fingers, but his mind went on: *Dammit, Maggie! I care for you! Don't you understand? I'm in love with you!*

The silent admission stunned him, and he felt suddenly dizzy. A tremor started in his toes and rocked its way through his body.

Maggie's left hand grasped the shoulder of Mark's sheepskin jacket while the other remained stubbornly clamped over his mouth. The feelings that had tormented her for months swelled until she felt she couldn't breathe. She couldn't bear it anymore— the anger, the desire, the love and hate that kept her teetering between ecstatic heights and miserable lows.

"If that's true," she said, staring into Mark's eyes. "If you truly care for me the slightest bit, then let me have some peace. Accept the fact that I don't want to be your latest paramour, and let me go."

"Let me go . . . let me go . . ." The words echoed through the surrounding oaks before being carried away on the wind. After a moment Maggie's hand left Mark's mouth and she stepped back into the shadows.

Mark's head reeled. His lips parted. He was *in love* with her. It was so simple. *That* was why he couldn't sleep! *That* was why he'd been cranky. Rachel and his mother had hinted at the idea, but he had dismissed them with a sneer. But it was true! Mark Fox, footloose bachelor, was thoroughly, consumingly in love.

Misreading his silence and the intent stare she could barely see in the darkness, Maggie felt her insides roil. The old suspicions of men reared up, and it hit her just what she was to Mark: just another woman, another lover in a long line that would carry on long after she became a thing of the past.

The cold night air burned its way up her nostrils and down her throat. Silence hung over them like a freezing fog.

Suddenly she was running, tearing across the lawn toward the welcoming light of the house, leaving behind the deafening silence that was all Mark could offer her.

She was yards away before Mark's vision cleared, and by then it was too late to go after her. He wondered what she would say if he hit her with this newest revelation. She wouldn't believe him. It would take time and much patience on his part before Maggie accepted his love. A feeling of jubilation burst through him. But accept it she would, someday.

Mark watched protectively until her slim form raced around the corner of the house. A slow smile spread across his face as he shook his head in wonder.

"Damn!" he muttered. It didn't matter anymore that she'd taken Foxcroft. He'd give her any damned thing she wanted!

Turning, he clucked to Sonny and started leading the stallion through the oaks. He would walk rather than ride across the field separating him from Foxcroft. The December night had grown frigid, but Mark Fox had never been so warm.

Tears rolled down Maggie's cheeks as she hurried along the dark, mill-stoned path of the vine-covered walkway. Never had she been so confused, so miserable, so frustrated! She questioned herself, despised herself, because in spite of everything, she wanted Mark, dammit! Not as a neighbor, not as an occasional lover! Suddenly it struck her just what she *did* want from him. She wanted him to love her! Mark Fox, who denied the very existence of love!

Maggie burst into the deserted library. Shrugging out of her jacket and gloves, she scaled the spiral staircase. Why should she try to forgive and forget, to sacrifice the pride that was the very core of her being, when the most Mark could offer was a fleeting affair?

Another pang of longing shot through her, but a determined look came to Maggie's tear-streaked face. Whatever it was that she felt for Mark—love or lust—it mixed with her spirit like poison, leaving her dizzy and sick and wishing she could go back to the safe, unfeeling existence she had before.

"It's *over*," she muttered grimly as she stalked to her worktable.

She worked late into the night in the studio. The old stove spat and sputtered nearby, and the overhead lights blazed. Still, the room seemed cold and dim as she painstakingly numbered the prints and signed them. Some collectors were finicky about the number of a print, claiming that the first to be screened had superior clarity. Often they collected one particular number from all of the editions they acquired. Her heart swelled anew as she examined each serigraph.

She had fifty left to do when she decided to take a break. With a sigh she slumped into the wing-back chair and opened the fourth journal. Margaret settled comfortably at her feet as Maggie removed the scrap of velvet to study it curiously.

It was then that a sound came from downstairs, and as quickly as Maggie's heart leapt to her throat, the Irish setter leapt to her feet, her barks splitting the air as she bolted to the closed studio door. Maggie tossed the forgotten book and cloth onto the desk and hurried to the door, grasping Margaret's collar as the dog continued to snarl and bark. She thought of Harold, and a chill of fright swept over her.

Maggie pulled open the door, her grip tightening on Margaret's collar as the dog lunged through the doorway, dragging Maggie with her onto the landing. She reached quickly behind her and flipped the switch at the top of the stairwell. A series of spotlights lit up the great library below. Margaret barked a few more times as Maggie's eyes searched the shadows. The dog sat down quietly, apparently satisfied there was no intruder.

A stiff wind rushed about the old building, causing one of the window iron grates to creak loudly on its hinges. The dog's ears pricked at the sound, and Maggie breathed a sigh of relief.

"See, girl? There's nobody here," she said, eliciting a friendly wag of the tail from Margaret. "It's just the wind. Come on. I've got more work to do."

The next morning the Thompsons drove up with a mammoth spruce tree in the bed of their rickety pickup. "Annie said you wanted a Christmas tree, Miss Maggie." Mr. Thompson grinned, as he and his brothers carried the hefty tree into the house. "We figured this one would measure up."

Maggie, Annie, and Rachel spent most of the day moving the tree to the far corner of the ballroom and dressing it with lights, strings of popcorn and cranberries, and a host of antique ornaments Rachel had found in the attic.

The crowning touch was a china angel with gossamer wings that shone brightly with glitter. It was afternoon when Maggie affixed the angel and climbed down the ladder Rachel and Annie held. No matter that competing shafts of sunlight poured through the French doors into the ballroom. When they turned on the strings of Christmas lights, the tree was brilliant, its colorful lights twinkling and reflecting along the walls of mirror until they seemed to quadruple in mass.

"Oh, Miss Maggie," Rachel said, "we haven't had a big tree like this in years!"

Maggie put one arm around Rachel's shoulders and extended the other to encircle Annie. "We will from now on," she assured her friends. "Every Christmas for as long as you want."

An hour later Claude and Dolly arrived. They admired the ballroom and the Christmas tree, and then took Maggie out to Claude's car where two parcels lay in the backseat. The folios— the protective sleeves in which the prints would be packaged.

Maggie was footing the bill, but Claude had overseen the design and ordering.

They were elegant. Each ivory-colored folio contained a printed guarantee that the work was an original hand-screened serigraph, one of a limited edition by Margaret Elizabeth Hastings.

"They're perfect," Maggie breathed to Claude and was rewarded with a beneficent smile.

Dolly was eager to see the reproductions of her likeness. As Maggie and Claude carried the boxes of folios, Dolly accompanied them with little need for her cane.

Laughing and chattering, they made their way into the library and up the stairs. Margaret trotted along beside them, wagging her plumed tail, leading the way to the tower room where she had spent so many recent evenings. It wasn't until the dog halted just past the studio doorway and began to growl that the three people realized they had surprised someone within.

Dolly was the first to speak. "John Henry!" she exclaimed.

Standing near William Fox's great desk, the man wore a heavy coat against the cold December day, but Maggie could see him straighten as he approached them with dignified calm.

"What are you doing here?" Dolly asked as Maggie and Claude continued to stare at the man.

One of John Henry's brows arched painfully high. "I couldn't contain my curiosity any longer, cousin," he said in his clipped voice. "I had to see for myself that it was true—that you're actually *brazen* enough to allow this event to take place."

"See here!" Claude broke in angrily. "I'll not hear you call this woman—"

"I shall call her anything I like," John Henry fired back. "I daresay I know my cousin better than you do. She's no longer mistress of Foxcroft, and she no longer has any control over what I do or say."

"Zut!" Claude spat, and stepped forward threateningly.

"It's all right," Dolly remarked, smoothly linking her arm in Claude's and drawing him back.

"No, it's *not* all right!" John Henry accused, his dark eyes glaring at Dolly as he took a few angry steps toward the door. "Look at you! Hanging on the man! Flirting with him! It was you and your men who started this whole mess in the first place!"

With that, John Henry whirled and stalked away. As Maggie and Claude and Dolly looked at each other in stunned silence, they heard his shoes clicking swiftly down the iron stairs.

When the door slammed below, Dolly—ever resilient—glanced at her companions with a smile.

"Never let it be said that we Alexanders don't speak our minds," she said.

Her comment dispelled the awkwardness, and after exchanging a rueful look, Maggie and Claude put aside their packages and began to show off the serigraphs to the woman who had modeled for the original so many years before.

The afternoon languished as Claude and Maggie discussed the reception while Dolly quietly toured the studio, seeming to depart the present as the sight of the long-deserted room took her back to another time. Slowly she moved among the towering print racks to linger at the blazing potbellied stove, the huge old desk that had been her husband's, the madonna portrait of Maggie and her mother. At one point, Maggie could have sworn she glimpsed the sheen of tears in Dolly Fox's midnight-black eyes.

As the couple prepared to go, they invited her to join them for supper in the city. They might even go to Captain Jack's if she would agree to come along.

"Come, Maggie," Claude urged. "You've been secluded too long."

How wonderful it would be to simply turn her back and walk out of the studio with her friends. It had been so long since she'd felt free to spend an evening frivolously. But soon all the work and preparations would pay off.

"No," Maggie said after a moment, her affectionate gaze darting from Claude's face to Dolly's. "I need to start packaging the prints in these lovely folios you've brought. You two go ahead and have a good time."

She watched them drive cheerfully away from the estate and spent most of the night in the studio with Margaret as her sole companion. Packaging the prints required several careful steps: positioning the paper on the support board, covering it with onionskin, sliding it into the folio, tying the gold cord.

It wasn't until she took a rest late in the night that she reached for her father's journal and discovered the odd scrap of velvet was gone.

Chapter Twenty-two

It was Friday, the day before the reception. In midmorning the phone rang, but it wasn't until Rachel came bustling in with coffee service that Maggie's eyelids stirred, then flew open as Rachel imparted the grim news: Early that morning a fisherman had discovered Harold's body floating face-down in the freezing waters of the Cooper.

"It's odd that poor old Harold should have gone close enough to the river to fall in," Rachel said. "Everybody knows he couldn't swim."

Rachel had known the man for years, but the sympathetic phrase, "poor old Harold," grated on Maggie's ear. When the old woman left, she fell back against the pillows, pulling the covers up under her chin as memories of the gruesome man whirled through her mind. His massive arm slashing with the machete at the limbs of a fallen oak, his malevolent grin as he lit the cord to the dynamite, his bloodshot eyes and foul breath as he accosted her in the garage.

From the beginning Harold had terrified her, and during the months since his disappearance, Maggie had fought the impulse to blame him every time something mysterious or frightening occurred. The wild chase through the pine forest, the violated slave hut, the vandalization of her mother's headstone. Somewhere in the back of her mind, she had stored the fearful idea that Harold was behind all those incidents. He had proved her instincts right when he threatened her in the stables.

After twenty-five years, the saga that had begun with a deadly fire had come to an end. Maggie shuddered. It was wicked to be glad someone was dead, and yet all she could feel was relief.

Several days before, when Mark had called the sheriff's office to report Harold's appearance, the two responding deputies had seemed only mildly interested. They had made a halfhearted tour of the estate, grumbling all the while about the wildman's wilderness know-how. It seemed Harold was something of a legend. The officers echoed Mark's sentiments about the futility of

trying to track him, expressed their relief that no one had been
seriously hurt, then left.

Now those same deputies, along with a horde of others from the
sheriff's office, swarmed over the grounds. Maggie rose, dressed,
and went outside. She spoke with the police, telling them what she
knew about Harold, then darted back inside as a familiar tall figure
approached from the stables.

But no sooner had she reached the foyer than her shoulders were
gripped firmly from behind. Her feet flew out from under her and
she was dragged, twirled, and swiftly backed up against the
private wall of the rose-colored parlor.

Mark's hands held the sides of her head, holding her steady as
his mouth swooped down on hers in a full-tongued way that was
instantly dizzying. Somehow Maggie slid up the wall, rising up on
tiptoe as his hips ground against her, letting her know of his
arousal, seeming to taunt her with the threat of consummation,
though the entire county police force stood just outside.

She pushed against his chest with all her might, but it was not
until he chose to end their embrace that she made any headway.

"What do you think you're doing?" she sputtered. He had on
his black leather jacket, the collar turned rakishly up to his ears.
The look he gave her was no less cocky.

"Kissing my woman," he said lazily, his hands drifting to her
shoulders.

She pushed so violently that his hands fell away and he
stumbled back. "I am not your woman, and I do not enjoy being
pawed by you!"

Mark slouched on one leg as his eyes raked her from toe to
head. "The hell you say."

Maggie felt suddenly naked. Her nipples still tingled from
having been crushed against him, and she fought the impulse to
cover her breasts.

From the foyer doorway came the distant sounds of the police
officers' voices. "Have you seen Mark Fox?"

"He said he'd be just a minute."

"Find him, will you?"

Mark ignored them. God, she looked great today with her hair
pulled back and her eyes clear and shining in a fresh scrubbed
face. He'd spent the past two days in a state of shock, knocked off
his feet by the realization that he loved her, remembering their
tempestuous times together and the mountain of mistrust she had
built against him.

As he looked down at her, he longed to blurt out the truth: *I love you!* But he held himself in check.

"Didn't our conversation the other night mean *anything* to you?" Maggie demanded.

Mark regarded her intently. "More than you know. But here I am, getting ready to join the posse to search for a murderer on a cold winter day with all those boring officials. Just wanted something to warm my blood before I went out."

Quivering, trying desperately not to show it, Maggie stood before him, a blush burning her face. She had forgotten the crowd outside until one of the deputies stalked into the parlor.

"Oh, there you are, Fox," the man said. "We're ready to go. Are you coming with us?"

"Yeah," Mark rumbled, breaking into a sardonic grin.

With a last smoldering look, he left with the officer.

Maggie watched through the parlor window as the posse set off toward the stables, led by a handler and a brace of bloodhounds. From there, they crossed the field toward the Cooper tributary, where they began to comb the riverbank. A few high-ranking officials remained behind in the kitchen, draining cup after cup of Rachel's coffee. Maggie joined them as they batted about the issue of foul play.

"Doc said there wasn't much sign of a struggle. Just a bump on the back of his head."

"If there'd been a fight, there would've been marks on the body. Harold Johnson wasn't too smart, but he was a big man. Mean, too!"

"He was a drinker. Mebbe he just got drunk and fell in the river."

"Yeah? Then how do you explain the missing machete? He was wearing the holster, but the knife was gone."

It was dusk when the search party returned. Mark was not among them. Straggling reporters began a fresh round of clamoring outside the gate, their hurried questions turning to disappointed grumbles when a deputy announced that the group had found nothing.

"We've been up one side of that river and down the other," the officer declared. "There is no evidence that Harold Johnson was anywhere near Foxcroft property in the past two days."

At his words, the reporters jammed their notepads into their pockets, climbed into their vehicles, and screeched up the avenue of oaks. With a feeling of relief, Maggie watched as the odd collection of officials and searchers followed.

That night, light spilled again from the windows of the studio as Maggie finished packaging the prints and stacked them neatly in boxes on the old double bed. Wearily she turned for a last look about the studio before turning off the lights. The coals in the old stove glowed red. The empty racks stood neglected, like tall metal skeletons. The prints were stacked securely on the bed, ready to be spirited away to Claude's gallery for sale.

What if something went wrong? What if the wealthy guests came only to gawk and not to buy? Questions rang through her mind, but she knew it was too late to worry about such things. She had done all she could do. The rest was up to fate. With a resolute sigh she closed the studio and left the library.

Stepping outside, she was confronted with the quiet, freezing night, yet there was no longer a reason to fear the dark. Harold was dead. Maggie strolled confidently through the darkness to the main house with Margaret trotting loyally at her side.

The next morning began when Annie shook Maggie awake with an alarming demand for the keys to the truck. It seemed the Irish setter had fallen ill, and Annie's narrow face was contorted with fright.

"I went into the kitchen a few minutes ago and found her lying on the floor as still as a stone," she cried.

By the time Maggie threw on a robe and raced down the stairs a few moments later, the Scotswoman had already taken the dog to the vet.

Margaret's illness cast a pall on the Foxcroft household. The morning newspaper didn't help. The story of Harold's death was on the front page, and with it all the old stories of the past—the fire, the deaths of William Fox and his mistress, the accusations against Dolly, and the tale of her amnesia.

Maggie took a last sip of coffee and, with a shiver, tossed the paper aside.

The hours ticked away. Trucks and vans pulled into the front courtyard, and service people filed through the house to the ballroom. The florist delivered three dozen poinsettias, and if he wasn't asking Maggie about placement, Captain Jack was bellowing about the hors d'oeuvres tables.

Claude Bouchard arrived in midafternoon with the easels, and Maggie helped him set up the original oil of Dolly, flanked on one side by an artist's proof, on the other, by number one of the print edition. When the veils were draped over the treasures, Claude turned to her with a wink.

"We must be prepared for a rush of business, *chérie*," he said encouragingly. "I have a feeling your work will be much in demand after today."

In the midst of the late afternoon hubbub the phone rang. Annie and Rachel were busily setting out candelabra and silver platters, so Maggie hurried to answer it.

"May I speak with Annie MacGregor?" came a businesslike male voice.

She glanced toward the ballroom. "I'm sorry, but Annie has her hands full right now. I'm Maggie Hastings. May I take a message?"

"Ah, yes, Miss Hastings. Annie mentioned you. I'm Dr. McFee, the veterinarian."

A flush of fear swept Maggie at the sudden memory of Margaret. "Is our dog all right?"

"I'm happy to report that she will be," he returned. "But it was a close call. It's a good thing Annie brought her here as quickly as she did. We were able to pump her stomach and get rid of most of the poison before it entered her bloodstream."

"Poison?" Maggie's hand rose to her throat.

"Yes, a form of arsenic commonly found in insecticides and weed killers. Your dog probably managed to get into it somewhere around the house. Unfortunately, it's not an uncommon occurrence."

Maggie replaced the receiver thoughtfully. All insecticides were kept locked in the toolshed behind the garage. And Mr. Thompson, the only person who had cause to use the chemicals, was a careful, responsible man. Maggie was sure he wouldn't leave anything dangerous lying around.

As she entered the ballroom, she decided to keep that part of the news to herself. There was no reason to mention the poison to Annie and Rachel while they were working so frantically. With a bright smile Maggie went into the room and announced only good news about the dog. A vaguely similar incident nagged at her memory, but as she fell back into the frenzied pace of preparations, it faded from her mind.

As evening approached, the workers departed. In the course of one afternoon, they had turned the ballroom into a magical place.

Now the great house was filled with an expectant quiet, like the lull before a storm.

By eight o'clock, a steady stream of Cadillacs, Lincolns, and Mercedes were lined up along the avenue of oaks. One by one, chauffeurs pulled their limousines to a stop in the courtyard and hurried around to help their blue-blooded passengers out. It seemed the combined lure of visiting Foxcroft and viewing Dolly Fox in the nude was too much to resist. Even those who normally refused to attend social gatherings had turned out for this one.

Claude stood with Maggie and Dolly at the front doors and suavely introduced the arrivals. In a demure gown of emerald velvet, Dolly smiled indulgently at the guests who greeted her cautiously, as if surprised that she should receive them in any fashion other than her birthday suit.

In contrast to Dolly's reserved gleam, Maggie sparkled like an icy morning in a dress she had bought long ago in Paris, a long-sleeved silver-sequined sheath that clung to her slim figure and shimmered with every move she made. Glimmering eye shadow enhanced the turquoise of her eyes, diamonds flashed at her ears, and the fiery hair was pulled up on the sides to tumble down her back.

The receiving line moved slowly, and by eight-thirty Maggie felt as if the smile were frozen on her face.

The Townsend-Harward party arrived fashionably late.

"Why, Isabel," Dolly said smoothly, "I never thought I'd see you here at Foxcroft."

"I can assure you, Dolly Fox," the chubby woman returned, "I wouldn't be here at all except to see with my own eyes just how gauche you can be!" With an imperious nod to Maggie, she swept toward the ballroom.

Maggie now found herself facing Alicia, who wore a scarlet satin dress that dipped in folds across her ample bosom. Her raven hair was perfectly in place, and her eyes were so perfectly made up that they seemed to leap from between blackened lashes. She was beautiful, powerful, dangerous.

"Maggie, my dear," she said with a sweeping look. "What an interesting gown. It's so difficult to keep up with sequins, isn't it? They fall in and out of fashion so rapidly."

"I suppose you're right," Maggie returned. "But then *some* things are never in fashion at all."

Alicia pursed her red lips and leaned forward to whisper, "You won't get away with this!"

When Maggie's reply was only a confident laugh, Alicia's hand closed on her husband's arm. Without another word she walked away, dragging her carefully smiling spouse with her.

Arthur was the last of the Townsend party. He greeted Claude and Dolly coolly, then took Maggie's hand and paused.

"How kind of you to rescind your edict," he drawled. When Maggie only looked at him questioningly, he added, "Don't you recall saying that I was never again to darken your doorway?"

"Ah, the impetuous days of my youth," Maggie replied with a mocking smile.

"And what about tonight?" Arthur pried. "Is this little venture going to prove just as impetuous?"

"You'll see, Arthur," she replied, drawing her hand from his soft grip. "You'll see."

When most of the guests had arrived and been greeted, Maggie walked with Claude and Dolly to the ballroom. As they paused at the entrance, Maggie's gaze swept the room. The hors d'oeuvres tables gleamed with candlelight and red poinsettias; the Christmas tree sparkled; the bandstand was a spectacle of black tuxedos and flashing brass. Through the whole of the room flowed a rainbow of colorfully dressed people, their conversation and laughter occasionally swelling above the big band sounds of the forties.

It seemed to be going more beautifully than she had dared to hope, and behind her back, Maggie crossed her fingers for continued good luck. The gesture didn't go unnoticed. Dolly reached over and patted her arm.

"You've done a marvelous job," she said encouragingly.

"*Madame, mademoiselle,*" Claude said, offering each of them an arm, "may I have the honor of escorting the soiree's two most beautiful ladies into the fray?"

If there was one thing at which Charleston's upper crust excelled, it was socializing. The food disappeared as quickly as Captain Jack could replenish it. The champagne flowed like water. The dance floor was brimming with couples as more and more guests succumbed to the lively standard melodies of the forties.

After Claude led Maggie through a flamboyant tango that drew applause, she found it impossible to get away as one man after another cut in. They complimented her, joked with her, and gradually she began to think of them less as targets and more as comrades. As the evening wore on, her spirits soared.

It was nearly ten when she excused herself and sank into a chair at the table where Claude and Dolly were huddled. With a quick smile at the infatuated couple, Maggie glanced at the velvet-draped pictures. "Do you think it's time for the unveiling?"

Claude turned an understanding gaze on her. "Patience, *chérie*, patience. Give it a little longer. They are having a wonderful time, and so they will be most receptive. Wait and see."

Maggie nodded, and as her eyes wandered casually over the crowd toward the ballroom entrance, her breath caught. "Mark!" she whispered.

Dolly quickly turned in the direction of her gaze. "Now, Maggie. He's the *one* guest I have here, the *only* person I invited."

Maggie looked at her blankly. "It's all right, Dolly." As if magnetized, her eyes strayed back to the doorway where he stood, his tall dark form devastating in a black tuxedo.

There was a momentary lull as a great many eyes turned to settle on Mark Fox, and not for the first time, Maggie noticed that the guests regarded him warily. It struck her that Mark's role was like that of the bastard son of a powerful lord. His influence was unquestioned, but his social position was uncertain. People couldn't afford to shun him, but they approached him with caution. He was a rogue from whom one never knew what to expect.

From across the crowded room, his eyes managed to find Maggie's. But it was Alicia's scarlet-clad form that moved to meet him. Maggie looked away in disgust, and at that moment Arthur stepped up to the table and asked her to dance. Without hesitation, she took the hand he offered and turned her back on Mark.

The band was playing a slow, romantic tune, and several of the couples swaying to the music smiled as Arthur, their fair-haired boy, led Maggie onto the floor. He took her smoothly into his arms and began a polished two-step, his eyes assessing her.

Maggie stared back levelly, and as she looked into his face, she found herself studying his faint resemblance to his half brother. The dark hair and light eyes were similar, but Arthur had none of Mark's hard, chiseled look, nor did he exude the haunting air of darkness.

"You look lovely tonight," Arthur said.

"Thank you."

"I often think of that night we went out together. If we'd met under different circumstances, without Foxcroft's being in the way, we might have become extremely close friends."

"Without Foxcroft's being in the way," Maggie returned, "I could have been friends with a lot of people."

Arthur's gaze became piercing. "You mean Mark, don't you? I wish someone would tell me how he manages to affect women this way. First, Alicia, now you!"

"I don't want to talk about Mark," Maggie said flatly.

"Neither do I," Arthur returned. With a smooth smile, he changed the subject. "Now, *this* is the kind of affair that does Foxcroft justice—music, dancing, high society having a high time. This is the kind of glamorous role I've always envisioned for Foxcroft. In a manner of speaking, Maggie, you've managed to bring my dream to life."

"Hardly," she said. "As I recall, your dream entails turning the house into an inn and the property into a playground for your friends. Foxcroft is not an entertainment palace, Arthur. This is only one night, one special night when I've invited people like you into my home."

Arthur gave her a hard look. "Settle down, tiger. I know this is your home, however *fleetingly*."

Her instinctive reaction was to snatch her hand away, but Arthur managed to recapture it. She looked up at him angrily, the sparkle in her eyes outstripping those that danced across the silver sequins.

"I thought we might be able to have a brief, civil dance," she snapped. "Now I see that I was wrong. All I represent to you—all I'll ever represent—is a means of acquiring Foxcroft. Let go of me, Arthur. I'm tired of dancing."

"Maybe it's not *dancing* you're tired of."

Maggie recognized Mark's deep, masculine voice before she spun to face him.

"Maybe it's just your partner," he added and glanced at Arthur's reddening face. "I'm cutting in."

Exasperation, resentment, competitiveness—Maggie could see them all on Arthur Townsend's face. She wondered just how many times this scene had been played out over the years, with Mark stepping in to wrench something away from his younger half brother.

"No, you're not," Arthur retorted, his grip tightening around Maggie's fingers.

"Oh, come now, Townsend," Mark said with menacing casualness. "Be a sport. You don't want to cause a scene here in the middle of the dance floor, do you?"

Maggie glanced about her. Dignified couples glided by, glancing curiously at the three of them. A picture of Mark punching Arthur at the Townsend party burst into her mind.

"No!" she interrupted quickly. "There will be no scenes *here*. Not tonight."

"Well, now, I guess that decides it, doesn't it?" Mark drawled, reaching out to rest his hand at the small of Maggie's back. "The lady doesn't want a scene, Townsend. Besides, there's a matter requiring your attention. Does the name Benny Tyler mean anything to you?"

Arthur flinched.

Mark caught the expression. "I thought so," he continued. "Tyler used to do odd jobs at Townsend and Company before he mysteriously disappeared from Charleston a few months ago. You really should be more careful, *brother*. The first thing any good criminal learns is to cover his tracks."

"You don't know what you're talking about!" Arthur snapped.

"Don't I?" Mark cocked a dark brow. "You see, Maggie, the New York consortium that bought Canadys Isle had narrowed the field of possible developers to two choices—Foxcroft, Inc., and Townsend and Company. The one virtue of Townsend's plan was that it offered more profits by proposing that the whole of the island be razed and developed. But those tantalizing profits were resting on shaky ground because, in fact, the consortium had no claim on the entire island. As long as the Gullah villagers held a legal deed to the southern tip of Canadys Isle, Townsend's plan wasn't worth the paper it was printed on. The solution was simple—hire a couple of men to make off with old Tom Canady's map."

Arthur? Maggie thought incredulously. *Arthur* was behind the theft at Canadys Isle?

"You can't prove that!" Arthur muttered tensely.

"I don't have to prove it. That's up to the authorities." Mark glanced smoothly at Maggie, who was witnessing the exchange with wide eyes. "I apologize for being late to your reception, Maggie," he went on. "As soon as I heard about Benny Tyler being arrested for robbery some miles north and then beginning to spill a story about Canadys Isle, I got in touch with an old friend and called in a favor. Officer Jerry Brown is in the foyer, Townsend. And he's waiting for *you*."

Arthur's narrow face drained of color. "Then by all means," he said with an admirable attempt at bravado, "let's go have a talk with Officer Brown."

They filed off the dance floor, drawing little notice as the band launched into a boisterous melody. Only one pair of almond-shaped eyes followed the progress of the two tall men and the fiery-haired woman as they made their way through the crowd and left the ballroom.

"See here, Officer Brown," Arthur began forcefully as they entered the foyer. "What's this all about?"

"It's about an incident that occurred some months ago, Mr. Townsend, a theft and assault on Canadys Isle. Maybe you remember it?"

"I recall hearing about the theft," Arthur returned, "but I was unaware there was an assault, and I fail to see what any of this has to do with me."

Maggie glanced at Mark, saw him fold his arms across his chest and level a mocking look on his half brother.

"An old woman was struck by one of two perpetrators," Officer Brown said. "The strange circumstances surrounding the incident all point to you."

"Preposterous!" Arthur exclaimed.

"What's going on here?"

The sound of Alicia's voice made Maggie jump, and the men turned with a start to the woman in red.

"Go back to the ballroom, Alicia," Arthur muttered. "I'll join you in a few minutes."

"Mr. Townsend," Officer Brown interjected, "I'm afraid I'll have to ask you to come along with me."

"You must be joking!" Arthur laughed, but the sound died as the patrolman shook his head soberly.

"I'll go inside and get Mother," Alicia said, as if the magic touch of Isabel Townsend could fix everything.

"No!" Arthur cried. This was not something he wanted the nominal head of his company to be aware of. "Don't go and get Mother! Just go back inside and keep your mouth shut!"

Maggie blinked. It was the first time she had heard anyone raise a voice to Alicia, who was looking at her brother in blank astonishment.

"This matter doesn't concern Mother or you," Arthur continued more calmly. "I can take care of it." As his sister melted away toward the lights and noise of the ballroom, he turned back to Jerry Brown. "Why do I have to go with you?"

"A man named Benny Tyler was arrested a couple of nights ago about fifty miles north of here. After talking with an attorney, Mr. Tyler decided to offer information on an unsolved case if the authorities dropped the robbery charges. The case was the incident at Canadys Isle. According to Mr. Tyler, you hired him and another man who's still at large to steal a certain document from a woman living on Canadys Isle. He claims you even told him the old woman kept the paper in her Bible."

"Ridiculous!" Arthur sneered, although telltale spots of red had appeared on his cheeks. "You say Tyler told you this? Well, I deny the whole thing! It's a question of his word against mine."

"Sorry, Mr. Townsend," Jerry Brown insisted. "It isn't up to me. You're wanted for questioning. So if you'll come along now?"

"I'm not going *anywhere* with you unless you have a warrant!" Arthur blazed.

Officer Brown sighed, reaching into the breast pocket of his heavy jacket. "I had hoped this wouldn't be necessary," he said, withdrawing a folded paper.

"That's what took so long this evening," Mark supplied. "Lining up the paperwork so you couldn't wriggle out of this."

Arthur glared at his half brother in helpless rage; yet when his voice came, it was low and steady. "I'll need my coat."

Maggie had to admire the control he forced on himself. Perhaps such composure was a reflection of his aristocratic upbringing.

"Come with me, Arthur," she said. "Your coat is in the parlor."

"Now, hold on just a minute," Jerry Brown objected as the two of them moved away.

Arthur glanced over his shoulder with a scathing look. "I'm not going to make a run for it if that's what you're afraid of!" He followed Maggie to the rose-colored salon with all the arrogance of a monarch.

Maggie watched as he selected a black cashmere topcoat and slipped the garment on over his tuxedo. Arthur Townsend had so much—wealth, social standing, good looks. Why would it be so important to him to rob the Gullahs of their land? But even as Maggie considered the question, the answer hit her with the force of a slap. Canadys Isle wasn't the issue, just as Foxcroft had never been the real issue. It was the personal rivalry between Arthur and Mark. If Arthur could torment Mark, could get the better of him by misusing a group of island villagers, she suddenly knew he wouldn't hesitate for an instant.

As he approached the doorway where she waited, she looked up at him steadily. "Do you really hate Mark so much?" she asked.

"More than you could ever know," he replied fervently, then strode away to join the men in the foyer.

When the police officer reached for Arthur's arm, the taller man snatched it away contemptuously and turned to Mark with an insolent smile.

"One phone call will extricate me from this sordid little mess," he said. "And then what will you have gained from all your machinations? Nothing. All this means absolutely nothing!"

"It means something," Mark returned, "to see you escorted out of here by the police. To know you'll spend at least one uncomfortable night in the jailhouse. That means something to *me*."

Arthur whirled away, threw open the double doors, and descended swiftly to the drive, where a patrol car waited. The cold December night air swept into the foyer as Mark and Maggie watched the car depart quietly along the avenue of oaks.

"Now *that* is what I call a rewarding sight," Mark announced.

Maggie shot him an irritated look and hurried to secure the doors, the movement causing the silver sequins on her dress to dance and sparkle like so many diamonds.

"You're obviously very pleased with yourself," she said, taking in his smug expression. "Now if you'll excuse me, I think I'll see if my reception has fallen apart!"

"What's the matter with you?" Mark demanded as she tried to hurry past him only to be waylaid by strong fingers curling about her arm.

"This is the biggest night of my life, Mark, and you've dragged your personal vendetta right into the middle of it! Did it ever occur to you that your grandstanding with the police could have caused a catastrophe?"

Mark's eyes glittered down at her like two hard green jewels. "But it *didn't*, did it, Maggie? Nothing is spoiled. Nothing is ruined. I thought you were just as anxious as I to see the Canadys Isle culprit get his just deserts, but I guess I was wrong. You're behaving like a self-centered child who can't see beyond her own selfish little concerns!"

Maggie glared at him in silent fury before wrenching her arm free and stomping off to the ballroom.

Chapter Twenty-three

The reception was going splendidly. If anyone had missed her during the short time Maggie was away, it didn't show. As soon as she entered the ballroom, she was whisked back onto the dance floor to remain there as one elegant male guest after another demanded her attention.

A half-hour glided by as Maggie observed the whole of the ballroom from her position on the dance floor. The tables were full, and the crowd had grown loud with the late hour, their laughter and conversation flowing through the room like a musical tide.

Captain Jack was performing with his usual efficiency. No matter how the guests clustered about the elegant refreshments, he managed to keep the silver platters brimming and enticing. The bar, too, was a popular gathering spot, and Maggie was thankful she had stocked it amply. It was there that she occasionally caught sight of Mark's tall form. At one point she saw him in heated conversation with Alicia and imagined that Arthur's headstrong sister was demanding an explanation of her brother's disappearance.

But if Mark had, in fact, related to her the bizarre facts, Alicia didn't seem to care. Moments later Maggie glimpsed the raven-haired socialite on the arm of her husband, laughing with a group of guests.

Finally Maggie excused herself from the dancing and walked to the table where Claude and Dolly were smiling into each other's eyes.

"Hello, you two," she grinned. "Mind if I join you?"

From a spot near the bar Mark watched her leave the dance floor, her silver gown sparkling as she made her way to his mother's table. Maggie was the most stubborn, the most volatile woman he'd ever known! At times she made him absolutely crazy! She smiled at something Claude said, her beautiful face taking on a glow. A warm feeling rose within Mark. Ah, but she was worth it!

"Maggie, *ma chérie,*" Claude breathed as she sat down, "your soiree is the hit of the season!"

"The soiree, yes," Maggie replied with a hint of reservation. "But the most important event of the evening has yet to take place. It's obvious these people like the food and drink and music, but what about the prints?"

"I'm certain they will be a huge success, my dear," Dolly offered.

"Soon, very soon, you will see!" Claude added with a confident smile.

So engrossed were they on the subject of the prints that they failed to notice the approach of the tall, dark man until he interrupted them.

"Mother, you're looking exceptionally lovely this evening," Mark said.

"Why, thank you, dear," Dolly responded, with the crooked smile so like her son's. "You look rather dashing yourself."

"Monsieur Bouchard," Mark continued suavely. "It's good to see you."

"Good evening, Mark," Claude answered with a nod.

The green eyes settled on Maggie, and she found herself beginning to squirm.

"May I have the honor of this dance?" he asked.

Maggie gave him a skeptical look. Apparently his little coup with Arthur had brought on a state of high spirits. "Now, why would you want to dance with a *self-centered* woman who has only herself on her mind?"

"It's not your *mind* I'd like to dance with," Mark returned, eliciting chuckles from Dolly and Claude.

"Really, Mark," she said. "I just sat down."

He dropped to one knee like a knight of old, drawing a fresh round of laughter from Dolly and Claude, as well as amused glances from the surrounding guests.

"I'll stay here all night if you insist on refusing me," he challenged.

Glancing around, Maggie saw that they were fast becoming the center of attention. "Oh, get up, for heaven's sake," she snapped, coming to her feet.

Mark took her arm, led her to the dance floor, and with a

self-satisfied expression, placed her hands behind his neck as his own found her waist.

"Why don't we start this evening fresh? Hello, beautiful," he said, his look sweeping appreciatively from her face along the lines of her body and back to her vivid eyes.

"Must you be so *flamboyant* about everything?" she demanded as they began to sway to the music.

"Flamboyant?" he repeated, the corner of his mouth dipping into a grin. "I like the sound of that." He encircled her with his arms, pulling her close against him so that she had to rest her cheek against the one he inclined.

A hand smoothed the mass of hair that tumbled down her back, then found its way beneath the curls to rest warmly on her back. "I guess you know what you look like tonight," he murmured.

"What?" she asked.

"Like a woman who's out to turn a man's head. Dare I hope it's mine?"

Maggie arched a brow. "There are many things I might think of doing with your head, Mark, but turning it isn't one of them."

He chuckled. "Very funny. But I prefer to believe what you let slip the other day when we were riding. You're too damned stubborn to admit it, but I believe you're in love with me."

Maggie's eyes widened. "Of all the conceited, arrogant . . ." The words trailed off, a defensive attitude flaring as she took in his look of amusement. When her voice came again, it was harder than she intended. "There's nothing between us, Mark, and there never will be. Not as long as I hold the deed to Foxcroft."

His cheerful look faded. "Don't you think that resolution is getting a little old, Maggie? I know I'm getting damned tired of hearing it. You think you know so much, but you're wrong about a lot of things."

Her turquoise eyes flashed up at him. "Am I *wrong* in thinking that you want the estate back? Am I *wrong* in assuming that you didn't want me to produce the prints or have this reception?"

"I've made no secret of my opinion of this whole thing," he replied steadily. "From the very beginning, I've thought it was foolishness."

"Thank you, Mark," she broke in, her body stiffening further in his arms.

He cupped her chin and raised it so his eyes bored into hers. "Will you let me finish? I was going to say I'm impressed. I mean, look at this place."

Maggie listened in surprised silence as he gestured about the room. "Look at this place," he said.

Maggie glanced about the ballroom. It was brimming with elegant guests, their laughter a friendly accent to the brassy sounds of the band. In the corner the huge Christmas tree presided over the scene, its lights twinkling across mirrors reflecting candlelight and gleaming silver.

"Your party is a success," Mark rumbled, drawing her eyes back to his face. "And from what I hear, your artwork is superb."

Maggie's surprise at his compliments showed clearly on her face. "Who told you that?"

He shrugged, his arm tightening about her, once again pulling her close. "People talk," he answered gruffly. "Rachel says you've been working day and night. Bouchard says you've done a hell of a job. Apparently you've managed to pull this thing off. Congratulations."

Maggie pulled away and gazed up at him. The lines of his face were solemn, but in his eyes she detected a hint of admiration. The familiar thrill began to stir within her. Before it could go any further, she tore her gaze away and leaned forward to bury her cheek in his shoulder.

Their bodies moved together instinctively, and as always, the nearness of him overpowered her senses. The slow love song came to an end just as she had nearly surrendered herself to the heady feeling of being held in Mark's arms. A hundred memories flooded her mind, but all were shadowed by the cloud of doubt that had always surrounded him.

The final notes of the melody died on the air. She and Mark pulled slowly apart, and as her gaze drifted up to him, she had an inkling it conveyed the dreamy feeling she continued to deny. She found herself staring as the bandleader's voice came from some faraway place to announce a short break. Then Alicia's syrupy voice poured into their private world.

"Mark, darling, if you're finished here, could you find it in your heart to escort me to the hors d'oeuvres?"

Mark looked down at her impatiently. "No, Alicia. I couldn't. Get your husband to take you."

"But I don't know where he is," she returned.

"Then find him!" Mark commanded.

Maggie looked at the woman and was annoyed that Alicia continued to impress her. The clothes, the jewels, and more than anything, the refined, imperious manner. Breeding—it showed clearly in everything about Alicia Townsend Harward.

"Why should I look for Grover?" she asked, her pretty face

tilted up to Mark. "What's the matter? Aren't I good enough for you anymore?"

Mark's hand fell from Maggie's back. She glanced up and caught the heated look he gave Alicia. A sinking feeling rocked through Maggie as her suspicions about the two of them flared anew.

"Don't be ridiculous," Mark rumbled to Alicia.

Aggression lit Alicia's eyes as she turned to Maggie. "Or is it simply that your taste is running to outsiders these days? To an imported little piece from New York, flashy enough to catch the eye, but too cheap to hold your lasting interest?"

Maggie's mouth opened to deliver a retort, but Mark was too quick.

"Stop it, Alicia!" he boomed, his voice drawing the attention of a few nearby guests. "You don't need to bring Maggie into this," he continued more quietly. "This has nothing to do with her. You and I both know who we are and where we stand. We agreed not to interfere in each other's lives. You've gone your way with Grover Harward. Now let me go mine."

Maggie glanced at Alicia and saw the heartbreak that shone in the heavily made-up eyes.

"All right," Alicia whispered. "But before I let you go, I want to hear you say it. Tell me you care for me. *Say* it!"

It was only an instant; yet it seemed long and tense. Maggie held her breath as she glanced furtively at Mark to find his eyes on her. But then he looked back at the raven-haired woman who stared up at him.

"I care," he growled, and Maggie's heart fell to her feet as her gaze was drawn irresistibly to Alicia.

A glitter of tears sprang to the almond eyes as they traveled rapidly over Mark's face. Yet when she turned from him, there was nothing pitiable about the victorious look she bestowed on Maggie. With a quick toss of her head, she sent her dark tresses flying as she walked proudly into the crowd.

Mark took a slow step and turned to face Maggie. The smile on his face seemed forced. "After all, she *is* my sister," he said.

Maggie folded her arms across her breast and looked him over. After all this time, the man continued to amaze her. With just a touch or a warm, searching look he could reach inside her, make her forget all she held against him. Just as easily, he could make her feel like a fool for having done so.

"Ever since we were kids, Alicia has tagged after me—"

"Don't bother to explain," Maggie cut in, her voice carrying an unaccustomed edge of jealousy. "I couldn't begin to understand the moral code to which the southern gentry subscribe!"

Mark caught the insinuation and scowled. "I was only trying to be diplomatic, Maggie. I've told you before that nothing ever happened between Alicia and me. Don't make something out of nothing."

Still, Maggie continued to study him, the doubt showing clearly in her eyes.

"I can talk myself blue in the face, Maggie, but it won't do any good unless you take me at my word." He gazed at her intently. "Not just about Alicia, but about everything. One of these days you're going to have to start believing in me."

Maggie stared into the beautiful green eyes that had captured her from the beginning. The urge to believe in him was stronger than he knew. But she found she could say nothing. Only stare.

At that moment, the sound of Claude's voice came through the microphone. "Ladies and gentlemen, now we come to the moment you have been waiting for, the pièce de résistance that has brought you out into the country on a winter's evening!"

A chuckle coursed through the crowd at his elaborate buildup.

"If you will, follow me to the mysteriously draped easels at the other end of the room."

The crowd gathered around the terrace doors, where Claude stepped onto the platform before them. "And now, if Dolly Fox and Maggie Hastings will come forward, please. You lucky people are about to see some beautiful handiwork these two ladies have accomplished together."

Maggie's breath began to come in quick, shallow gasps as a wave of nervousness swept over her. This was it. The time had come.

"Go ahead," Mark rumbled from nearby. "This is your moment."

She glanced at him fleetingly, long enough to find the familiar, dark look on his face. She made her way through the crowd until she reached Dolly and Claude.

"What you're about to see," Claude continued over the microphone, "is an original oil that was painted quite a number of years ago."

"You didn't have to say *that*," Dolly broke in teasingly, having caught her beau's light, joking mood. The crowd roared, and deep inside, beneath layers of twitching nerve endings, Maggie rejoiced.

"I beg your pardon, *madame*," Claude returned with a smile for Dolly. "As I was saying, William Fox was a gifted artist. Since his work was never shown publicly, he was an unknown. But his talent was discovered recently by a young lady who is herself an artist, Miss Maggie Hastings. She has created a magnificent serigraphic edition from William Fox's original, a limited, signed and numbered edition. It is those serigraphs we offer."

"Are you telling us we can buy them *tonight*?" came Alicia's challenging voice from the back of the crowd.

When Maggie's gaze leapt to her face, she found the almond eyes leveled on her.

"Tonight is merely the unveiling, *madame*," Claude returned. "We are showing the edition and taking reservations for numbers. I am happy to announce that La Galerie Bouchard will act as vendor."

The crowd murmured appreciatively. Claude Bouchard's gallery had one of the best reputations in Charleston, and he had never before offered reproductions of any sort. As Maggie watched with satisfaction, the sneer on Alicia's face turned to shock.

"And now, ladies and gentlemen," Claude continued dramatically, "I give you William Fox's portrait, *Dolly: Au Naturel*!"

With a swift movement, Claude swept the drapes apart to reveal the three pictures. The crowd surged forward, necks craning, eyes straining. There followed a hushed moment, and then the hoped-for oohs and aahs. Someone began clapping, and the applause spread through the group like wildfire. "Bravo!" a man called. "Bravo!"

All eyes seemed to turn to Maggie—smiling, admiring eyes. With the relief of a prisoner who has received a reprieve, she took a deep breath. Time seemed to freeze as everything registered bit by bit.

She surveyed the sea of faces and saw the cream of Charleston society. By habit, they were lavish, by heritage, gracious and genteel. As she looked at them, Maggie realized with surprise that she liked and admired a great many of them. They were not all like the Townsends. They could not be lumped together as a breed. They were only people, people who were celebrating her efforts.

Around her, the guests applauded and cheered loudly, but Maggie felt as if she were enveloped in a silent vacuum. She looked about the room. Next to her, Dolly and Claude were smiling proudly. Near the buffet tables along the mirrored wall, Captain Jack and Annie applauded wildly. Rachel wiped her eyes with the corner of her apron.

The applause went on, dying only as clusters of people pressed forward to examine the art more closely surrounding Maggie and Claude and Dolly, and cutting them off from the rest of the guests.

"I'll take one of them, Bouchard," came a strong male voice. "Number thirty-eight. But how are you going to handle this?"

"I've got my reservation book right here," Claude explained over the heads of the guests. "And you can pick up the print any time next week at my gallery." He scribbled a quick notation in his book. "You're down for number thirty-eight, Mr. Tate."

"I'll take any number in the first ten," called another man.

"And I want one of the artist's proofs," Mrs. Crenshaw shrilled, the sight of her bulky purple form causing Maggie to break into a laugh. "But I want it signed by Miss Hastings!"

Her remark elicited a chorus of similar requests.

In the midst of the commotion, Claude leaned over to Maggie. "Where are the prints?" he asked quickly.

"They're in the studio."

"Get them, *chérie*! Get them! And some pencils, too!" he added excitedly. "Your public is clamoring for you. I didn't anticipate this, but if things go on this way, we'll have a sellout! I'll get someone to clear a table where you can do the signing."

Maggie looked at him blankly. "But is it legal?"

Claude's blue eyes were dancing. "*Chérie*, almost anything is legal so long as no money changes hands." Maggie hurried out the side door of the ballroom and dashed toward the library.

Overhead the stars twinkled against the black December sky. Maggie's breath emerged in small clouds as she rushed across the lawn, her silver heels clicking lightly across the frozen ground.

Maggie's ears rang with applause and the sound of voices calling out for her work. Her heart swelled with relief and pride. Blind to her surroundings, she saw only the smiling faces of her patrons. As she ran along the vine-covered walkway, she failed to notice the door ahead swinging stealthily closed.

She hurried into the library and had nearly reached the stairwell when she came to an abrupt halt. Something was wrong. She breathed in the unexpected smell of oily smoke, heard a faint crackling sound growing ever louder against the library silence as her gaze flew to the studio door—open and emitting an ugly orange glow.

"No," she whispered, still frozen. And then she raced up the stairs.

"No!" she cried as she reached the top.

Far below, in the dark recesses of the foyer, a manicured hand reached around the oak door and slid the massive dead bolt securely into place.

Maggie stumbled a few paces into the studio, looking wildly about the room. Three of the tall metal print racks were lying on the floor. One of them had crashed into the old stove, which lay awkwardly on its side, having been ripped from its ceiling anchor. From its belly spilled embers and coals, their red shapes turning into a flaming trail across the braided rug. Patches of fire licked at the hem of the old quilt on the bed. As Maggie watched in horror, the fabric caught, rising in a sheet of flame near the cardboard boxes containing the prints.

"No!" she screamed as she flew toward the fiery corner and grasped the box nearest the flames. She heaved it from the bed, set it down a few safe yards away and returned for the other. Her gaze swept madly about the room and lit on a towel hanging by the worktable. Snatching it up, she began to flail at the blaze that leapt ever higher from the bed.

Minutes flashed by like seconds. She didn't hear the ruckus below as the sound of the fire before her swelled, its heat leaping out to embrace her with each futile swipe of the towel. Throwing the useless rag down, she raced across the room, grabbed the trash can and, after tossing the contents onto the floor, set it in the sink and turned on the tap.

"Come on," she urged as she watched the level of water creep too slowly toward the top.

Mindless of the liquid that sloshed from the can, she hurried back to the fire and tossed the water on the burning bed. For only an instant, the flames receded as if fearful of their watery enemy. Then they encircled the wet spot, their crackles seeming to be filled with laughter as they burned hotter and brighter in the otherwise dark studio. Maggie retrieved the blackened towel and resumed her fight with new vigor. She was deaf to the sound of an approaching step on the cast-iron stairs.

She was looking around for a new weapon against the fire when she saw him in the doorway. "What are you doing here?" she asked blankly, then turned back to the bed, her eyes on the half-burned quilt. She snatched the burning cover from the bed as flames shot up from the old mattress.

"Help me!" she cried as she thrust the burning quilt on the flaming rug. Quickly she soaked the towel in the small amount of water remaining in the can, and began to beat the mattress.

"Help you?" came John Henry's crisp voice. "Don't be silly."

Maggie glanced in his direction, her look conveying only mindless panic before she returned to her task. John Henry's voice floated again through the room, but she failed to grasp the meaning of his words.

"Why, I was just on my way out when I saw you running in this direction. That was when I realized what was meant to be. That was when I surrendered myself to fate. Deep in my heart, I suppose I've known it from the first time I saw your face. Everything comes full circle. At last, it will all be over."

Maggie continued the battle for the bed, though it became clearer each second that the fire was to be the victor. It wasn't until John Henry spoke sharply that he managed to pierce her consciousness.

"Stop that! It's really quite pointless, and you *do* look so ridiculous!"

She paused, stepping away from the furnacelike heat, turning to him with glazed eyes.

The man closed and locked the studio door, then walked calmly into the hot, smoky room. "It's really quite amazing how everything has fallen into place," he said. "So many years, so many incidents and interactions, all leading up to this one final moment. I can assure you it will be quite painless. You'll fall asleep, and the smoke will spirit you away long before the fire reaches you."

At last, Maggie's mind began to register what he was saying. Abruptly she realized she was looking into the face of a madman.

"What do you want?" The brittle words came through her lips as she began to back toward the far wall, away from the fiercely burning corner where the blaze was reaching for the ceiling, eating away at the plaster.

John Henry regarded her imperiously from his position in the center of the room. "My dear, you really are slow. They'll find us here, and there will be a frenzy of scandal, and then they'll confirm who we are. They're quite good about those things nowadays, you know. Dental records, and all that! Yes," he added with an impassioned look. "Eventually they'll figure it all out, and they'll speak about it for years in shocked whispers. Let them be shocked. Let them remember John Henry Alexander of Foxcroft with awe!"

Maggie's eyes were wide open as her feet halted in their retreat. "You're crazy," she mumbled.

"Crazy, am I?" John Henry returned, insulted. "Not crazy enough to risk falling into *their* hands! Common folk have no more understanding of Foxcroft's people than *you* do! Ours are not the ways of peasants. Our tragedies and destinies must not be judged by their small minds. We are above their petty justices. *This* is justice! *This* is dignity!"

"You're *crazy*!" Maggie shouted. "There are two hundred people next door! Someone could walk in here any minute!"

John Henry chuckled dryly. "No, someone *couldn't*. No one can get in and no one can get out until it's far too late. There are a couple of empty cans lying around downstairs. I'll leave it to your imagination as to what was in them. Relax, my dear. We have all the time in the world." He chuckled again, the sound harsh and discordant. "All the time in the world."

The towering fire grew louder, but Maggie's mind was wiped suddenly clear of the inevitability of the fire and the threatened artwork. Her life was in danger. Her survival instinct took over, and she lunged toward the door. Just as swiftly, John Henry raised one arm threateningly. Maggie halted as she recognized Harold's machete in his hand, flashing wickedly in the light of the fire.

Cringing against the wall, her eyes riveted on the machete, Maggie became paralyzed as waves of terror began washing over her.

"Harold," she managed to whisper.

"Yes, *Harold*, that stupid oaf!" John Henry sneered the words as he lowered his arm and took a few steps closer. Smoke unfurled through the room, hiding his face until he was only a few feet away.

"Stupid, greedy Harold. He actually believed I was going to bring him a bundle of money down by the river—'keep quiet' money for a small job he did more than twenty-five years ago. *I'm* the one who planned everything! *I'm* the one who set everything up so it was quick and clean and untraceable. All Harold had to do was put a match to it, and he couldn't even do *that* without being seen! How anyone believed that ignorant man could have planned that fire is beyond me. Now, *William*, he knew better. He figured the whole thing out. Didn't you read about it in his last journal?"

With shocked, jerky movements, Maggie shook her head.

"Well, you *would* have," John Henry pronounced with conviction. "But now you'll never have the chance. It was the first thing to go," he concluded with a nod at the fire.

Maggie's eyes turned to the south side of the room. It was engulfed in flames, which raged as they consumed the old furnishings. She watched them overtake the wing chair, the old upholstery igniting like the head of a match. The heat was a ponderous weight in the air; the smoke was suffocating. And then came the crashing sound of splintering glass as one of the old north-facing windows burst from its frame.

The flames leapt toward the broken window, a shaft of cold air pulling them across the floor behind John Henry. He waved the machete threateningly in her direction, then calmly continued his earlier train of thought.

"Yes, with all his faults, William was a scholar. Even so, I didn't remember he kept a journal until you brought the books to Mark that night. William wrote down everything, and I read it all before I burned it. All his suspicions—beginning with the day I poisoned the dog, to the time he found that scrap of velvet in the barn. He knew at once what it was. After all, it came from one of *his* old smoking jackets, a hand-me-down he'd given me years before.

"I suppose I must commend your father after all. He was the only one who ever figured it out, even the reason I was trying to frighten that redheaded jezebel away from here. He realized too late that I could see what would happen: If he took up with *her*, then Dolly would lose Foxcroft. And so would *I*! He was too late, but nevertheless William wrote everything down, right up to the night he dismissed me from my position and ordered me off the estate, the night before he died."

Without realizing it, Maggie had pressed herself flat against the wall next to the madonna portrait. The horrified look on her face was a stark contrast to the sweetly smiling visage of her mother.

Her breath caught in her throat. Her father! Margaret! Poison! A memory stabbed at her—something Captain Jack had recalled from a conversation with her father. "We found the dog poisoned." Around and around the words ran in her head until a loud groan interrupted them. She turned in time to see the blazing bed crash out of sight as a patch of the old wooden floor gave way.

With stinging eyes she looked at John Henry. "This is *insane*! We've got to get out of here!"

He only waved the machete menacingly, the madness spilling like water from his dark eyes as he seemed to ignore everything that was happening around him. The old stove followed the path of the bed and fell into the library below. Behind him, the small trail of fire was turning into a wall that reached to the northern windows. Another pane smashed to the floor as the flames raced up the drapes and across the valence, mushrooming into a red, smoking cloud.

John Henry coughed in the blinding smoke, but his eyes remained locked on Maggie all the while. When he found his voice again, he resumed his feverish tirade.

"Everything was fine until you showed up. Dolly didn't remember anything about the fire! And I knew it was a sign. My cousin was dense—beautiful, but dense. She didn't accept that Foxcroft was her destiny. If she had merely stopped drooling after Art Townsend and concentrated on her own husband, all of us could have been happy. But no! She had to pine for Townsend and neglect William so that he was ripe for that gold-digging harlot! Dolly deserved to take the blame. It was *her* fault! But still, all those years I took care of her and Foxcroft. We were fine, *fine* until you showed up with that damnable face of yours!"

John Henry's gaze darted to the portrait hanging next to Maggie. "It's quite remarkable, really," he added. "The resemblance you bear to that mother of yours. As if you were some sort of unholy reincarnation."

With a sob that turned into a racking cough, Maggie turned her back on the madman and pressed her face against the smoothness of the wall. It seemed to grow warmer even as her cheek lingered there only for a moment. Slowly, her tearing eyes rose to meet those of the copper-haired woman in the portrait.

The sounds of the fire and John Henry's horrifying voice receded as her mother's features registered one by one—the clear, hopeful look, the pure, loving smile. Suddenly, out of Maggie's suffocating fear burst a ferocious anger. As if from outside herself, she watched two slender hands reach for the heavy frame of the portrait.

"Ashes to ashes, dust to dust," came John Henry's voice from just behind her. "Tonight the final scene of an old drama will be enacted. And we, my dear, shall watch together as the curtain comes down."

And then Maggie whipped the painting off the wall and whirled around, wielding the heavy portrait like a sword. The heavy wooden frame connected with a resounding crack against the side of John Henry's distinguished face, then flew out of Maggie's hands to clatter to the floor.

The man's head twisted grotesquely with the blow. The machete flew from his hand, twirled several times in the air, and fell across the room. But even as his knees folded, John Henry's head swiveled back to Maggie. A stream of blood gushed from his temple, and his eyes burned red with the light of the fire, as if some hellish thing looked out from within. There was an instant that stretched to infinity as his gaze fixed on her, his look filled with shock and hatred and the illogical semblance of triumph. His eyes rolling back, he crumpled to the floor.

Tears streamed down Maggie's face, and she put her hands over her ears, blocking the roar of the fire, blocking the scream that ripped from her throat as her gaze locked on John Henry's motionless form. The night wind suddenly howled through the broken windows, sending the wall of flame toward the worktable and several jars of flammable chemicals that stood on its surface. It was only then that she became once again capable of thinking.

She looked to the door where a pool of flame was spreading, then to the body that lay only feet away, blocking her exit. Nearby, another portion of the floor broke away. Soon the whole room would fall into the library below.

Maggie kept her eyes on John Henry as she stepped over his body. She was about to run for the doorway when an iron hand clamped itself around her trailing leg.

She screamed as long, bony fingers bit into her ankle, the force of John Henry's grasp making her stumble and fall. Her legs began to thrash wildly, the sequins of her dress catching the light of the fire so that she herself was a reflected flame. Still, the fingers held her captive.

Rolling onto her back, she glimpsed John Henry's insane face, where blood had painted one side of it crimson. Yet even as her eyes froze, Maggie instinctively began drawing back her free leg. She drove the spike heel of her shoe into the unsuspecting man's midrift and heard a gust of expelled breath. The grasping hand fell from her ankle.

She scrambled away on her knees and was on her feet by the time she reached the door. The blaze was waist-high. With quick, darting movements, she turned the old lock and grasped for the doorknob. Finally she had it, the hot brass burning her fingers as she speedily twisted the knob and drew the door open through the flames.

The air from the library rushed in, and the fire surged up around the doorway. Maggie raised her arms protectively and stumbled back. The smoke furled through the room like a dark, heavy banner, and as she looked toward the door, she found the exit had become invisible. There was only a wall of fire.

She glanced behind her and saw that John Henry was struggling to his feet. A hopeless sob racked her even as she realized she had to move, had to get downstairs. Taking a deep breath, she held her hair close to her head, covered her face, and bounded through the flames to the landing.

She raced to the stairwell and looked below only to find an inferno. The remains of the bed and other studio furnishings blazed at the south wall, their flames encompassing long shelves of old books. In the foyer the velvet drapes were afire at the barred windows, and a towering bonfire blocked the door. At the foot of the stairs, several odd containers lay awkwardly about, containers her shocked mind finally recognized as gasoline cans.

It was then that a banging noise reached her from beyond the fire. Springing onto the spiral stairwell, Maggie raced heedlessly down the metal steps which were beginning to glow with heat.

The noise was resounding as she reached the foyer where flames reached halfway to the cathedral ceiling.

"Maggie!" came a deep, booming voice she immediately recognized as Mark's.

"I'm *here*!" she screamed at the door, invisible behind the brightness of the flames.

"Maggie!" he called. "Open the door!"

She stumbled around the edge of the fire in helpless confusion. "I *can't*!" she cried, her voice breaking. "The fire!"

She lingered at the edge of the blaze, separated from her salvation by twenty feet that might as well have been twenty thousand. Her chest heaved with sobs as she caught the sound of voices from outside.

"Where's the key?"

"There's no time to go to the house for the key! Has anybody got a gun?"

"I do!"

"Come here! Let him through!" Mark's voice rang out. "Give me the gun! Maggie! Maggie, do you hear me? Get away from the door! Get away from the door *now*!"

She staggered out of the blazing foyer toward a row of bookshelves the raging fire had yet to reach. She was nearly there when John Henry's maniacal laughter rang through the smoke-filled room. She screeched in terror and crouched quickly behind the shelves, her gaze flying to the dark form at the top of the stairwell.

"So near and yet so far!" he called in sarcastic reference to her plight, and though Maggie couldn't see his face for the smoke, she could envision the mad eyes glaring down at her.

"I'll see you in *hell*, Maggie Hastings!" came his final challenge.

With a groaning crash, the remainder of the studio floor gave way and fell in great chunks to the floor below, bringing with them a rain of fire. The spiral staircase teetered, then broke away from the fractured ceiling. Maggie stared toward the iron stairs, where John Henry was perched at the top like a great bird on a ship's mast. The staircase began to fall, and the man sailed through the air, a fierce cry following him and ending abruptly as he thudded to the floor.

The old iron staircase collided with the first of the bookshelves. Like dominoes, the tall structures began to topple against one another, gaining force and speed until they reached the spot where Maggie cringed. The shelves that had sheltered her began to fall. Something struck her temple, and she fell with them.

A heavy weight was upon her. She barely heard the sharp crack of shots as they split the air. The sound of the raging fire was deafening; smoke singed her nostrils. She tried to move an arm, but it wouldn't respond. The heat was searing her lungs, and flames crept ever closer to the spot where she was pinned—where the ancient manuscripts and books of Foxcroft had nearly buried her.

From somewhere far away, above the howl of the blaze, a voice called out her name.

"Here," she whispered, her throat burning with the effort. "I'm here." But as she spoke the futile words, she knew they carried no farther than the pile of books.

"Maggie!" The voice was urgent, drawing her briefly from the seductive darkness and heat that smothered her, threatening to take her to the sleep John Henry had promised.

"Here!" she gasped defiantly, even as the air delivered only smoke to her burning lungs.

So this is what it's like to die, she thought, but she felt no fear as she surrendered herself to the wonderful images of Mark that waltzed through her mind. An angry look changed to a crooked smile. A boyish expression melted into a hot look of desire.

"Maggie!"

The voice came from somewhere nearby, piercing the roar of the fire.

"Maggie! Open your eyes and look at me!" the voice came again, carrying the odd sound of a sob within it.

Still, Maggie couldn't move, although she felt herself suddenly being grasped and lifted.

"*Look* at me, Maggie!"

The deep, sobbing command refused to be ignored. Maggie had to force her eyes open. Above her, she caught sight of dark brows and brilliant green eyes.

"Mark," she whispered.

The fire was blazing about him like a furnace, lighting up his handsome face with flickering red light. A rush of feeling overtook her. In life, she'd been unable to master her resentment and suspicions, letting pride overrule every thought and emotion. In death, she effortlessly swept all that away, freeing the pure sweet feeling that had survived beneath it.

With tremendous effort she forced herself to focus on his eyes, making sure that he looked directly at her.

"Mark, I love you," she managed, expending her last bit of strength as she watched the light of acknowledgment come to his face.

A black circle appeared in her head, swelling rapidly to block out everything but its own dark void, and Maggie sank with relief into the shadowy world that sought to claim her.

Chapter Twenty-four

"A mild concussion. A broken arm. A few bruises," Dr. Myers announced.

The painkillers were powerful, and Maggie's eyes remained shut, but for the past hour, she had lain awake in the blackness listening to the quiet sounds of the house, the hushed voices of Rachel and Annie, Captain Jack and Jonas.

Rachel's voice rose from the foyer. "I tell you, she's *sleeping*, Mr. Fox!"

"She's been sleeping for a day and a half!"

"And she's *still* sleeping," Rachel returned promptly. "Besides, she doesn't want to see anybody."

"I'm the one who saved her life, for God's sake!" Mark thundered. "I'm going in there. I don't care—"

"No!" Rachel commanded. "Now, you listen to me, Mark Fox. You're not going in there and get that child all rousted up. Not in the shape she's in!"

There was a moment of silence.

"All right, all right," he eventually grumbled. "Just tell her not to worry about anything but getting well. Everything's going to be all right. She had no business trying to take this place on anyway. From now on, *I'll* handle everything!"

Despite the pounding in her temples, Maggie turned her head, a tear sliding off her cheek to wet the satin pillowcase. She succumbed to the drugged sleep that beckoned.

The room was gray, the color of a foggy day. The shades were pulled as Maggie had requested, and shadows blurred the familiar shapes within the room. Her only companion was Margaret, who lay quietly by the bed. Both of them had been John Henry's victims, and both had retreated to the sanctuary of the green bedroom.

Rachel entered quietly. Maggie watched the old woman deposit a fresh glass of water and quietly leave without realizing Maggie was aware of her ministrations.

Maggie's eyelids fluttered closed again. A noise caught her attention just before the bedroom door flew open. With a start, she opened her eyes to behold a female form standing majestically in the doorway.

"The doctor said she was supposed to rest!" came Rachel's objection from behind the formidable Dolly Fox.

"That's exactly what he told *me* twenty-five years ago!" the woman snapped as she swept into the room.

The setter growled threateningly.

"Hush!" Dolly scolded, then strode to the French doors and threw aside the drapes so that brilliant morning light flooded the room.

Maggie squinted against the strong light. She glared at Dolly Fox.

"Aha!" Dolly exclaimed. "I see you're awake after all. And about time, too! You've been locked up in here for a week. Refusing to talk to anyone! Denying visitors! Really, Maggie!"

"There's no one I want to see!"

The sound emerged as a harsh whisper, although Maggie would have screamed it had she been able. The doctor said her laryngitis would gradually disappear as the singed tissue of her throat and lungs healed. The arm that rested uselessly in a cast would take longer.

Dolly looked stylish in a tweed suit and felt hat with a pheasant feather at the crown. Her polished appearance only intensified Maggie's sour mood as she pictured her own dirty hair and pasty complexion.

"There's no one you want to see," Dolly repeated pensively. "Well, to quote a friend of mine, 'That's just too damned bad!' I don't care if you want to see anyone or not. I've been where you are, and I know that what you need is to get up out of that bed and *live* again!"

"I didn't realize you were a doctor!" Maggie whispered snidely.

"There are a lot of things you don't realize," Dolly replied. "But one thing at a time. Perhaps when you discover you can't frighten me away with insults, you'll listen to my advice!"

Against her will, Maggie's lips began to tremble as tears welled up in her turquoise eyes. Dolly regarded her bitter fight for control, then sank to the bed and gathered Maggie into her arms.

"There, there, Maggie," she murmured.

The embrace of the older woman unleashed all the fears and misery Maggie had locked inside herself. "But I can't forget!" she cried in a raspy tone. "I can't forget anything about that night. It keeps circling through my mind when I'm awake. And when I sleep, it's all I dream about!"

"But don't you see, Maggie? That's good. In time it will fade to only a vague memory. You'll see. Everything will be fine."

"No, it *won't* be fine!" Maggie whispered between desperate sobs. "It will never be fine again. I've lost Foxcroft!"

Dolly Fox stroked the wild hair that spilled over Maggie's distraught face. "Sometimes you have to let go of something before you can really have it," she replied enigmatically.

The visit from Dolly brought Maggie back to the land of the living. She climbed out of bed that afternoon and went downstairs for the first time since "the accident," as Rachel termed it.

But Dolly's presence had also reminded Maggie of a vow she'd made months before. "If you ever part with the estate," Dolly had demanded, "you must *promise* to sell it to Mark."

With a defeated feeling, Maggie remembered her reply: "I promise."

Annie and Rachel were thrilled to see her up, but their happy smiles turned to concerned glances as they saw the depths of Maggie's despair. In their anxiety over their mistress's well-being, they had forgotten about the loss of the prints. Neither of them had stopped to realize that she would now be forced to sell the estate.

Early the next morning Rachel took up a tray of coffee to discover that Maggie wasn't in her room. After looking through the house, the old woman finally found her on the side lawn, gazing at the charred remains of the library.

"Come along, Miss Maggie," Rachel urged. "It ain't doing you no good to stand out here in the cold."

Deep in thought, Maggie took a moment to reply. "But it reminds me of what I've done, Rachel. What General Sherman started a century ago, Maggie Hastings has finished. The wing is completely leveled. Nothing is left. No books. No paintings. Nothing!"

The morning was damp and chilling. Rachel pulled her shawl more closely about her. "Miss Maggie!" she scolded. "The things you're talking about, they don't matter! The things that matter are life and people who care about you. Not old books and old rooms!"

Maggie chuckled dryly, the sound like that of rustling weeds. "You're a good friend, Rachel. But no matter what you say, I know the truth. I'm a fool. I've been a fool all along. I swooped in here like an avenging angel, determined to take over the whole of Foxcroft. All I've done is destroy it."

The old woman's dark eyes snapped behind her bifocals. "You talk like this *place* is the important thing, Miss Maggie. Foxcroft is just a house, just a building. *You're* a human being, and if it hadn't been for Mr. Fox, *you'd* be the one that went up in smoke!"

Mark. As Maggie surveyed the blackened ruins of the library, she imagined his face. Mark had saved her. He had risked his life to rescue her.

"By the time all of us got there, Miss Maggie," Rachel continued, "Mr. Fox was walking out of that burning place with you in his arms. Wouldn't put you down. Carried you all the way up to your room and stayed until Dr. Myers came running in. Why, he waited up all that night just to make sure you were all right."

Maggie had heard the story a dozen times. "So you say," she replied hoarsely. "You'll notice he hasn't been around since then."

Rachel looked at her impatiently. "There you go again. I've already told you he had to go over to that island with those businessmen. That's the reason he hasn't been here. The first few days when he was here all the time, you wouldn't even see him!"

Couldn't see him, Maggie thought miserably. What could she have said? That he'd been right all along? How could she face Mark now that she'd lost it all, including any hint of equal standing with him?

During the time she'd known Mark, Maggie had put up with his various moods—the indifference, the anger, the passion. She could even have shouldered his hatred. But she couldn't bear the idea of those emerald eyes looking down on her with pity. She would rather remember him as he was on the night of the reception—brazenly seductive as he held her on the dance floor, powerful and determined as he plucked her from the engulfing flames.

Only a week and a half ago she'd confronted him in the freezing darkness of the oak grove. All he seemed to be able to offer her was a string of one-night stands. As usual, his silence had told her more than any words. Yet now, Maggie found that it didn't really matter. Her feelings for Mark had changed that fiery night in the library. Now they were selfless and uncondemning, undemanding of anything except the joy of existence. If she never saw Mark again, it would remain the same. A brush with death did wonders when it came to sorting out what was important in life.

A sad smile came to Maggie's lips. Funny how she'd changed. The memory of Mark she would cherish above all others was the sweet look of surprise when she told him she loved him. Through all the cold, empty days and nights ahead, she would wrap herself in that recollection and feel lucky that once in her life she had known the rare, dizzying elation that many never knew.

She loved Mark, and she'd made a promise to Dolly. It was time to give in.

Maggie took a final sweeping look at the crumbling skeleton of the studio where she had labored so diligently. The fantasy of her life at Foxcroft was dying. A dull ache pounded within her as she surrendered to the inevitability of leaving the plantation, leaving the vibrant, tempestuous life she had shared with Rachel and Annie, Dolly and Claude, *and* Mark.

A biting wind added a final accent to the desolate moment as she resolved to move back north where she belonged, putting behind her the memories of a long-dead mother and father, and the vicious nightmare that had nearly claimed her life. With a feeling of resignation, Maggie turned from the remains of the library and walked back to the house with Rachel.

Settling herself in the dining room with coffee and the newspaper, she scanned the headlines, not stopping to read an entire story until she reached the local pages. It was then that the picture of a familiar face seized her eye.

"Ground breaking at Canadys Isle," read the headline. "Yesterday builder and developer Mark Fox of Foxcroft, Inc., sank the first shovel at the site of the multimillion dollar resort facility he will develop on Canadys Isle . . ." The story went on to extol Mark's earlier successes in real estate, and concluded with the information that the ground-breaking ceremony would culminate that evening in a black-tie dinner at the City Club.

Maggie's eyes returned hungrily to the grainy photograph. Mark's smile was brilliant, carefree, exhilarated. He had gotten what he wanted, and success obviously agreed with him. Her eyes moved to the crowd that pressed in behind him. In the background, just at Mark's shoulder, was the dark-eyed face of Alicia Townsend Harward.

A wave of resentment washed over Maggie. Alicia had won

after all. Maggie was on her way out, and Alicia was in, right behind Mark all the way. Dolly had said that Alicia would inherit from Mark. Perhaps one day the socialite's children and grandchildren would play in the halls of Foxcroft.

A few hours later when Rachel and Annie ventured into the green bedroom, they discovered that Maggie was nearly packed.

"Please don't rush off like this, Miss Maggie," Rachel pleaded, and blew her nose fiercely into a hanky.

Annie blinked back the tears in her pale eyes. "It's not right," the Scotswoman sniffed.

Maggie regarded her two friends, an ache starting in her throat. "It's best for me this way," she replied. "I'll stay with Shelley until I get settled, and then I'll send for the rest of my things."

Rachel and Annie followed their mistress to the veranda with the few suitcases she had packed. As Maggie stepped into the cold December air, a harsh breeze lifted her bright tresses and stung her eyes. She glanced up at the gray sky, then took a sweeping look across the courtyard.

The fountain was still; the red geraniums that clustered at its base were long gone. Beyond the brown lawns, the twin rows of live oaks looked lonely, their barren branches reaching across the drive to each other. She was lost in melancholy thought as she stared up the drive, looking for the taxi. But it was not a cab she saw coming up the driveway. It was a truck, followed by a cavalcade of vehicles.

A questioning look came over her face as she turned quickly to Annie and Rachel. "What's this?" she murmured, and received only answering shrugs.

Maggie's eyes returned to the odd caravan, and as the assortment pulled into the courtyard, she began to recognize them. Mr. Thompson and Jeremy were in the lead truck, followed by a group of their relatives. Captain Jack's van was followed by Jonas's old flatbed, and then Naomi's station wagon.

There must have been a dozen cars and trucks in all, some of them loaded with lumber and tools. As Maggie watched in awe, people began to spill out of them and make their way toward the veranda. Captain Jack, Jonas, the Thompsons, and then Naomi with a group of Gullah villagers including Juba and Pheby. Captain Jack, Jonas, and Mr. Thompson came to stand before her, smiling at her obvious surprise.

"We've come to build it back for you, Miss Maggie," Mr. Thompson began.

"It'll be just like an old-fashioned barn-raising," Jonas said, and a cheer issued from the crowd behind him.

"We expect to have us a good start by sundown, young lady," Captain Jack concluded, his blue eyes twinkling. But then those bright eyes fell on the suitcases behind Maggie.

"Here now, what's this?" The old man's gaze rose to Maggie's face.

With a feeling of guilt, Maggie looked at the captain, then turned to the crowd of smiling faces. "I can't thank you all enough," she ventured hoarsely, "but a taxi is on its way. I—I'm leaving."

A murmur coursed through the crowd.

"I told her she ought not to rush off," Rachel sniffled.

"Me, too," Annie chimed in.

Captain Jack was looking Maggie over assessingly. "I never figured you for a quitter," he said finally.

Maggie's eyes took on a bright sheen. "I haven't quit, Captain Jack. I've been beaten."

"You could do *something*," Jonas accused.

"What?" Maggie demanded.

A thoughtful look crossed the young man's face. "You could take out a loan," he suggested.

Maggie gazed at him. "And how would I pay back a loan, Jonas? And you of all people should know the bank won't lend me money on my looks."

"You could paint some more pictures!" Mr. Thompson offered.

In spite of her heartache, Maggie smiled at the gruff farmer, then pointed to the cast on her right arm. "I appreciate your suggestion, Mr. Thompson. But it will be weeks before I can use this arm."

At that moment, a yellow taxi puttered into the courtyard, its driver honking impatiently.

"Just a minute!" Maggie called in her gravelly voice. Her gaze traveled from face to face until it came to rest on Captain Jack.

"So that's it, then," the old captain muttered.

Maggie took a deep breath. "That's it," she said softly. Before the trembling of her lips could give way, she began to circulate through the crowd, bestowing handshakes and thank-you's on the crowd of people who had turned out to help her.

When she came to Naomi, she looked hopelessly into the warm

dark eyes and sensed that she found understanding before turning to Pheby and Juba. The old woman's face reflected indignation.

"I come all the way over here from home just to find out you're leavin'!" Juba accused. "I thought I *knew* folks. Didn't think you were that kind!"

Maggie looked at her with such blatant despair that it stunned the old woman into silence. "Believe me," she murmured soberly. "If I could stay, I would." The turquoise eyes shifted to Pheby.

"I hate for you to go, Miss Hastings," the girl said sadly.

"So do I, Pheby, but I want you to keep painting. Don't stop for anything. And when you're ready for that showing, ask Naomi to get in touch with Mr. Bouchard."

"Hey, lady," the taxi driver finally called. "Can I at least get your stuff loaded?"

The crowd looked on as Captain Jack and Jonas piled the luggage into the trunk. Rachel and Annie stood with Maggie at the car door. They stared at her so dolefully that Maggie found herself smiling tearfully. She stepped over and gave each of them a hug.

"I'll never forget you," she whispered. Raising her voice as much as she could, she spoke to the crowd. "I'll never forget *any* of you!"

As if her limbs were weighted, Maggie climbed into the taxi. She quickly lowered the dirty window. "Rachel," she murmured, "tell Mark to mail the papers to my attorney. Tell him there won't be any delay in my signing them."

The taxi cruised up the avenue of oaks as Maggie bit her lip to stop its shaking, clenching her teeth until she drew the salty taste of blood. They had turned out of the estate and onto the highway before the uncontrollable weeping began.

Mark dawdled by the glossy antique bar of the City Club, his gaze sweeping across the crowd of thirty people. City and county officials, builders and developers. In a far corner, his New York associates were gathered around Sally Ann, obviously entranced by her flirtatious wiles and her southern charm. Closer by were Grover Harward and Alicia, who smiled dazzlingly at her husband while somehow managing to send Mark several sultry, inviting looks.

He thrust a forefinger inside his constricting formal collar, loosening it and the black tie with one deft stroke. He had come to like these social affairs less and less, but this one was necessary. The scandal that had tainted Arthur Townsend's connection with Canadys Isle had quickly swayed the consortium. By the time Townsend had lined the pockets of an attorney or two and extricated himself from trouble as he'd predicted he would, it was too late. The investors had already signed with Foxcroft, Inc. Soon the building on Canadys Isle would begin in earnest, and a dream would come true.

Taking a gulp of scotch, Mark turned his thoughts to another dream. He hadn't been to Foxcroft in days, hadn't seen Maggie since the night of her ill-fated reception. Yet the thought of her filled his waking hours and crept into his sleep.

Maggie was recovering, Rachel assured him, but she continued to refuse to see him. Well, it was time for things to be settled between them. Tomorrow morning the furies of hell wouldn't be able to keep him out of Maggie's fortresslike sanctuary. He had nearly lost her once. It wouldn't happen again.

Especially now that he knew how she felt. Once again he recalled her face, glowing in the light of the raging fire. "I love you," she'd whispered, her incredible eyes on his before they closed and she fainted. It was the only memory he planned on saving from that hellish night. It had taken the fear of death to make her part with her pride, but she had done it. She had finally admitted her love!

The thought brought a smile, and in a new buoyant mood, Mark drained the last of his drink and turned, almost bumping into the ancient maître d' of the City Club.

"Excuse me, Mr. Fox, but there's a call for you in the study."

"Thanks," he said and with a sense of relief, left the crowded bar behind and made his way into the stately room next door.

"Hello," he said into the phone.

"Mr. Fox, I been trying to find you all afternoon!" Rachel's voice was shrill and stricken. "Lord have mercy," she went on. "She's gone!" the old woman cried.

Mark didn't have to ask who.

Snow began to fall shortly before midnight on New Year's Eve. Shelley and Nathan had tried to badger Maggie into accompanying them to a party at a friend's home in Kensing, but Maggie held firm in her refusal.

"It's enough that you're putting me up until I find a place of my own," she had remarked. "I don't expect you to drag me into your social life."

She watched the couple—happy together now that Nathan had

settled down—stroll out to the car arm in arm; then she turned on the television and, like countless other Americans, tuned in to watch the New Year's celebration in Times Square.

As the huge apple descended, she poured a small glass of champagne. The countdown began, and at the stroke of midnight a band struck up the nostalgic chords of "Auld Lang Syne," accompanied by a chorus of cheers and firecrackers.

The people on the television screen were embracing, and for an instant, the image of Mark drowned them out. What was he doing at that moment? Was he in the midst of some posh celebration? Perhaps kissing in the New Year with the shapely blonde from the polo match? Maggie took a hasty gulp of champagne and pushed the thought away.

The next morning, Albert Morely called. The Foxcroft documents had arrived and would be delivered shortly, he said in a clipped manner. A bit surprised by the attorney's eagerness to do business on a holiday, Maggie wrote it off to his overwhelming conscientiousness. She had known the papers would be coming, but the idea of them was still a bitter pill. Knowing that Shelley and Nathan would sleep late, she donned layers of clothes and set out on a brisk morning walk.

New Year's Day was clean and shining, the white-blanketed landscape crowned with a flawless blue sky. Sunlight sparkled on the ice-laden trees, and as Maggie returned from her walk an hour later, her boots crunched through the crusty top layer of snow. Though she was bundled up in a coat, scarf, and mittens, her nose and cheeks were red from the breathtaking cold.

A young boy dashed by with a sled. She watched him race away toward a group that had gathered on top of a hill.

A stone church stood on the hill, its spire reaching high against the blue sky, seeming to preside over the children who played cheerfully in the snow far below. It was beautiful, like the picturesque, wintry scene one might find on a postcard. Yet all Maggie could find herself thinking was how different it was from the quiet, sweeping grandeur of Foxcroft.

A block ahead was the house where Shelley and Nathan lived, and as Maggie glanced up the street, she wondered if perhaps Albert Morely had arrived with the papers that would dissolve her claim on Foxcroft. It was then that her glance fell on the solitary figure standing outside the door.

The tall man wore a long navy overcoat, and his dark hair shone in the sun. As she approached, Maggie's gaze lingered on him.

The shape of his head, the breadth of the shoulders, the confident stance. Her heart began to pound at her ribs; she caught her bottom lip between her teeth. The sound of her crunching footsteps reached the man's ears. He turned, and Maggie froze in mid-stride.

"My God," she whispered, her eyes glued to the face of the man who stood only yards away. A stiff wind whipped his dark hair raggedly across his tanned brows. Above cheeks stained red by the cold, a pair of green eyes burned through the January morning.

"My God," Maggie whispered again as he strode up to her, his eyes locked on her face.

"You are the *most* troublesome, the *most* stubborn woman I've ever come across," he began in the deep southern voice that still echoed in Maggie's dreams. "Do you know that son of a bitch Morely wouldn't tell me where you were until I dragged him out of bed this morning?"

"What are you doing here?" Maggie managed to say, her wide eyes searching his angry expression.

The anger turned to incredulity. "What am I . . ." he repeated, then rolled his eyes and slouched on one leg as Maggie had seen him do a hundred times. He stared down at her for a long moment.

"I came to offer you a deal," he finally drawled.

Maggie's breath had gone shallow at the sight of him, but she bristled at his remark. "I don't want your charity," she snapped.

A cold wind rushed by, whipping their hair into their faces, but neither paid it any heed.

Mark folded his arms across his chest and scrutinized her thoroughly. "I can't believe you took off like that without any warning. I thought you had more spunk."

"It's not a question of spunk," Maggie replied stiffly. "I just finally had to admit you're right."

"What do you mean?"

"I don't belong there," she answered softly, the words tearing at her so that tears started in her eyes.

Her discomfort seemed only to annoy Mark, who reached into his breast pocket and withdrew the familiar-looking documents that granted title to Foxcroft.

"Let's get this straight once and for all," he said. "When we're finished with this agreement, when I've paid you, there's nothing I could possibly want from you, right?"

Maggie's eyes darted between his in silent confusion.

"Am I right?" he demanded, waving the papers in the air. "After this, I have nothing to gain from you. No reason to lie or use you? Correct?"

"I . . . I guess not," she finally stammered. As she watched in awe, Mark tore the papers in half and released them so that they fluttered quietly to the snow.

"Sign or don't sign," he stated. "I don't really give a damn!"

He stepped swiftly forward and took Maggie's face in his gloveless hands. The abrupt gesture smacked of anger, but the pleading look in his eyes removed the bite.

"Just come back," he said thickly. "The place is empty without you. My *life* is empty without you."

Maggie's knees lost their strength, but Mark's cold palms held her steady. Still, she could only stare, doubting her powers of reason, that he could actually mean what he seemed to be saying.

"I told you there was only one answer," he went on. "One day, I said, you'd just have to start believing in me. Well, *today* is the day."

His eyes searched hers as her heart pounded in her throat.

"Damn it, Maggie! I *love* you!" Mark thundered. "I have all along!"

A moment of suspenseful silence ensued as they looked at each other in silence.

"I . . . I love you, too." Maggie managed the unfamiliar words, and the age-old shackles that had bound her heart fell away.

Mark released a sigh of relief, the corner of his mouth dipping into a crooked grin. "I know," he rumbled.

He was so damned cocky! An answering smile spread across Maggie's features as her spirit soared into wild, free happiness.

Maggie's eyes raced over his beautiful face, loath to give up the sight of the sparkling green eyes and the dark hair that lifted with the breeze.

"Happy New Year," he murmured, his mouth so close his breath mingled with her own.

"The happiest," she whispered, her eyes closing as his cold lips found hers.

The cold was banished as their kiss grew warm with the passion Maggie had tried so often to banish from her mind. Her left arm reached up to clasp him to her, and she was crushed as Mark's arms closed desperately around her.

The tears that flowed heedlessly down her cheeks were those of joy, the cast beneath her coat, the only barrier that would ever again stand between them.

"Mrs. Fox?" Smythe called out in his clipped British voice. The new butler-chauffeur was a stickler for convention, and Maggie wondered with a grin just how long it would take him to fall into the comfortable habit of calling her "Miss Maggie" as everyone else around the estate did.

"Yes, Smythe," she answered as she walked heavily into the parlor. She had never been more beautiful, the fiery hair pulled back from a face glowing with maternal radiance.

"Where would you like me to put the playpen?" the distinguished butler asked.

Maggie's eyes slid to where Dolly and Claude sat comfortably on the settee. Above their heads hung the surviving artist's proof of William Fox's portrait of Dolly. Number one of the print edition now hung in Dolly's town house; the original was on exhibit at La Galerie Bouchard.

"Put it in the nursery," Maggie replied in answer to Smythe's inquiry. "If you can find room."

She gave Dolly and Claude a scolding look. "Honestly," she teased, "between you two and Captain Jack, the nursery is beginning to look like a toy store! You really *must* cut back on the presents."

"I intend to do exactly as I please," Dolly responded. "I deserve to celebrate. After all, how many women have the chance to become a grandmother and a bride all in the same month?"

"We plan to spoil our grandchild *mercilessly, chérie*," Claude said with a bright look at Maggie, "so you might as well get used to the idea."

He and Dolly looked toward the door as Mark strode in from the veranda.

"Hi," he said to his mother and her fiancé, then continued to Maggie. He produced a late rose from behind his back and pressed it into his wife's hand as he kissed her lightly on the forehead. He did a lot of that sort of thing nowadays, as if the affectionate tendencies he had stored up for a lifetime were impatient to be free.

"How are you feeling?" he asked, looking into Maggie's eyes.

A brilliant smile came to her face as she returned her husband's loving look. "Wonderful."

With a satisfied grin, Mark placed his arm possessively about
Maggie's shoulders and turned to Dolly and Claude. "If you want
to see something pretty, why don't you come out front?" he
suggested. "Jeremy is bringing Yankee Lady over to the courtyard
so Maggie can have a look at her."

At a year and a half, Gray Lady's filly had turned out to be the
most beautiful horse Maggie had ever seen.

"*Yankee* Lady?" Dolly questioned with a knowing glance in
Maggie's direction.

"Named for the fire in her eye," Mark replied with a grin.

Chatting gaily, the two couples wandered into the foyer and
toward the veranda. It was then that Claude noticed the painting
hanging near the front doors.

"*Mon Dieu!*" he said. "Where did *this* come from?"

It was an odd work. Against a barren winter landscape, a single
Red Fox stood with its head raised proudly. Red eyes, like those
in the ring on Mark's finger, regarded the viewer challengingly.
And at the bottom Maggie had inscribed the words: "Valor in
Adversity."

She blushed modestly as, within the circle of Mark's arm, she
moved along to the doorway. "Mark insisted we hang it there."

"*Bien!*" Claude pronounced. "It's wonderful!"

"You see?" Mark chimed in, as they stepped outside into the
mild evening air. "I *told* you it was good!"

At that moment Jeremy strode onto the drive with Yankee Lady.
The dark filly pranced proudly toward the veranda and whinnied
happily upon spotting Mark. With a quick squeeze of Maggie's
shoulders, he bounded down the stairs and began to point out the
horse's excellent lines to Dolly and Claude.

After a moment, Maggie went over to the porch swing and sat
down. Rachel came out to sit in a neighboring rocking chair as she
snapped green beans. She was followed closely by Annie, who
flopped into another rocker and began busily stitching on a gown
for "the honeymoon babe."

Maggie had retrieved the embroidered clothes from William
and Stella's old chest. With a sense of reverence, Annie had taken
it on herself to repair a few of the garments that had grown fragile
with age. Stella's grandbaby would laugh and coo in clothing
stitched by her own hands.

Margaret trotted up the stairs to curl up at Maggie's feet.
Everything was so peaceful, so right. It was a feeling that had
eluded Maggie for most of her restless life, but now she was

certain she would never have another day without it. She had found her place. Occasionally, when she toured the new construction on the library, she experienced a chilling memory. But those memories were the only sourness in her life, and even they were gradually fading away.

So much had settled into place since her return. The household was warm and cheerful and filled with laughter. Claude and Dolly were wildly happy, planning a November wedding which would only shortly precede that of Jonas and Naomi. Since Mark had hired him on at Foxcroft, Inc., Jonas had begun receiving a salary that allowed him to build a promising future for himself and his bride.

Pheby's summer showing at La Galerie Bouchard had been a sellout. And now, Juba took pride not only in her granddaughter's celebrated talent, but also in the wonderful changes that were taking place in the Gullah village as Mark's development of Canadys Isle began to take shape.

Just after the turn of the year, Isabel Townsend had closed up the great house on the Battery and whisked her son away to an exclusive Swiss resort. Despite Arthur's success in vindicating himself in the Canadys Isle affair, it seemed his mother had been furious at the scent of scandal that had befallen the corporation of which she was chairperson. They were gone seven months, and since their return, Arthur had stayed away from everyone associated with the Foxcroft household.

Even Alicia had contributed to Maggie's overall peace. She had, as Dolly said, been "forced" to move to the state capital with her politician husband. Beyond a surprised doubt that Alicia Townsend Harward could be "forced" into anything, Maggie had given her husband's half sister little thought.

She was too preoccupied with her own happy existence. She was at Foxcroft—beautiful, mysterious Foxcroft—long the scene of intrigue and tragic secrets, now a bright home filled with love and laughter. John Henry's poisonous plot had ultimately been foiled. He had managed to wreak tragedy long ago, but survivors carried on.

As she reached down to stroke the setter, Maggie savored the poetic justice. After all the years of heartbreak and loss, it would be the blood of William and Stella that carried on the Fox line.

Contentedly, she settled back against the swing and surveyed the courtyard, where fireflies brightened the dusky September evening still laden with the scent of honeysuckle. Indian summer.

She had come to love the southern season when the low country clung to the laziness of summer days and nights.

Her eyes lit on Mark's tall, lanky form, and once again the familiar rush of love welled up. The cold grimness she had once seen in him had vanished. He was a wonderful man, and he would be a wonderful father.

Maggie's thoughts turned to her earlier life—the skittish wandering, the careless whirl of romance, unknowing days when she had predicted she would always be a loner. Her fingers strayed lovingly to the mound that was her baby. In only seven weeks, he would arrive.

The tests had shown that the child was a boy. Perhaps he would be an artist like his grandfather or a real estate tycoon like his father. Perhaps, she thought dreamily, he would travel an easy, uncomplicated road through life. But as he chose that moment to resoundingly kick his mother, Maggie thought that idea improbable.

More likely, he would be proud and stubborn and headstrong. He would make mistakes and learn most things the hard way. But whatever adversities the fates threw in his path, Maggie felt confident he would meet them valiantly. So it had been; so it would be. It was the mark of a Fox.